A Touch of
Morning Calm
A Sam Jenkins Mystery

Wayne Zurl

Published by
Melange Books, LLC
White Bear Lake, MN 55110
www.melange-books.com

A Touch of Morning Calm ~ Copyright © 2016 by Wayne Zurl

ISBN: 978-1-68046-301-9

Cover Design by Lynsee Lauritsen

For Bazzie:
To remember the days on the banks of the real Crystal Creek.

Long before there was much ado about the division of North and South Korea at the 38th parallel, that land was known to the rest of the world as Koryeo.

In those ancient days, a dynasty existed in Koryeo called Chosun. To those people, the loose English translation of Koryeo meant The Land of Morning Calm.

If you've ever been to the Korean countryside, you know the phrase is appropriate. The same could be said for the Smoky Mountains of East Tennessee.

But not all the time.

Chapter One

For the last two years, I've spent nearly one third of my life with Sergeant Bettye Lambert, my administrative officer and occasional partner. We get along famously—most of the time.

At my age, you'd expect I'd know how to deal with women, but experience shows I'm not as smart as I think. If I inherited the ability to handle the opposite sex efficiently, I would have taken a different job—like a hairdresser. But apparently in that area I'm hopeless. So I remain a cop.

The main telephone rang on Bettye's desk. If the caller wanted me, she would buzz my phone and forward the call. Nothing happened. Moments later, she stood in my office doorway, looking a little miffed.

I could always tell when things weren't going her way. She cocked her left hip to the side and rested a hand there. I thought she looked attractive. With her right hand, she leaned on the doorjamb and scowled at me.

At least she isn't holding a gun.

"It's your friend—that cheap blonde," she said.

"Who?"

Bettye shook her head, and her blonde ponytail swung back and forth. "You know who."

"I'm sorry, I don't. Who are you talking about?"

"Well, you seemed to get along with her just fine. It was me she didn't like."

"Huh?" I remained in the dark.

"You damn well know who I'm talkin' about, Sam Jenkins. That

1

blonde we met on the Cecil Lovejoy case—that one from Chicago."

"Ah-ha." A light in my brain switched on.

"Yes, *ah-ha*. Now pick up your damn phone."

Bettye gets away with saying things like that because we both know how important she is to my little police department. And hearing a note of jealousy in her voice boosts my ego.

"You're beautiful when you're angry," I said. "Just why are you angry?"

"Lord have mercy, you're pathetic."

I tried a smile. "That may be true, but you're still hopelessly in love with me."

"Not after today, darlin'. I said answer the phone. *That* one's waitin' for ya." She turned and walked away.

Sergeant Lambert made reference to a woman named Veronica Keeble. Two years ago, after a local man, one Cecil Lovejoy, was murdered in Prospect, Bettye and I interviewed Mrs. Keeble. Sort of a suspect at the time, Veronica was thirty-five-years-old, blonde and absolutely gorgeous. Did I mention she was an ex-hooker?

I answered my phone, curious to learn what 'that one' had to say.

"Hello, this is Chief Jenkins."

"Well, hello there. It's been a long time." She sounded friendly.

"Yes, it sure has. How are you?"

"I'm fine, thanks. Were you the police chief when we first met, or have you been promoted from detective?"

I remembered the time I interviewed her. On a warm July day, we walked down the street where she lived, and I listened to the intimate details of her earlier life.

"Yeah, I was the chief back then. We only have thirteen cops here, so I get to play detective at times. I'd have to sweep the floors, too, if the mayor caught me not looking busy."

She laughed briefly, something a little husky and a whole lot sexy. "I see. You must have a tough boss."

I thought about Bettye. "Sometimes I wonder who the boss is around here. What can I do for you, Mrs. Keeble?"

"The last time we spoke, I thought we agreed on Sam and Roni." Her voice sounded soft and inviting.

Another memory—before we parted company, she asked my first name, shook my hand and left me gazing into the most incredibly blue eyes on the planet.

"We did. Okay, Roni, how can I help you?" I wondered what I might be getting into.

"Did you ever find out who killed that awful man?"

"That's a long story—sort of."

She called me to learn the outcome of a two-year-old case?

"You'll have to tell me some time."

"Sure, but first tell me why you called. I want to know if I should be flattered because you remember me or act totally professional."

"Wow, how do I answer that?"

"Try the direct approach. Remember, I'm a civil servant. You pay my salary. I, madam, am at your disposal."

She used that soft and inviting sound again. "That opens up all kinds of possibilities."

The woman really had a way with words. I thought I'd play along. I wasn't busy.

"But," she said, "I guess I should tell you why I called before I forget."

"Yes, ma'am. It's your dime."

"Well, I have a friend who just opened a business in Prospect. I think she may need police assistance."

"Really? Why didn't she call?"

"I told her you and I had already met. I know it's been a while, but I still remember how nice you were. You listened to my story, and you weren't judgmental like someone else might have been. I thought you were okay for a cop. I told her I'd call and see if you would help her."

"Okay for a cop, but not so hot for a plumber or delivery man?"

"Oh, stop, you're just looking for compliments."

"Maybe. I could be suffering from self-esteem problems." I allowed a few seconds for her to enjoy my self-deprecating humor. "If she's in some kind of trouble and it's a police matter, of course I'll help. But I'm sure you understand I have to hear her story first."

"I knew you'd do it."

Roni Keeble didn't say, 'Yipee,' but I could envision her smiling. I still have a good memory. Did I mention the girl was gorgeous?

"Will you have lunch with us? I'll introduce you, and Sunny will explain everything."

"Having lunch with a complainant and her friend isn't the usual way a policeman starts an investigation."

"Lunch would be nice though, wouldn't it?"

This is how a cop gets into trouble.

"Yes, I'm sure it would be, but you two could come to my office."

"Sunny is Asian. They like to conduct business over a meal."

I remembered thinking about not being busy. And her story sounded intriguing. Or was I just in the mood for a little more flattery?

"Ask her if having tea would work. It's culturally appropriate, and we can mingle with the gray-haired ladies at Tillie's Tea House here in town."

She laughed again. "Okay, tea is fine. Would this afternoon at two be convenient?"

"Sure. That gives me time to get a purple rinse and a perm. I want to fit in with the local girls."

"Sam, I can't wait to see you with purple curls."

* * * *

At five-to-two, Bettye came back from lunch. She may have forgotten about Mrs. Keeble; I hoped so. Bettye didn't ask what Veronica wanted, and before leaving the office, I conveniently forgot to mention that I planned on having tea with her.

It's nice having women like you, but I'm glad I'm not single. Juggling girlfriends isn't easy for a guy at any age.

I bounced down the steps of the municipal building and strolled across the town square to a cozy, Americanized version of an old English tea house. Tillie's looked like something you might find in Devon or Stratford-upon-Avon, but with a little down-home Tennessee flair. Tillie's Tea Shop occupied an old building with wide heart-pine floorboards and rough hewn beams someone must have found in an ancient barn. Fancy chintz cloths covered all the tables.

The owner, a colorful local woman named Tillie Spoon, operated the business with the help of a baker and a few waitresses. Tillie held

Prospect's over-seventy female social crowd in the palm of her hand. She served tea and coffee and delicious homemade cakes, pies, scones, cookies, brownies, blondies, and melt-in-your-mouth lemon bars—all of which could plump up your waistline and stagger your cholesterol level.

The frosted glass oak-framed door looked taller than the usual six-feet-eight-inches. I opened it and walked in. Nine or ten gray-haired ladies stood in front of me at the entrance; Tillie stared back at them.

"Christ's sake, Bernetta," Tillie told the leader of the gray contingent, "if ya called me, I woulda had tables set up."

"Oh, Tillie, you shouldn't take His name in vain." Bernetta looked aghast.

"Don't worry about it, Bernetta. Now, jest wait here while I drag these tables t'gether."

Then Tillie saw me standing in the doorway. She shook her head and continued to look frustrated. "Sheriff, you couldn'ta come at a better time. Git on over here and he'p me move some tables t'gether fer these ladies...who didn't call in advance."

Tillie Spoon was in her fifties, short and what a kind man would call cuddly—from sampling too many lemon bars, perhaps. Her dark blonde hair showed lots of bright yellow highlights, and she wore a frilly print dress. Tillie had a pretty face, and if you liked good-looking, busty women with attitude, she was the girl for you.

"I'm not the sheriff," I said.

She tried to shake that off, but couldn't. "Do what?"

"I'm the police chief. Someone else is the county sheriff."

"I know that. I jest see you kindly like Matt Dillon, the town's lawman."

"Matt Dillon was a U.S. marshal. *The Lawman* was Dan Troop. Different show."

Tillie wrinkled her nose. "Oh, I don't care."

Probably before her time.

She slapped one hand on the tabletop and waved me closer with the other, her impression of someone exasperated with a situation. I didn't buy it for a minute.

"Come over here, and lend a hand," she said. "Come on. These ladies don't have all day."

I assumed that the old girls could spend all kinds of time sipping their tea, but didn't want to contradict Tillie. I excused myself while passing through the gaggle of senior citizens and smiled like a politician. Tillie continued to wave impatiently, getting women out of the way and me into position. I helped her move four tables together, set out ten chairs and rearranged the placemats and a few vases full of bachelor's buttons, black-eyed Susans and Queen Anne's lace. Just thinking about the decorative weeds made me want to sneeze.

I brushed a few specks of dust from my sport jacket. "Miss Tillie, I'm here to meet a couple of young ladies, not sign on as your hired hand."

She shook her head and snorted silently. No carpetbagging Yankee cop would intimidate her.

"Well, thanks for your he'p, Sheriff. One of your ladies is already here. By the way, does your wife know about your girlfriends?"

"Get lost, Tillie." I turned to look into the almost crowded tea room and spotted Roni Keeble at a table near the back wall. She raised a hand and gave me a quick wiggle of her fingers. I walked over.

"Hello," I said. "Nice to see you again."

She extended a hand for me to shake.

"I see Tillie put you to work," she said. "You weren't kidding about that civil servant thing, were you?"

"What can I tell you? I'm a sucker for a damsel in distress."

She smiled, and I fought back a need to gasp at how stunning she looked. The last two years had been kind to her. She didn't look older; she looked better. Her hair was a little shorter than what I remembered, and she neither needed nor used much make-up. She wore what I thought you call a peasant blouse—loose and made of unbleached cotton; it looked like something a sexy Mexican bar girl would have worn in a western movie. She remained seated, so I didn't see her tight khaki pedal-pushers until later.

I sat, and she spoke. "Sam, it's good to see you. Thanks for coming. Sunny called and said she'll be a few minutes late."

Roni's smile was enchanting; she could turn heads at the Playboy mansion. And I'm getting too poetic.

It felt almost like being on a blind date. I would have preferred

6

conducting business on a strictly professional basis, but we were going to have tea and meet her legally distraught friend. And somehow we had to fill the intermittent moments. I'm really lousy at small talk and didn't want to hand the ball off to her, so I broached the subject I use any time a good-looking woman backs me into a corner.

"How's your husband doing? His name is Dwight, isn't it?"

Her smile faded, and her striking blue eyes lost a little sparkle.

"His name *was* Dwight. He passed away about six months ago."

I shook my head. "I'm sorry for your loss. That's a shame. What happened?"

So much for the clever line I use on married women.

"He was home one day and out of the blue had a stroke. An ambulance took him to the hospital, but on the way, he suffered a massive heart attack. Dwight died later that night."

I did some quick math and remembered he would have been about fifty-four. At my age, I hate to hear things like that.

Above Roni's head, a Regulator wall clock ticked away loudly, the second hand snapping into place over and over again. Perhaps the news I heard and what I saw might have been symbolic.

"I'm shocked," I said. "As I remember, you were very close." I repeated the standard policeman's condolence. "I'm really sorry for your loss."

She half shrugged and looked sad. "Thanks. Dwight and I were very much in love. I felt awful for a long time."

Okay, Jenkins, what do you do for an encore?

Fortunately, my socially inadequate brain didn't have to come up with something either sympathetic or witty.

"Oh, here's Sunny now," she said, and her smile returned

An Asian woman in her mid-thirties walked to the table. I looked at her and immediately knew she was Korean. Fifteen years ago, she could have won the title of Miss South Korea; she looked that beautiful—high cheekbones, clear and intelligent almond-shaped eyes and just the right amount of fullness to her lips. Those two women looked like the best pair of bookends a guy could find, and I was getting paid to hang out with them.

Anyone who's spent time in Korea would have known with one look that Sunny Kim was a city girl. Generally, the food and hygiene are better in the cities than in the poorer agricultural regions. City girls tend to have better complexions, their teeth are nicer, and most often, their legs are shapely and straight because their mothers haven't carried them tied piggy-back around their hips during the years their soft bones were forming.

That all may sound like I'm evaluating a race horse, but I'm someone who notices things about people. I've always remembered the observations I made during the fourteen months I spent in South Korea many years ago.

Like many Korean people, Sunny Kim was short. My guess, about five-foot-two. Her hair was almost black, and I estimated that, at 2008 prices, her haircut cost almost as much as it takes to fill the thirty-six-gallon tank in my pickup. She wore an off-white and yellow striped cotton sundress that ended just above the knee. Ivory-colored high heels and a matching soft leather purse completed her outfit.

I stood up, as any gentleman would.

"Sam, this is Sunny Kim. Sunny, Sam Jenkins, the man I told you about."

She extended her hand. "Hello, it's nice to meet you." She spoke with just a hint of accent and flashed a dazzling smile.

"Ahn yong hash imnikka, Miss Kim." I made the traditional Korean greeting.

She looked surprised. "Oh, you speak Korean?"

"Nay, Han-gul mal, chokem mal imnida." I told her I spoke a little of her language.

She tilted her head. "I think maybe more than just a little."

I smiled. "Maybe better than the average GI, but not enough to say I'm fluent."

"You have a very good accent for an American. I'm impressed."

"Com op sumnida," I thanked her, again in a formal, traditional way.

Sunny returned my smile. "You are very charming, Mr. Jenkins. Did Roni tell you that I was Korean?"

"No, I guessed."

"You are very smart. How did you know?"

I tilted my head. "I'm a police chief. I know everything."

Sunny laughed and touched my fingertips.

She was being more than charming herself. Many Korean women are. They aren't afraid to speak their mind. But they're also easy to embarrass, and I never minded cashing in on that. Every time I'd tease a Korean girl, I felt like an affectionate big brother.

"Hago tae-dahnie ipumnida, Miss Kim." I said she was very pretty.

As most Korean girls might do when someone complimented them, Sunny Kim put her hands over her face and acted shocked.

I tapped my finger on the table to get back her attention. "Don't be shy. It's true."

She shook her head like a schoolgirl. "I think you are a slicky boy, Mr. Jenkins."

I laughed. "I haven't heard that term in almost forty years. What's your full name...in Korean?"

"Kim, Soon-Wha."

"I'll bet your mother calls you Sun-Mi."

"She does! How do you know?" She sounded surprised, and her Korean accent thickened a little.

"I knew a girl named Soon-Wha. People called her Sun-Mi."

"She was your yobo?" She asked if Soon-Wha was my girlfriend.

"Sun-Mi was the sister of my house girl. I had a round-eyed girl for my yobo—an American secretary at KMAG." I looked at Roni Keeble and said, "I think Sunny may know what I mean, but that's the Korean Military Advisory Group, an Army command in Seoul. She was my wife—still is."

"Oh, how nice you were married then," Sunny said. "Did you like Korea?"

"We loved it."

She beamed, showing more than a little pride in her country.

"From the DMZ to Cheju Island. I was sorry to leave," I said.

"Roni never told me you were in Korea and spoke the language."

"We've not discussed it."

Just how friendly does she think Veronica and I have been?

"It seems you two are getting along famously." Roni said. "You can be charming in two languages, can't you, Sam?"

Maybe more than two, Mrs. Keeble.

"I'm sorry," I told Roni, "When I meet someone from Korea, I can spend lots of time talking about my stay there. I didn't mean to ignore you. I apologize."

"You didn't ignore me. I'm glad you two get along so well."

I assumed she said that to be gracious, but still sounded a little put off.

Some people may think that I can't help myself where women are concerned. Honest, I was just there to help.

I looked from one pretty face to the other. "Okay, ladies, what can I do for you as a cop?"

Sunny exchanged glances with Roni. After a brief moment, she looked at me.

"I've just opened a business in Prospect," Sunny said, "Kisaeng Massage Therapy. Perhaps you've seen it?"

Kisaeng is the Korean equivalent of the more familiar Japanese term, Geisha. It identifies a well-trained and well-bred lady who provides companionship and the touch of class gentlemen desire when they gather. Traditionally, none of these terms signifies a call girl, bimbo or slut. That's a common Western misconception. However, thanks to a few publicized illicit operations, Korean massage parlors haven't gotten the best press over the last few years, especially in Blount County, Tennessee.

"I have," I said, "and I should have made the connection. I also should have stopped in to say hello to a new person in town. Me ahn homnida," I apologized.

"E hay homnida." She said she understood. "Can chom isumnida." And my oversight didn't matter. Then she gave me another big smile.

Roni interrupted, almost impatiently, bringing us back to the important business. "Sunny has only been in business a few weeks now, and she's already gotten shaken down by a man from Knoxville."

I frowned, and my eyes narrowed. I don't like to hear about shake downs. "Explain that one. I don't understand."

"His name is Mr. Park," Sunny said. "Park, Hee-Chul. He is Korean, of course. He is…what would you say?" She thought for a long moment, "a powerful man in the Korean community."

I understood her euphemistic description perfectly. "A gompay?" I used the Korean word for gangster.

"Yes, Sam, a gompay. You know the word."

"You mean Knoxville has a branch of the Kimchee Mafia?"

Sunny laughed, sardonically. "Yes, the Kimchee Mafia. Exactly. He and his hired man came to visit me. He said he would protect me from...whatever I needed protection from. There would be a monthly fee, of course."

The Korean Mafia should be considered as corrupt, brutal and effective as any organized crime faction in the world. And because of the physical properties of kimchee, the famous Korean pickled cabbage, their breaths may be enough to knock you over as easily as a well-placed screw punch.

"I thought I left all this back in New York," I said.

"And me in Chicago," Sunny said.

Aha, the Roni/Sunny connection finally dawned on me.

"Did you and Roni know each other in Chicago?" I looked at Veronica and then back at Sunny.

Her expression changed. "Yes, we worked for uh...the same person."

"Oh."

Roni, the very high-priced call girl, married one of her former clients and moved back to hubby's hometown. Sunny just admitted to being a coworker.

"Tell me about your new business here in Prospect," I said.

Sunny frowned and shook her head. "Oh, Sam, I know what you must think, but my business here is one-hundred-percent legitimate. Like Roni, I am no longer living that life. I had enough money to open an honest business. I swear to you. I found good girls who wanted to work for me. I sent them to school. They are all certified massage therapists. I even accept insurance payments."

When Korean women get excited or emotional, their voices get a little whiney. Sunny was no exception. She may have thought her former occupation would change my mind about helping her.

I thought about what she just said to legitimize her business. I would never have admitted being in cahoots with medical insurance people if I wanted to sound innocent.

I smiled for her. "Okay, I believe you. Number-one honest business,

11

huh?"

She laughed and nodded. "Yes, number-one business," repeating the Anglicized Korean term for good.

"So, this Mr. Park wants to sell you protection? How do I find Mr. Park so we can have a talk?"

"You mean you will help?" she asked.

Her smile came back—full force. The small amount of pink rouge she used on her high cheekbones accented her almost black eyes; when she smiled, they lit up. I wondered what had happened in Sunny's former life that would make the little favor I offered so important.

"Of course, I'll help you. No one comes into my town and shakes down a business owner. Mr. Park has insulted me and offended you. I'll take care of this."

I thought Matt Dillon might have said something like that to a couple of saloon girls in Dodge City. Both women looked relieved and happy. Tillie walked over to the table.

"I didn't want ta disturb you folks while ya were talkin', but this ain't the library. What can I git for y'all?"

I looked at Tillie and frowned. She countered my stare and then turned to the ladies.

"Since the sheriff ain't talkin', what kin I git fer you ladies?"

Veronica wanted coffee. Sunny asked for tea. I was more difficult.

"How many different types of tea do you have?" I asked.

"Jest how many can ya drink at one time, sugar?"

"Have you got that stuff from the Charleston Tea Plantation?"

"Well, o' course I do. Would ya like that?"

I shrugged. "No, I was just asking."

Tillie saw through my act. "You're just another impossible man. I'll bring ya that." She turned her attention to Sunny. "Would you like the same, miss?"

"I think the sheriff must know what's good. Yes please, same for me."

After two cups of tea and enough chit-chat with two personable women to hold me for a while, Sunny said she had to get back to her business. We said good-bye, and I assured her I'd find Park and resolve the situation. That left me sitting with a half-empty tea cup and the lovely Widow Keeble.

I remembered my inability with small talk.

I smiled and sounded like a moron. "Life sure can be interesting."

She ignored my statement. "You two certainly hit it off, didn't you?"

"Sunny seems like a nice girl. I'll do what I can to help. I think I can fix this up quickly, and she won't have to worry about Mr. Park anymore." I tried my cute, but harmless, little boy smile.

"That's not what I meant."

Uh-oh.

"Help me out then. What do you mean?"

"I told Sunny you were a nice guy, but I never thought you'd flirt with my friend like that. I felt foolish sitting here."

I didn't respond quickly enough.

"Was I mistaken about when we first met?" she asked. "I mean, you were very professional—the perfect gentleman, but I thought we made, oh, I don't know, sort of a connection?"

I wondered if, at that moment, she also thought I was a moron. She played with her napkin while she spoke, all the while looking down at her hands. I glanced back at the Regulator. We'd been there a long time. She raised her eyes again and stared at me for a moment before continuing.

I wish I'd left first. Why do these things happen to me?

"You knew I was married," she said, "and you respected that. You didn't come on to me, even after I told you what I used to do for a living. Most guys, especially cops, would have tried to take advantage of that. But when we shook hands and said good-bye—I don't know about you, but I sure felt something."

Especially cops?

Responding to a statement like that wasn't easy, and she was right, sort of. But when you think you may have to arrest someone, beautiful blonde or not, you tend to act professionally...or at least you should. But I saw her point. I admit, just one handshake was enough for me to feel an attraction.

"I'm flattered—a lot. And, yes, a guy would have to be more than a little off center not to feel something...nice after meeting you. I guess I

Wayne Zurl

just act like an old married man most of the time." I paused for a moment, needing to get back that professional barrier. "It's been good to see you again, and I'm genuinely sorry you lost your husband. How about I do my best to help your friend? I'll be sure to let you know how I make out. I'll call you and her, too."

"Did I just get a brush-off, Mr. Jenkins?"

"No, ma'am, not from me. I'm just acting like a good little sheriff."

She laughed. "You're certainly not little, and does anyone other than Tillie call you Sheriff?"

"Only when I starred in cowboy movies."

"I guess they were before my time."

I shrugged and felt old. "I understand. And I won't ask how old your father is."

"And I'll be sure not to tell you."

"Good idea. Okay, I'm going to see what I can learn about Mr. Park."

She waved to Tillie and made a gesture for the check. Tillie dropped it off, and I picked it up.

"Please let me pay for this," she said.

I hate when girls do that.

I shook my head. "No, I'm an old-fashioned guy. When I have tea with two beautiful women, I do my chivalry act and take care of the check."

"You were my guest."

"Doesn't matter. I'm happy to be here, and I was doing my job, so we have to do this my way."

She dipped her head an inch. "As you wish, sir."

After that smile, I understood why men paid eight-hundred-bucks for her company.

"Good girl."

She stood and tucked a few strands of blonde hair behind her right ear. I peeled a few bills off the wad I carried in my pocket to pay the check, and we left together.

As I walked back to the municipal building, I suspected the next few days might be difficult.

Thirty years ago, it would have been a piece of cake. Why should I worry now?

Chapter Two

"Ralph, as soon as the word *intelligence* came to mind, I thought of you." I swung my big swivel chair around, changed the phone to my right ear and settled into a more comfortable position.

"Oh yeah? You always start a conversation like that when you want a favor. Sounds like a load of crap to me."

"Partner, I'm shocked...and hurt."

"Gimme a break." He added a typical note of sarcasm.

Special Agent Ralph Oliveri from the Knoxville FBI field office is overly cynical for a guy his age.

"Jeez, I called to say hello," I said, "and...I just happen to have some legitimate business to discuss."

"Yeah, what else is new? Whaddaya want this time?" Ralph speaks with an unmistakable New York accent.

"Intelligence information. What do you know about a Korean named Hee-Chul Park or Park, Hee-Chul if you do it the Korean way? You may also use Pak as the family name." I spelled it out. "Sometimes they've Americanized...

Oliveri interrupted my lecture on Korean folkways. "Yeah, we know about him."

"You do?"

"Sure, he came up a few years ago. Our small-town version of Korean organized crime. But he's also a big man in the Korean community here in Knoxville. Very philanthropic, or so it seems."

"How so?"

Ralph had piqued my interest. I moved my feet off the edge of the

16

desk and sat upright, anxious to hear the skinny on my Korean gangster.

"He either gives or loans money to start businesses and churches," Ralph explained. "He finds jobs for people, helps newly arrived Koreans locate homes—many altruistic tendencies."

"So he's a loan-shark and labor padrone, a shady character who fancies himself an ethnic block boss. What's altruistic about that?" I put my feet back up and relaxed again.

"Haven't had any complaints on him. Nothing from Knoxville PD either."

"Of course."

I told Ralph how Sunny Kim received a visit from Mr. Park and his henchman, who had yet to be identified, and been given the word about his protection racket. Park allowed Sunny seven days to get her finances in order before his goon squad made their first collection.

"And this Miss Kim comes to you," he said. "Figures you're the white knight who'll run Park off and save her day?"

I rarely take offense to Ralph's sarcasm.

"All the girls think that about me."

"Is she crazy?"

"Hey."

"So what are you going to do, confront the goons Park sends? They'll say Kim misunderstood. They'll say one of Park's enterprises is building security. If Kim doesn't want someone looking after her business, she has no obligation. Maybe you have her wear a wire, but nothing incriminating is ever said, and you got nothin'."

"Who said this would be easy?" I asked.

"These guys are pretty smart, pal. Everyone knows what the real story is, but you never get enough probable cause for an arrest. If you stretch that just to break Park's balls, you lose it in court because reasonable doubt abounds. And, Mr. Smart Guy, what happens next? Windows get broken, employees get tuned up or if Park is really pissed off, there's a midnight fire."

Ralph is twenty years younger than me; I hate it when he acts parental.

"I know all that, Ralphie. I thought I'd have a friendly chat with Park."

17

Ralph continued his sarcastic act. "And you'll just get him to roll over and mend his evil ways?"

"I can be persuasive. And I get along great with Asian people."

"You might put the Korean woman in deep shit by going toe to toe with this bird. I hate to say it, but for the time being, that protection money may be a necessary overhead and good insurance. What kind of business does she own anyway?"

I wished he hadn't asked. "Uh...massage therapy."

"Oh, for chrissake, Sam, is this some kind of sex shop the county deps will be raiding in six months?"

"She says not."

"And you believe her because…?"

Ralph was an accountant before he became a federal cop. He's got a conservative streak.

"She's an ex-hooker."

"Oh, Madonna mi'. Are you for real?"

"I've always thought so."

"A Korean ex-hooker opens a massage parlor and you believe her business isn't just as shady as Park's?"

"Yeah, I do."

"Mannaggia!"

"So, Ralph, can you send me a full package on Mr. Park? Will you get the current poop from INTERPOL as well, or shall I?"

There was a moment of silence. Oliveri always bitches about doing me favors, but he's gotten involved in a few very interesting cases because of me. I looked at it as good training for the kid.

"Yeah, I'll send you a complete story. Gimme a couple hours."

"Thanks. By the way, goombah, you wouldn't know anyone at the embassy in Seoul who could run this guy through the Korean National Police, would you?"

"I really wish you didn't know so much about the resources we have."

"Too smart for my own good?"

"Nuts."

He hung up.

18

* * * *

Ralph's couple of hours spilled over into the next day. Of course, he had someone to call at the US Embassy in Seoul. There's always an FBI spook lurking around embassy corridors, no matter where you go in the world. And there were quite a few time zones to consider between East Tennessee and South Korea, not to mention the International Date Line to delay my information.

I soon learned that Mr. Park had been born Pak, Hee-Chul in 1955 and grew up in the post war Yong Kong Dong section of Seoul near the Han River. At an early age, he fell into league with one of the many gangs of real slicky boys that roamed the streets of Seoul, doing anything they could to make a few won—either honestly or not. Stealing from the U.S. military has always been one of the easier and more lucrative ways to garner cash...and thereby power.

Stories of the illegal prowess of the slicky boys were always entertaining when 1 served in Korea with the Army. Pak, later calling himself Park, grew in stature among the crooks of the capital city, ultimately organizing his own gang. The Korean National Police arrested him many times, but sustained only a few convictions. Surviving the jail time only enhanced his reputation among the thugs and street people of Seoul.

In 1986, Park immigrated to Vancouver, British Columbia. The Mounties and city police there documented his assimilation into Korean organized crime and monitored his activities. He had no arrests in Canada, but was high on the suspect list for several murders.

An officially clean record in Canada allowed him to enter the U.S. in 1991. He spent a little time in Seattle and then moved on to Los Angeles. Police and FBI intelligence followed him through 2003 when he came to Knoxville. In 2008 he was about to meet yours truly.

* * * *

"Sammy, you've got a call on the main number. It sounds like another one of your New York people." Bettye put the call through.

Since the New York person wasn't female, I assumed Bettye and I were friends again.

"Chief Jenkins, may I help you?"

"You certainly may, big guy. How the hell are you?"

I recognized the voice. "Freddie? You big chadrool." That's the Italian word for idiot.

"Now is that nice?"

"No, but it's true. How ya doin'?"

"I'm okay. Police chief, huh? Hot damn, you're really coming up in the world."

"Yeah, from a dick lieutenant making lots of money and twenty-eight detectives to watch over, to a chief with twelve cops and one operations aide. Anyway, the title's nice. By New York standards, the pay sucks, but what the hell, I've got status now."

"I hear ya. You like it?"

"I complain, but...yeah. There are some good people here. How about you? What're you doing?"

"I work for my kid now," he said. "He owns a construction company. I go out and do estimates. I like it, too. Better than that gig I had as a maitre d' and occasional bouncer. This thing helps the kid out, keeps me outta trouble, and I end up with a few honest bucks."

"I haven't heard from you since those e-mails you sent a couple years ago. Nice of you to call. You want to just shoot the breeze, or is there something I can do for you?"

"A favor actually."

"I thought so," I said. "Sure, anything you need. Well, almost anything."

"I'm gonna come up and see you. I hear the Black Cloud works for you again. Shit, you poor guy. It'll be good to see you two again."

John "Black Cloud" Gallagher, currently my operations aide at Prospect PD, had been a detective who worked with me in New York. Retired Detective Fred Mazzio, another former member of my herd, was the one speaking on the phone.

"Good. You need a place to stay? We've got a guest room. I'll let you have it cheap."

"You're a real sport, boss. No, I need you to find some place nice to park my forty-foot motor home. We're coming up for a motorcycle rally. I'm dying to ride that thing you hillbillies call The Dragon."

I'm no motorcycle buff, but I know all about The Dragon. It's a winding stretch of US 129 running between Tallassee, Tennessee and Fontana Lake on the North Carolina side of the Smokies. Every motorcyclist or sports car enthusiast worth their salt wants to drive that road.

"You'll like that," I said. "You might get dizzy and drive off a cliff, but you can give your bike a real workout."

"Great. Can you get me a spot for seven days?"

He gave me the dates.

"I certainly can. I've got great influence over the people in this neck of the woods. How's Mary? The woman is a saint if she's still living with you."

"She's okay for a grandmother of three."

"Congratulations. You always looked like the grandpa-type."

Fred cleared his throat. "Speaking of looks, Sam, I've gained a little weight since I retired. I say this because I don't want to walk into your place and listen to you break my balls."

"You were no lightweight back on the job. You must have been what, two-twenty-five?"

"Yeah, and I gained about fifty pounds...or so."

I tried to picture that.

"Jeez, Freddie, what did you do with all your expensive suits?"

He laughed. "Only you would think of that."

I thought of his old comrade. "I'll call you back about the RV spot. Hang on a minute. I want you to talk to someone." I buzzed honorary detective John Gallagher's phone.

"Hey, John, I've got an obscene phone call for you." I switched it over.

Ten minutes later John Gallagher walked into my office.

"Whaddaya think, Boss? Freddie'll be up here day after tomorrow. You gonna offer him a job?"

And people say there is no such thing as a stupid question.

"Doing what?"

"You need another clerk-typist with a gun?"

"One is all I can handle."

And I have trouble with him at times.

21

"Anyways, it'll be good to see him again," he said.

"Yeah, it will." I nodded and thought about something job related for a moment. "You know, John. That gives me an idea. Maybe I will offer Freddie some work. Just for a day. I've got a job for him. What would I do without you? Damn good thought."

"Oh, yeah? Thanks, Boss. You're not gonna fire me and hire him, are you?"

"No, John, as long as you find him a campground to park his RV, your job is secure."

Chapter Three

I pulled off the Pellissippi Parkway at Exit 3 and made a right on Westland Drive. After traveling east less than two miles, I turned between a pair of tall brick columns that created the entrance to a subdivision called Kensington Gardens.

Attached to those columns, five-foot-tall brick walls provided the backing for a botanical garden that stretched several hundred feet, decorating the outside of an upscale housing development. Twenty yards of manicured sod lawn preceded the flowers and met the two-lane blacktop. Kensington Gardens showed lots of curb appeal.

A white unmarked Chevy Impala sat on the side of the entry road facing Westland Drive where Knoxville Detective D.W. Renfro waited for me. I parked my Ford across from the Impala, walked to the passenger's side and opened the door.

"Detective Renfro?"

He nodded.

"I'm Sam Jenkins."

"Figgered that."

We shook hands. Renfro appeared to be in his early forties, had a medium build, wore summer clothes appropriate for a detective, had a thirty-dollar haircut and what the British would call a neat, military-style mustache, a couple shades darker than his sun-bleached blond hair. He looked professional and competent.

"Park's at home," he said. "Up ta the next corner, make a left, third place on the left. He's usually got two ol' boys with 'im. They's called Boo and Ha. Some names, ain't they?"

I smiled.

"Those two look like a couple o' middleweight sumo wrestlers," he said. "Ya want a li'l back-up?"

"I wouldn't mind if you sat at the curb and kept your eyes open. But I'd say you may not want to listen in on our conversation."

"Uh-oh." He grinned. "Okay, jump in. I'll take ya up there. My radio'll git us he'p quicker 'an yours. If ya need it, that is."

Park's house was large, perhaps five to six thousand square feet on two floors. The façade of sandstone-colored brick contrasted nicely beneath a dark brown, tabbed shingle roof. All the homes around it were large, and the lots were small—a sign of the new millennium. I pressed a bell button, and Westminster chimes sounded within the home.

A dark haired, middle-aged Korean woman answered the door wearing a gray shirtwaist dress that looked like a stylish domestic uniform. I greeted her in Korean and handed her my business card. Not the one that says *Have Gun Will Travel*; I save that for special occasions. She smiled. I showed her my badge, and in English explained what I wanted. In fluent, but heavily accented English, she asked me to wait. She bowed slightly and disappeared.

I waited in a slate-floored foyer, looking up at a modern glass chandelier slightly larger than a Smart Car. A few minutes later, a tall Korean man in his thirties walked up to me.

Without a greeting or even a smile, he spoke. "I am Mr. Ha. Mr. Park is busy. He is not seeing anyone until he finishes business."

Mr. Ha was a good-looking man. He wore a brown suit and white shirt, but no tie. His shoes were square toed and unmistakably Korean, probably custom-made. About six-foot-tall, Ha and I stood eye-to-eye. His broad shoulders and narrow waist reminded me of the ROK Marines I used to see marching with the 8th Army Honor Guard—all the same size and appearance. His clothing looked expensive, but even an experienced Korean tailor has trouble compensating for the bulge made by a large automatic hanging under the arm in a shoulder holster.

His vacant eyes bothered me, a typical thousand-yard stare. I got the impression that Mr. Ha cared for nothing or no one but himself. I wouldn't have been surprised to learn that he'd been endowed with neither a heart nor soul.

"Does Mr. Park have an attorney?" I asked.

"Of course. Why do you ask?"

I took out my cell phone, flipped up the cover and prepared to tap in a number.

"I'd like to call him. He should be present when I have a dozen Knoxville detectives assist me in executing a search warrant. I plan on ripping Mr. Park's house to pieces unless he sets his business aside and speaks with me...now. Not later."

Ha scowled at me. A small mole marred the surface of an otherwise smooth right cheek. The corner of his right eye twitched involuntarily. I assumed it would every time someone annoyed him. Something good to remember.

I tried to look friendly. "I promise to take very little of his time if he reconsiders."

"What are you searching for?" Ha asked.

"Nothing if he speaks with me. If he refuses, I'll tell his attorney, not you."

He considered me for a long moment. When we locked eyes, I lost the smile.

"Wait here," he said.

I'd seen enough of the oversized lighting fixture, so I walked into the living room. Everything there appeared angular and modern—grays, whites, and blacks—cold and uninviting. There were several impressive oriental paintings on the walls. I took a closer look. Money seemed to be no object to Mr. Park and his interior decorator.

In a few minutes, Ha returned. We stood close again, eye-to-eye. He didn't immediately speak, but rather tried to stare me down. We were playing chicken, and he wanted me to blink first. The tick at the corner of his right eye came back into motion. I'd seen similar facial imperfections in other sociopathic individuals whose minds functioned on levels beyond what the average person comprehends. I thought life would be simple as long as the ticking continued. Once it stopped, I assumed Ha would take action. I've had a lot of experience with bad guys, so screw him, I thought, and kept right on staring.

Finally, our game ended. He said, "Follow me."

We left the living room, walked down a short hallway, past the kitchen and dining room and into a wide family room. This adjoined an equally large, glassed-in sunroom. Beyond that was a covered patio and swimming pool.

When I entered the sunroom, a short Korean man in his fifties stood from where he'd been sitting on a black leather sofa. A younger man with a wide powerful body, short hair and a face scarred from adolescent acne, stood behind the couch. He looked more like the sumo wrestler Renfro spoke of.

The older man smiled warmly. "Mr. Jenkins, I'm Hee-Chul Park." He pointed over his shoulder adding, "And this is my associate, Mr. Boo. You've already met Mr. Ha. How may I help you?"

Park and I shook hands, and we bowed slightly. I said hello in Korean and added my thanks for seeing me.

"You speak Hangul nicely for an American. Very polite, very good accent. That is not typical GI Korean."

"Com-op sumnida," I said, thanking him.

"Please sit, Mr. Jenkins. We are in no hurry."

I loved his voice and the benevolent despot act.

Park looked like a typical Korean businessman, not a criminal. He was about five-five and stocky but not fat. His skin was ruddy, and his thick, brush-like hair was cut perfectly and almost fifty-percent gray. The light gray silk suit he wore may have cost as much as the annual rice crop from Kimpo. Beneath the jacket, he wore a black golf shirt buttoned to the top.

Intricate wrinkles at the corners of his eyes made me think he smiled a lot. I took him to be a wily old bugger. His countenance made me believe he was always thinking of an inside joke the rest of the world knew nothing about.

"Would you like tea?" he asked.

"Yes, thank you very much." I sat in a black leather easy chair, facing him across a narrow glass and chrome cocktail table. I decided I'd smile a lot, too.

"In-som-cha or ok-su-su-cha?" he asked, testing my language skills and giving me the choice of two Korean teas.

"I like old-fashioned corn tea," I said. "but it gives me heartburn. The ginseng would be lovely."

26

"In-som-cha, choo say oh, Ha she," he said to Mr. Ha, who immediately left the room.

"I keep a supply of corn tea," Park said. "It reminds me of my humble beginnings. But I'm sorry to say not many guests wish to drink it."

"Your beginnings in Yong Kong Dong?"

"Yes! You know where I lived as a young man. Very good. I assume you have not only been to Korea, but have spent some time in Seoul?"

"You're correct. I know Yong Kong Dong, also Ma-po Ku, Shin Sol Dong, Hu-am Dong, Yong San Ni...many parts of Seoul the average American never visits."

He nodded for a moment before asking, "And where are you from, Mr. Jenkins? You do not sound like the natives of Tennessee."

Mr. Ha returned and stood next to Park's sofa. Boo, still behind the boss in general support, looked like a stone temple guardian in a black, three-piece suit.

"I've lived here for a number of years," I said. "But I'm originally from New York."

"I thought I recognized a bit of an accent. I've been to New York."

Probably for Korean mob in-service training.

"It is an exciting place," I said.

"Did you live in the city?" he asked.

"No, on Long Island, but, of course, I spent a lot of time in the five boroughs."

He nodded. "I remember Long Island having many beautiful parts. I was invited on a boat trip once—on Long Island Sound."

Probably to send a colleague, who fell into disfavor, on a one-way trip to live with the fishes.

I smiled and nodded. The Korean woman who had answered the door brought in a tray holding a pot of tea and two cups without handles. A plate of sweet Korean cookies sat between the cups. I made a point of thanking her when she poured for me. Like Sunny Kim, she giggled and covered her face because of some incomprehensible embarrassment.

"Mrs. Shin is a good housekeeper," Park said. "I employ her as a favor to her son. He owns a market in Oak Ridge."

I dipped my head to acknowledge his statement and to show respect

27

waited until Park sipped his tea first, then drank from my cup.

"So, Mr. Jenkins, what shall we talk about? What was so important that you came all the way from Prospect to visit me?"

"We have a mutual acquaintance, sir—a Miss Kim, Soon-Wha. She's a new business owner in Prospect. It's on her behalf that I come to see you."

"I see." Park nodded thoughtfully and sipped from his cup.

I glanced at Ha and Boo. Ha stared at me scowling, angry perhaps. His body language made me think I wouldn't be getting a birthday card from him. But Boo stood impassively without expression. Boo was the guy to worry about.

It was time to practice my Oriental diplomacy. If I wanted cooperation from Park, even compliance grudgingly given, I'd have to allow him to make it seem like this acquiescence had been his idea—the old saving face game.

"I believe Miss Kim may be under a misapprehension," I said. "One which has her upset, and even frightened enough to come to me as a policeman and ask for my protection."

Park feigned surprise. "How so?"

I let the question slide and continued my monologue. "I have no doubt that after a conversation with you, I can return to Prospect and tell Miss Kim she may rest easy and continue her business without fear."

Park tilted his head and cracked a slight smile. He seemed willing to let me talk and didn't press for an answer. "I've met this Miss Kim," he said. "She is a beautiful woman. Are you involved with her on a...personal level?"

"No, I've only recently met her. Our association is strictly professional."

"Do you know the nature of her business, Mr. Jenkins?"

"She employs massage therapists."

My answer sounded lame. Park allowed himself an even bigger grin to say he thought the same. A gold tooth on his bottom right quadrant twinkled in the bright room.

"I happen to know that Miss Kim engaged in a more...recreational business for years," he said. "Do you think she will run a legitimate physical therapy practice in your city?"

28

"At this point, yes, I do."

His smile changed to a frown. "And what are her fears?"

"As I said, probably unfounded and undoubtedly a misunderstanding. She thinks that for some reason, she must pay you money to stay in business."

Park shrugged and tried to look dumbfounded. He had quite an act. "It is true that I paid a visit to Miss Kim, as one Korean welcoming another to the area. I wished her luck. Perhaps you are correct, and she misunderstood my good intentions and my offer of assistance as a security consultant at a reasonable cost."

I tossed my head back and grinned like the village idiot. "Ah, there's the answer then."

Park nodded twice. "If we are both wrong about Miss Kim, and she is about to engage in some immoral activity, would she be able to continue to do so in Prospect?"

I shook my head. "No. I wouldn't allow that."

"Forgive me, Mr. Jenkins, but I am not all that familiar with your laws and customs. Is there some means where she could perhaps make a donation, to whom I'm not sure, to allow her to expand her business, shall we say, beyond simple massage therapy?"

I shook my head again and sipped more tea. "I understand what you're thinking, Mr. Park. No, that's not possible. I don't operate that way."

"Simply put, Mr. Jenkins, is there some way that perhaps both you and I—together—could provide Miss Kim with the security she might need to do business in Prospect?"

I allowed myself another sip of tea to make him wait for my answer. "No, sir. Beyond normal police protection, none of our help will be necessary. If Miss Kim establishes a legitimate business, I hope she lives long and prospers. And I've already made her feel welcome in our little city." I placed my teacup on the table and sat forward, giving Park an intense stare. "But if your suspicions are correct and she returns to this illegal business someone told you about, I will either make her time in Prospect extremely uncomfortable or I'll arrest her and close up the shop. It's that simple."

Park let out a silent laugh. "Then I assume your visit here was a courtesy. If you learn that she does have some illegal intentions, you will inform me. I would not want to be involved with someone like that in any way—Korean or not."

"That is a wise thing for you to say, Mr. Park. I'm glad we understand each other. And I will tell Miss Kim about her misapprehensions."

He nodded and sipped more tea. We must have looked like two old diplomats sitting across the "ribbon table" at Pan Mun Jom.

"Miss Kim mentioned your associates, Mr. Ha and Mr. Boo," I said. "She was fearful that they, for some unknown reason—you know how these women are—may wish to do her harm or damage her property or intimidate her employees. I can't imagine why, but now that we are friends, and because they are in your employ, I thought it would be appropriate for me to count on Mr. Ha and Mr. Boo to be...how shall I put this? Oh...my security consultants and assistants."

Park frowned. "I don't understand."

I turned two palms up. "If I were to learn that something has happened to Miss Kim—her property becomes damaged or any of her employees are bothered, I could hold these men personally responsible for what happened. I need you to promise me that they will insure nothing I could object to would *ever* happen to my new friend, Miss Kim."

"You ask a lot at our first meeting, Mr. Jenkins."

I thought we'd come to a point in our relationship where I should test Park's resolve. "I'm very protective of the people in my town, Mr. Pak."

Hi head jerked up. "My name is Park, Mr. Jenkins. I Americanized it when I became a citizen."

It was my turn to nod and grin. "I understand. Your former president, Pak, Chung Hee called himself Park when he dealt with Americans. I had a friend who knew Pak quite well. I met this man in Korea...on a professional level. I think he liked me. We were both soldiers then, and I learned things from him. Unfortunately, after I left your country, this friend and President Pak had a...falling out, shall we say? My friend was General Kim, Jae-Gyu. Most people called him CIA Kim."

Park looked startled. "That man killed Pak, Chung-Hee and was hanged for it." He couldn't shake the surprise from his voice.

I raised my eyebrows. "I said I learned from him, sir. I never said I didn't grow to know more than he did." I followed my comment with another big smile.

Park laughed out loud, a real belly-laugh. "So, you come here to keep me from your city. Okay. Have the Kim girl for yourself if you want her. You are very personable and polite for an American. You speak Korean as well as I've heard any foreigner do so, but I should be offended. I should not agree to anything. How could you stop me? Now, you told Mr. Ha you had a warrant to search my house. Why do you want to search me? What is it you are looking for?"

I touched my nose and lowered my eyes trying to look like someone just caught in a lie. "Did I say that? Perhaps it's a warrant to search the home of another Mr. Park I'm going to see today." I dipped my head a quarter of an inch. "My apologies, sir. Just another misunderstanding, I suppose."

I stood up. "Thanks for your time, Mr. Park, and for the tea. I hope you never find out how I deal with people who refuse to work with me."

Park scowled at that. Ha never changed his expression, and Boo still did his impression of Old Stone Face.

I took a step to my left and stood in front of Mr. Ha. He fixed me with a badass stare. His eye ticked away, faster this time than before. Park remained seated. Boo stood fixed in position, but his head moved to watch me.

"As a gesture of good will, I won't arrest Mr. Ha for carrying a concealed handgun," I said, still looking into Ha's eyes. "But only today. And only because he's now personally responsible for Miss Kim's safety."

Ha tensed up like a steel spring. I exaggerated a smile.

"Nice to meet you, Mr. Ha. See you again some time."

When I spoke the last word, I feinted with my left hand. Ha dropped his look and automatically shifted his right leg to the rear, giving him a more secure stance—a move someone familiar with tae-kwan-do might use. His open legs now provided me with the target I needed and I drove my knee into his groin—hard and with determination. He let out a

31

whoosh of air and doubled over in pain. Ha should have kept watching my eyes.

I wanted to make a point, and that saving face crap can go just so far. I brushed my sport jacket aside so Park and Boo could see the Smith & Wesson on my belt and my hand resting on the grips. Park was standing now. Boo began to move from behind the sofa, but Park held up a hand. Boo stopped. Ha leaned against the wide arm of the couch, still moaning and holding his crotch.

"Nice to meet you, Mr. Pak," I said. "Please say good-bye to Mrs. Shin for me."

A smirk began to form on Park's face. I looked at Boo and his wide, square body. His expression reminded me of a good mystery, one that's tough to figure out. There was something going on behind his hard eyes, but that something seemed impenetrable, something known to him alone. Of those three hoods, Boo was the scariest. I pointed at him with my left index finger and let my thumb fall like the hammer of a gun.

I winked. "Have a nice day, chingo," and called Boo *friend* before I left, without an escort to the front door.

Outside, I dropped into the front seat of Renfro's police car and let out a little air.

"Hmmm, I guess that went off well enough." I felt like I just ran two miles, flat out.

Renfro looked at me and frowned. "I don't even want to know."

I raised my eyebrows. "No, you don't."

He shook his head, started the car and drove me back to the subdivision entrance where I had parked my Ford in the shade.

As I drove back toward the Pellissippi, I couldn't help telling myself, I *really* was getting too old to do things like that.

Chapter Four

As a younger man, I could pull off stunts like a confrontation with Park and his hired yo-yos without skipping a beat. Now, the stress of those shenanigans takes its toll on me. I've always said that if you're sharp and have good experience, being a cop is like riding a bicycle. I only need to realize that my tires may be losing some tread.

By the time I got back to the PD, I felt tried, hungry and needed a drink to neutralize the massive dose of adrenalin that surged through my veins and helped me through the discussion with Park. I said hello to Bettye and John, didn't tell them what I had done and retreated to my office.

It would have been bad form to break out the bottle of Glenfiddich I kept in my desk drawer during the middle of a day, so I settled for a cup of the coffee Bettye made earlier. That week we were drinking a fifty-fifty mix of House Italian Roast and Manitou Blueberry from the Leelanau Coffee Company in Michigan. I like buying mail-order things.

I held my cup and leaned back in the big swivel chair, closing my eyes and trying to clear my head of the throbbing I felt as a result of taking on the local Kimchee Mafia single-handedly.

Sipping the coffee was easy. Clearing my head was not.

An adrenalin spike doesn't just evaporate after you engage in the action that naturally produces the hormone. With sufficient dosage, you emulate the Energizer Bunny until you crash. When you crash is anyone's guess.

I've tried to learn all sorts of things like meditation and other methods of straightening out my head for times like these or when I have problems sleeping. But I'm not very good at any of them. Often, things race through my mind, overwhelming my ability to relax. Sometimes, I'm amazed at what filters into my brain when I'm trying to think of nothing.

I placed the coffee cup on the desk, closed my eyes tightly and attempted to put myself in a quiet place. I gave it a few tries and several minutes. Having no luck pulling off that trick, I ended up in a place that was anything but tranquil. I may have fallen asleep or slipped into an intense daydream. My mind took me on a trip I could have done without. The miles and the years spun rapidly in front of me. The present faded out of my mind and what replaced my thoughts of the current situation, seemed no better than what I had just experienced.

I relived one of the more frustrating and unsolvable dilemmas of my younger days. It seemed odd that I didn't recall something that happened to me in Korea—my current dilemma involving so many of those people. Instead, I saw myself as a young soldier in Vietnam, a place full of terrible frustration at the best of times.

I'd been assigned as an advisor to a company of South Vietnamese irregular infantrymen. Five other American GIs served with me. The Viets were led by a captain from their LLDB—the Luc Long Dac Biet or South Vietnamese Special Forces. If you didn't know any better, you'd say that a Special Forces captain would have been one of the superior soldiers on their payroll. But with the prestige attached to the LLDB and because their officers had the potential of becoming a provincial military governor and advisor to the Regional and Popular Forces, the troops called Rough-Puffs by the Americans, there was also the potential of substantial political kick-backs far above their meager ARVN salaries. So, these positions were passed on, not to the elite soldiers of the Army of the Republic of Vietnam, but rather to those with political horsepower and impressive connections.

We worked in Tay Ninh Province, an area rife with Viet Cong activity. Almost two hundred of us patrolled the jungle countryside looking for a VC stronghold. We'd received intelligence obtained by Vietnamese members of our U.S. detachment called roadrunners, brave men who went undercover, mingling with villagers and hardcore Viet Cong, to gain information. It was our job to exploit that intelligence.

Our company headed to an area where we hoped not only to find a large group of enemy soldiers, but also a cache of weapons, ammunition and supplies that would keep *Charlie* in business for a long time. Pulling this off would be a feather in everyone's steel pot, and it would ultimately save lives.

Not long into our patrol, scouts found the VC camp. We deployed in an ambush formation and crouched uncomfortably waiting to fight. I recommended that skirmishers be sent forward to fire on the Viet Cong, draw their attention and run back toward our lines, attempting to lure the larger force of VC into chasing them back toward our main body and thereby into a crossfire. It would have been a classic maneuver and looked like it would work until one of the LLDB sergeants ordered his squad to fire prematurely, long before the bulk of our opponents were within the killing zone.

The VC spooked and never advanced far enough to be enveloped by our guns. Wisely, they retreated. To counter that, I suggested sending two platoons forward, attempting to flank the fugitives and cut off their retreat. The LLDB captain hesitated...and then waited some more. He seemed happy to let them escape. I wondered who had taken money to undermine our trap. I screamed at the captain. He still waited. I screamed again. Nothing happened. I became furious, and everyone around me knew it. I hoped like hell another large VC unit wasn't in close proximity and couldn't join forces with those who were pulling back, prepared to dig into their base camp or disappear into the jungle. I envisioned being caught between two units of superior strength and cut to ribbons by their AK-47s and rocket propelled grenades.

In my dream, I began to see everything in slow motion. I looked around at the Vietnamese and U.S. soldiers. They stared back. I thought they were waiting for me to take charge, but I was only an advisor and not the unit commander. People wanted me to make things right, but I was unable to do so because of things beyond my control.

In the background, I heard Kyu Sakamoto singing *Sukiyaki,* one of my favorite songs from the early '60s. The VC had disappeared into the bush. Two U.S. sergeants recalled any troops who had advanced beyond our line, insuring that our men didn't get caught in the same type of trap we had intended for the opposition. The SVN captain still sat there

35

thinking about his next course of action. He talked to the sergeant who ordered the early shooting in hushed tones. I was furious and ripped off my little boonie hat and threw it on the ground. A veteran sergeant-first-class came over and put his hand on my shoulder.

"Come on, L.T.," he said. "It don't mean nothin'."

I was young and emotional. I cared. I wanted everything to come out perfectly because we could do it. I knew how to do it. And there was no reason why we shouldn't except for that miserable captain. The sergeant tried to calm me down. The captain walked away, not wanting to be anywhere near me. Later, he would complain to my C.O. about my disrespect.

Sakamoto finished his song, and Nancy Sinatra began singing *You Only Live Twice*. I found myself sitting at a window seat in a Boeing 707, banking to the left over Fuji-Yama on an approach to Tachikawa Air Base near Tokyo. The sky around us was the color of gray steel, littered with massive cotton ball-like cumulus islands. Lower down, a wispy stratum of clouds hung around the summit of the volcano like webs, just as I'd seen in old photos and post cards.

The music stopped, I blinked, and the scene switched back to the jungle. I felt angry. Tears filled my eyes. I could have cheerfully strangled the officer who disregarded my plans.

I felt a hand on my shoulder. It wasn't SFC Joe McKinney.

"Sammy, are you okay?"

I raised my head and looked at Bettye Lambert. Concern and confusion showed on her face. I sat forward and pushed my coffee cup out of the way, across the desktop.

"Yeah, sure, Betts, I'm okay. I was just daydreaming."

"Darlin', you've got tears on your cheeks. What's the matter?"

I smelled her perfume and stared into her hazel eyes. Not wanting to get into a lengthy explanation, I finally shrugged. "Uh, allergies, I guess. My head feels like it's going to explode. It just happened. I'm okay though. Thanks."

Bettye tilted her head. I wasn't sure she bought my story.

"Did you need something?" I asked.

"No, sugar, I didn't need anything. I was just walkin' by and thought somethin' was wrong. Sure you're okay? Your ears are red."

I tried to shake off the embarrassment. "Yes, ma'am, I'm fine. Thanks for your concern. I'll just finish this coffee and...I guess I'll do something...that needs doing."

She still looked dubious. "Be sure and tell me if I can help you with anythin', you hear. And, Sammy, please take medication for your allergies."

"I will. Thanks again."

As she left my office, Bettye's blonde ponytail swayed back and forth—so did her backside.

* * * *

"He had a pair of henchmen with him named Ha and Boo." I added salt, pepper, fresh dill and butter to the pan of Yukon Gold potatoes sitting on the range.

"Henchmen? You may be the only person on earth who uses that word, sweetie," Kate said.

"You're probably right. Old-fashioned words are getting lost in today's culture. People would rather say bad dudes than henchmen, minions or my all-time favorite, myrmidons."

"Oh, God, I know you're the only one who'd say myrmidons." She laughed as she finished quartering the last of the fresh boiled beets and began mixing them with sour cream and other ingredients. "Forget about the traditional meaning of Achilles' faithful soldiers at the siege of Troy, you had your own loyal followers or should I call them hired ruffians? Why should this Korean hood be any different?"

"Yeah, I love that word. You ready for more wine?" I held up a bottle of New Zealand sauvignon blanc.

"Yes, please." She pushed her empty glass a little closer on the kitchen counter.

"I actually liked this guy, Park. There's no doubt he's a criminal, but he had class. We could deal with each other."

"Sometimes you make me feel so liberal."

"What are you talking about?"

"Well, I don't seem to think anything is wrong when my husband tells me he's friends with a beautiful ex-prostitute who was once a murder suspect."

37

She hesitated, and I interrupted.

"We're not friends. She said I seemed trustworthy."

"Oh, please!"

"What?"

"And she introduces you to her Korean friend, also a former hooker, also beautiful and now owner of a massage parlor."

"So?"

"So, this gorgeous Hangook tells you she's being shaken down by a local representative of the Kimchee Mafia. You visit him, threaten him and kick his *henchman* in the crotch. And I'm supposed to listen and say, 'I'm so glad you had an interesting day, dear.' And I do. You're unbelievable!"

"You think so?"

"May I have more wine, please?"

"I just filled your glass."

"I need more, thank you."

"Someone might think you had a drinking problem."

"A reasonable person might think I had a marital problem."

"Jeez."

Chapter Five

The stores and commercial buildings around Prospect's town square and along the side streets that spider from it are not new. Thanks to a pushy Chamber of Commerce and a zealous code enforcement department, the physical appearance of these establishments would be acceptable to all but the most obsessive/compulsive evaluator of small urban settings. The carefully preserved buildings all smacked of the period between world wars. Prospect began to grow and develop in the 1920s as a community near the Aluminum Company of America, the area's major employer since 1919.

This particular store sat directly across the street from Kisaeng Massage Therapy. The sign above the front door and a large picture window read:

The Brothers Fine
Diamonds…and other Fine Jewelry

The owners, Bernie and Irving Fine, were identical twins and former residents of Brighton Beach. They relocated to East Tennessee after their father, a well-known diamond wholesaler, died, leaving a business named for them. Bernie and Irving were a few years older than me, and as ex-New Yorkers, we spoke often. I considered them friends. I walked into the shop and found one of the brothers waiting for customers behind a glass fronted display counter.

"Hey, Bernie," I said.

He put on a big smile that looked more than half way genuine.

"How ya doin'? How ya been?"

Bernie was a short, slightly built man with thinning red hair streaked with gray. He reminded me of Woody Allen with a bad haircut. Irving, not then in attendance, looked almost identical, but Bernie wore the glasses in the family.

I returned the smile. "I'm okay. How's your brother?"

"Uhh, he's driving me crazy. I can't deal wit him."

"You heard from your sister lately?"

"Oy, don't ask."

Strike two, I shrugged.

"Have you got a minute? I need some help."

"Hey, you're always a gentleman. Whatever you need, just ask." Bernard always seemed eager to accommodate.

"Tell me about your new neighbors across the street."

"Heh, heh, heh." He pronounced the words with a snicker rather than laughing. "You mean Prospect Bait and Tickle?"

"What?" Prospect Bait and Tackle, a store for fishermen, was in another part of town.

"The massage parlor you're talking about?"

"Yeah, right."

"Whadda you wannna know?" he asked.

"What does bait and tickle mean?"

He slid off the stool where he'd been perched. "I'm jus' kidding. You know what they say about massage parlors."

"Is something going on over there?"

He did a long exaggerated shrug. "Not that I know."

"They've only been open a couple of weeks, but does it look like a legitimate business, or are the clients all sleazy-looking men?"

"You mean like a den of iniquity? Heh, heh, heh."

"Yeah, like sex for money," I said.

Bernie pushed his hands out to the sides and turned the palms up. "I can't say that. I don't see many customers, but so far I've seen only old people go in there."

"Bernard, you and I are old people. Be more specific."

"Old, old people, men and women…both, with canes maybe."

"So the customers seem like people who really need some kind of physical therapy?"

He shrugged again. "I guess, but how should I know?"

"Good. Thanks for the help."

"Ya welcome, anytime. So do you need any jewelry fuh *huh*? Some beautiful opals I just got in from that Burmese Jew my brother knows."

"*Her* had a birthday the end of last month. Remember the brooch I bought? *Her* does not need any more jewelry at the moment. I'll see you at Christmas time."

His grin seemed almost lecherous. "I love Christmas."

"I can imagine. So what can you make with those opals?"

* * * *

I left Bernie Fine to his jewelry, crossed the road and headed toward Kisaeng Massage Therapy. The air was clear, smelled clean, and Prospect looked like the perfect place to live and work. It was a good morning to see what Sunny Kim had decided to wear.

Until recently, the space now occupied by Kisaeng Massage had been a father-daughter family dentistry business. Those two had since moved to a modern, upscale professional building near the city park. The floor plan in the suite consisted of reception and waiting areas, several private treatment rooms and, as I learned later, a separate office for the owner.

Sunny had added a few subtle East Asian touches when she redecorated the building.

Where a half-wall separated the reception desk and counter from the waiting area, she built a wood-framed, opaque paper wall where diffused, recessed lighting created a soft, relaxing glow seen by the waiting patients.

The items hanging on the walls were not modern bits of schlock obtained from an ethnic restaurant supply catalog. Something most people from Korea called a Pusan plate, a fourteen-inch, white porcelain platter with a hand painted kisaeng wearing a chima-chogari, the classic Korean dress, and playing a stringed musical instrument called a kai-ah-goom, hung above a dark brown leather covered settee.

A large brass plate showing four old men in high relief, wearing old-style hats and clothing, playing the game Go, hung over two matching armchairs.

Framed, original artwork elsewhere on the walls all looked to be pre-World War Two with colonial Japanese influence evident. I assumed Sunny's former Chicago apartment donated those things to the office decor.

I stepped up to the reception counter where Roni Keeble smiled and greeted me.

"Hi, welcome aboard." She looked like a cruise director on the Love Boat.

"What are you doing here?" I know I sounded surprised.

"I work here. Sort of a silent partner. Did you come for a massage?" She tilted her head and offered a sexy smile.

"You didn't tell me you worked here."

"We say hello every couple of years, and I have to call and tell you what I'm doing?"

She wore a blue knitted top that clung to her body like a wet T-shirt.

"No, Veronica. Of course not." I must have sounded offended. I wasn't.

"I didn't mean it to sound like that. Sorry."

"It's okay. No offense taken. I have no feelings, so they can't be hurt." I returned the smile. "I paid your friend Mr. Park a visit yesterday."

She squinted at me with those sapphire blue eyes, perhaps not believing the remark about my feelings, but perhaps more interested in the outcome of my meeting with the gangster.

"Not my friend, handsome," she said. "What did he have to say for himself? Denied everything, I bet."

"Is Sunny around? I'll tell my story once, and both of you can enjoy my company."

"Oh, brother." She shook her head, picked up the phone and pushed two buttons on the console. A few seconds later, she said, "Come up front if you have a minute. Someone here wants us to fall in love with him."

I wiggled my eyebrows and gave her the cutest smile I could muster up. She stuck out her tongue like a little kid. A lot of the women I know do that. Maybe it's me.

"Sunny will be here in a second. Did everything go okay?"

"Park and I got along famously. He thought I was charming—said so, too. His friend Mr. Ha may not like me too much, but I think Park will leave Sunny alone."

Sunny Kim walked out from somewhere in the back of her shop, an office I'd get to see in the future. She wore a lovely black tank top and snazzy white slacks she didn't purchase in Kmart. I smiled at her.

She returned my smile. "Hello, Mr. Sam. You have good news?"

I tilted my head like a matinee idol and showed her more of my pearly whites. "The mister isn't necessary, and yes, I have good news. Ladies, Mr. Park said in essence, he will leave you alone. Now, we just have to wait and see of he's good at his word."

Sunny looked at me questioningly.

Roni asked, "Do you really think he'll leave her and the place and the employees alone? We all have a stake in how much you tend to believe him."

"It's impossible for me to know, but we had a long talk, Korean style, over tea and with much formality. He didn't argue and volunteered to no longer pursue what he originally wanted. I believe he had a misconception about your business here, if you know what I mean."

Both girls nodded. The difference between Roni's blue eyes and Sunny's almost black eyes could startle and arouse the Dali Lama. They looked like four polished stones.

"I'm guessing that he may write you off," I said. "And I think I left a lasting impression on him. But if something happens or you just see something you don't like the looks of, call me. Call 9-1-1 first. A car will be on the way before I get here. I'll look out for you anyway I can." I gave them another grin that implied I wanted to be their hero.

Sunny sighed and looked relieved. Veronica gave me a look designed to cloud men's minds.

"You're a pretty good guy...for a cop," Roni said.

"Tae-dahnie com-op sumnida, Sam," Sunny said.

"Chom ahn-ayo, Miss Kim." I bowed. "And thanks a bunch, Ms. Keeble." I winked at her. "It's a pleasure doing business with you ladies."

Three things in the world stir my emotions—vintage British sports cars, old wooden sailboats and beautiful women. I had two of the latter within inches of me and a '67 Austin-Healey in the garage. Two out of three ain't bad.

* * * *

On my best or most ambitious day, when four o'clock rolls around I would rather sit at my desk with my feet up and prepare myself to go home at five than do any meaningful work. I refer to this as my personal out-briefing time.

I was doing just that when I heard two grown men, neither of whom would ever see sixty again, acting like juvenile fools.

"Oh, yeah, Gallagher, you're almost as big around as me," one said.

"You're not the Italian stallion any more, Freddie. The Italian hippo, maybe."

"No one ever liked you, John, because you always had a big Irish mouth."

"Everything about you is big, Freddie," the other countered.

I walked out to the lobby.

"Gentlemen, gentlemen." I raised my voice and interrupted their display of adolescence. "You're disturbing Sergeant Lambert's tranquil environment. In language you both understand, shut up. You," I pointed at Gallagher, "back to work. And you," pointing at Fred Mazzio, "my office...now."

"Jeez, you're acting like I'm back on the job," Mazzio said.

"You've always been a discipline problem, Mazzio Junior. Man, have you gained weight."

"Nice of you to mention that in front of the young lady." He turned and flashed a sleazy smile at Bettye.

In my room, we shook hands and sat in the two guest chairs in front of my desk. I felt a twinge of jealousy looking at Fred's thick hair, combed back without a part. Hardly a dozen strands of gray interrupted the rest of the almost black waves. But the waist of his jeans measuring well over forty inches made me feel a little better, as did the round belly beneath his plum-colored golf shirt.

"You prick," he said, "you don't look any different than when I saw you years ago. More gray maybe. And didn't you gain a little weight, too?"

I twisted my lip into a sneer. "Yeah, I wear size 32 ½ pants now. Nice try. You look good though. Got a nice tan. Does your son know how to keep you in line?"

He shrugged.

"Should I give him a few pointers?"

He smiled like an Italian wedding singer. "You're the only one I ever let supervise me."

"I'm honored."

We spent a few minutes catching up on personal trivia before I asked if he knew where to park his RV.

"It's parked, hooked up, and Mary is shopping in the campground store as we speak. John called and gave me the 4-1-1."

"Ah...cell phones."

He shook his head. "You really are a freakin' dinosaur."

"You rode your bike here?"

"No, I drove our Hummer. The bike is still hooked to the back of the motor home."

"You brought a motorcycle *and* a car with you?"

"Certainly."

"You are such a wop."

"Speaking of *I-tralians*," he said, "you got any good restaurants around here, or do I have to eat owl soup and roasted 'possum or some other hillbilly shit?"

"Gombah, I'll take you to a restaurant that will make your Sicilian ears wiggle. A guy from Hoboken and his family opened up a place in the next town west of here—The Villa Napoli. Top shelf all the way. Tell your wife. I'll get the Black Cloud and Mrs. Cloud and Kate and the six of us can have dinner before you leave."

"I'm not Sicilian. I'm Calabrese. How many times have I told you? Stop killing off your brain cells with that scotch, and you'll remember things. You buyin'?"

"Yeah, why not? I've got a job and a couple of pensions. And somebody has to see that John stays well fed."

"I'll get the drinks."

I nodded. "Sounds good."

Fred gave me a look. "Hey, Sam, that was good of you to give Gallagher a job. I heard he had big money trouble down in Boca."

I turned my palms up and shrugged. "He's doing okay now. Likes the job. Bettye likes him. It's like she's got a big son...one that's older than her father."

Mazzio shook his head. "That's one good-lookin' desk sergeant, pal. You doin' that?"

"You're a low-class swamp guinea, Frederick. No, I'm not *doing* that. She and I are married and not to each other."

"Still the straight arrow, huh? Live it up. You'll be dead soon."

I changed the subject. "How'd you like to be a cop again? Just a quick job—maybe half a day's work. I need an unknown face for a little undercover work."

He frowned. "Whaddaya talkin' about?"

"I've got a job that you were born to do."

"I can hardly wait. How do I get screwed this time?"

I still wasn't one-hundred-percent sure Sunny Kim's business was legitimate. I guess I'm just too cynical. Now that I knew Roni Keeble worked there, I had even more doubt. Would two former eight-hundred-dollar-a-toss hookers settle for wages paid after a medical insurance company sent them the checks? I needed an independent source to assess the situation.

"I want you to check out a massage place that just opened in town," I said. "See if you can get more than your lower back tended to, if you know what I mean."

"You think it's a skivvy joint and want me to try and get a toot?"

"Crudely put, but yes."

"Are you paying?"

"I'll reimburse you for a basic massage. I think it's seventy-five bucks. If you offer some additional stipend to the masseuse, and she accepts, and you take advantage of her, uh...services, I'll only pay if you testify in court...as some kind of expert witness."

"How the hell am I going to testify if I'm in Florida?"

"I'm just interested if she'll take the bait. If she does, make some excuse. Tell her you forgot your Viagra."

He scowled. "Hey, I don't need any o' that."

46

"Oh, I forgot. The company has no customers from Italy."

"I'm tellin' ya. I'm not kiddin'!"

"Of course you're not. Who cares? You in or what?"

"I go for a massage, and you pay?"

I nodded. "Yeah. Simple, huh?"

"If I proposition the broad and get lucky what happens?"

"It's a long story. Actually, I like the woman who's running the place, so I'll probably just give her the opportunity to close up and leave."

"You're a real gentleman."

I shrugged. "When do you want to do this?"

"I just drove here from Florida. My back and shoulders are killin' me. Lemme call Mary and tell her I'll be late for dinner."

* * * *

I called Katherine and told her I'd be late for dinner, too. Then I waited. And I began to think. Fred's simple question of what would I do if Sunny's business turned out to be as dirty as the back alleys in Seoul was a good one. If I simply ran her out of town, I could open up a can of worms. The local politicians who weren't exactly in love with me could level accusations of hanky-panky with the two ex-hookers, and there goes many years of a somewhat shady but always untarnished reputation as an all-American crime fighter. Locking up a young Korean woman for a sex crime and Sunny Kim for at least suffering and permitting the illegal practice would make me feel bad, but I'd probably get over it. I picked up an old copy of Car & Driver and looked at the pictures.

At twenty-after-six Fred walked back in, all smiles. I wondered if he brought back enough evidence for me to take police action or...

"You get lucky?" I asked.

"I feel great." He dropped into a guest chair like a palate of ammunition kicked off the skids of a cargo plane flying over a jungle landing zone. "It was almost like in-country R&R in Saigon."

"So now I'm in the nostalgia-for-sale business?"

"You oughta go there, and try it. I mean this little girl—couldn'ta been more than ninety pounds—said her name was Miss Cho. She had the face of an angel and the hands of a pipefitter. That girl got out every ache and kink, and I...

I interrupted his enthusiasm.

"Bottom line it for me, Frederick. Are they running a sex shop over there? You were gone a long time."

He shook his head vigorously. "Hold your horses, madman. I walked in there, and this gorgeous—and I mean luscious—blonde is at the reception desk. You know her?"

I nodded. "Uh-huh. Her name's Veronica Keeble."

"Veronica? Jeez, sexy name," he said. "Va-va-voom. What a piece o' ass." He raised his eyebrows twice and leered for a moment. "Anyways, she asks me what I wanted. I tell her I just drove here from Florida, and my back is killin' me. She asks if I'd be paying cash, or did I have a prescription from a doctor and be submitting to insurance. I figure, hey, if some guys can get a vitamin V prescription paid by insurance maybe I can put in for this. But I behave and say charge card."

"Your honesty is overwhelming."

"Yeah, right. I try to save you a couple bucks, and you crack wise." Fred rolled his eyes. "Okay, she hands me a couple of forms." He shrugged. "I've never been in a whorehouse before where you get medical history forms to fill out. So I'm doing all this, and this Oriental girl comes out. Shit, she's as good-looking as the blonde, but in a different way. You know what I'm saying?"

I nodded again. "Uh-huh. She's the owner of record. I know her, too."

"Oh, Christ. And you're passing up those two? I hope you don't mind me sayin' you're nuts."

"Do you mind?"

"Yeah, sure. Anyways, she's, I don't know, Chinese, Korean or something. You know that movie star, too, huh?"

"Yeah. She's Korean. Her name's Sunny," I said.

"Mannaggia mi'! So, *Sunny,* escorts me to a room. I figure it's time for me to strip down and wrap a towel around me, but she gives me a pair of gym shorts and says I should change, and when I finish filling out the forms, put them in the little rack on the hall side of the door to the room I'm in. They'll know I'm ready.

"I do that, and I'm layin' on this table, just in these shorts, when this

48

Miss Cho comes in. She asks me questions like where I'm hurting and all, and I tell her. And she starts working on my legs and then my back. That girl had hands of gold, Sam, I'm tellin' ya."

"A real pro?"

"You bet. Then I turn over on my back, and she starts working on my legs again, and I'm starting to get really hard. You know what I'm sayin'?"

I shrugged. "Uh-huh."

"So I ask her if I can get a *special massage*. You know, hinting around that I want at least a hand job. She smiles and says in my hour there that I'll have all my sore muscles taken care of. Not exactly what I wanted to hear. So, in a minute or two, I try again, and point to my crotch and tell her I'll pay extra if she takes care of that for me. She giggles and says, 'No, can't do that. Go see wife or girlfriend.' So I say, 'Sorry for the misunderstanding', and she goes to work on my shoulders and neck. You know how they twist your head back and forth and all of a sudden make your neck crack?"

"I can guess."

"Hands o' freakin' gold, Sam. Hands o' gold! I feel great. But I couldn't get to first base in the sex department—couldn't even pay for it. What a shame."

"You think one of them made you?"

"I doubt it. Do I look like a cop anymore?"

"You look like the Godfather."

"You think?"

I tossed my hands in the air. "Actually, I'm glad they're legit. It makes my life easy. Thanks. How much did you have to pay? Seventy-five?"

"Yeah, plus a tip. I threw her a ten—cash. Here's the credit card receipt, and I need you to take care of this for me. Who's Davis Huskey Jr.?"

He handed me the Visa receipt from Kisaeng and a copy of a parking ticket written by PO Junior Huskey.

"What's this?" I waved the ticket in front of him.

"I parked in a handicapped spot. I was on a job. For chrissake, I didn't wanna walk."

49

Wayne Zurl

Chapter Six

The next day, I came back from lunch and settled into reading the ream of paperwork lying on my desk. Bettye went out to run a few errands, and John Gallagher answered the phone and took the radio calls from the sector cars.

My intercom buzzed.

"Hey, Boss, there's a Mrs. Keeble on the phone for you. Says it's important," John said and put the call through.

"Sam, I think we have a problem." Roni sounded concerned. "One of our girls didn't show up for work today."

"When did you hear from her last?"

"She worked yesterday from noon until eight o'clock. Now she's an hour late, and that's unlike her. There's a patient waiting, and I can't get her to answer the phone. I'm worried, Sam. She lives with two of the other girls in a trailer park off Sevierville Road.

"What's her name?"

"Rosie—uh, Rosalind, Rosalind Cho. She's about twenty-five or twenty-six."

"Give me the exact address. I'll send a car."

She did.

"Did her roommates come to work?"

"Started this morning. They said Rosie was okay when they left. I hope this doesn't have anything to do with Park."

I hoped the same thing. But since I didn't have my crystal ball in gear, I couldn't comment until someone checked further. "I'll call as

51

soon as I hear from the patrolman I send. Is Sunny with you today?"

"She is."

"Everything else okay?"

"Yes, I think so."

"All right, lady, I'll get back to you as soon as I know something."

"Thank you, Sam. You're being so sweet."

I walked out to the lobby. John Gallagher sat at Bettye's desk. Fred Mazzio lounged in John's chair with his feet on the desktop and his hands folded over the mound he called a stomach. I looked at him.

"What the hell are you doing here?"

"Slummin'." I figured I'd stop by and see when you're going to take us to dinner."

I made a face and ignored him.

"Who's working the northeast sector today?" I asked Gallagher.

"Johnny Rutledge," he said.

I slid the desk microphone toward me and depressed the transmit bar.

"Headquarters to unit five-eleven, five-one-one."

"This is five-eleven," Rutledge said.

"Check a residence at Prospect Farms Mobile Home Park, spot sixty-four. See if you can find a Miss Cho. Last name spelled, charlie, hotel, oscar. Call me from that location."

"Ten-four, boss."

"John, do a DMV search for her. The first name is Rosalind. See what you get on her personally and on any registered vehicles."

Fred asked, "Did you say Cho? She the girl I know from the massage place?"

"Maybe. Cho's a common Korean name. There may be more than one over there."

"Yeah, that could be." He nodded. "So when do you want to go out and eat Italian?"

Fred and I talked, while John piddled around on the computer. Ten minutes later, I heard Johnny Rutledge.

"Five-eleven to headquarters."

John keyed the mike. "Go ahead, five-eleven."

"I'm here at this double-wide, but cain't get nobody ta answer the door. They's a black Kia parked on the blacktop next ta the mailbox fer this place. Tag number is hotel, bravo, alpha, nine-three-seven."

"Tag number?" Fred asked.

"Yeah, that's Tennessean for license plate number," I said. "Run the reg, John. See what you get."

He did and learned it was a 2005 Kia Spectra registered to Rosalind S.S. Cho at the address where Johnny Rutledge waited.

I picked up the phone and dialed the number for Kisaeng Massage Therapy. Roni Keeble answered.

"Can you get me a set of keys for Rosie Cho's trailer home? The cop there gets no response from anyone inside."

"Sure. Well, I guess so. I'll ask one of her roommates."

That wasn't good enough. "I'll be there in five minutes. Get me the keys."

"Yeah, sure."

We hung up.

"John, tell Rutledge I'm getting keys for the trailer. I'll be there in less than fifteen minutes."

"Ten-four, Boss," John said.

"You want company, big guy?" Fred asked.

"I thought you were on vacation."

"I am. I just like to watch you work."

"I'll bet. You just want to learn how to be a real cop again."

"Oh, spare me."

"Come on, Slim. I'm on the case."

* * * *

"Nice car," Fred told me as we drove north on Main Street in my unmarked Crown Victoria.

"All part of the package."

"This thing's almost new. You really stepped in it."

"I got it new. It's worked out to be a nice job."

I crossed over the Crystal Creek Bridge where the name of Main Street changed to Prospect Road.

Fred shook his head and looked at me. "That blonde is a freakin' movie star."

Wayne Zurl

"So you said. Happy to see her again?"

He tilted his head like a dog hoping to get a biscuit. "She gave you some look. Just how well do you know her?"

It was beginning to sound like an interrogation.

"She was a homicide suspect a couple of years ago."

He blinked a couple times. "Homicide suspect?"

"We eliminated her quickly."

He shook his head. "She likes you, you Scotch bastard."

"Because I'm nice."

"Shit. You're old enough to be her father."

"Sugar daddy, maybe."

He waved a hand dismissively. "Shit."

At the corner of Prospect Road and Sevierville Road, I turned right. A mile and a half more and I turned into Prospect Farms Drive. In another minute, I saw Johnny Rutledge's white and blue police car.

"Hey, boss, how's it goin'?"

"Hi ya, Johnny." I poked a thumb to the side in Fred's general direction. "This is Detective Fred Mazzio from New York. He's sort of on a ride-along."

"Hello, sir," Johnny said.

"Hi ya, kid. You think your boss knows what he's doin'?"

Rutledge smiled like a proud son. "Oh, yes, sir, he shore does."

Fred laughed. "Well, you got him snowed, big guy."

"Shut up, and watch my back," I told Mazzio. "Johnny, walk around to the rear door for a minute while we open the front."

I looked on a ring of several keys for one that might open a front door. I tried one in the doorknob lock, and it worked.

I took out my old Smith & Wesson and looked at Freddie.

"You packing?"

"Nah, it's back in the RV. I got no license to carry in this state."

"You can wait here if you'd like."

"Bullshit. There can't be more than six of them inside. You've got a gun and six rounds. I trust you."

I pushed the door open and listened—nothing but the air conditioner fan spinning outside and to the left of where we stood. I stepped inside and heard more nothing, but could see clearly into the living room. A

54

closed door stood to our right—to a bedroom, I presumed.

"Keep an eye on that door, sport."

Fred nodded.

I took a couple of steps toward the kitchen-dinette. A half wall separated that from the living room. I moved slowly. Fred followed. The closed door behind us bothered me, but I couldn't look everywhere at once, Fred was unarmed, and we couldn't split up. Instinctively, I looked for a place to take cover if something or someone popped up behind us. I knew Fred was doing the same. It all comes from years of practice; years of doing exactly what we were doing that afternoon. A year each in Vietnam didn't hurt either.

When I looked around the half-wall, I saw a pair of small, bare feet. I pointed to the floor. Fred nodded again. A young woman lay face up on the linoleum with four bullet holes in her torso. Blood had soaked the oversized white tee shirt she wore and spread over the embossed tile of the linoleum. I checked her carotid artery for a pulse. It was a day of nothing in the doublewide; nothing but bad luck for that little girl.

We continued toward the bathroom and the additional two bedrooms at the far end of the house and found no one present. We retraced our steps and moved up to the closed door that presented us with a mystery.

That door represented the kind of thing that makes a cop nervous— an unknown. We had no way to learn anything about the room beyond without opening the door. Simple, you'd think. Unless the guy who fired those four rounds into Rosie Cho was hiding inside. The entire place was clear except one spot, a room closed as tight as my Scottish grandfather's wallet. The door opened on the right with the knob placed along the outside wall. When I opened the door, most of the room would be obscured on our left and only a limited portion visible on the right, an exterior wall being all we'd see. If someone was waiting in that room, we wouldn't know it until we, make that I, exposed myself to the open space. But I didn't have much choice and pushed the door with my left hand. It traveled about two feet and stopped.

"Shit," I hissed. I wasn't sure why I had whispered.

"I hear ya, big guy." Fred whispered, too.

I used sign language to indicate that I'd go low and fall to the left after I passed inside the doorframe. Fred would stay ready and retreat to the front door if necessary. At times like that I wanted to be home sweating in my vegetable garden. I shrugged and made the move. I felt stupid when I saw an empty room and only a big, stuffed toy tiger jammed behind the open door blocking its progress.

I stood up and felt the strain in my lower back. "This kind of stuff always seemed more swashbuckling years ago," I said.

"It's a bitch gettin' old."

"You'd think I'd know when to quit."

"Not you," he said. "But think how stupid I feel. I'm here with ya."

I let out a long breath and shook my head. "You think we should start a therapy group for adrenaline junkies?"

"I think we ought to take another look at our body," he said.

"Hold that thought while I check this closet."

I yanked on the bi-fold door. Still nothing and no one. I shook my head again.

"Ready to do it, Holmes?" Fred asked.

"Lead the way, Dr. Watson."

Back in the kitchen, Fred said, "Son of a bitch. That is the girl from the massage parlor…the one who did me."

It seemed like such a waste. "Man, she's young."

"Yeah. I thought she was a nice kid."

I shrugged. "Right. Do me a favor, and get Johnny back in here."

"You got it."

A few moments later, that pair walked up the wooden steps of the tan mobile home. Fred followed Johnny inside to where I stood.

Johnny looked at the body. "Oh, Lord have mercy. Ya cain't git much deader."

"Get on the radio, and tell John or Bettye to call for an ME and a crime scene unit."

"Yes, sir," Johnny said and walked out to his car.

I looked at my watch for a second time and scribbled a few notes on a scrap of paper I found in my jacket pocket. Then I looked at the area around the corpse.

"Four shots in the body," I said. "And not a very good group. The shooter jerked the trigger. There are two stray rounds up here." I pointed to the splashboard above the counter and the frame on one of the upper kitchen cabinets. "Looks like a .22. Six rounds, no ejected shells. Probably a revolver fired double action. He sprayed the rounds all over."

"You sure it's a he?" Fred asked.

"No."

"Somebody was mad—or wanted to send a message. Got any ideas?"

"Maybe. A Korean hood approached Sunny Kim, the beautiful Korean you met at Kisaeng, and wanted protection money. I sort of interceded. He's got two nasty-looking thugs he uses as enforcers. Either one would kill you as quick as look at you."

"I've never known a gook that could shoot any good. Might explain the spray of rounds."

"I guess we'll find out. But any hit man who uses a .22 is usually a pretty good shot."

"What else you notice?" he asked.

"Nothing."

"You're loosin' it, Sam."

"No, I notice that there's nothing…nothing but the body and the two stray rounds. Nothing is out of place. Nothing looks like the shooter forced his way in here. No one tossed the place. Nothing's weird."

"See, years ago I did teach you something."

"Up yours."

"Ha."

As Fred and I stood over Rosie Cho's body, Johnny Rutledge walked back inside.

"Crime scene heard my transmission. They'll be here in jest a minute. ME's on the way, too."

"Good boy, Johnny," I said.

Rutledge looked at the body again.

"She Chinese?" he asked.

"Korean."

"You can tell?"

"Yeah."

"How?"

"I just can. I spent two years in Asia. Koreans look different than

Japanese. They both look different than Chinese. You can tell the difference between northern and southern Chinese. Vietnamese look different again. So do Cambodians, Thais and Malaysians. I don't know much about Laotians."

"Show off," Freddie said.

"Johnny, why don't you take Detective Mazzio and start a neighborhood canvas? See if someone saw or heard anything."

"Yes, sir."

"Come on, kid," Freddie said. "Let's solve this thing while the boss stands around scratching his gray head."

They left. I called Bettye and asked her to brief the mayor and send John Gallagher to see Sunny Kim and get statements from Rosie's roommates and question the other people at Kisaeng. Then I made a second call. The Knoxville number rang seven times before the answering machine kicked in.

"I know you're on vacation this week," I said, "and I'm sorry to call on business, but if you're listening, pick up. It's important." I spoke to Rachel Williamson's answering machine like an old friend.

I finished my message, and the receiver clicked as she lifted the phone off the cradle. "What's so important that you disturb my week off?" She didn't give me an opportunity to answer. "Are you finally ready to take me on that picnic in the mountains you promised so *very* long ago?"

I couldn't let her get away with that. "It's too hot for a picnic, and if we drive around with the top of the Healey down, your hair would blow all over. We should wait for another time—October maybe, the leaves will be colorful and... Hey, I've got a good story for you. A fatal shooting of a Korean girl who works in town. Even if you're not working, your partner can get it on a bulletin, and he'll have film and the whole nine yards for the six o'clock show. Interested?"

"Of course I'm interested, lover. But Jack can drum up his own stories. I'll be there in half-an-hour. I'll call and get Leckmanski to meet us there with his camera. Where are you now?"

I told her and then asked, "Aren't you doing something with your husband or kids on your days off?"

"Boyd is working. Some kind of big client meeting. The boys went to Splash World with the neighbors."

"Splash World? God, can you imagine how loud that must be?"

"Sometimes you can be so stuffy."

"Who's stuffy? I have no patience for a brigade-sized hoard of children screaming and splashing in a communal pool. Yuck."

"You make it sound so appealing."

"Time's a'wastin', woman. Call your cameraman and get your lovely ass down here. If you hurry, John can film the ME taking the body out."

I gave Rachel, East Tennessee's favorite TV anchorwoman, the address and directions to the mobile home park and started looking around. Before I got too far, a single, muffled siren blared in the distance.

In only moments, the siren sounded closer and trailed off in a stifled moan as a white Ford Expedition with county sheriff's logos on the doors stopped in front of the doublewide. I looked out the front door. Jackie Shuman and Neal Brickman were the duty crime scene investigators. They carried kit boxes and camera bags into the trailer.

"Hi, guys," I said. "I've got a gunshot victim over here."

"Howdy, Sam," Jackie said.

"Whaddaya say, boss?" Neal added.

"Neal, what makes you so lucky today? Your lieutenant mad at you and made you work with Jackie?"

He laughed.

"Where's Sparky?" I asked, inquiring about Jackie's regular partner, David Sparks.

"He's vacatin' this whole week. Done took his wife ta Myrtle Beach." Jackie said.

"Jeez, Myrtle beach in July. Must be over a hundred there," I said. "I'd go to Alaska."

"Hard ta figger some people, ain't it?" Jackie looked at Rosie's body. "Chinese?" he asked.

"Korean."

"You kin tell?"

"Yeah. Don't ask how."

* * * *

Fred and Johnny returned to the doublewide. I introduced Fred to the evidence technicians; they already knew Rutledge.

When it comes to being pushy, Fred Mazzio is higher on the food chain than young Rutledge.

Mazzio spoke first. "That was a goddamn waste of time. Almost everybody is working. Two young mommies were home, but too far away to know shit, and the one woman that's nearby was probably bangin' her boyfriend. That one works nights at Walmart. Hubby works days—same place. Co-worker *just happens* to be on the scene having ice tea or some shit, while the broad is in her nightgown. Real class operation."

"So you've got nothing?"

"Worse than that, I got all sweaty. This was a very clean shirt when I left the RV this morning." Using two fingers, he pulled the white and yellow luau shirt away from his kahuna-sized body to illustrate the point.

Another county vehicle, the morgue wagon, pulled up and parked on the blacktop road close to the steps of the trailer. I told Johnny to start an official crime scene log and handed him the scrap of paper I had been using to record times and personnel.

Doctor Morris Rappaport was the deputy medical examiner on duty. As usual, Earl Ogle acted as his driver and helper.

The pathologist entered the house, looked at the body and spoke to no one in particular. "A young Japanese girl. Such a shame."

"She's Korean, Mo." I couldn't control the urge to say it.

"How can you tell?"

I let my chin hit my chest and grunted. "You explain it, Freddie."

"Me? What?" He looked at Morris and smiled. "Hi, my name's Fred Mazzio. I used to work with Sam back in New York."

I looked out the open front door. The air conditioner hummed incessantly. The fan spun as fast as the tail rotor on a helicopter.

From the surrounding trees, the buzz from hordes of cicadas made their presence known, sounding like the army of chanting Zulus that surrounded a company of famous Welsh soldiers at Roark's Drift.

The overhead sun didn't allow for many shadows or much shade in the mobile home park. It was one of those lazy, hazy, crazy days of summer I remembered Nat "King" Cole singing about—days of soda and pretzels and beer. For poor little Rosie Cho, it was the first day of her afterlife.

A white mini-van with WNXX TV identification on the sides pulled up, and I stepped outside. The driver, John Leckmanski, was the senior cameraman from Rachel's station. We shook hands.

"You've got plenty of time before the competition gets here," I said. "As far as I know Bettye's just now writing up the first general press release. No one else knows."

"Good. It's too hot to hurry."

"Where is she?" I asked, referring to Rachel.

"Don't know. I spoke to her and left Knoxville forty minutes ago. She's closer than me."

"She didn't mention making a stop. Maybe she had to do her hair."

John made a face. "You think she'd sit around the house with messy hair?"

"You've got a point," I said. "The ME just got here. He'll be a little while before they bag the body."

John nodded. I started for the steps again, and my phone rang. I listened for a couple of moments and then continued to the doorway.

"Gentlemen," I said, to the people inside, "an emergency just came up, and I've got to leave for a little while. I hope I'm not too long. Johnny, you hang out until everyone's finished, and then secure the place. Take the keys back to Mrs. Keeble or Miss Kim at Kisaeng Massage." I gave Fred a questioning look.

"I'll hang around here a bit longer," he said, "if you don't mind. Things are just getting interesting."

"Suit yourself. Johnny can drive you back. And thanks for the company."

"Anytime. Hey, you don't have another opening for a clerk-typist, do you?"

61

Chapter Seven

Rachel put her head on my shoulder and sighed. "I never thought this would happen." I smelled a fragrant shampoo on her dark brown hair.

"Well, I won't say this was inevitable, but all things considered, it was always possible."

"Oh, Sam, I feel awful."

She moved her head and looked at me. The dimple on her chin has always fascinated me.

"I know," I said. "You have this guilt thing."

"I have to tell my husband. I mean I can't hide this from him. He won't react well. I just know it."

She wore a pink short-sleeved knit blouse, a pair of tight jeans and high heels. When she finished speaking, she crossed her left leg over her right knee. Her shoe touched my leg.

"I'm afraid he's got no choice. He's got to accept it. It happened. It's not like we can undo anything."

"Oh, I wish I could. I wish someone could." Rachel had been in Tennessee for more than fifteen years, but she still spoke with a Pennsylvania accent.

"We can take care of everything. I know these people. They're good." I shrugged and tried to look sympathetic. "Life'll go on. The best I can do right now is be here with you. Help you get the ball rolling."

"I know. Thanks. You're the best, Sammy."

She kissed my cheek. I wanted to do more.

"Maybe not the best. I do feel responsible. If it wasn't for me...

"Oh, don't. Please don't. I had to—you knew I would."

"Yeah, I suppose."

"Are you going to tell Katherine? She'll think I'm awful. I feel so stupid."

"She's pretty understanding, and I doubt she thinks you're stupid. It's not like she hasn't been in the same position herself."

"Really? I didn't know. Now I feel sorry for you."

"Ancient history."

She gestured with her hand, sweeping around the waiting room. "What can these people think?"

"They see this kind of thing all the time. We're nothing out of the ordinary."

"This is really more my problem than yours."

"As soon as you called...you knew I'd help. I couldn't leave you alone."

"Thanks so much."

"Uh-huh."

"Do they think it's yours?"

"I doubt it. I know these people. One look and they'd know. Anyway, it's not my style."

"What do you mean by that?"

"Well, no offense to Boyd, but you know, like I said, not my style."

"I don't understand."

"Now really, do I look like I'd drive a Lexus?"

"What's wrong with a Lexus?" She sounded offended.

"Nothing's *wrong* with them. I drove a rental once—comfortable, but about as much fun as driving a lawn mower."

She frowned.

"That thing you drive...it's a nice girl's car—good for a soccer mom like you."

"I'm not a soccer mom!" She punched my arm.

"I just don't look like I'd drive Boyd's convertible. It's ah...very formal. Like I wouldn't wear a shiny silk suit either. Neither one fits my personality."

"Oh." She looked very unhappy.

"Hey, it was an accident. His car was damaged, but you weren't hurt. It wasn't your fault. The car can be fixed. I'm glad you wear a seat belt."

She nodded and folded the strap of her purse like she was mad at it. "I just wish he never needed my car to take three people to lunch. I wish he drove a car with more than two seats."

"Like I said, the guys here are good. Boyd will never see the repair. He'll be happy you're not hurt. I'd look at it that way. I'll take you over to the airport for a rental car and you'll be ready to get back to the station with the story on the murder."

She nodded, but still looked sad.

"Something like this happened to Kate? She didn't wreck your Austin-Healey, did she?"

"No, I didn't have the Healey then. It was an old MG. A guy ran a stop sign and creamed her right front fender."

"Was she hurt?"

"No, just the car."

"Were you mad?"

"Well..."

"See what I mean?"

I couldn't think of anything more clever to say. "Boyd will be fine."

I hope the schmuck asks if she got hurt before wanting details on the car.

"I hope so." She didn't sound like she believed that.

On the way to Prospect from Rachel's home in Knoxville, an old lady driving a big Buick Park Avenue plowed into the rear end of Boyd Williamson's shiny black SC430. Rachel and I were sitting in the office at Ralph Fleenor's body shop waiting for an estimate and a guess at the time frame for completing the repairs.

* * * *

I pulled my big Ford off US 129 and into the lot of the Budget-Rent-A-Car agency across from McGhee-Tyson Airport in Alcoa.

"This place is pretty big for a rental office," Rachel said.

"They sell used cars, too."

"Oh." She still looked distraught and hugged her purse. "I'd better get this taken care of."

64

I nodded. "The customer counter is inside. I'll be right with you. I want to look at a couple of the Mustangs they're selling."

"You want a Mustang now?" Rachel sounded like she thought I was crazy.

"No, I just want to look."

She slung the strap of her purse over her right shoulder and trudged into the office looking like a G.I. after a major battle. I checked out two fastbacks and two of the ragtops parked on the sale line.

In less than ten minutes, I met Rachel in the office. The clerk handed back her license and credit card while she initialed a contract several times and signed the bottom of the form.

"Finished already?" I asked.

She nodded.

"Okay, Ms. Williamson," the clerk said, "here are your keys. The car is in spot 24. Thanks very much for using Budget, and have a nice day."

She took the keys, pushed her wallet back into the purse and forced a smile for the young man. I opened the door and held it for her. We stepped back into the bright sun. Rachel put on the big shades she uses to go incognito. It took a moment for my eyes to acclimate to the glare.

To the left of the office, the ready lot was almost empty. Three subcompacts sat in the first row that had eighteen numbered spots. We walked to the second row, past a couple minivans, and found a metallic purple PT Cruiser in spot 24.

"This is what you rented?" I sounded surprised.

Rachel snapped her head around to look up at me. Even with high heels, she only comes up to my nose.

"Other than one of those little things," she pointed toward the row of small cars, "and those *real* soccer mom vans, it's all he had available."

"Did you know what you were getting?"

"Not exactly, but it was all he had." She sounded short on patience.

"Do you want to be seen in...that?

She didn't respond.

"You look great in purple, but not driving a purple car."

"It doesn't matter," she said. "It's all he has."

Her pink blouse fit snugly and had a low, scooped neckline. She has a great figure for a mother of two.

"Never say all." I turned and started back to the office.

"Where are you going?"

I didn't answer.

"Sam."

I guess she expected me to make a scene.

"Find some shade. I'll be right back."

Rachel sighed, and her shoulders dropped two inches.

The clerk, a twenty-something-year-old, good-looking black kid wore a white shirt, striped tie in the Budget company colors and black trousers. He smiled when I stepped up to the counter.

"Yes, sir. Is something wrong?" he asked.

I grinned, trying to look friendly. "Is that really the only full-sized car you have? It's sort of juvenile-looking."

"Yes, sir, I'm afraid so. We're cleaning up a mid-sized Dodge right now if Mrs. Williamson would rather drive that. It should be finished in less than half an hour."

Waiting was not an option.

"You've got a black Mustang against the fence next to the shop. It looks pretty clean. How about that?"

"Oh, that's a Cobra special rental. It's going to be picked up in a couple of days and taken back to Chattanooga."

Not if I can help it.

"Isn't this a first-come first-served business?" I asked. "Mrs. Williamson is a famous person in this area. She really shouldn't be driving an eggplant-colored kid's car. Her insurance company is paying. How about the Mustang? Let Chattanooga wait. You've got a customer who needs a cool ride."

He looked like he was mentally preparing to deal with a pain in the ass.

"Sir, someone is scheduled to be here and drive that back to Chattanooga. It's not ours. It's just a drop-off.

I hit him with an irresistible smile. "How about I promise you something your boss will love?"

He looked at me skeptically. "I don't understand."

"The next time I'm on TV, when I can fit it in appropriately, I'll tell everyone how accommodating you Budget people were at a time of great importance. What's your name? I'll mention you personally. You'll get points with the boss."

"Are you on TV with Ms. Williamson?"

"All the time."

"I don't remember seeing you."

Think quickly, Sam.

"Do you watch her 11 o'clock show?"

"I open up here at seven. I'm usually in bed before that."

"Well, there you are. Trust me. I'll make you famous." I crossed my heart with a right index finger.

He looked like he trusted me as much as the last guy who hacked his credit card number. "How long will she need the car?"

I leaned forward over the counter. "Who knows? Who cares? She has insurance and Triple A." I tilted my head and blinked a couple times. "Don't you think she'd look good in a Mustang? Screw Chattanooga."

He sighed and didn't appear happy about giving up. "Okay, I guess so."

I read his name tag. "You're a good man, James. I appreciate the hell out of this. Call Chattanooga and put them on hold."

"Yes, sir," he sighed again, as if he felt the weight of the world on his shoulders.

James wrote out an amendment to Rachel's contract. I initialed and signed for her, and he handed me the remote opener.

"I'll bring back the other paperwork and keys for the PT as soon as she drives off. She's got to get back to Knoxville and prepare a hot story."

James nodded, and I left the office.

I smiled and handed Rachel the new contract and dangled the locking thingie in front of her.

"Dump this grape, baby. You're driving that Cobra GT back there." I pointed at the Mustang sitting thirty yards away.

"Cobra?"

"Yeah, cool, huh?"

"You want me to drive a car named after a snake?"

"You're too conservative. Live it up. Insurance is paying."

She closed her eyes for a moment. "You're impossible."

We walked over to the Black fastback parked in the shade. I opened the door, switched on the ignition and goosed the accelerator. The tuned exhaust would make any girl feel a surge of romance. I cranked up the air conditioner.

"This does look pretty sharp, doesn't it?" she said.

"Hot wheels for *the* local TV hottie."

"Oh, God, sometimes you act so juvenile."

"You love every word I say."

She slid into the black leather bucket seat. I closed the door after she swung her legs into the driver's compartment. Rachel rolled down the window and looked up at me.

"Be careful," I said. "Don't let this thing run away with you."

She smiled, wiggled her fingers to say good-bye and burned a little rubber merging onto Route 129. My friend, the soccer mom, was not used to a hot car.

Chapter Eight

"Where the hell did you go this afternoon?" Fred asked, treating me like a suspect.

Six of us were sitting at table thirty-five in the Villa Napoli. The owner, Nick Cutrone, had just taken our dinner orders, and his grandson, Vinnie the bartender, returned with our drinks.

Not waiting for an answer to his question, Fred raised a hand. "The Jack and water is mine." He sounded impatient and thirsty.

Vinnie handed each of the girls a glass of white wine, and then Fred got his whiskey. I had asked for a Peroni Italian beer. John received a tall glass with red liquid over ice.

"What did you order, John?" I asked.

"Vodka and cranberry juice."

It sounded like something for an alcoholic health nut. "Is it any good?"

"Yeah, and good for you." He cracked an adolescent smile. "Cranberry juice is a...

"I know, I know."

I thought I might have avoided Fred's question.

Mazzio slammed his glass down and licked his lips like a hungry vampire. "Answer my question, big guy. Where'd you go?"

Tenacious bastard.

"A friend had a traffic accident. I helped out."

"Who?" Kate asked. "You didn't tell me. Was anyone hurt?" She sounded concerned.

I felt like smacking Mazzio.

"No one was hurt," I said.

Someone from work?" Kate asked.

Reluctantly, I answered. "An old lady in a big car rear-ended Rachel. She was driving her husband's Lexus on the way to the murder scene."

"Oh, Rachel," Kate said, without a hell of a lot of enthusiasm.

"Who's Rachel?" Fred asked.

"Sam has a girlfriend. She's a TV news reporter," Kate answered with an expression any film director would have loved.

It's a good thing my wife is so good-looking or her smug act would have annoyed me.

"You bum." Mazzio gave me a lecherous grin and sucked down half of his Jack Daniels.

Table thirty-five was situated at the back corner of the restaurant, sharing an elevated platform with three other tables. Italian opera posters hung on the stucco walls; a harlequin-dressed Pagliacci looked down on us, his arms stretched out in song.

The server's door to the kitchen swung on two-way hinges less than fifteen feet behind us. If I moved quickly, I could toss Mazzio off the platform and make it out the back door before anyone noticed where I'd gone. We sat no more than four feet above the main floor; he'd only bounce.

"The Boss doesn't say much about his girlfriend," John began, making sure everyone saw his smug and obnoxious grin.

Apparently it was going to be gang up on the boss night.

"It took me almost a month working at the PD to find out who Rachel was," he said. "I think the Boss has some kind of animal *magnitude* over these women."

Freddie was always willing to stick up for me. "Animal magnetism, you idiot. But I don't believe it."

Barbara Gallagher jumped into the conversation defensively, but sounding child-like. "I don't think John is an idiot."

She was an attractive, middle-aged woman, but sometimes said things as if she had the mind of an eight-year-old with as much intelligence as a garden toad.

"You know, John," I forced a smile, "I should have made you sign a confidentiality clause when I hired you, one with the death penalty for opening your big mouth."

"Sam, you know John can keep a secret if you want him to," Barbara said, like her husband was the G. Gordon Liddy of my administration.

I should have left them in a Florida debtor's prison.

"It's not a secret, Barbara," I said. "It's just that people automatically take it the wrong way, especially when my wife calls her *my girlfriend* and when a guy like Frederick, whose mind has always been in the gutter, comments on it and leers like a homeless pervert."

Kate sipped her wine with an innocent smile and a dazzling feminine look. If she hadn't decided to show a little cleavage that night, I would have gotten really angry.

She looked at me and fluttered the lashes over her big brown eyes. Diligently, she used a finger to smooth her right eyebrow. She looked like any one of those conniving but beautiful women I remember from the 1940s movies.

"You've got that right," Mary Mazzio said. "Fred's mind has always been in the gutter." She drained half her first glass of wine. A few strands of blonde hair fell forward over her right eye. She tried to blow them away, but missed.

I finished the bottle of Peroni, signaled for Vinnie to bring me another and steeled myself for a long night.

Kate decided she'd clarify her statement. "Sam's right. She's really *not* his girlfriend. She's just a friend... So he says, and a girl—a rather pretty one, it so happens. How old is she, Sammy? Forty-two-ish?"

Her smile turned a little malevolent. Kate was enjoying herself; she reminded me of Lucretia Borgia.

"This is kind of a sensitive subject with me," I said. "If you people don't mind, let's talk about something pleasant...like the murder."

Mazzio and Gallagher sipped their drinks, grinning like Brutus and Cassius. *Bastards.*

* * * *

The next morning, we awakened to rain, an intense, soaking rain. No doubt the plants and trees liked it. The animals and birds liked it. I kind of liked it. When I took my dog for a walk, she thought it sucked. For a Scottish dog that should have been born with a toleration of rain naturally present in her genes, Bitsey hates it. She hates to feel it beating on her fur and hates to walk in wet grass. But she took care of her morning necessities and did her best to act tolerant.

On my way to work, I passed a sheriff's traffic enforcement unit handling a one car spin-out on US 321 in the Walland Gap. The deputy stood next to a maroon Ford Focus stuck in the soft shoulder mud. A wall of rock on the south side of the road rose above the ground for more than a hundred feet just behind the Focus. A shaken-up young lady sat in the driver's seat. The deputy wore his police slicker with the orange side out, and a plastic cover over his summer campaign hat. He looked like he had everything under control.

The usually dark gray asphalt road appeared black and shiny in the rain. Some folks drove carefully; others did not. Listening to the radio, it sounded like a busy rush hour for the road cops.

The back roads to Prospect and the countryside seemed quiet and peaceful. A few horses grazed in a field, oblivious to the rain. The inmates of a Llama farm hid under an overhang of their barn; most of them chewed on the hay packed into the wall racks on the plywood siding.

As I approached the town square, I smelled the fragrant air cleared by a five mile-an-hour breeze and cleansed by hours of gentle rain. It was the kind of day where I'd prefer to sit in front of a big window and watch the drops fall. But I had a murder to solve and didn't have time to dawdle like a retired old fart living in the Great Smoky Mountains.

I'd get right down to business, right after I smacked John Gallagher in the head with a phone book for his wisecracks the night before.

* * * *

I felt almost responsible for Rosie Cho's death, but not totally. That was all contingent on knowing if Park, Hee-Chul had sent one of his henchmen to kill an employee of Kisaeng Massage, thereby sending a message to Sunny Kim and her friend, the knight errant and zealous police chief. Originally, I thought Park had been straight with me when he said he'd leave Sunny alone.

Now, I entertained the idea he was not only an ethnic gangster, preying more upon his own countrymen than others, but also a liar. In Korea they say, koogie-mal. I was ready to work on convicting Park and at least one of his thugs for the murder of little Rosie, whose only apparent problem stemmed from being an employee of the person from whom Park wanted to collect protection money. Only at the moment, nothing linked Park or his goons to the crime except my half-hearted hunch.

If Park wanted to send a message that Sunny and I received, he'd done so—very efficiently. I wished he had just called.

I telephoned Detective D.W. Renfro at Knoxville PD and told him what happened and that I wanted to confront Park. I thought doing so in a public place would keep Mr. Ha and Mr. Boo on their best behavior, assuming it was they who accompanied their boss on his outings.

With only a few words, I hooked Renfro. This business was getting more interesting each day, and Renfro agreed to help by keeping an eye on Park's home. He agreed to call after he followed him to a place where I could get Park's undivided attention, and we could have a serious chat.

At 6 p.m., my phone rang. Renfro and his partner, Detective Witford Maples, had followed Park to a Korean restaurant near the West Town Mall in Knoxville.

I picked up Sergeant Stanley Rose, my nighttime road supervisor, and after he changed into civilian clothes, we headed for Knoxville. Just before seven o'clock, I turned off Alcoa Highway onto Kingston Pike and drove west. We passed the mall, and I turned left on Montvue Road. Only a hundred yards from the corner, a wide driveway opened up on my right. I turned in and drove between two strip malls with a communal parking lot in the center.

The Korean restaurant was situated in the south line of storefronts, and a Korean grocery store sat directly across the blacktop. Other shops flanked both places. I parked in a spot near Renfro's white Impala, which faced the restaurant. Stan and I walked over to the detective's car. Renfro rolled down the window.

"Hey," he said.

I nodded. "Thanks for tracking down this guy. This is Stan Rose," I pointed a thumb at my partner.

Renfro said, "Hey, Stan. This here's Wit Maples." He did the same thumb routine.

Stan nodded to both the Knoxville cops. "Gentlemen."

"Hi ya, Wit. I'm Sam Jenkins."

"Hey," Wit said.

After we finished our hardboiled cop dialogue, we got down to business.

"Park's inside," Renfro said. "He's jest got the big'un, Mr. Boo, with 'im tonight. Been here fer almost an hour, I guess."

"I'm lucky he's a slow eater," I said.

"Uh-huh."

"We'll take it from here," I said. "I just want to talk with him."

"Okey dokey. We'll hang out fer a while, case somethin' interestin' goes down, and y'all kin use a hand."

"Appreciate it."

"Uh-huh."

Stan and I entered the restaurant and stopped at the sign asking us to wait to be seated. I'd been in the place before. It was an excellent restaurant frequented mostly by Koreans and a few occidentals who appreciated the atmosphere and the food. For me, it felt like stepping into an upscale eatery off Ulchi Ro in downtown Seoul.

In an establishment where a tall patron is a five-and-a-half-foot tall Asian, Stan Rose, whose driver's license says he's six-four and I estimate at a solid two-hundred-and-thirty-five pounds, stuck out like a very large sore thumb.

After a moment or two, a middle-aged Korean woman wearing lots of makeup greeted us. She wore a black cheongsam, a Chinese dress, not a Korean design. It wasn't traditional, but it gave her an exotic, dragon-lady look.

"Good evening. Table for two?" She spoke in heavily accented English.

"Ahnya hash ayo," I said, greeting her. She smiled, possibly used to Americans who could speak a little Korean. "We'd only like to talk with one of your customers, Park, Hee-Chul."

She spoke a little apprehensively. "I will have to check with Mr. Park first."

I palmed my badge and showed it to her without drawing attention to myself. "We'll only be a moment, pu-yin. I think Mr. Park is anxious to see us."

By now Park, who sat at a low table in one of the private tatami rooms on the right side of the dining area, was looking our way. I looked back and grinned.

"Yobo-sayo," I said loudly and waved at Park.

"Excuse us, pu-yin. My friend knows we're here." I started walking to Park's table. Stan followed closely. The hostess didn't object. Mr. Boo, seated to Park's right, stood as we approached. He was barefoot. Light gray socks stuck out beneath the cuffs of his black trousers.

"Ahn yong hash imnika, Mr. Jenkins?" Literally, Park asked if I came in peace.

"Nay, ahnya hash ayo, Mr. Park," I affirmed that I did indeed come peacefully.

I smiled again. Boo looked at me carefully.

"Please sit, Mr. Boo," I said. "We'd like to join you two for just a minute."

Boo looked at Park who nodded. Boo sat with more grace than I expected from a guy almost as big as a small SVU.

"Gentlemen, please sit with us," Park invited.

"Mr. Park, Mr. Boo, this is my colleague, Sergeant Rose."

"How do you do, Sergeant?" Park said.

Stanley nodded at Park. Boo nodded at Stan, still playing Mr. Stone Face. Stanley returned the nod, also without smiling. It was a face-off of the big guys. I placed my money on Stan. He had height, weight...maybe and lots of reach...not to mention his .40 caliber Glock.

And it would be a good guess that somewhere under his double-extra-large sport jacket Boo carried a gun of his own.

Stan and I removed our shoes, left them on the step in front of the room with the grass floor mats and sat on cushions called pong sook, next to the short-legged table. I felt sorry for Stan trying to get his bulk that low to the ground. But he pulled it off with remarkable ease.

"Mr. Park," I said, "I thought when I left your home we had a gentleman's agreement. You said you would no longer bother Miss Kim or any of her employees."

He tilted his head questioningly. He wore a dark gray suit with a maroon golf shirt. Before speaking, he smiled, and his gold tooth sparkled.

"I told you I would leave Miss Kim and her massage shop to you, Mr. Jenkins. I have no wish to aggravate the police in your city in what is obviously such a personal matter to you."

A waitress stopped at the table, bringing extra tea cups for Stan and me. Park waived her away with a little visible annoyance as she set down menus in front of us.

"Yesterday a Miss Rosie Cho, an employee of Kisaeng Massage, was found murdered. Would you know anything about that?"

Park looked at me and frowned. Boo blinked several times, wrinkled his forehead and appeared a little shaken by my statement.

"I'm sorry, Mr. Jenkins," Park said. "I don't know this Miss Cho. And I am sorry to hear she was murdered. You are sure this wasn't an accident?"

"Four bullets in the chest are rarely an accident...or a suicide."

Park shook his head, showing either real or feigned concern. Boo took a deep breath and allowed himself a slight change in expression, back to the stoic warrior.

Park must have felt a need to elaborate. "Put yourself in my position, Mr. Jenkins. I thought I could do business with Miss Kim. You are an intelligent man. I am sure I need not explain further. I had no idea she could muster such an enthusiastic champion as you to her side. I have not encountered such a personal commitment from a police chief before." Park decided to smile for us, perhaps to show no hard feelings. "I wrote Miss Kim off as a poor economic risk. She is hardly worth the cost of gasoline for my associates to pay her periodic visits. So, my friend, you won. Why would I go to the expense or bother of revenge?"

Economics play an important part in organized crime. But there are other factors that influence a thug. I allowed myself a half grin. "Reputation."

Someone in the kitchen dropped a pot. Many of the patrons looked toward the noise. Boo didn't flinch, and Park didn't skip a beat as he shook his head.

Park trumped my smirk with a wide smile. "I am quite happy with the reputation I enjoy in the local Korean community," he said. "Ask the people. You speak our language wonderfully. They will tell you Park, Hee-Chul is a good man." He nodded once for emphasis. "Go ahead. Ask."

Obviously, I was getting nowhere. I really didn't expect Park to stand up and confess, then volunteer to jump into my handcuffs. But I learned long ago that guys like Park need occasional visits to keep them on their toes. And if you stir a pot, sometimes the oddest things float to the surface. So, the ride to Knoxville wasn't a total loss.

I shrugged and nodded. "Thanks for your time, Mr. Park."

Park's smile continued broadcasting at high wattage. He pointed to the table covered with small dishes full of hot and cold vegetables. "Won't you join us for dinner, Mr. Jenkins? As you can see, we have not received our main meal yet. Perhaps Sergeant Rose would enjoy the Korean food."

I dipped my head an inch, still looking into his eyes. "Thank you, but no. Perhaps I'll order some yaki mandu takeout to keep my large friend happy. I'll see the hostess before we leave."

Park laughed silently. Boo looked unhappy. Maybe the big guy was beginning to like me, and my abrupt exit disappointed him.

"Enjoy your meal, Mr. Park," I said. "Nice talkin' with you, Mr. Boo. Ahn yong-ee kay sipsio, gentlemen."

Out on the sidewalk Stanley said, "Glad I didn't have any holes in my socks."

I laughed.

"You can really rattle off that baba-baba shit, can't you?" he said.

"Baba-baba shit?"

"Any language I can't speak is baba-baba shit to me. I learned that phrase from a drill sergeant in basic training. He was a bad dude."

"They have drill sergeants in the Air Force?"

"Uh-huh."

"I thought you had den mothers."

"Easy, white man."

"Touchy tonight."

We stood on the curb at the edge of the parking lot.

"You believe Park?" he asked, looking like I'd be crazy if I did.

"Sure, and I used to believe John Gotti was just another garbage man. I really don't know, Stan. I just don't know."

"I hear ya."

"Well, let's give the pros from Knoxville a sit-rep," I said and started walking across the blacktop to chat with Detectives Renfro and Maples.

After we finished, Stan and I sat in my car and watched Renfro drive out to Montvue and make a right, heading toward Ray Mears Drive. I looked over to the first row of parking spots near the restaurant. A new, black Lincoln Town Car sat conspicuously in a handicapped spot.

"That must be our boy's wheels," I said. "Some balls, huh? If I had a parking ticket and the authority, I'd write him up."

"It wouldn't matter. A fine's nothing compared to the juice he gets from displaying his cool and contempt for the local cops."

"How cool would he act if I dropped a grenade in his gas tank?"

"Lordy, but you bees in a bad mood, massah."

I grunted.

The sky still looked as light as if it were five in the afternoon. A little haze in the distance mixed with the setting sun and the city smog created a hint of pink behind the clouds.

"Let's go somewhere and get a drink. That might cheer me up," I suggested.

"Aren't we supposed to wait until after sundown?"

"If that were true, half of the adult population of Alaska would have the shakes all summer long."

Stan shrugged. "I guess it's dark somewhere in the world."

He's easy.

"By the way, sahib," he said, "what make you think I didn't want to eat no Ko-rean food?"

I chuckled. "I figured another ten minutes curled up on those mats, big feller like you'd be permanently bow-legged."

"You always lookin' out fuh me. I feels priv'lidged."

We adjourned to the bar at Chesapeake's restaurant, less than fifteen minutes down the road. I ordered a double Famous Grouse on the rocks, and Stan drank his usual Canadian Club and Cola. After ten minutes on the bar stool, Stan ordered a plate of fried mozzarella sticks.

78

I ate almost half of Stan's cheese sticks and we sucked down a pair of drinks each. Nothing helped solve the case, but we felt a lot better.

* * * *

Before leaving Prospect for our chat with Mr. Park, Stanley told Officers Junior Huskey and Will Sparks to re-canvas the trailer park that night looking for residents, home after a day's work, who might have seen or heard something near Rosie Cho's place that morning. If the boys uncovered any information, I'd deal with it tomorrow. A second interview with the ladies and gentleman at Kisaeng massage was also on my list.

Chapter Nine

Kate had turned out the light on her side of the bed and fallen asleep some time ago, but I continued to read. She lay there breathing audibly but not snoring. Bitsey, on the other hand, was cutting wood like a twenty-inch Husqvarna chain saw. I got out of bed, stepped over to the dog's small oval mattress and shifted her slightly. The chain saw switched off, but Bitsey remained asleep. It's difficult to disturb a sixteen-year-old dog's rest.

After a few more pages of *Double Play,* a novel about Jackie Robinson, I turned out my light. The digital alarm clock showed ten-to-eleven.

I should have known the conglomeration of cases I'd been working on would get to me. I try not to let the amount of stress complicated work generates affect my private life, but I have a better track record of accomplishing that while awake. It's getting an undisturbed night's sleep that often eludes me.

Sometime after drifting off to sleep, the first scene of a dream placed me on a rural road in Korea, standing patiently, waiting for a bus. In the distance, a rooster tail of dust announced an oncoming vehicle. A robin's egg blue, battered thing that looked like a 1950s school bus stopped a yard from where I stood. After a breeze blew the dust away, the driver opened a pair of hinged doors; I moved to the entrance and mounted the three steps into the bus. I nodded to the driver and dropped a handful of change into the glass-sided coin catcher. He nodded back and used his head to point toward the rear, indicating I should sit before he started up again.

I looked back at the passengers filling many of the occupied seats. Scattered about on the moth-eaten benches, all of the girls from Kisaeng Massage sat and looked back, but no one seemed to recognize me. Park and Boo sat in the last seat on the right with their backs against the rear bulkhead. Park smiled like a satisfied vulture, while Boo showed his usual sphinx-like countenance. Another twenty Koreans sat scattered around, all showing blank expressions.

I took a seat about midway into the bus. The door closed, the driver mashed the gears, and we started again, rolling slowly over the gravel road. As he shifted up, the clutch chattered, the bus lurched forward, and clouds of dust began to swirl behind us. I listened to the crunch of gravel under the bald tires. It was a warm day, but only two or three of the windows were open; the rest may have been jammed shut. The inside of the big vehicle felt hot and stuffy. I had no doubt why Americans called them kimchee buses. The smell created by the road dust, mixed with the pungent odor of pickled cabbage breath, and the garlic sweat oozing from the pores of the passengers created a unique smell.

We made a few quick stops, and the remaining seats filled rapidly. At the next village, a place with only two dozen mud walled cottages, thatched with reeds, several people boarded, half of them forced to stand in the aisles. One man brought his goat along for a ride. Two women carried large bundles on their heads.

There was no room for the carefully wrapped and tied packages on the racks above the seats or on the floor up front, so the passengers passed them overhead toward the rear seats. The people sitting there didn't object to keeping them on their laps.

A few miles further and more people jammed in. A crate of chickens was passed hand over hand backward. Two more neatly tied bundles traveled the same way. A man behind me ended up with one.

I calculated that two additional people could push their way onto the bus with some effort before we reached sardine can capacity. An old woman sat next to me at the window seat. The brakes squeaked, the bus stopped, and three more people pushed on, one a woman holding a baby. The driver objected to the woman standing forward of the white line while she held her child. As often happens in Korea, a simple conversation can sound heated and become animated. The driver told the

81

woman to get off and wait. She said she couldn't wait. More chatter emanated from the other passengers. The driver shook his head in disgust, pulled the doors closed and drove on.

Then the baby travelled rearward, hand over hand from passenger to passenger, above everyone's heads, until it ended up in my lap. The little boy looked at me and grinned. I made a face and stuck out my tongue. The kid laughed and wiggled his arms. The mama-san next to me showed a toothless smile and said the little boy was cute. I think she liked me, too.

The bus jerked forward as the driver double clutched and shifted gears. I made another face and gently poked the baby in the stomach. He laughed and gurgled simultaneously.

We were chugging along again, the bus kicking up swirls of dust. The goat behind me made noise. One of the chickens said to the other, "Did you hear the one about the priest, the rabbi and the Arab?" The little kid passed gas. At least I hoped it was only gas.

Then the bus stopped. A flooded rice paddy spanned the acreage off to our left. I craned my neck to see out the other side. A narrow, loam-colored, dirt track led between several ancient cottages called *choga chips* on the right. Where the lane ended was anyone's guess. I pushed a little bowlegged man out of the way so I could see through a small section of windshield.

My eyes popped in surprise. Mr. Ha stood in the middle of the road a dozen yards in front of the bus. He wore the same brown suit I saw the day we met at Park's house. Across his chest in a proper port arms position, he held an old M3 "grease gun", a cheaply made American sub-machine gun—a Korean war leftover. The driver beeped the horn. Ha didn't move. The driver tried another beep. With a quick snap, Ha raised the little sub-machine gun, jamming the bent wire stock into his shoulder, his left hand grasping the stick magazine.

"Turn the bus!" I yelled.

The driver did nothing.

"Goddamn it. Turn right! Wen chugaro toro!"

Still nothing. But Ha hadn't fired. I looked around and heard incessant Korean chatter. The women became animated, some putting their hands over their eyes, some waving their arms trying to get someone to do something.

I looked behind me. Park and Boo were standing now. Park had a bigger grin on his face. Boo just stood there, as stolid as ever. Park pointed at me, threw his head back and laughed. He waved like a long-lost friend. The little boy in my lap looked at me and giggled, but now he had Park's face. I heard and smelled the gas expelled by my young companion and thought I'd retch from the stink. Bile began rising in my throat. I tried to shake off the feeling.

"Wen chugaro toro ka sipsio!" I shouted at the driver, pleading. I envisioned the .45 caliber, military hardball ammunition shattering the windscreen, decimating the passengers. Ha's weapon held thirty-five rounds in the stick magazine. I assumed he carried extras.

I passed the baby to the old woman next to me and fought my way to the front of the bus. Two rows from the driver's seat, a manicured hand grabbed my wrist. I looked down and to my right.

"Be careful, Sam!" Roni Keeble said.

Next to her Sunny Kim sat and looked up at me with dark searching eyes. I nodded reassuringly, pulled free and yanked the lever, opening the narrow double doors.

I stepped down and stood next to the bus looking at Ha. He shifted his point of aim from the bus to me. Marshal Dillon, eat your heart out. This was the real deal. Only I stood there unarmed.

I bent down and picked up a baseball-sized stone from amongst the gravel. I looked at Ha. Ha looked at me. I wound up and threw—like Andy Carey nailing a batter running to first who just sent a sizzling grounder deep along the third base line. Ha pulled the trigger. The .45 caliber round popped and traveled slowly down the stubby barrel. I watched it approaching, spinning toward me. I woke up.

The alarm clock showed 2:24 in the morning. I was wide awake. More awake than if the buzzer had sounded at 6 a.m.

I lay there for a few minutes trying to regroup. I knew I'd never get an ending for the dream, and wasn't sure I wanted one. Stones are a poor match against a machine gun.

I blinked a few times, squeezed my eyes tightly shut, opened them and decided to make a trip to the bathroom. I took a long drink of cold water and three valerian caplets, hoping to get back to sleep with herbal assistance.

Back in bed, I tried to clear my head and envision a quiet, peaceful place. I've made no secret of the fact that I'm lousy at meditation and all that other new age, progressive relaxation crap. I remembered where it got me when I tried at work.

Everything except a peaceful place began racing through my head, things I had to do, things I should have done, dead Korean women, Korean gangsters, Korean restaurants, farting babies, laughing goats, talking chickens.

I got up and walked into another room, turned on the computer and found no more emails than what had been there at 7:15 when I last looked. Even the spammers hadn't sent me anything new. I thought I'd find some light reading about on-line universities, replica watches or male-enhancement products, but no such luck.

I went back to bed and thought of what we did earlier that evening. Just before dinner, I turned off the satellite radio and switched on a CD—*Mob Hits*. Don't ask why. That was a big mistake. For the rest of the night I remembered Lou Monte singing *Lazy Mary*. The jaunty Sicilian tune wouldn't leave me alone.

C' 'na luna mezz' u mare
Mamma mia m'a maritare ...

La lari ula' pesce fritte' baccala
Uei cumpa' no claamare c' eggi 'accatta.

Then Lou told me in English he was about to embark on the 'second stanza' and sang something similar all over again.

Having finished that, Lou said, "For those of you nice ladies and gentlemen who don't understand the I-tralian language, I'll sing a few choruses in Britissssh."

Lazy Mary you better get up
She answered back, I am not able.
Lazy Mary you better get up
We need the sheets for the table...

Silently, I sang along. If I fought and tried to block Lou from my mind, I was afraid I'd only get into it with Julius LaRosa—or, God forbid, Louie Prima. Madonna mi!

At 6 o'clock the alarm sounded. I turned it off and grabbed onto Kate.

"What a night," I said.

She turned and kissed me on the forehead. "Good morning, sweetie. You sleep okay?"

Chapter Ten

I had read through more than half the list of residents at Prospect Farms Mobil Home Park looking for something to spark a brilliant investigative inspiration when Bettye buzzed my phone.

"There's a Dee-tective Dee-Dubyah Renfro from Knoxville on the line for ya."

"Dee-tective Dee-Dubyah? Y'all sound so all-fared country t'day, li'l darlin'."

"Watch yer step, city-boy." She laughed and transferred the call.

"I figgered ya'd want ta know about somethin' called in early this mornin'," Renfro said.

"I'll bet if I'm exceedingly patient, sometime in the not too distant future you'll enlighten me about this new development, won't you?"

"Y'all talk funny, ya know? Anyways, a detective on another shift, feller name o' Gabe Earlywine, got called ta where two kids found a body right near the fishin' dock at I.C. King Park offa Al-coa Highway."

"That place is right off a major road. Anyone see anything?"

"It's near the highway, 'cept the dock and that parkin' lot is low down and blocked by some big hedges. Cain't no one can see nuthin' from the road."

"Is this body a former resident of Prospect?"

"Nope, he's not. Used ta live right here in Knoxville."

"Okay, I'm interested, but don't know what it's got to do with me. What's the punch line?"

"Dead man's one Chang-Hai Ha—the tall feller that worked fer yer Mr. Park."

I pushed back in my swivel chair and propped my foot on the open desk drawer to my right. "Son of a gun. How'd he die?"

"Two shots, one in the chest, one twixt the eyes."

That really interested me. "From a .22?"

"Not hardly, .45 ACP. M.E. says holler points. No casin's left near the body. No blood ta speak of. Musta been killed elstwheres and dumped in the park."

"Interesting. How can I get in touch with this Detective Earlywine?"

"Comes in at four. He was on standby overnight and got called out at ten-past-five this mornin' when them two kids called 9-1-1. They's there ta go fishin'. Me and Wit's next up, so we'll be handlin' this one, but Gabe, he done all the preliminaries."

"Any good ideas or suspects yet?"

"Beats me. Cause when ya got a professional thug gets killed, ya got a good chance another thug done the killin'. I thought y'all might have some words o' wisdom fer me, you bein' so familiar with them Koreans."

"Give me a few minutes to look up wisdom on Google, and I'll get back to you. I like your idea of another bad guy taking him out. Some kind of rivalry between Asian hoods maybe? Could also be hooked up with this Rosie Cho business here in Prospect. I don't suppose the uniform cop who responded or Earlywine found a .22 revolver in Ha's pocket?"

"No such luck. We're a'fixin' ta search the apartment where he lived and then go see Mr. Park. If we find anythin' connected ta the girl's murder, I'll holler at ya."

* * * *

I walked across the square to Kisaeng massage. In addition to my re-interviews, I wanted to see their reactions to Mr. Ha's demise. Sunny Kim looked shocked. Roni Keeble didn't skip a beat and made some caustic remark like good riddance to bad rubbish. *My kind of girl.*

The other young woman working there, Kum-Ok Kyeung, said she didn't know Mr. Ha. I spent some time with Kum-Ok, who had been one of Rosie's roommates. She was a shy, young-looking girl who could add nothing to what she told John Gallagher the day before. I found it difficult to believe a masseuse could be shy. Kum-Ok repeated that she had seen Rosie at approximately 8:30 on the morning of the murder and left for work while Rosie made her morning tea.

There were two more employees to talk with, Lee, Chun-He, a third roommate, and Prater McKendry, a physical therapist's assistant, both due in at noon.

On my way back to the municipal building, I waved to Irving Fine who stood on the sidewalk outside his jewelry store admiring the display upon which he must have just finished working. Irving opened the door to the shop and waved for me to join him. I'm curious by nature, so I walked over.

"Hi, Irv. What's up?"

"Sam, hello. My brother, he told me you were asking about dat place across da street." He spoke in a nasal, hushed voice. No other person was in earshot, so I guess he liked the idea of being a truly confidential informant.

"The massage parlor?" I found myself whispering, too.

"Yeah, I heard a girl from dare got killed." Irving wasn't *exactly* a mirror image of his brother, but he had the same red hair mixed with gray and the same nervous energy. Even if threatened with a penalty of death, Irving wouldn't wear the same clothes as his twin.

I raised my volume a little. "That's right. Were either of you working the night before it happened?"

"We were bot' here. We got new stones and had to book dem in."

"Is Bernie here?"

"Him! He's in da back on da phone. He wants to buy and sell old toys now. He's crazy!" Irv's voice raised a few more octaves.

"If you've got a minute, get him, please. Let's talk."

"Hey, for you anytime—you're always welcome." He turned toward the back room and screamed, "Ber-nard!"

From behind the wall, a voice answered, "Whaaat?" Not exactly a blood-curdling scream, but much louder than necessary.

"Sam is here! Whattsamatta wit' you? Come out here!"

From the doorway, Bernie emerged.

"Shut up already! I'm coming!"

When he saw me, Bernie's expression changed to a big smile. He wore a Mets cap tilted back on his head and used a middle finger to push his glasses to their original position on the bridge of his nose.

"Hi ya doin'? How ya been?" he asked.

"Hello, Bernie," I said.

We started talking about the night before Rosie Cho's murder and hadn't gotten to first base when Bernie grabbed an eighteen-inch bag of popcorn from beneath the counter. He offered me some.

"Here, it's kettle corn. At da flea market I got it. Yesterday I went."

"Yeah, he's looking fuh toys!" Irving almost yelled. "He's stupid!"

I fished a half-dozen kernels of corn out of the tall bag and popped two into my mouth. It tasted good, sweet from caramelized sugar and salty at the same time.

"Whadda you know?" Bernie screamed. "It's not stupid. They're wort' good money." He took a mouthful of popcorn and loudly crunched a couple of un-popped kernels.

Irving scolded his brother. "Stop chewing dose t'ings. You'll break ya toot!"

"Shut up! It's my teet!" Bernie said.

"If you go ta da dentist, I gotta pay." Irving scowled and shook his head. Bernie smiled again and ate more popcorn.

"Guys. Uh...can we talk about that night?" I asked.

"Tell him about da motorcycle!" Irving spoke as if Bernie were a hundred yards away.

"What motorcycle?" Bernie asked, back again to 180 decibels.

"You know what motorcycle, stupid. Da one on da sidewalk!"

"Heh, heh, heh." Bernie grinned. "Oh yeah, da black t'ing, a Harley I t'ink."

"On the sidewalk? By the massage parlor? When?" I asked.

"Yeah, by da massage parlor—all afternoon," Bernie said. "We left...what time did we go?" He looked to Irving for help.

"How should I know? Seven-t'irty, eight o'clock? We got home, and I missed Jeopardy. It was your fault."

"I t'ink seven-t'irty or eight." Bernie said. "No, we got home at eight. I picked up Chinese from Wah Lum. He's very good. Very fresh. Not too oily. Den NCIS I watched."

I tried to assimilate all the information and segregate the banter about kettle corn and antique toys. I closed my eyes momentarily and shook my head. "So this black motorcycle, maybe a Harley-Davidson, was on the sidewalk from afternoon until at least 7:30?"

The Brothers Fine nodded.

"Did you see who was driving the bike?" I asked.

"We try not ta look. Dat would be nosy," Irving said with a concerned frown.

I wanted to call Ingmar Bergman and ask him to explain what just happened, but instead I thanked my friendly jewelers for their input and continued back to the office.

* * * *

I asked my two henchmen, or more properly henchpersons, since one of them was our female desk sergeant, to run a complete background on Rosie Cho. This would include a list of friends, enemies, boyfriends, group associations, churches, bank accounts, debts and financial obligations, credit cards, telephones, computers, insurance companies, personal effects in her room, contents of her car, personal papers, relatives in and out of the area, and any known recent arguments. I also asked Bettye to check if any officer from Prospect PD or passing county deputy or state trooper wrote a ticket on a black motorcycle parked on the sidewalk that afternoon.

All that would keep her and John Gallagher busy and out of trouble for a long time. Then I jumped in the Ford and headed to Knoxville.

* * * *

I met Ralph Oliveri in the parking lot at the Olive Garden in a shopping center the size of a small city. Turkey Creek provided every possible department store, boutique, eatery or specialty shop the population of West Knoxville, Farragut and Concord would ever need. I hoped Ralph would have more information I could use. Besides, I owed the man a lunch for some favor of long ago.

I wore a snazzy tropical weight, beige, herringbone sport jacket over a light blue button-down shirt and brown slacks. Ralph appeared in typical FBI uniform: a Wall Street gray suit, white shirt and somber blue tie.

A young woman led us to a booth in a quiet room decorated like a Neapolitan patio with artificial grape vines hanging from an overhead trellis. As we sat down, Dean Martin began singing *Ain't That a Kick in the Head.*

The hostess handed us several folders; a lunch menu, a dinner menu, a specials menu, a desert menu and a wine list. If I read them all, I'd qualify for a master's degree in restaurant sciences.

A cute but slightly overweight brunette wearing a white shirt, garish tie and black hip-huggers walked up to the table.

"Hi, I'm Shannon. I'll be taking care of you today. Can I start you off with my favorite wine? It's $3.95 a glass." She said that all without talking a breath, as if it was one sentence.

She showed me a half-full, sweaty bottle of an inexpensive white zinfandel.

"No thanks, Shannon," I said. "That's a little too sweet. How about a couple of glasses of water while we figure out what we're having for lunch? We'll pick the wine later."

"Okay, no problem." Shannon sounded like her zip code was 90210.

Shannon disappeared, and Ralph spoke. "How do you know that wine is too sweet for me?" He tilted his head and squinted. His dark eyes became narrow slits.

I think Ralph affected that look when he interrogated suspects. It didn't influence me.

"How many Italians drink white zinfandel?" I asked.

"I don't know." His expression softened, and he looked like a little boy with his dark hair parted on the left and combed in a timeless, conservative style.

"You like dry reds. Don't break my balls."

"Maybe you should ask first." He tried to act offended.

I thought he was going to sulk.

"If you were my wife or girlfriend I'd ask."

"You got a girlfriend?" He grinned lecherously and raised his eyebrows.

"Figure of speech, moron."

"How come you make me drive all the way out here? You can't get any further west and still be in Knoxville."

91

"I'm buying, and I like this place." Obviously, his parents never taught him about looking a gift horse in the mouth. "Gimme a break. I drove further than you. Listen, that's Al Martino singing now. When did you hear Al Martino last?"

He ignored my musical question.

"The waitress sounded like an idiot," he said. "I hope she gets the order right."

"Don't worry. I'll make sure. The food here is good. You'll like it." Sometimes I treat Ralph like a son because he's twenty years younger than me.

"What are you having?" he asked.

"I haven't looked at the menu. You've been talking too much." Sometimes he acts fifty years younger than me.

"Jeez."

We spent a few minutes reading the dinner selections.

"Have you ever had this stuffed chicken marsala?" Ralph asked.

"Yeah, it's excellent. You can ask for pasta if you don't want the garlic mashed potatoes."

"You gonna have that?"

"I don't know...maybe."

"I'm having that. With... What pasta would go with that?"

"Farfalle."

"What's that?"

"Bow ties. What the hell kind of Italian are you?"

"I'm having that. How about you?"

I rolled my eyes and dropped the menu. "Since I can't read while you're talking, yes, I'll have the same."

"You want Chianti?"

"No, something heavier, I think. Wait a minute." I looked at the wine list.

"How about a valpolichella? This is a nice one." I pointed to one of the choices.

"Sure. My old man used to drink valpolichella."

"Your old man was smart, like me. You, you're a putz."

"Jeez."

Shannon returned with our water, a communal bowl of salad and a basket of bread sticks. She set those down in the center of the table and again spoke with her machine-gun delivery. "I forgot them, so I'll be, like, right back with your salad and bread plates. Would you like fresh grated cheese on your salad?" She stood with a death grip on a large hand cranked grater suspended above the salad bowl.

"Do black bears stroll through the Smokies?" I inquired.

Shannon appeared confused, but remained steadfast, grater at the ready.

"Ralph, cheese?" I'd be polite to my touchy friend and ask first. He only nodded, chewing on a bread stick. I looked up at Shannon. "Yes, please."

"Tell me when," she instructed.

I waited for the opportune moment.

"When!"

I think that startled her. She blinked and took a breath, put down the grater and picked up her order pad.

"Are you, like, ready to order?"

"Sure, but ask my father first." I pointed at Ralph.

Shannon tilted her head and showed more signs of confusion, but we made it through the ordering process without serious incident.

Half way through the first plate of salad, she brought the wine. Since Ralph isn't as fatherly-looking as I am, she opened the bottle—with some difficulty, poured me a drizzle and waited for my approval.

"Oh, God, this tastes like vinegar," I said.

"Vinegar? Like, really?"

I smiled. "No, I'm just kidding. It's lovely. Thanks very much."

She sighed, and her shoulders dropped two inches. She looked relieved. "Like, I've never heard anyone say something like *that* before."

"He's unique," Ralph told her.

I smiled again, as if we were, *like*, old friends.

She poured two glasses of wine. As she walked away from the table, I noticed that for a young girl she had a wide backside. Too much pasta. No phys. ed. classes. I took a sip of valpolichella.

"What do you make of this second murder?" I asked Ralph.

"Hell of a coincidence, but I don't know enough to see a connection."

"Me either. There aren't that many Koreans around here. I mean, Knoxville ain't Flushing, you know."

"I do know, and I anticipated your questions. Like I said, we're not in the loop with this Mr. Ha killing, but here's a little general info for you. According to the census people now, let's take Knoxville and the three metro counties…Knox, Blount, and Anderson. It seems the Asians represent less than two percent of the population in the area, but that still accounts for almost twelve thousand people. People who answer the census questions. That isn't counting people who throw away the questionnaires or the undocumented aliens who never get them."

"Fascinating." I finished a forkful of salad, bit off the end of a bread stick and sipped more wine.

"It is, really. Now, as I was about to say, in any ethnic enclave of the U.S., there are always your assorted hoods who try to make a quick and illegal buck exploiting and shaking down their brethren. As a matter of fact, we have Chinese, Korean, Vietnamese and maybe one or two Filipino thugs trying to do just that in the aforementioned jurisdiction. We're sure not like L.A. or Seattle, but we manage a little blip on the radar.

"Even more fascinating," I said. "And it's amazing what you can learn when you hang around with a Fed. Where does that leave me?"

"In a good position to pass the bread sticks."

* * * *

That afternoon I went back to Kisaeng Massage. Chun-He Lee sat down with me and talked about her former roommate, Rosie Cho. I said Kum-Ok Kyeung was shy; Chun-He definitely was not. Kum-Ok was a cute girl, but not a beauty. Chun-He certainly was. I called it a toss-up who was the prettiest, Chun-He or Sunny Kim. Both were Miss Korea material. I would have picked Sunny, but only because she was older. Regardless of how pretty and personable Miss Lee had been, she provided no information that shed any light on who killed one of her trailer home companions.

When I finished speaking with Chun-He, I waited for Prater McKendry while he dealt with a patient—or client—or whatever you call those who visit a massage therapist and PTA.

To kill time, I leaned on the counter of the reception area talking with Roni Keeble, admiring her colorful 1970s retro blouse when my cell phone rang.

Bettye said, "Sam, John just found a parking ticket on a motorcycle that Junior wrote that day. He...ah...neglected to turn it in until two days later. It's not on a Harley though. It's an '07, black Honda Shadow. Place and time are right."

"Thank John for me, and when you see Junior tell him I'm going to shoot him in the foot, and after I'm finished, I'll beat him to death."

"You want me to tell Junior that?"

"No, don't tell Junior that. He's too enthusiastic to yell at. Who's the owner?"

"It's registered to Prater McKendry, DOB 6-30-79, with a Rockford address. You want more?"

"No, that's the guy who works here. I'll get what I need from him. Thanks, kiddo. I'll be back to the barn shortly."

"You take care, darlin'. John and I'll be here."

I went back to waiting for Prater and shooting the breeze with Roni. She complained about a fuel injector problem on her Audi, thinking I'd know something about modern cars.

Before I had to embarrass myself and admit I didn't know what a fuel injector looked like, a middle-aged man on crutches hobbled down the hall, said good-bye to Roni and left. Moments later, Prater approached us carrying a bundle of rolled up linens that he tossed into a hamper behind the counter. Roni introduced us, and we moved into Sunny's office so our conversation would be private.

I learned that Prater acquired his physical therapy skills courtesy of Uncle Sam's Air Force. Since separating from active duty, he continued his education by going to school for massage therapy. After working simultaneously at Baptist Hospital in Knoxville and two other physical therapy practices—all part-time jobs, he landed his first full-time gig at Kisaeng.

He confirmed that he had worked with Rosie the night before her murder and apologized for parking his 750 Shadow-Aero, a classically-styled motorcycle that might have looked enough like a Harley-Davidson to fool the likes of Bernie Fine, on the sidewalk. He promised to pay his ticket in advance of the scheduled court date, but offered nothing more that helped me.

It seemed almost like these people worked hard to know nothing about their fellow employees.

As often happens in the life of a police investigator, I was once again stymied.

* * * *

It felt like one of those times when I was sick and tired of my job. I teetered on the verge of saying screw it. If no one saw anything and no one wanted to tell me anything, the things someone obviously knew or had seen or might guess at concerning Rosie Cho's death, then maybe she'd go into that great repository of unsolved cases the FBI reports on each year, and I'd move on.

I was sick of Ralph Oliveri not having the answers I needed, sick of Dee-Dubyah Renfro and the other Knoxville dicks not being able to connect the Cho and Ha murders and sick of being old enough to collect Social Security. As Mel Brooks once said, "Life stinks." So, I wanted to say screw it.

* * * *

"You're awfully quiet, sweetie," Kate said, as she diced boiled red-skinned potatoes into little cubes, before adding sour cream, crushed garlic and other seasoning.

"I'm thinking about how annoyed I am, with myself and the rest of the world, over this Korean fiasco."

I acted as souse chef by slicing half-inch slabs of cymling squash destined to be grilled between the Teflon-coated jaws of a device named for the former heavyweight champion, George Forman.

I had XM Radio tuned into the 1950s station. Little Richard Pettyman sang *Lucille,* and I sort of bopped to the music.

"Things aren't going as you'd like them to go?"

"I think I may have started an avalanche."

"You've never done that before, and it would seem unlikely you did this time," Kate said, more soothing than Little Richard's song.

"I see this as two connected incidents. No one else does yet, but this would be too much of a coincidence if two Koreans, both loosely on the same line, aren't somehow related to each other by other than national ties."

Bitsey always stayed under foot while Kate and I cooked. Kate bent over and popped a little potato cube into the dog's mouth. She wagged her tail. Bitsey did, not Kate.

"Remember what you used to say when we lived in Korea? When things happened and the reason wasn't apparent?"

"I was young then. I said a lot. Did I say something meaningful?"

"Of course you did, sweetie. You said something like, "When things like this happen in totally different places but appear to have a common link, in the end we'll learn that they're all tied together...all related."

"Thank you, Madam Nu, for your inscrutable oriental intelligence."

"Madam Nu was Vietnamese."

"I know that. You think I said something similar back then?

"I know you did. And you were always right. I hate to admit that, but it's true. It's true now. You have some uncanny knack. It's why I hate you. Look for the connection, Sammy. Somewhere in those two murders, there's more of a connection than just the nationality of the victims."

"No woman hates me. You're just saying that."

"Of course I don't hate you. It's just that you're obnoxious when you're always right. Who wouldn't hate that?"

"Huh?"

"Never mind."

After a recent cut, Kate's salt-and-pepper hair looked even whiter. The color wasn't important. She was beautiful. And she could cook— almost as well as me.

"Yeah, right," I said. "This hood Park is the connection. I just can't put reasons to what happened yet. Suppose Park had Rosie killed to send a message? Would Sunny Kim kill Park's man in retaliation? Park says he had nothing to do with Rosie Cho, and I believed him. Would Sunny, thinking Park was involved, kill Ha herself or hire someone. She seems non-violent to me."

"She seems quite beautiful to you as well. Would you stereotype your suspect and overlook something because of that?"

"I don't think I ever have. Perhaps you remember a beautiful Irish girl whose behavior I had doubts about?"

"Sorry."

"That's okay."

Little Richard finished screeching about *Lucille*, and The Pony Tails began telling us they were *Born Too Late*. I started taking spice jars and a small bottle of olive oil out of a cabinet.

Kate continued. "I know it's easy for me to say, but keep looking for the exact connection. When you find it, this will all make sense and fall into place. The connection is out there somewhere."

"Yeah, I guess. I'm not exactly tripping over a basket full of clues that will kindle any lucid theories." I took a fry pan out of the lower cabinet and placed it on a burner. "I'm ready for the chicken cutlets, but I'll wait for your potatoes."

"Hang in there, sweetie. I'll only be another minute."

"It's at times like these I'd rather hang onto you." I stepped behind Kate and put my arms around her waist.

"Careful! I don't want a chunk of my finger in with these potatoes."

"Just a little extra protein." I nuzzled between her neck and shoulder.

"Are you going to be able to control yourself and eat dinner?"

"I'm in love, but I'm also hungry."

"Ah, a hopeless romantic, but good. Eat first. Love later. After the sun goes down."

"I hope that isn't like Stan's idea of drinking in Alaska."

"What?"

"Forget that. I think you're so sexy when you're cutting vegetables."

"Thank you, Chef Jenkins. I understand your sauces are aphrodisiacs."

"I guess that means I should go easy on the garlic?"

"Well, like, yeah!"

Chapter Eleven

Jackie Shuman's crime scene package arrived in the morning mail. A report, sketches of the doublewide and the lot around it and a stack of 8x10 glossies were in a large Priority Mail envelope. I was looking at the photos when Bettye walked into my room.

"You're not going to believe this," she said, shaking her head and peeking over the tops of her glasses.

I looked at her waiting for the news. She wasn't smiling so I assumed she didn't plan on telling a joke.

"You just bought that new color lipstick and got it on sale?" I said.

"Well, it *is* a new color, Sammy. Thank you for noticin'." She blushed for a moment and then gave me a smile before continuing. "No, Bobby John just called in. Workers at the greenhouse on Doc Beasley Road found an abandoned car parked on the property. There's a dead Asian girl inside."

I put a hand over my eyes and wanted to plotz. "You're right. I don't believe it. Do we have some kind of genocide going on here?"

"Lord have mercy. I sure don't know. I wish I could help you."

"You can. Give me the fat Irishman for the morning and run this place while I'm gone."

"Of course I will. You two leavin' now?"

"We're already on the way."

"I'll tell Bobby," she said, "and then get the county boys rollin'."

"The new kid is riding with Bobby this week, isn't he?"

"He is."

"He'll get his feet wet before he gets near the academy."

99

"Any idea when the next class starts?"

"They cancelled the one scheduled in April," I said. "Not enough enrollees. Probably hold one after the busy season."

"He should do well."

I nodded. "He's working out so far. Let's see how he handles the heavy stuff."

"I hope he keeps his breakfast down. Bobby says it looks bad."

"Good training for the boy. We'll make a cop out of him...or not."

"Be nice, darlin'. Dallas is a fine young man."

"I've been nice. I'll just hate his uncles for the rest of my life."

"You are a difficult man, Sam Jenkins."

"And you love me anyway."

"Yes, I do. Now get out of my police station."

"Yes, ma'am. I'm on my way."

* * * *

I drove up to Sevierville Road and turned northeast toward the adjoining town of Seymour in the neighboring county. The greenhouses sat close to the end of our jurisdiction at the intersection of Doc Beasley Road and stretched for almost three hundred yards in both directions.

It wasn't the neatest commercial property I'd ever seen. Derelict vehicles, pieces of rusting equipment, stacks of wooden pallets and old boxes and enough tall weeds to hamper the progress of an infantry squad were scattered around in no particular order. Long plastic-covered and uncovered half-round growing sheds stood in haphazard rows. Some of the plastic was shredded and torn and looked like a ship with tattered sails. If someone tried, they couldn't create a more abandoned look for an active business.

I pulled off the blacktop near the driveway entrance. Two open gates allowed access to a compound surrounded by a six-foot chain-link fence. Bobby John Crockett had parked his police cruiser across the entrance, blocking the driveway from the rest of the property. He and our rookie police officer, Dallas Finchum, stood a few yards from a white Hyundai Elantra speaking to a tall gray-haired man in his early-fifties. I parked my car in a small patch of shade. John and I walked over.

"Howdy, boss. Hey, John," Bobby said. "This here's Mr. Chester

Suttles. He's the manager. His daddy, Amos Suttles, owns the business. He was in first this mornin' and found the car just like it is—didn't touch nothin'."

"Hello, Mr. Suttles. I'm Sam Jenkins, chief at Prospect PD. This is John Gallagher. He'll be conducting the investigation with me."

"Good ta meetcha."

"How's it goin'?" John said.

"You know the woman in the car?" I asked.

"No, sir. Never seen her before. Course I ain't got a real good look at her."

"Any idea when this car may have been dropped off here?"

"We closed up last night at six. I got here jest b'fore nine this mornin'. Weren't nobody here all night."

Thick clumps of weeds grew on both sides of the gates. It looked like a team of mules couldn't move them. "You ever close these gates?"

"No, sir, ain't been shut in years. No need ta, really."

I looked at my three colleagues and knew the inevitable had fallen upon us. Warm overnight temperatures and the car sitting in plenty of bright morning sun would have hastened putrefaction of the victim.

Being a lead investigator sometimes has its disadvantages. "Well, I guess it's time to take a look."

I stepped over to the passenger's side of the Hyundai expecting to give myself a little distance from the body to see clearly. I was surprised and felt foolish.

"She's in the passenger's seat and slumped to the left," I said, "but she was shot in the right temple. There's blood on the inside of the steering wheel, but not on the window. No exit wound. She was probably moved from the driver's side."

No one commented.

I took a pair of latex gloves from my pocket and pulled them on. John had already done the same.

The little car sat on a stretch of three-quarter-inch blue stone that provided no chance of a usable foot impression near the vehicle. I walked back around and tried the driver's door handle and found it locked.

"Bobby, pop the lock with your slim-jim. Dallas, pay attention to what he does."

Crockett dug out a twenty-inch, flat stainless steel bar from a plastic milk crate in the trunk of his police car. Dallas Finchum followed him around like a shadow.

"Dallas," I said, "watch us from the driveway. I don't want more people walking near the car than absolutely necessary."

The kid's face changed from wide-eyed and enthusiastic to just this side of crestfallen. He looked like I just told him there was no Santa Claus, and he believed me.

"Yes, sir," he said and stopped in his tracks.

Once Bobby unlocked the door, and I opened it, I automatically grabbed my nose. "Jesus H. Christ!" A wave of warm putrid air overwhelmed me. It felt like over a hundred-and-twenty degrees in the closed automobile. I took two steps backward. "Thank heavens for the good ol' summertime. Otherwise we'd find bodies that didn't stink enough to gag a maggot."

And young cops think it's glamorous being a detective.

"Open the other door, Bobby," I said, "let's get a cross breeze. If I reach in there now to look at her face I may throw up on our crime scene."

Crockett opened the right side door and moved away quickly. I held a handkerchief over my nose, reached in and turned the girl's head. There appeared to be only a single gunshot wound to her temple. I immediately recognized the victim.

"Mr. Suttles," I said, "it's not going to get any prettier from here on. The crime scene investigators and medical examiner will be here shortly to do their work. I assume your people use the other driveway in back of the retail shop and park in the big lot?"

He nodded.

"Would you tell everyone to keep clear of the area? We're going to tape off this driveway and the section of the gravel."

He nodded again, began to look a little woozy and took a handkerchief from his back pocket to hold over his nose. Chester Suttles stood more than six-foot-tall, but weighed less than one-fifty. His pale complexion and bony frame made him appear frail and vulnerable.

"You doing okay?" I asked. "Dead bodies and hot weather do not make for a pleasant work environment."

"Yes, sir. I'm fine."

I didn't believe that for a minute.

"Do me another favor," I said, "and ask everyone working if they've ever seen this car before or if anyone drove past your property after they left work."

Suttles mumbled 'Okay' from behind his hankie and looked like he might become ill.

"Maybe, with a little luck, we can narrow down the time the car got here. We'll have to speak with everyone sometime later. Don't let anyone leave, even to make deliveries, until we do."

He nodded once more and offered no objection.

When Suttles left I said, "This is another girl from Kisaeng. Her name's Kum-Ok Kyeung, a roommate of the last victim."

"Some box of worms, huh Boss?" John opined.

Bobby snickered. Even Dallas smiled. Everyone at the PD enjoyed John's brand of English.

"*Can*, John. It's a can of worms. You, on the other hand, are a box of rocks," I said.

He smiled and fluttered his eyelashes. "Boss, how can you say that?"

If I found out John did his nitwit act just to get a laugh, I'd kill him.

Within thirty minutes, all the forensics people arrived at the scene. Jackie Shuman and Neal Brickman again represented the county sheriff. Mo Rappaport and Earl Ogle were present at the pleasure of the medical examiner.

Bobby called in the plate number, and Bettye confirmed the Hyundai was registered to Kum-Ok.

"What is this, Sam?" the doctor asked. "Same crime, different location? Another Chinese girl?"

I corrected the doctor. "She's Korean, Morris. Same continent, different country."

He shrugged. "Whatever."

Morris set his black bag down and reached into the car to tilt Kum-Ok's head for a better look at the bullet hole. The death-smell had dissipated a little with the breeze, but nothing like that ever seemed to faze Mo.

"This gunshot wound looks like a .22. Might be the same weapon from the other shooting," he said, "but who knows? The four rounds in the other girl were lead hollow-points. Hard to tie to a specific gun though. High velocity, soft projectile. They mushroom back a lot. Tough to see clear rifling marks."

"Do your best, ui-sah."

Morris looked at me and frowned. "What's that mean?"

"It's Korean for doctor."

"Oy, such a worldly guy for a small-town cop."

I smiled. "Think of me as an international man of mystery."

"If you say so, Samilah."

John and I left Mo and Earl to do their thing. Neal had cordoned off the necessary areas with yellow crime scene tape.

Jackie asked, "You git my report? The one on the Rosie Whatshername murder?"

"Arrived in this morning's mail. Thanks," I said.

"Read it yet?"

"Just started when this came in."

"Y'all will see that I mention the shooter usin' a cloth ta wipe off a couple o' things. Your prints were all that's on the outside front door knob, with nothin' much on the inside and nothin' on the bathroom door. I believe he...or she...maybe threw up in the commode. Might git some DNA from the swabs Neal had took. Got a partial off the flush lever, but don't see more'n three points. Ain't the victim's or the other girl's. We got elimination prints from them."

Jackie took off his BCSO ball cap and wiped the perspiration from his forehead. Dallas Finchum walked over and listened to our conversation with as much interest as a teeny bopper listening to her favorite rock star.

"No stomach for killing, but maybe he did it a second time," I said. "The lousy shot group and vomit sure doesn't say professional killer, does it?"

"Not hardly."

"One shot in her head's more efficient."

Jackie nodded.

"But check the weeds and span out a bit looking for more vomit, just in case they haven't toughened up any."

Gallagher had a big grin on his face when he spoke to Jackie. "Go over the area with a *five tooth comb*, kid. Want me to show you how it's done?"

Jackie laughed. He took off his cap again and fanned his face. His short dark hair was soaked with sweat.

"We'll git'er done fer ya, Dee-tective Gallagher," he said. "Don't y'all worry."

The legend of John's vocabulary had spread to the sheriff's office, too.

"Thanks, partner," I said to Jackie. "You're a fine American." I looked at Dallas. "Jackie, if you've got any grunt work, let Officer Finchum help. Teach him how to be a world-class evidence technician."

Jackie grinned. "Works fer me."

Dallas looked so happy I thought he might wet his trousers.

* * * *

When we got back to the PD, neither John nor I knew any more than when we first found Kum-Ok slumped in her car. There were no neighbors to question. None of the workers knew anything. And the forensic reports were at least a day away.

I found a Harley-Davidson Road King with Florida plates parked in the spot reserved for Prospect's one and only police chief.

"Mazzio, you miserable bastard," I growled to no one in particular.

I parked in a visitor's spot, and we headed for the back door.

John walked directly into my office. I stopped at Bettye's desk and gave her all the information I knew so she could make a blotter entry and send out a press release.

"Don't hurry with that news release," I said. "I want to make a phone call first."

She smiled and knew what I wanted to do. "I'll let you know when it's ready."

I joined John and found Fred Mazzio sitting behind my desk. The bum still had hair darker than a Labrador retriever and a big matching mustache. He sat there smiling, waiting for me to act annoyed because he

105

used my parking spot. He looked like a Polynesian kahuna in his black and white Hawaiian shirt and blue jeans.

"Who are you supposed to be? Magnum F.I.?" I asked.

"F.I.?"

"Yeah, fat investigator."

He laughed. "You're pissed, aren't you?"

"For what?"

"Yeah, for what?"

"What are you doing here?"

"I wanna take you to lunch."

"What a sport. I thought you were getting ready to go home."

"I'm not going home."

"Ever?" I felt the surprise show on my face.

"No, not ever...never...whatever. I like it here. I rode the Dragon yesterday afternoon. What a freakin' blast. I want to do it again, early in the morning sometime, without a helmet. I paid for five more days. Same spot."

"You better wear a brain bucket, sport. You can't afford to take any more knocks on the head."

"See, you are pissed."

"Why should I be pissed at a guy who's buying me lunch?"

"Yeah, right."

"Give me a few minutes. Talk to your father," I pointed to John, "while I make a couple of phone calls. He'll tell you about our new murder." I sat in the guest chair next to my desk phone.

"New murder? Shit, this doesn't look like a dangerous place, but in two days, you've got more killings than Detroit."

I called Roni Keeble. Sunny Kim picked up a second phone, and the three of us spoke. They were suitably shocked at the death of Kum-Ok. I told them that I planned to have officers escort them and the remaining two live employees home each night until we had the killer in custody. They didn't argue the necessity of that.

I said I'd stop by sometime during the afternoon and try to jog something loose from someone's brain. They said they'd be waiting.

Then I called Rachel, told her about the second murder and suggested she get a cameraman on the road so she could 'scoop the competition'.

She laughs when I sound like Walter Winchell.

"Are you close to making an arrest?' she asked.

"Honest answer? No. I haven't any idea who did this or the other murder. I only assume it's the same person, and I think it may be related to the fatal shooting in Knoxville."

"Can I say that on the air?"

"I hate to admit it, but I guess it's all I've got for the moment. Sure, go ahead, and say that. I'll live with the smirks and snickers among the law enforcement community."

"I have to say something, Sammy."

"I know. It's okay. Maybe the killer or killers will get a false sense of security."

"You're sure?"

"Yeah, I'm sure."

"Oh, I feel so sorry for you. But thanks for the call."

"You're welcome. How's your Mustang?"

"You had to ask?"

"What do you mean? That's a nice car. You didn't have an accident, did you?"

"No." She sounded offended. "I'm just not used to all that power. I found myself doing eighty up Broadway before I realized how fast it was going."

I chuckled. "If you get stopped for speeding, tell them you know a cop."

"You're so helpful."

"I am, and I treat you too good."

"I should take you to lunch, shouldn't I?"

"You should. You owe me so much."

"Oh, boy."

"I'd suggest a Korean restaurant, but the surroundings might give me feelings of inferiority."

"You'll solve these cases like you solve all the others."

"I hope so, or we'll have quite a dent in our Korean population."

"You'll find the killer. Be patient."

"Thanks for the pep talk. I'll see you."

She said good-bye and hung up.

"Let me guess who that was," Freddie said, raising his eyebrows and grinning in an obnoxious way.

"Why bother?"

"The first call was the blonde across the street and the beautiful Dink. Am I right?"

"She's not a Dink, Frederick."

"Okay, gook, slope, Korean, whatever. The other was the reporter you have the hots for, right?"

"You're so fucking smart you should tell fortunes."

"What's the reporter look like? I wanna see her. What channel?"

"She's on vacation this week. You can't."

"I'll be here next week. I want to see her."

Persistent bastard.

I wanted to change the subject. "What does Mary do while you're out screwing around?"

"I don't know…this and that."

"I hope she has a boyfriend."

"I'd kill him."

"Let's go to lunch," I suggested. "Chinese is close, but if you want a beer, there's a barbeque joint down the road a'piece."

"Boss, I told you, I can't do Chinese anymore," John said. "The *suitamol maglucinate* gives me a *relergic* reaction."

Fred and I looked at each other and shook our heads in unison.

"He means MSG, right?" Fred asked.

"Exactly," I said. "John, just tell old man Lum not to use any MSG in your meal. They can make Chinese food without MSG."

"I'd rather go to Howell's," John said.

I knew when to give up. "Okay, barbeque it is."

"Ye-haw," Freddie squealed. "I want me some Tennessee ba-ba-que."

"Sometimes you act like such a child, Frederick Junior," I said.

"What?"

"What what?"

"I'm happy. I loved that freakin' Dragon. These mountains are cool. I like it here. What can I tell you?"

"You're not thinking of moving here, are you?"

After we bought our property in Walland I used to tell the people back home that Tennessee sucked so more New Yorkers wouldn't move in.

"I don't know. Why?" He frowned at me. "Maybe I'll buy a summer place. It's cooler here than Florida. And I'd look good in a log cabin."

"If you lived here and I caught you parking in my spot again, I'd throw your ass in jail."

"Aha! See? You are pissed. I knew it." His adolescent smile came back.

"Aha, your ass."

"See? What did I tell you, John?"

"I don't know, Boss. You sound pissed to me." John always joins in; he's susceptible to mob mentality.

"Shut up, John. Do you ever wonder why nobody likes you?"

"Everybody likes me, Boss. Ask the Sarge."

"What does she know? Let's go to lunch before motorcycle boy decides not to pay."

"Ha! I knew it!" Fred said. "I just knew you'd get pissed. You're so easy."

I only play along so those two feel wanted.

* * * *

We sat in the dining room at Howell's pub at a sawbuck-style table made from unpainted 2x4s. A sixty-inch flat screen TV played a continuous loop of country and western music videos. A skinny young guy wearing a black oversized cowboy hat strummed an acoustic guitar and sang about how much he missed his repossessed pickup truck or some other nonsense. More than half the tables in the room were already filled, while plenty of noise filtered in from the barroom.

"So what are you going to do?" Fred asked while we discussed the two Prospect murders.

"What do you think? Investigate."

I drank from the pint mug of black-and-tan I had ordered. Fred took a long pull from a pint of Bud Lite, and John sipped diet Coke through a straw. We waited impatiently for our lunches.

"Just you? You got any help to call in?"

"John will help, and so will Bettye. Maybe some of the cops will, too. But they have patrol to take care of."

"Little place like this? Are the cops busy?"

"Busy enough. You know, all the typical bullshit. It's summertime. The touristas and locals need assistance with the usual crap. It'll be mostly me and John. Bettye will run the department while we're out."

He pointed at himself. "You want some help?"

"You?"

"Yeah, me. What's wrong with me?"

"Nothing's wrong with you. I can't hire you."

"Who said anything about getting hired? I volunteer, okay?"

Dossie, the waitress, walked up balancing our three platters on her arms. We'd been easy and ordered the same thing, hand-pulled smoked pork sandwiches the size of a half soccer ball, homemade cole slaw and baked beans. Those things did not come from the dietetic side of Howell's menu.

After Dossie left I asked, "You think we can close this in five more days?"

"If the three of us work on it, sure, but you'll owe me."

"Owe you what?"

"Buy me lunch. And I wanna *meet* the reporter."

"Your ass."

"Come on. I can help. Send me and John out. We'll do all the road work. You do all the boss work. Just like the old days."

"You're crazy."

"You knew that years ago." Mazzio grinned like a nincompoop and drank more beer. I wish Reggie the bartender had given him a dribble glass.

"You want to work with him, John?"

"Then you'll owe *me*, Boss." John always smiles like a bad little kid when he thinks he's been clever.

"Jesus H. Christ," I said.

"You can even forget the lunch." Fred said. "I just want to see the reporter. I mean what kind of self-respecting TV star would fall for you?" He sounded desperate.

"Nobody has fallen for anyone. We're just friends. We do each other favors."

"Who are you kiddin'?"

I closed my eyes for a long moment. "I don't know who I hate more, you or John."

"You love us all, Boss," John said.

"Bullshit.   I   should   have   stayed   retired."

Chapter Twelve

"Set up in the squad room," I told Fred. "There's more space there. If one of the patrolmen makes an arrest, they can use the little juvenile room."

We walked down the hall, and I showed him the workspace.

"Ask John or Bettye for any office supplies you need," I said.

"You think your two murders are by the same killer who did the gook in Knoxville?" he asked.

"Probably connected. I don't know how, but it's too much of a coincidence. Different guns, but we'll see."

He began spreading out the crime scene photos from the Rosie Cho murder on an eight-foot folding table I asked the building custodian to bring up from the basement. Jackie Shuman promised to hand-deliver a set of the Kum-Ok Kyeung murder photos and his reports before noon.

"Do we have PD wheels, or do we have to use that piece o' shit John drives?" he asked.

"Use one of the spare marked cars unless you need an unmarked car. Then you can use mine. If I catch you smoking in my clean Ford, I'll kill you. I swear. I'll shoot you and cut off your ears."

"Easy, madman. I haven't had a cigarette in three years."

"Oh yeah?" That surprised me.

"Yeah, I'm clean and sober. Well, I'm nicotine free."

"Good for you. Tell Bettye if you need anything from the computer. She knows a lot more than John."

"My granddaughter knows more than John."

"If you're on the road, call in once in a while." I remembered what he was like years ago.

"Didn't I always?"

"No."

"Yeah, well."

John Gallagher walked into the squad room.

"Okay, John, you and your new partner can get to work. Let me or Bettye know exactly what you need," I said. "If I'm not here and you need a decision, she'll make it."

"Okay, Boss. We'll be very *explisive*."

"I know you will, buddy." I shot Fred a sidelong glance and saw him smiling.

"You want us to call you at lunch time?" John asked. "We'll meet you somewhere."

"Only if you've got something worth saying. More work. Less food."

"You're still so serious about this shit," Fred said.

"It's a double homicide, Mazzio Junior, and the third Knoxville murder is still unsolved. Find me the connection."

"Bitch, bitch, bitch."

"Don't make me fire you."

"You never hired me. How can you fire me?"

"Don't confuse me with technicalities."

* * * *

I plopped down in the chair next to Bettye's desk. She'd been preparing the monthly vehicle reports for Earl Biggins, the city mechanic. She stopped, took off her granny glasses and looked at me.

"Another unofficial detective, Sammy?"

Sometimes I think she questions my decisions...or my sanity.

"Freddie's good. Between him and John, they'll get the road stuff done. That leaves you and me to do the inside stuff. We need to find the connection between those two girls and Chang-Hai Ha."

"How do we do that?"

"Let's start with an Immigration Investigator. Call INS or ICE or whatever Homeland Security calls them this week, and see what they've got on all three victims. Then you can run down all the other Koreans who are in the cast, no matter how little they've been involved so far. I'll call Renfro and tell him about our new murder and see what he's come up with."

"That's it?"

"Unless you've got a better idea. You can't just sit here and look pretty."

She smiled and fluttered her eyelashes. "You thank I'm purty, sugar?"

"Oh, Lord have mercy. Someone teach me how to deal with women."

"Thank yew, Sammy. Y'all are so sweeeet." She did her Daisy Mae act on me.

"Ugh."

* * * *

D.W. Renfro was out of the office when I called, but Wit Maples told me they had nothing new on the Mr. Ha killing, but a couple of reports had come in.

TBI ballistics said the .45 slugs found in Ha's body most likely came from a Series 70, Colt Government Model semiautomatic or something similar, capable of using a barrel from that gun. That narrowed it down to only a half-million pistols that could have been bought over the counter at a licensed gun store, purchased legitimately from a dealer at a gun show or illegitimately from someone selling a pistol out of the trunk of his car in the parking lot at some gun show. Handguns are not difficult to purchase in the great state of Tennessee.

A .45 automatic is a potent handgun. I used to carry one in the Army. In spite of all the myths about the Army .45 being notoriously inaccurate, even a run-of-the-mill GI gun can be tinkered with to make it shoot extremely well. The slide can be tightened, a new barrel bushing installed, better springs added, and the trigger can be stoned down for a smooth let-off. All that work cost me a six-pack of beer and little more than an hour of socializing with my friendly armorer one day around 1968. But in today's world of high-capacity nine millimeters and double action .40s, a 1911 model, GI .45 is an outdated weapon. I'd have to look for a killer whose personality fit this piece of nostalgic weaponry—

perhaps an anachronism himself. Or, if I had to be a politically correct investigator, herself.

In between phone calls, I gave Bettye a complete list of all the persons spoken to during our investigations, the Koreans, the potential witnesses, the neighbors, anyone with whom a cop had contact.

After Bettye's preliminary work with Immigration, the Tennessee Bureau of Investigation, and NCIC—the National Crime Information Center—and our own motor vehicles information section at the Department of Safety, John and Freddie could start on the credit card bureaus, military records and other places where a clue might be hiding.

I was tempted to call Park, Hee-Chul and question him about my second murder. But I had no doubt he'd deny any involvement and cause my blood pressure to sky-rocket. I also doubted he'd become civic-minded and volunteer to do a little detective work for me within the Korean community. I'd leave Mr. Park alone for a while.

* * * *

Jackie Shuman was prompt in bringing us his reports and photos on the Kum-Ok murder. He and Neal Brickman spent an hour with John and Freddie kicking around possibilities.

I went back to Kisaeng and did my best to push the theory of a connection for all three murders. The four people left at that business were willing, but not eager to agree with that possibility. But no one would come up with anything to make the connection. I'm afraid my grasping for straws didn't inspire much confidence in those folks.

After hearing Rachel's newscast telling the world that her favorite police chief admitted being baffled, the remainder of the Knoxville viewing area would be equally confident.

Just when additional pressure and impatience were the last things I needed heaped upon my shoulders, Mayor Ronnie Shields summoned me to his command center.

When I arrived at the second floor office, Ronnie's secretary, Trudy Connor, greeted me with a businesslike smile. I complimented her new dress, and she beamed me aboard the Starship Prospect.

At first glance, I found no new furnishings in the mayor's office, but since I'd been there last, a bank of several file cabinets had swapped places with the burgundy leather couch.

The stuffed, nasty-looking fish, a pike I think, still snarled at me from its place on the east wall, and an eight-point buck with sorrowful eyes hung reluctantly across from Ronnie's massive mahogany desk—something just a little larger than a regulation ping pong table.

The only new fixture was a young overweight, dark-haired specimen dressed in a pearl gray suit, electric blue shirt with a starched white collar and yellow paisley tie. In addition to thinking how much I hated shirts like that, I figured him to be somewhere around thirty years old.

Ronnie sat behind the desk, while Chubby stood off to his left in front of a bookcase.

The mayor smiled as I entered, so I returned it. The other party said and did nothing. I nodded at him and said hello. I saw no reason for us both to act ignorant.

"Hello, Sam," Ronnie said. "Come on in, and sit down." He pointed to one of the green leather guest chairs. "Relax."

I took a seat and crossed my legs.

"Jest wanted ta talk about progress on the murders o' those Ko-rean women," he said. "But first, I need ya ta meet our new deputy mayor."

That caused my eyes to click open a notch. Prospect has never had a deputy mayor before.

"This here's Darnell Means." Ronnie extended a hand toward the Pillsbury Dough Boy and smiled. "Darnell, this is Sam Jenkins, our po-leece chief."

I readied myself to get up like a gentleman and shake his hand, but he made no effort to move. So, I smiled, wondered what other enjoyable things might happen in the next few minutes and relaxed my shoulders.

Darnell dipped his head a quarter inch, but didn't crack a smile. "Mr. Jenkins, good ta meet ya."

I assumed that was his way of acting managerial and self-important.

I offered a half grin, half sneer. "Charmed, I'm sure." *You mutt.*

He never even allowed his eyes to twinkle.

I looked at Ronnie, raised my eyebrows and tilted my head. It was his dime.

"Uh, right, uh. Case ya didn't know, Sam, Darnell's been a county commissioner fer a couple years and before comin' here worked at

116

Amherst, Loudoun and Gage in Murr-vull." That was Ronnie's attempt to pronounce Maryville, the town just west of Prospect.

Perhaps the mayor thought mention of an old and established law firm would impress me.

I nodded. "Uh-huh. Never heard of him." And waited.

"I been readin' yer file, Mr. Jenkins," Means said. "Seen ya used ta teach law at a police academy back in New York and a community college part-time. You an attorney?"

If he'd read my file, he knew damn well I wasn't, but I couldn't resist the opening. I smiled to soften the coming slur. "No, my parents were married when I was born."

Ronnie grimaced, but came back quickly and picked up the conversation. He began with a forced laugh. "Darnell, ya gotta watch ol' Sam here. He's got more jokes and funny lines than a pro-fessional comedian."

Obviously Darnell didn't agree. "I see. I graduated UT Law in '03."

"And now you're a politician." I forced a friendly grin. "Good luck to you."

Darnell recognized the left-handed compliment. He blinked twice, but did nothing more.

Ronnie looked as uncomfortable as a mouse sneaking through the reptile house of the Knoxville Zoo. "Uh, the Council figgered I could use a deputy. Give me a li'l he'p with administrative things and more peace o' mind when I take vacation time."

"Uh-huh," I said with as much enthusiasm as Sydney Carton when he mounted the tumbrel.

Ronnie didn't come back with one of his typical witty remarks like, 'Boy howdy' or 'You betcha.' The brief lull in conversation hung in the room like a cloud of mustard gas over the trenches of Passchendaele.

"Well, uh, I guess we oughta talk about those murders," Ronnie said.

I had nothing to hide, so I took that as my cue to report. And, since during an investigation truth is a flexible thing, I felt no obligation to say I didn't have the slightest idea who killed whom.

"I was just about to interview an important subject when I got called up here. Things are coming together, and we're learning more material facts quite rapidly. This should break very soon." I paused and looked at Ronnie with a crooked smile. "I wouldn't be surprised if we cleared our two murders, and possibly an additional case from Knoxville, very shortly."

The mayor didn't even try to comment before Means stuck in his two cents. "You said *may*. In other words, the cases are still up in the air?"

"No," I lied. "We're making good progress, and our cases may be cleared by arrest in a matter of days."

He smirked and looked even more obnoxious than before. "Mind if I ask why y'all didn't hand a big and complicated case like this over ta the county sheriff's people?"

That started my hackles rising. "Actually, I do mind. How I handle felonies in Prospect is my decision. But I'll explain an important reality about criminal investigations in Blount County."

I shifted in the chair and tried to look more comfortable. Actually, I wanted to cold-cock Darnell and step on his neck.

"With the exception of a good detective named Stallins," I said, "the next senior man at sheriff's CID is the unit lieutenant who's only got eight years on the job—none of them as an investigator. The other two general service detectives have three years apiece. They're nice kids, but they're political hacks, not exceptionally good cops. The uniformed crime scene investigators over there are more qualified to work felonies than the plainclothes detectives."

Means shot a few daggers at me, crossed his arms over his chest and looked out the picture window at the town square below.

"Y'all are usin' *some* county he'p now, right, Sam?" Ronnie asked, probably hoping I'd find a way to mitigate my insubordinate remark.

"Of course. Two of those competent evidence technicians I mentioned did the forensic work, and Dr. Rappaport is performing the post mortem exams."

"Could ya use he'p from this man Stallins? I might be able ta git him assigned here on temporary duty."

I shook my head. "Bo's got his own cases that never stop coming in. And if I'm not mistaken, he's the one who holds that whole section together. I've got competent help right here. We don't need outside people at this point."

Ronnie followed up with one of his looks meant to convey the message, 'Jenkins, you bastard. Don't let me down, or I'll have a stroke, and you can report to this new guy while I'm on sick leave.'

I took his point, but the idea prompted me to ask, "Ronnie, where does Darnell fit on the table of organization? Is he your assistant and 'of counsel', or does he get a spot in my chain of command?"

Ronnie stared at me like I had two heads. "Do what?"

I made it simple. "Do I report to him or you?"

"Uh, why, uh, ta me. Same as always, Sam."

I stood slowly. "Okay. If we have no further business to discuss, I'll go downstairs and see if I can clear a few murders."

* * * *

The first thing out of my mouth as I cleared the double doors that separate our lobby from the rest of the municipal building was, "Grrrr!"

Bettye looked up—not especially surprised because I often growl, but concerned none the less. "What happened, darlin'?"

"Did you know we now have a deputy mayor?" My question sounded slightly accusatory since the feminine grapevine within city government is often better than my own internal intelligence sources.

"A what?"

Her answer and surprised look smoothed me over. While Bettye may not gossip, she wouldn't withhold important information from her favorite boss.

"A new position—deputy mayor. Filled by some whippersnapper named Darnell Means."

"Never heard of him," she said.

"Says he was a county commissioner, but he's obviously not from our district. Also says he worked for Amherst, Loudoun and Gage. What kind of law do they practice? I know it's not criminal defense."

"I'll find out."

I nodded and remembered Bettye had been a Prospect court officer prior to becoming a cop. "Can you call your old contacts at the county court, and see what kind of a lawyer young Darnell is? He any good or what?"

119

"Okey dokey."

I looked at the clock. "It's almost five o'clock. Those civilians will be running for the parking lot in a few minutes."

She nodded. "First thing tomorrow mornin'."

"Okay. I'll see what the Yellow Pages say about this den of shysters. Then I'll call Joe Costello for a professional opinion," I said and headed for my office.

* * * *

That night, I sat in my favorite wingback recliner sipping a large gin and tonic. Kate had turned on the 60s station, and I listened to Glen Campbell singing. The words took me back to a replacement depot at Long Binh, South Vietnam where I sat on a bunk waiting for a driver to take me to my new unit. Pat Sajak or some other AFVN disc jockey played the same song, *Galveston,* then, too. Glen sang the same words, "I am so afraid of dying," and "I clean my gun, and dream of Galveston." It still sounded good now, but seemed more appropriate back then.

After Glen Campbell finished, the Monkees picked up with *The Last Train to Clarksville.* I wondered how many people today would connect that song with the bustling Army installation Fort Campbell and Clarkesville, Tennessee of the late 1960s.

Kate walked into the living room and handed me a small dish of mixed nuts. She wore a white cotton sleeveless blouse and a pair of denim shorts. She looked cool and fresh with not a hair out of place.

"Have you cooled off yet?" she asked.

"Yes and no. I'm not looking to chew anyone's head off at the moment, but I know this young creep is going to be trouble."

"But Costello told you the man wasn't even a lawyer. Why did they hire him?"

"Well, he is a lawyer, technically. He graduated from UT Law, but after a few tries, he still hasn't passed the bar exam."

"So, what kind of place would hire him?"

"God knows why Prospect hired him as a deputy mayor, but no one hired him as an attorney. He'd been working as a paralegal for this outfit in Maryville. The Yellow Pages says they're a general practice going back to when Clarence Darrow was just a child. Joe told me they're big, with lots of young associates handling things like bankruptcy and financial problems, disability cases, worker's comp, medical malpractice, divorce and custody…mundane stuff like wills and closings. They have a platoon of ambulance chasers sniffing out personal injury cases. They do just about everything but criminal law."

"And this young twerp had the nerve to question your judgment in a murder investigation?"

"He doesn't know squat about criminal law. What can you expect? He's a politico and an asshole."

"I don't think those two are mutually exclusive."

I laughed. "Thanks for the nuts."

She smiled. "You're welcome."

"You took a good haircut the other day."

"*Took* a haircut? You sound like an old man from Brooklyn."

"I am an old man from Brooklyn." Kate is a Long Island girl; they talk differently.

"You don't look so old to me," she said. "But thanks for the compliment. It wasn't much of a haircut…just a trim. You know…a little snip here…a little snip there."

"Now who's talkin' like Brooklyn? You make Barbra Streisand sound positively gentile."

"I'm strictly a Long Island girl."

I thought I said that.

"And a cute one."

She looked at the pages of bond paper I held and asked, "What are you reading?"

"The cast of characters in a murder mystery."

"Can I see?"

"Sure. I'll take help from anyone."

She took the papers from me and read over the list.

"I can't find any relatives among the bunch," I said. "Or any connections based on proximity. The only thing that ties them together so far is their national origin and Park's attempt to shake down Sunny Kim. But you'd think if he wanted to make a second attempt to collect protection money, he'd have contacted Sunny after the Rosie Cho killing and made some euphemistic remark about her safety or the possibility of losing another employee. For some reason, I believe Park. I think he's lost interest in Prospect. But why did Mr. Ha get snuffed? And who punched his ticket?"

"I don't have answers for you, Sammy, but maybe I have a connection. Your first victim was Rosie Cho, right?"

I nodded. "Uh-huh."

"Now here's someone—Boo, Cho-Hung. See?" She pointed to Mr. Boo's name on the list. "Sometimes Korean men are given first names referring to related family names. Maybe Boo's mother was a Cho."

I shrugged. "Anything's possible, but there are less than three hundred family names in that whole country. They must have a hell of a time making sure you don't marry your first cousin."

"I understand," she said. "And I think you're going to need parents' names from all these Koreans. Remember, a Korean woman does not take her husband's family name when they marry?"

I nodded. "I do."

"Children get their father's family name," she reminded me. "So, you could have a mother and daughter on your list and never know it until you knew the names of spouses and children."

I slapped myself in the forehead. "Ah, Watson, what would I ever do without you? I am ashamed of myself and have been a great bloody fool. Don't tell my brother, Mycroft. He'll laugh."

"Cheer up, Holmes. Your secret is safe with me."

Chapter Thirteen

The next morning, I dropped an administrative bomb on Bettye. "I hate to do this to you, Betts, but I'd like you to get back on the phone with INS and ask them for all the relatives listed in the files they have for this batch of Koreans. Mothers and fathers will have different surnames. The children get the father's family name."

"Oh, Lord have mercy."

"I'm sorry, but see if they can find any connection with Rosalind Cho, use her birth name of Cho, Sung-Sook and Boo, Cho-Hung—Mr. Park's Boo. If you're speaking with a non-Korean, tell them to run the same name spelled a few different ways, like Sung-Sook and Song-Suk. Boo could be Bu. Soon-Wha could be Sun-Wa." I spelled each out. "Get the idea?"

She shook her head and looked a little frustrated. "You make life interestin', Sammy."

I raised my eyebrows. "Think of how tranquil it might be if we didn't have to solve another department's murders as well as our own."

"Darlin', I know you just hate to show other cops how clever you are by doin' what they can't."

"That sounded incredibly insincere."

"Don't you believe it. Now just leave me ta sort this out."

"I'd rather you work on this than the county court thing. I know enough about Darnell Means for the moment. But when you get a chance, see if you can dig up some deep, dark secrets about the guy."

"I really wish you'd learn how to use a computer."

I smiled. "Remember that proverb about not teaching an old dog new tricks?"

"I don't believe that for a minute."

"Dig up some really good dirt I can use when the time is right."

"You are bad."

"No, ma'am. I ain't bad, but the bad don't mess with me."

"Then you're just an egomaniac."

I shrugged. "Well, there is that."

She smiled again, and I retreated to my office.

At ten o'clock, D.W. Renfro called.

"Now I know y'all ain't gonna believe what I got this time," he said.

"Go easy. I'm an old man."

"Are ya sittin' down?"

"Don't pamper me."

He laughed. "Me and Maples, we got us another homo-cide. Cain't believe this. Knoxville's gettin' ta be like Washington DC or one o' them vi'lent places. Lord have mercy, all these bodies."

I knew he'd get around to telling me, but I asked anyway. "Who's the lucky corpse of the day?"

"Your friend and mine, Mr. Hee-Chul Park. Deader than a doornail. Right here where I'm standin' in his own home."

I felt like someone just told me pieces of my jigsaw puzzle were missing. Bummer. Life just got more complicated.

"Shot?" I asked.

"Yep."

".22 or .45?"

"Big ol' .45. One ta the head. He's a'settin' right here in his easy chair, glass o' scotch on the table, TV a'playin'."

"Let me guess—no forced entry, no struggle, no signs of robbery, no nuthin'."

"Sounds like ya already been here."

"Who found him?"

"Housekeeper, Mrs. Ahn-Na Shin. She got here jest a'fore nine this mornin'. Walked in on her boss, who's now got a big ol' hole in his forehead."

"Where's Mr. Boo?"

"Ain't here yet."

"Mrs. Shin broken up?"

"She's a'cryin' an' a'rockin'."

"That sounds upset."

"You wanna come up here for sumthin'?"

"I'd like to speak with Mrs. Shin sometime, but it doesn't have to be while you're working up your crime scene. Will you get me an address and a couple of phone numbers?"

"Shore thing."

"I guess Boo is worth talking with, but I'm not sure he'd tell us the sky is blue on a clear day."

"That ol' boy looks like a mean one."

"Ask Mrs. Shin how the tall, dark and handsome cop who spoke Korean to her can get in touch with Mr. Boo."

"And who might that cop be?"

"Oh, that hurt."

"Jest kiddin'. You kin really speak that lingo?"

"Better than the average soldier."

"Well, I never."

"You got anything to go on yet? Anything like a clue?"

"A clue? Shoot, I ain't seen a decent clue yet. Oops, I tell a lie. Wit done talked with a neighbor who said they seen a red Audi parked at the curb last night 'bout 9:30. Not much of a clue. Only said he recognized the grill. Don't know a model or a tag or nuthin' more."

"An Audi?"

"Yep, red Audi. That mean anythin' ta you?"

"It might. I'll have to call you back."

"I ain't fer away."

"You have a time of death?"

"ME figgers late last night. He'll have a closer guess after the post."

"Thanks for the call. Let me know if the same gun killed Park and Ha."

"I'll do it."

* * * *

I interrupted John and Fred while they studied the crime scene photos. Reports, pictures, diagrams and soda cans lay scattered all over the table and desks in the squad room. John wore a white shirt and tie with his sleeves rolled up, and Fred again looked tropical, but professionally intense in a Hawaiian shirt and Bermuda shorts.

"Just as it was told to me," I said, "I'll tell it to you," I put on an East Tennessee accent and quoted D.W. "'I know y'all ain't gonna believe what I got this time.'"

"Not another one!" Freddie said. It sounded more like a statement than a question. He dropped a handful of photos onto the table.

"Don't keep us in suspense, Boss," John plead.

"Park got whacked last night," I said. "He took a .45 in the head, sitting in a leather chair, drinking scotch."

"I hate scotch," Fred said. "It tastes like iodine."

That sounded dreadfully irrelevant to the case.

"What else does Knoxville know?" John asked.

"Not much. Maybe a car, but a poor description at best."

"I think we've got something here," Fred said, changing the subject. "Not about Park, but look at this picture."

He showed me one of the shots Jackie Shuman took of the wooden steps to the doublewide at Prospect Farms.

"What am I looking at?" I asked.

"This is from the Rosie Cho murder. Besides the obvious, look at the blacktop, right here between the black Kia and the grass." He pointed to a place on the photo.

"You've got me. I see blacktop faded to gray and spiky crab grass."

"Look at the spot."

"Spot?"

"It's an oil spot, Boss," John interjected.

"The photo shows one clear oil spot," Fred said. "And look where it is. Even if this Kia or one of the other cars the girls usually parked there had an oil leak, they would not drip that close to the grass. Even if one of those broads parked all the way over to the right, an engine drip would still be further left. I thought we should drive over and look."

"When we did, know what we found, Boss?" John asked.

"Don't keep me in suspense, John." I tried to imitate his way of speaking.

"Two drips," he said.

"Two drips?"

"Yeah, two drips," Fred said.

"Maybe I'm concentrating on Park getting iced," I said, "but I don't see..."

"The Kia is still parked there," Fred continued, "locked up—hasn't moved since before its owner Rosie Cho got killed. We checked with Earl, your mechanic here at the garage. The Kum-Ok car, the white Hyundai that Crockett impounded, it's locked up in our lot. Neither of those cars have an oil leak."

"Aha!" I said.

"Yes, aha. Now we want to see the third girl's car—the other Korean roommate."

"Her name's Chun-He Lee," I said.

"Okay, whatever," Fred said.

"And you want to check for an oil leak?"

"Exactly. And I want to know why a second spot appeared after the first murder."

"You know, Boss, these Korean girls all buy Korean cars," John observed.

"Does Chun-He drive a Korean car?"

"I don't know, Boss, but isn't that interesting?"

I wondered where he was going with this.

"Do you own an Irish car, John?"

"Do they make an Irish car, Boss?"

"No, and who cares if all Korean people buy Korean cars?"

"I just think that's very *calvanistic* of them."

Fred squeezed his eyes shut and shook his head. "Calvanistic?"

I took a shot at interpreting. "Chauvinistic, John. It's chauvinistic. Are you trying to drive me nuts on purpose?"

He smiled like a naughty child.

"Come on, John," I said. "Only a nitwit would say Calvinistic."

"I wish you wouldn't say those *dispatchatory* things all the time, Boss. You hurt my feelings."

Fred and I looked at each other. I shook my head. Fred laughed. John smiled. I work with two village idiots.

"Bettye's just run everyone we've met so far through DMV," I said.

127

Wayne Zurl

"Ask her what kind of car Chun-He drives. I have to go over to Kisaeng for a few minutes anyway. I'll see if Chun-He is working and where her car is."

"Gonna see the blonde, huh?" Fred asked.

"Yeah, her and Sunny. And by the way, sport, Chun-He looks like a movie star herself."

"You bum. I'll bet you're—"

"If you don't clean up your brain, Mazzio, I'm going to call your father and tell him about the pervert he raised."

"He already knows, but he'd be happy to hear from you anyway. He liked you for some reason. Maybe because you were a good shot."

Fred Mazzio, Sr. had been a uniformed cop with our department for years before either Freddie or I were hired. Now, he lived in Port Saint Lucie, peacefully retired and not trying to solve weird murders in Tennessee.

"I liked your father, too." I sneered. "More than I like you."

He laughed again.

"Can we get back to the oil spot?" I asked.

"Sure, great white leader. Anything you want."

"If it didn't come from one of those cars, and you're telling me that's not probable, what are you looking for?"

"Duh! What would fit in a spot that small? Like…a motorcycle?"

That sparked an infusion of enthusiasm. "Sit tight. I'll be back, or I'll give you a call."

Fred bowed and pulled his forelock. "We await your orders, fearless one."

What would life be like without a bunch of smartasses?

* * * *

I walked out the front door of the municipal building and crossed the road to the town square. The city's department of buildings and grounds workers had mowed the big rectangular lawn the day before and that unmistakable fresh cut grass smell lingered in the air. Two young couples lay on blankets sunning themselves, an old man fed peanuts to a pair of squirrels, and a pretty young redhead walked a miniature poodle along the brick path.

128

The digital thermometer on the Citizen's Bank and Trust told me it was eighty-two degrees, pleasant, but too warm for the sport jacket I wore to hide the gun and cuffs hanging from my belt. Most plainclothes cops in Tennessee don't bother with coats in the summer, but I'm old-fashioned and don't like to walk around looking like a gunslinger.

I crossed another street and approached Kisaeng Massage. I opened the door and heard the little bell attached to the frame tinkle. Finding the reception desk was easier than finding a killer in a small town.

Roni Keeble sat there looking fresh, efficient and as usual, very pretty, her blonde hair pulled back behind her ears. She wore a white blouse with a neckline just begging to be looked down.

"Is Sunny here?" I asked, skipping the normal amenities.

"Yes, in the back room." Her smile disappeared when she saw me frowning.

"How about Chun-He?"

"She's with a patient…a woman with fibromyalgia."

"Where's Prater?"

"In at noon. He has a patient coming in, too. Tendonitis of the shoulder."

Her answers began to show a little attitude.

"Wonderful," I said, with too much emphasis.

"What's the matter?" Her question came out soft, but she looked worried.

"Come with me. We're going into Sunny's office." I had plenty to do before questioning Chun-He.

"What about the phones?"

"You're not that busy."

"Why are you mad?" She sounded more apprehensive.

I jerked a thumb in the direction of Sunny's office. "Let's go."

"I only asked a simple question, and you bite my head off. I really don't need this."

No one could accuse Veronica of being timid or short on attitude.

We walked into the back office and found Sunny sitting at her desk, a stack of papers on her right and an open ledger in front.

"Sit," I said to Roni.

"What is wrong with you?" she asked, getting more agitated.

I ignored her question.

"Sam, what's the matter?" Sunny asked. Her wrinkled brow and lack of usual smile made her look troubled.

"Okay, ladies," I said. "Tell me why I shouldn't be terribly disappointed with you two?"

They glanced at each other and then stared at me. They sat almost immobile, looking guilty, like two little girls caught with their hands in the cookie jar.

"What do you mean?" Roni asked.

"You seem so mad," Sunny added, her voice taking on more accent than usual. "What is wrong, ad-josh-ee?" She used the Korean term of respect for an older man.

I looked at Sunny. "Don't give me that uncle stuff. And you, young lady," I switched my look to Roni, "What the hell was your car doing in front of Park's house last night?" I thought a little creative questioning was in order.

"How did you know?" she asked.

My bluff paid off.

"How many red A4s with your plate number are there in this neck of the woods?"

"Well, ah..."

"Yeah, I know," I said. "I get a phone call this morning telling me Hee-Chul Park has been found dead, and your car was seen outside his house. What am I supposed to think?"

"Mr. Park is dead?" Sunny sounded as if I just told her Buddha was a serial killer.

Roni's ex-call girl attitude resurfaced as she bounced from a minor state of shock quickly and easily. "Since you're so upset and serious over this, shouldn't you be advising us of our rights or something?"

"Don't even entertain the idea that you have *any* rights." I heard my voice elevating and checked it. "I went out on a limb for you two. What the hell were you doing at Park's house?"

They did the look at each other act again.

Then Sunny decided to speak. "We wanted to ask if he would reconsider taking money from me. I thought it would stop the killing...if I just paid him. I can afford it and thought it would be the best way."

I sighed with frustration. "And you two decided to make all this right by paying protection money?"

Roni answered. "You didn't seem to be making any progress."

I took that one hard. It stopped me in my tracks, but just for a second.

"Oh, I wasn't quick enough for you, you two law enforcement experts?"

"I didn't mean that, Sam," Roni said. "I'm sorry."

Her attitude disappeared. She gave me a look that could have melted the Mendenhall Glacier.

"We thought we could stop all this killing," she said. "We thought Park was responsible."

"And when Park laughed at you, you killed him."

"No!" they answered in unison.

"What did Park tell you?" I asked, on the verge of losing patience.

Sunny dropped her eyes, an old Korean custom for a child who's getting scolded by an older person. Normally, I would have smacked a subject and made sure we had eye contact while we spoke, but I respected the cultural thing. Sometimes I'm so liberal I can't stand myself.

"He said...you were more trouble than I was worth to him."

"Did he elaborate on that?"

She hesitated again, looking a little embarrassed. "He said you were the craziest American cop he'd ever met. He thought you might try and kill him if he continued to shake me down."

I couldn't suppress a smile. Park had flattered me. It may seem strange to many people, but I took Park's statement as a compliment.

Police work is the only profession where if your colleagues or opponents refer to you as a psycho, it's meant as a term of endearment. Park had made my day—posthumously.

Both women stared at me, waiting for my next comment.

"Then who killed him?" I asked.

They turned to each other and then back at me. Those two women, who had been around the block more than a few times, looked genuinely upset. But all that collaboration before speaking made me think they were concocting a phony story.

Wayne Zurl

"We...I...don't know," Roni said and threw her hands up in the air.

"Sam, please, we did not kill Mr. Park. Please believe us," Sunny's voice took on the emotional whine of an excited Korean female.

"I didn't tell the Knoxville cops that I knew the owner of the red Audi," I said, wanting to keep the pressure on for a few more moments, "but they're not stupid. I can't keep them from driving down here and taking you two into custody and sweating a statement out of you."

Neither woman spoke.

"Goddamnit," I continued, "this isn't some lousy misdemeanor the Chicago vice cops can make up. You were there during the time the medical examiner says Park died. How do you explain that?"

"We didn't kill him, Sam," Roni said. "Honest!"

"Please, ad-josh-ee, please! Please believe us."

"From the very beginning of this," I said, "you people here have held something back. I can feel it. You told me half stories, half-truths. What are you not telling me?"

Again they looked at each other. A single tear ran down Sunny's cheek.

"Well?" I asked.

"Okay," Roni said. "Give us a few minutes, and talk to Chun-He. She told us something this morning. She's very frightened."

"And what is she going to say?"

"Something that will help you. Two things, actually."

"For chrissake, Roni, this isn't quiz night at the local gin-mill. What is she going to tell me?"

For a moment, I thought she might cry. Her voice wavered. "You're being such a bully."

"I haven't gotten cranked up yet. Wait until I really think you killed Park."

"I...didn't kill anybody," Roni said. "Why won't you believe me?"

"The last thing I want to believe is that one or both of you killed that gangster. Give me an alternative. Otherwise, I'll have to turn you over to those two Knoxville dicks. When they do a background investigation on you, what do you think they'll assume? They're a couple of good ol' boy, evangelical Christian detectives investigating a pair of ex-hookers involved in a murder. Do you think either the police or the media will side with you? Who's your only ally here?"

Roni's baby blues and Sunny's almond eyes darted between me and each other, but neither answered.

"Me, right? Start talking, damn it."

Roni looked at her watch.

"For God's sake, Sam, she'll be finished in five minutes. If she doesn't tell you something you want to hear, I will. I promise. But let Chun-He talk."

My right hand went involuntarily to my forehead in frustration, and I shook my head. But I knew Roni wouldn't say anything before Chun-He had her turn. I gave up...for the moment.

"Five minutes. Okay. And Prater is due in at noon?"

"Yes," Roni said.

"That's in thirty-five minutes."

"Noon...yes." Roni raised her eyebrows. "That's what I said."

I took in a deep breath and looked at my two former hookers. "One more question before Chun-He comes in, and look at me while I'm talking to you."

They both did.

As I spoke, my eyes moved from one face to the other. "Did you, either of you, kill Park? Even in self-defense? Or did you have someone do it for you?"

Roni answered first. "For the umpteenth time, Sam, no!"

"Anyo, ad-josh-ee, I swear!"

Fool that I am, I believed them.

"That had better be straight talk, ladies." I gritted my teeth for a brief moment. "I hope it's the truth because it was your last opportunity for a good deal."

"Sam!" Roni said.

"And you want me to believe you only learned this new information from Chun-He this morning?"

"It's true! If we knew this before, we would have told you," Roni said.

"I must have missed your phone message."

She began to protest, but I went first. "Five minutes, Roni. That's what you asked for. We'll wait." My blood pressure began rising again.

133

I felt hot and stifled, even in the air conditioning. I peeled off my jacket, hung it on a doorknob and stepped into the hallway where I used my cell phone to call Bettye.

"How are you making out?" I asked.

"I'm having problems getting the clerks at INS to care about our project. I don't think the last one put in much effort. Her supervisor wasn't any help either. I just don't know the right questions to ask. Maybe if you called..."

"Betts, I can't take the time right now, but I'll get you someone who understands all the intricacies of the Korean name system. Just hang in there. How are the Bobsey twins doing?"

"John called the motorcycle dealer up on the Motor Mile. He learned that Prater McKendry bought a new Honda from them last year. Recently, he complained about an oil leak and took it in for repair. They replaced a seal or something, but he told them the leak wasn't fixed. He's scheduled to take it back. Fred said that's good to know."

"It is. Tell those two that McKendry is due in here at noon. Have them wait for him in the parking lot. See where he parks and look for oil drips. Tell Freddie to make a big production of taking an oil sample with a Q-tip or something and a little evidence bag. Have a uniform guy back them up. Is Junior available?"

"He's working a three car accident on McTeer Station Pike. Might be a while."

"How about Bobby John?"

"He and Dallas are free."

"Good, use them. Tell Bobby to keep the marked car away from the back of Kisaeng until the last moment. I don't want McKendry to get scared off and have to chase him on that motorcycle. Fred and John can take him into custody. We'll question Prater at the PD. Now hang on a minute."

I asked Roni Keeble where Chun-He parked her car, learned that it was in the first row of the municipal lot behind the row of shops and a couple of spots away from the infamous red Audi A4.

"Tell John while they're waiting for McKendry, they'll find Chun-He Lee's car in the first row behind Kisaeng. Make sure they have the right description and plate number. I want them to make sure there isn't

134

an oil drip there, too."

"Okey dokey, boss."

"I'll get you another partner in a minute."

"Yes, sir. I appreciate it."

I dropped the cell phone back into my jacket pocket and spoke to the two women. "Do you have other patients scheduled for this afternoon?"

"We have two," Roni said.

"You'll have to call and reschedule them. Chun-He might be able to take Prater's patient, so let him wait. Prater's going to be busy at the PD for a while. If I end up arresting Chun-He the patient will have to come back."

"You're going to arrest Chun-He?" Sunny sounded surprised.

Chapter Fourteen

The two women looked at me like I planned on molesting Mother Theresa.

"I don't know," I said. "You two won't give me a hint about what she's going to tell me."

The ladies said nothing. Five minutes later, Chun-He Lee knocked on the office doorjamb. She wore a white polo shirt and tan slacks, looking every inch the health care professional. I motioned for her to come in and sit. I remained standing and refused to return her smile. Her expression changed, and she looked like someone who just stepped into the on-deck circle for the gas chamber at Alcatraz.

I addressed the three. "Okay, ladies, here are the ground rules. You two," I nodded at Sunny and Veronica, "stay here while we talk. I may want to ask you questions. But, you only speak when I need an answer. This is not a participatory discussion. Chun-He, when I ask you questions I expect honest, direct answers. No more evasions and no half-truths. Do not look to them for help. Keep your eyes focused on me. You tell me everything. Understand?"

She nodded.

"We've waited this long, so we'll wait for Roni to cancel the rest of the appointments for today. I don't want people walking in here while we're doing business." I turned my attention to Veronica. "Will you take care of that while I make another phone call?"

She agreed.

I looked from Sunny to Chun-He. "While I'm on the phone, I do not want you two talking, giving each other signals, or even looking at each other. We clear on that?"

Sunny spoke for the pair. "We promise."

I needed to make a call and thought the silence would create a few more minutes of pressure on the girls. It couldn't hurt.

Roni walked out to the reception desk, and I stepped into the hall, grabbed the phone from my jacket pocket and called my home number.

"Kats, are you busy?"

"Just finished making a pot of okra stew, and I was going to fix myself lunch."

"I have a job for you...an important one. You mind waiting for lunch?"

"What's my important job?"

I took a few extra steps into the hall for a little more privacy. From where I stood, I could see three papasans depicted on their brass plate, playing an ancient bead game.

"I need you to help Bettye." I went on to explain that I wanted her to talk the INS clerks through a search of the Korean names, looking for family connections.

Like the good trooper she is, Kate agreed. "I'll call Bettye first. I can pick up Chinese takeout once I get to Prospect. We can work and eat at the same time."

"Spoken like a real cop. Bettye can call INS back and ask to speak to an agent first. She can try to get him or her hooked on the murder investigation aspect. Maybe the agent can handle the clerks. You make all the explanations on how you want them to search names, Okay?"

"Sounds easy. Where will you be?"

"Not far. I'll see you at the PD shortly."

"You're so mysterious sometimes."

"My second compliment this morning."

Kate hung up, and Roni stopped next to me in the hall.

"I spoke to the two people with afternoon appointments," she said. "But couldn't reach the man scheduled to see Prater at twelve."

"His problem. We can live with it."

Roni passed me and took her seat in Sunny's office. I closed the office door, stepped further into the room and turned to Chun-He. Like the other ladies in attendance, she, too, hung her head looking as if she

137

was waiting for an ax to fall. Chun-He still looked pretty, but her big seductive smile of the other day was conspicuously absent.

"Okay, what do you have to tell me, Miss Lee?" I asked, standing close to keep the pressure on and get the maximum psychological advantage.

She looked over at Sunny who lacked the friendly smile Chun-He wanted to see. Sunny gave her a curt nod prompting her to begin.

"I-ee-goo, o-nee-ah!" Chun-He stretched out every syllable to a maximum, making the words both guttural and nasal at the same time, something I think only a Korean woman can do. Roughly translated, she said, "Oh shit, big sister!"

I looked at Sunny. "I hope that was only an honorary reference."

"Yes. It was," she said.

I felt a little relieved. I didn't need more family connections and complications.

"Chun-He?" I prompted her to start her story. She knew what I wanted to hear.

"Oh, ad-josh-ee, I am so embarrassed." She hid her face in her hands for a brief moment, and then looked back at me. I waited patiently.

"There is nothing I haven't already heard." I tried to sound worldly and unconcerned about her explanation. "Just start at the beginning. Once you get going, it becomes easy."

She sighed and while looking down at her hands told me, "We were business girls."

"Jesus Christ." It came out automatically. When I finished shaking my head, I looked directly over at Roni. I knew exactly what the euphemism meant.

Roni also knew what Chun-He meant. "Not here! And not with us." She shook her head and raised her hands. It looked like a sincere response.

"This is an honest business, Sam!" Sunny added.

To Chun-He, I said, "You mean sex for money business?"

"Yes, ad-josh-ee. I am so sorry. I had to. Had no choice."

I was someone else's uncle again.

"Who are *we*?"

"Rosie, Kum-Ok and me."

138

"Kum-Ok, too?"

"Yes, Kum-Ok, too."

I shook my head and looked at Sunny.

"We didn't know, Sam! Honest! Roni told you we only found out this morning. That's true."

I didn't bother to ask when they were going to let me in on this insignificant detail.

"Did you have a madam or a pimp, Chun-He?"

She looked questioningly at Sunny who rattled off a translation in Hangul.

"Mr. Ha," she said.

"Mr. Ha was your pimp?" I couldn't keep the surprise out of my voice. "Was Mr. Park behind this?"

She shook her head. "Mr. Ha work on his own. I don't think Mr. Park knew."

When hired thugs skim profits off the top of a criminal enterprise, crime bosses are rarely pleased with their initiative.

"Did Park have Ha killed because of that?"

"I don't knooow," she whined.

The possibilities started to seem endless.

"Do you think Park learned that Ha worked on his own, not giving him a cut of the money?

"I don't know that either."

"Did Mr. Ha kill Rosie and Kum-Ok?"

"I don't knooow."

"Then who killed Rosie and Kum-Ok?"

"I am not sure. I can prove nothing."

"You're not a cop or a lawyer, Chun-he. You don't have to prove anything. What do you think and why?"

She hesitated. The liar's stall? She looked up at me and then at Sunny.

"Oh, o-nee!" she whined.

"Chun-he?" I said. "Stop looking at Sunny. Tell me."

"I don't know!"

I bent at the waist and put my face close to hers. "You maybe?"

"No! Me kill Rosie? No, Rosie was best friend! I don't kill Rosie or

Kum-Ok!"

It was time to change the topic.

"Why did Prater McKendry come to your home more than once?"

Her eyes widened. "You know?"

"I know he was there. Before Rosie died and also after. Why?"

She did her scanning the faces in the crowd act again. Her face had contorted. She looked to be on the verge of tears and appeared frightened. Being a bully was getting easy.

"Prater and Rosie wanted to get married," she said.

Son of a gun!

I tried not to look surprised, but any one of those girls could have knocked me over with a feather.

"When were they going to get married?" I asked

"Soon? I don't know."

I looked at Veronica and Sunny wondering when someone might think it important to tell me that one. But they were busy checking the condition of their nail polish.

"That explains why he came to your house before Rosie was killed," I said. "What about his visit after Rosie was gone?"

"I was not there when he came. Kum-Ok was there, maybe. I do not know when or why he came to our house-su. No one told me." Her Korean accent began getting thicker, and the frightened expression prevented her from looking too good. Pretty girls never appear most attractive when you're grilling them about a murder they may be involved in.

"Do you think Prater killed Rosie?

She began to cry.

"No one is going to hurt you, Chun-He," I lowered my voice and tried to sound fatherly. "Did Prater learn Rosie was a business girl?"

"I think yes, maybe."

I glanced at Roni and Sunny. Still checking cuticles.

"He'd be angry," I said. "Were you there when he learned?"

"I was there when they fought. He follow Rosie one night. He saw her go to motel. He wait and then follow her home to our house-su."

"Where did she go? Tell me how you girls did business." I continued with my soft, even tone.

"Mr. Ha work with desk clerks at motels by airport. When a single man check in, the clerk ask if he want girlfriend for the night. If man say yes, the clerk call Mr. Ha. Mr. Ha then call us."

"How could you work all these nights and still work here during the days?"

"They catch us for short-time only. No overnight."

"Convenient." No one commented on my observation. "What did Prater say to Rosie when you saw them argue?"

"He say, 'You stop, or you will be sorry.'"

"Did he hit Rosie?"

"No, just tell her that and leave mad. Very mad."

"Rosie didn't stop doing business at the motels, did she?"

"Rosie go to Mr. Ha. Tell him she has to stop. Want to get married. He say she *can't* stop. Have-ou no choice."

"You think Prater followed Rosie again?"

"I think maybe."

"Did Prater know about Mr. Ha?"

"Who knows? I don't know."

"The same gun that killed Rosie also killed Kum-Ok. Why would Prater kill Kum-Ok?"

"I don't knooow!" She started whining again. "When Kum-Ok get killed, I was afraid for my life!"

"Did you speak with Mr. Ha after Rosie died?"

She nodded. "Yes. Next day."

"Did he say something to frighten you? Something like, Rosie died because she wanted to quit?"

She shook her head. "No."

"Any chance Ha killed Rosie or had her killed?"

Chun-He took a long moment to compose herself. She sniffed sadly, brushed away a few tears with a nicely manicured hand and tried to look serious.

"If Mr. Ha kill Rosie he would lose money. Same same Kum-Ok."

That made sense. And Ha didn't look like he'd throw up if he killed his mother, much less one of his whores. Where did the vomit come from? Prater began looking better for killing both Rosie and Kum-Ok.

"Any guess who killed Mr. Ha?"

She shook her head violently. "Nooo. How can I know this?"

"Mr. Park was killed last night. With maybe the same gun that killed Mr. Ha, but different than the one that killed Rosie and Kum-Ok. What do you think about that?"

"Mr. Park, too? I-ee-goo!"

She looked shocked. I nodded.

"Prater's not smart enough or tough enough to take out either Mr. Ha or Mr. Park. Who do you think?"

"Take out?"

"*Take out* means to kill. Who do you think killed those men?"

"I don't knooow!" she stretched her words for emphasis and cried intermittently; eye makeup ran down her cheeks.

"How about you two ladies? Any ideas?" I looked at Roni and Sunny.

Both shook their heads.

"And you didn't know about these three hooking on the side before today?"

"No, Sam, honestly. Not until this morning," Roni said.

"No, Sam, I swear!" Sunny said.

"We never told...anyone about working for Mr. Ha," Chun-He added, sticking up for her older sisters.

I felt like walking out, throwing up my hands, and like Darnell the dipstick suggested, let the county dicks or TBI agents take over. But instead, I put on my jacket, opened my cell phone again and called Bettye. It was ten minutes after noon.

"Are Fred and John back yet?"

"They came in a couple of minutes ago."

"Did they get their man?"

"Just like the Mounties."

"Did Kate get there?"

"She did. We're two busy beavers."

"I'll bet you are."

"You'll be pleased with our progress."

"I can't wait. See ya in a few minutes."

"Bye." She often makes bye sound like something a sheep would say.

I turned back to my audience. "Roni, you were right. I bullied all three of you. I apologize, but it was necessary."

I got two nods immediately. Chun-He sniffed again and finally managed a nod.

"I'll make a suggestion...something for your own safety and good." I looked at Roni. "Are you still living in Yorkshire Dales?" I remembered the large house she and her late husband owned.

"Yes, the same place."

"Then you have at least two guest rooms?"

She nodded. "Three."

"I'd like the three of you to stay together until I sort this business out." I pointed at Sunny and Chun-He. "Following you home and to work isn't good enough any longer. I'll have a policeman drive you two home so you can get enough things for at least a couple of days. Someone will watch Roni's house at night, pick you up in the mornings and bring you here. Under these unfortunate circumstances, you'll need to recruit new help to take care of your customers. I hope you can keep the business going."

"You will use your policemen to protect us?" Sunny asked.

"When the word gets out what you three look like, I won't have a problem getting volunteers. Everyone working will drive by Roni's house whenever they can."

I didn't exactly see three ecstatically happy women looking at me, but they all managed halfway decent smiles.

"I'm going back to the police department and speak with Prater. I'll call and let you know what progress I make."

I opened the door to Sunny's office. A man in his late 50s sat patiently in the waiting area. He was engrossed in a copy of *People* magazine. I closed the door again.

"Roni, your noon appointment is here. He doesn't need to know any details of your business. Tell him Prater had an emergency to take care of, and Miss Lee isn't feeling well. Let him reschedule."

Roni said she'd arrange that.

Before opening the door, I said, "If you talked nicely to me I'd understand, even if I didn't believe you."

She had enough confidence to smile and push me. "Just get out."

On my way to the municipal building, I checked the sidewalk where Prater McKendry had illegally parked his motorcycle. An unmistakable spot of engine oil darkened the concrete where the bike sat for an entire day.

I looked around the quiet town square. It was another beautiful July day, clear and temperate. A few cars circled the landscaped center of the little city. A few people walked the streets. I felt confident enough in my colleagues to say Prater McKendry would rather be on a picnic in the Great Smoky Mountains National Park than in the squad room with Mazzio and Gallagher.

Chapter Fifteen

Prater was not even close to being tall, about five-foot-six by my calculation, but he exaggerated on his driver's license application and called himself five-eight. He had a medium build and short brown hair. A good-looking boy, he and Rosie Cho would have made a nice couple. He wore a yellow polo shirt and dark gray, casual pants. I stood on the side of the room as Fred Mazzio interviewed him.

"Let's go over it again, kid." Freddie growled. "You expect us to believe you just happened to stop by at that doublewide to be sociable with your co-workers and then stopped again after the Cho woman was killed...just to offer your sympathies?"

"It's true," the boy said.

Fred threw it right back at him. "You couldn't do that at work?"

"No, sir. I'm telling you the truth."

Fred blew out a little air to show his disbelief, frowned and shook his head.

John Gallagher took a turn. John would be the good cop. It was easier for Fred to play the tough, bad guy.

"First you told us you weren't at the trailer park. Then, when we told you the lab boys analyzed that oil drip we found and can match it to your motorcycle, you remembered being there...twice. I think you were there more than twice."

Prater looked at Gallagher and blinked rapidly, as his Adam's apple travelled up and down his throat like an out-of-control elevator car.

"I can't help you, and I won't speak up for you if I catch you lying again," John said. "Just tell me, were you doing those girls or what?"

John doesn't sound like the goofy malapropian guy we all know and love when he interrogates a suspect.

"Honest, sir. I don't know what y'all are talkin' about," the kid said and sounded convincing.

I pushed off the wall, took a step closer to the desk where they sat and interrupted. "Excuse me, but I don't think that's true, Prater." He shifted his look from John to me. "You know exactly what he means. I believe you were personally involved with one of those Korean girls." His eyes widened. "I believe you were pretty serious about her. That true?"

He didn't answer.

"Look," I said, "I'm sure these gentlemen have explained that you're mistaken if you think you can stonewall us and we'll believe your lies, and then we'll just let you go."

As I said the word *go*, I slammed my palm on the desktop so hard Prater jumped, John flinched a little, but good old Freddie knew what to expect and just stood there starring into Prater's eyes grinning. He didn't skip a beat.

"If you think any of that, you're crazy." I wanted to vary my act somewhere between his Dutch uncle and the insane neighbor all the kids on the block feared. "Or you're stupid, and we're going to get genuinely pissed off."

Prater looked at me like a child waiting to get hit by his father.

"Now," I continued, "in a moment, I'm going to ask you a couple of questions. You're supposed to answer truthfully. No big mystery…right?"

He nodded.

"If you lie to me once, I'll try again. If you lie to me twice, you'll see me get annoyed. If you lie to me a third time, I'm going to tap this mean-looking, Italian man on the shoulder, and he's going to know I want him to beat you until we hear the truth. That's pretty simple, too, isn't it?"

He nodded, looked a little more frightened and started to speak.

I snapped at him. "Don't answer yet. That was a rhetorical question. Keep listening because I want you to understand the law. I'll quote from the Tennessee Code for you. 'A person who knowingly and intentionally

146

causes the death of another person who was born and is alive is guilty of murder.'"

His face contorted at the mention of murder.

I let that sink in and then continued to explain, "Depending on circumstances, in this state you either get life in prison, or you get the *death* penalty for murder. Bad stuff, huh?"

He moved his mouth, wanting to speak.

"Shut up! That was another rhetorical question."

Prater wasn't a hard-core criminal and keeping him off balance was too easy to be a challenge.

Each time I spoke, I took a few steps to his right and then to his left, to keep his head moving and make him uncomfortable. "When someone stonewalls us and makes our lives difficult, he pisses us off. I'm sure that doesn't surprise you. By lying and making us think he considers us stupid, we do not, under any circumstances, want to give that guy a break."

He wrinkled his brow and tried hard to listen and follow me.

I continued to speak slowly, but raised my volume with each sentence. "We will not tell a district attorney that the guy cooperated. We will not allow him to be charged with less than the maximum crime. We *will* enjoy seeking the death penalty."

That got another visible reaction. His blinking increased. It looked as if he was having difficulty swallowing.

"We will not allow this guy's lawyer to plea bargain down to a lower charge. We *hate* guys who stonewall us!"

Prater's face contorted more with each of my statements as he saw his future sliding into a bottomless sewer. Tears welled up in his eyes. I left all traces of the Dutch uncle at the gate long ago and didn't give him a chance to regroup.

"When guys like that are convicted, we go to the prison and watch them get that lethal injection. Later on, we go to lunch and celebrate. Do you understand what I'm telling you?"

He said nothing. I put my psycho act into high gear and slapped the desk, this time even harder than before. He squeezed his eyes shut, shuddered. His shoulders rose four inches as he jumped a second time.

"Now's the time to answer, goddamn it! Do you understand?"

Wayne Zurl

"Yes, sir." His response was somewhere between a whisper and a croak.

I noticed a dark thread, about an inch-and-a-half long, on his left shoulder. It annoyed me. I wanted to pick it off and throw it away.

"Would I be here talking to you like this if I didn't think you had something important to tell us?" I said.

"No, sir."

"Do you want me to charge you with a capital crime and demand the death penalty when you may be guilty of a lesser crime?"

"No, sir."

"What lesser crime are you guilty of?"

"Do what?"

"Don't *do what* me, you little piss ant! I won't slap the desk the next time. I'll slap the shit out of you, goddamn it!"

Prater said nothing. The first tear ran down his cheek. His hands were strangling each other in his lap. I wouldn't have been surprised if he had soiled his pants.

"More education now, Prater, so listen up." I spoke calmly again. The friendly Dutchman was back in the driver's seat. "When you cause the death of another person, *but*," I emphasized the last word, "*but* you do so under extreme emotional distress, you're probably not guilty of murder." I shook my head and tried to make the idea sound so elemental even a child should understand.

Sitting in the armless chair next to the scarred up gray metal desk, he looked like a small lost boy on the verge of screaming for his parents.

I gently placed a hand on his shoulder. "You understand what I'm saying, son?"

He still looked confused.

I removed my hand and slowed my speech even more so he could grasp the important point. "Okay, listen carefully. Here's a bit of free legal advice. If you're in such a confused and troubled state of mind that you are emotionally unstable—you might even be called temporarily insane—then you are *not* responsible for your conduct. Nod if you heard that."

He did.

"If that's the case, what you did was not intentional, it was reckless.

148

Your culpability changed. The crime changes. Understand?"

He nodded again. I knew he heard me, but I doubted he knew what I was talking about. I looked at the thread again. It was still there. I got more annoyed, but I pressed ahead. I was on a roll, and Prater looked so far off balance it wouldn't take much more to get a confession.

I pulled an armless chair to within a foot of his knees and sat. I slowed and softened my delivery even more. "That emotional distress thing sets up a whole different possibility. Then, if under certain circumstances you kill someone—someone who you were romantically involved with, someone like Rosie Cho. Then you may not be guilty of murder. You could be guilty of manslaughter. And that's a much less serious crime—much less of a penalty because it's *not* murder."

Prater didn't know the differences between *murder* and *manslaughter* any more than he could compare a Riesling with a Gewürztraminer, but when I said, 'not murder,' his eyes opened a little wider.

"A sharp lawyer can get a guy like that off with only a couple of years in jail." I smiled and touched his shoulder again. My friendly act. "And then he has the rest of his life ahead of him. No death penalty. No life sentence. Am I getting through to you yet, son?"

"Yes, sir, I think so."

I didn't see any light bulbs go off. It wasn't a horribly difficult concept to grasp. At least I didn't think so. I tried again to help tutor him through criminal law 101.

"So," I continued, "if some guy who was in love with a girl, loved her enough to marry her, intending to spend their lives together, found out that she had a secret life, let's say as a call-girl, would I be correct to assume this guy might then feel at least a little emotionally distressed?"

He didn't answer, but more tears rolled down his cheeks. I just hit center with a sharp arrow. He used the back of his hand to wipe the tears away, hung his head and looked down at the hands in his lap. They were still now, no longer doing the Lady Macbeth routine, and he was thinking. Prater wasn't a tough guy, and he was on the verge of cracking. He sniffed loudly.

I didn't look at either Fred or John, but I knew they'd be wondering about the call-girl remark.

"Knowing your girl stepped out on you once would be tough to take," I said, "but if you learned about her taking money for sex and told her to stop and all would be forgiven, and then you found out that she didn't stop—man, that would be intolerable. It would be for me anyway and probably for any man on a jury. Guys understand things like that."

He looked up at me momentarily, then hung his head again and wiped his nose with the back of his hand.

"Let's say this guy was a really hard-working, decent young man. Let's say he followed his girl one night just out of curiosity and saw her prostituting herself again, a second time or even more. How many juries in the world wouldn't feel sorry for this guy?"

He lifted his face, and I held his gaze.

"Every man *and woman* on the jury would see him as the injured party."

I looked toward John and then Fred. "Right?" Both nodded in agreement. Prater looked at them, too.

"That's a whole different ballgame, kid," Mazzio said. "You're no murderer."

"Wouldn't any one of those twelve people think that hard-working, decent guy, that military veteran, was at least upset or emotionally distressed?" I asked.

Still no answer, but a lot more tears.

Softly and gently, I said, "It's time to answer again, Prater. Wouldn't that guy be so upset he might go *crazy* and kill the girl who was having sex with other men while he waited at home, still in love and faithful to her?"

He blinked a couple of times. I knew I had him. I continued speaking like his best friend. "Have you ever heard a lawyer say his client was temporarily insane? The newspapers report stories like that all the time."

He could barely speak, but managed to nod his head and croak out, "Yes, sir."

"It's a very good defense." I swept my hand around, taking in the three of us in the squad room. "Do you think *any* of us blame you for killing Rosie? Do you think we don't know how you must have felt?"

It was barely audible, but I heard, "Guess not, sir."

"Prater, you were so upset when you shot Rosie that you had to throw up. We know about that. That's emotional distress, my friend, plain and simple. It's something everyone on a jury will understand. Damn it, son. We feel sorry for you."

"Yes, sir...thanks."

"I want two things from you, Prater. I want the gun you used, and I want to give you the chance to tell your side of the story. You're not a criminal, son, so I'll allow you to write it all out in a statement. You can tell everyone how much you were hurting, how you took action because you were crazy with love for Rosie and frustrated when you saw what happened. Are you ready to do that?"

"Is that what I should do, sir?"

"You get three things when you write the statement, Prater. You get the chance to tell everyone *why* you did what you did. Next, you get me on your side. I'll tell the DA you cooperated. Believe me, that goes a long way in your defense. And *finally,* you get this problem off your shoulders and your conscience. You free up your soul, my friend. You get to sleep again. You won't always be looking over your shoulder waiting for a cop to take you in at gun point. Understand?"

"Yes, sir."

"Where's your gun?"

"In my apartment."

"Will you give me your keys?"

"Yes, sir." He dug into his pocket and placed a ring of keys on the desk.

"Where do we find the gun?"

"Under my mattress."

"Good. Are you ready to start writing your statement?"

"Yes, sir." He wiped his eyes again and sniffed.

John handed him a handkerchief.

"Do you want to just start writing, or would it be easier for you to tell me the story and let me help you write it?"

"I guess I could use some help."

"Okay, let's take a break first. You want something to drink? A soda?"

"Yes, please."

Wayne Zurl

"I'll get you a soda. You understand we have to put handcuffs on you now. Just one on you, the other to that ring attached to the desk. Okay?"

He looked at the steel ring and nodded. "Okay."

"John, do me a favor, and hang out here for a few minutes. Keep Prater company."

"Okay, Boss."

John got up from the edge of the desk where he'd been sitting. He stepped close to Prater and picked the thread off the kid's shoulder, dropped it on the floor and then patted him on the back. John turned to look at me and smiled. I looked back and scowled. I left the squad room, and Fred followed.

"Still got it, don't you, big guy?" Freddie said. "You were always good with head games. That was some line o' shit. You got him good."

"Yeah, poor kid. Stupid thing for him to do though, wasn't it?"

"Yeah, that's life." Mazzio always was a compassionate bastard.

I bought Prater a Pepsi from our soda machine, told Bettye what had happened and gave her Prater's key ring. She and Kate were at her desk in the reception area. I asked Bettye to call Jackie Shuman and have him retrieve Prater's pistol and search the rest of his home. I didn't take much time to see what progress the girls had made with the Korean names.

Fred poured himself a cup of coffee. I took a large glass of water and three Advil. I *wanted* a double shot of the scotch in my desk drawer. Two minutes later, we went back to the squad room.

It took more than an hour to get the kid's initial statement on paper. I had missed lunch and was starving. When I'm hungry, I'm not happy. I had a headache that wouldn't quit, but I needed to move on with phase two of the interrogation.

Sitting next to Prater, I pushed the yellow lined pad to the side.

"Now you should think of how you want to tell your reasons for *needing* to kill Kum-Ok. That's all part of the same incident. Probably one continuous state of mind, right?"

Prater looked at me and said nothing. I didn't want to lose him at that point.

"It's time to get *all* your thoughts on paper. Tests will show that one gun was used twice. Start by telling them you were scared for some reason. You were confused. Compelled beyond your control—*crazy* with emotion. Isn't that right?"

He closed his eyes and nodded.

"Tell me what happened and why. I'll write it out for you. I'll help you explain."

Prater took a king-sized breath before speaking. "Y'all were there so quick after it happened. I thought you'd connect me to Rosie. I figgered one of the other girls would give me up—tell you I loved Rosie."

I sat back and crossed my legs, getting ready for a long story.

"I tried to talk with Kum-Ok," he said. "She was easy to talk to. She was nice. I went to see her, but she wouldn't listen. She said she wouldn't talk to me. Told me to go away. I think she knew I shot Rosie."

More tears appeared at the corners of his eyes. His head sounded congested, and his nose ran a little more. He used John's handkerchief to wipe it. Prater's voice sounded thick and unrecognizable. He feared for his life and may have thought of me as his only friend.

"I was afraid she'd tell someone somethin'," he continued. "The next night, I followed Kum-Ok to the motel where she met a man. Later, I followed her back towards her place. When we were on that lonely part of the road, I pulled my bike up next to her car. She was drivin' slow. I had taken my helmet off so she could see it was me. When she looked my way, I pointed for her to pull over. She did, and I sat in the car with her and tried to get her to listen to what I had to say. I wanted to explain, but she still wouldn't listen. She said if I didn't leave her alone she'd go to the police and say it was me who shot Rosie. Then we argued, and I shot her once." His admission came out with no more inflection than if he had told me what he ate for breakfast.

"Why did you do that?"

"I was scared that sooner or later she'd tell someone. Then I figgered if two call girls were killed you might think it had somethin' to do with their pimp. I put her in the passenger's seat. It was easy. She didn't weigh much."

"How many people knew they were call girls? Did someone connect them with Mr. Ha, the pimp?"

He shook his head. "I don't know. I just figgered... Maybe it wasn't a good idea."

153

Time to act non-judgmental. I shrugged. "What happened next?"

"Then I drove the car off the main road to that spot by the greenhouse and walked back to my bike. It was only up at the corner. Then I went back home. I was sick again when I got there. That matters don't it?"

"Sure it does. Be sure to write that down." I smiled to keep him hopeful. "You parked your bike on the corner of Sevierville Road and Doc Beasley?"

"Yes, sir."

I'd have someone check for an oil drip. Lots of physical evidence is good even with a confession.

"Is that how you want to tell your story?"

"Yes, sir, I guess so."

I wrote it up and had him sign the statement, the form giving us permission to search his apartment, and his waiver of counsel. Prater placed my pen on the desk and finished his Pepsi.

But I still wasn't finished with him. "How well did you know Rosie's pimp?" I made it sound like a casual question, something barely relative to the murders. "Did you meet him more than once?"

"I never met no pimp, sir."

"You didn't know a man the girls called Mr. Ha?"

"No, sir."

"How about another Korean, a Mr. Park?"

"No, sir."

"This isn't the time to start lying again, Prater. If you knew those men, tell me now. If I find out you had anything to do with them later, all deals for leniency are forgotten. You understand?" I still spoke softly.

"I don't know either of those Korean men, sir."

I shook my head. "I hope to hell you're telling me the truth."

"I am, sir. I swear."

Frustration again showed in his voice. He had been stressed to the breaking point once, got a chance to relax and now had no toleration for more pressure. When he told the truth and I questioned his honesty, he got excited. Sometimes that's called the ring of truth.

"What kind of guns do you own?"

"Just one…a .22 revolver. I bought it to carry when I go fishin'."

"Only one gun? A revolver? No automatic?"

"No, sir. Just that one. It's a little Smith & Wesson."

I stood up and laid a hand on his shoulder. "Thanks, kid. I'll take that soda can for you. You'll start feeling better real soon."

I wondered how long it would have taken Prater to decide he needed to kill Chun-He, the only remaining person who knew that he and Rosie had argued.

Fred and I left the squad room again. John would fingerprint and photograph Prater and enter his name in Bettye's booking log. I'd give the Pepsi can to Jackie Shuman, and he'd ask the lab to look for a DNA match with the vomit.

After John finished an arrest report, I'd write the prosecution worksheet and the court informations, and then I'd have one of the cops take Prater to the Justice Center for arraignment. It would be after the 3:30 deadline, but in Blount County, a double homicide arrest would bring the on-call judge back to the bench.

In the hallway Freddie said, "You lyin' sack o' shit. You schmooze him into copping to Rosie's murder with that extreme emotional distress horse manure, you write that up, and then you squeeze in the other murder. And he tells you he capped Kum-Ok to try and throw us off. I love it. He believed every word you said."

"Yeah, I know. I feel sorry for him. How do you think he feels after we ganged up on him and scrambled his grits?"

"You're getting old." He slapped my shoulder.

I shrugged. "I am, but I still fit into my old uniforms."

"That hurt, you bastard."

"My old Army uniforms." I sneered at him.

"Ouch! Even worse. You can be a real prick when you want to."

We just tucked two of the murders under our belts, but still needed to think about who killed the Korean hoods.

"Remember the car that a witness saw parked outside Park's house the night he was killed," I asked.

"Yeah?"

"I hate to tell you this, sport, but it was Roni Keeble's."

"No." Fred sounded crushed. "She didn't whack Park, did she?"

"I don't think so, but I don't like her and Sunny second guessing me and talking to Park about the girls' murders. It wasn't a good time to be seen with a dead man."

"That would be one waste of a fine looking woman if she's guilty."

I nodded. "You heard about Rosie hooking on the side?"

"Yeah, that's new. Tell me about it."

"The three hired girls from across the street worked a little side business with Ha as their pimp."

"Son-of-a-bitch, Rosie was a hooker, and she wouldn't let me pay for it? What the hell was that about?"

"Apparently, this business was all after hours and in the motels near the airport. It had nothing to do with Sunny's operation. Ha worked deals with some of the desk clerks and sent the girls where they were needed."

"I'll be a son-of-a-bitch."

"It's a long story and a little complicated. Chun-He told me about it when she gave up Prater as Rosie's boyfriend."

"Jesus, Rosie was alone with me in that room. Why do you suppose she wouldn't do me? I offered to pay."

"Just not your day."

"If you were pros, wouldn't you do me?"

"Frederick, I don't believe you asked that question."

Chapter Sixteen

Fred stayed with John while he wrote up McKendry's arrest report. I walked to my office with a handful of notes on the murders. As I neared Bettye's desk in the reception area, I saw that she and Kate were eating Chinese food from round aluminum trays—signs of Wah Lum's house specials. Kate used chopsticks, while Bettye wielded a plastic fork. I imagined that after all the telephone work they did and the usual interruptions, their food may have gotten cold, but the office smelled good, and I assumed someone had cranked up the microwave. The smell made me even hungrier than only minutes earlier, so I decided to call for a delivery. I dialed the back room first.

"Squad room, Mazzio," he growled, in typical detective fashion.

"You sound like you belong here."

"I could get used to this."

"You hungry?" I asked.

"Dying."

"Chinese?"

"Works for me."

"Tell bean belly we'll get him something without MSG and ask the kid if he wants lunch."

"You buying his last meal?"

"I'm all heart."

"Where is this place? You want me to pick up?" Freddie said.

"They're right across the square. I'll ask them to deliver. I've got a menu in my office. Take a look."

"Be right there."

Wayne Zurl

I took the Wah Lum folder from my library of local menus and tossed it on the desktop.

Then I called Bobby Crockett, a single cop who would owe me big-time for assigning him to escort the Kisaeng trio of beautiful women around. He and Dallas Finchum were on patrol, but I rang Bobby's cell phone. The assignment was not something I wanted broadcast over the radio. And those two could transport Prater to court before tying up with our resident beauties.

When I finished with Bobby, I called Rachel at home. Her phone was ringing when Fred sat down in a guest chair. I tossed him the menu.

"Hi." She sounded out of breath. "I just opened the door and heard the phone. I've been out running."

"How far did you go?"

"Three miles today."

"Wow. It's hot out there."

"Tell me about it."

"I'll bet you're all sweaty."

"I am."

I tilted back and smiled. "Oooo."

"Stop that!"

"You glad to be back at work?" I asked.

"Actually, I am. I was alone most of the week. Kind of boring."

I sensed a hint. "I can cure your boredom. Want a big story?"

"You arrested someone?"

"Hook your phone to that recorder thingie."

"Okay, wait."

I heard the appropriate noise that goes with thingie hooking.

"It's an Ipod, not a thingie," she said.

"Who cares? I hate technology."

"Okay, I'm ready. Tell me."

I did and then added new information about the Ha and Park murders that she didn't already know.

"All that happened in Prospect?"

"Beautiful downtown Prospect."

"Of course. I didn't know that much about the Knoxville murders."

"The Knoxville cops don't call you like I do."

158

"I know. You're good."

"Better than you know, baby."

Fred looked at me and frowned.

"We can fix that," Rachel purred.

"Don't go there."

"Coward."

"Sad but true."

"Oh, well. Do you know who committed the Knoxville murders?"

"I might in a day or so."

"Are you going to arrest him or her or them?"

"I'll want to be there, but the Knoxville guys can have the collar."

"Collar?"

"That's New York language for arrest."

Mazzio shook his head, tossed the menu onto my desk and stood.

"Will they call me?"

I snickered. "If I tell them to call you, they'll call you. Then you'd owe them something. But if something happens, I'll call you. Maybe we'll both call you."

"Then I'll owe you."

"Of course."

"I owe you a lot, don't I?"

"Um. When do I collect?"

"You said not to go there."

"Whoever listens to me?"

"You're bad."

"I'm also hungry. I've got to go eat, and you have to file your story or whatever it is you do with stories."

"Okay, I'll talk to you when you catch the Knoxville killer."

"Yes, you will. Are you going to take a shower now?"

In the background Fred mumbled, "Oh, for chrissakes."

Rachel giggled. "None of your business."

"But you owe me." I tried to sound plaintiff.

"Byeee."

"Uh-huh. See ya."

I hung up and settled back into my big chair, feeling relaxed for the first time that morning. Fred was walking around looking at some of the things hanging on the wall.

"Let me guess who that was," Fred said.

"Shut up, Frederick."

"Your wife's in the next room."

"That's why I behave. We're just friends. We have a good professional relationship."

"Oh, you and your *friend* are just into phone sex?"

He sat in the chair next to my desk. The seat looked a little too small for his bulk.

"Shut up, and pick out your lunch."

"Already have. So did John. There's the list." He pointed at my desktop.

"I'll call," I said.

"I thought you might."

I grabbed the menu and the scribbled list.

"What channel?" he asked.

He can be terribly persistent.

"Channel?" I asked.

"Yeah, she's back at work. I heard you say so. What channel? I want to see this broad."

"Don't call her a broad."

"Touchy, touchy."

"Up yours."

"What channel? I will not go away."

"You are such an asshole."

He laughed, and I told him. Too tired to fight.

"What time?"

"Six and eleven."

"I'll watch."

"John doesn't give me this much trouble."

"I know. I'm not John."

* * * *

I grabbed the side chair next to Bettye's desk, spun it around and sat. "While I'm waiting for my Chinese food, ladies, tell me what you two have been doing."

Kate spoke first. "I think we've done quite well actually."

She thinks she's so smart sometimes. Bettye looked at me with a satisfied smile.

"Are you going to just sit there acting proud of yourselves or tell me?"

"What's it worth to you, big boy?" Kate asked.

"Standard rates. Lunch at a place of my choice. If I pay, I take all the credit."

Kate looked at Bettye. Bettye frowned and shook her head. Kate shook her head. It all looked so prearranged.

"I think we should hold out for more," Bettye said.

"While you're holding out, think about this," I said. "Remember, I'm the guy who takes care of you ladies. You," I pointed at Kate, "might have to quit your cushy volunteer jobs and be a cashier at Walmart. And you," this time pointing at Bettye, "might get to enjoy your new assignment as the foot-patrol sergeant on steady midnights." It was my turn to smile.

"You always play dirty," Kate said.

"We deserve better, you old grouch," Bettye said.

"I'm the boss. I need to win. Now tell me, or I'll make you work with Freddie."

Bettye put up her hands. "We give up. Go ahead, Kate."

"You remember Mrs. Shin?" Kate asked, as if she were addressing a numbskull.

"There's no quick way to this answer, is there?"

"Patience, Sammy, patience."

"Yes, dear, I remember Mrs. Shin."

"Well, do you know what her husband's name was?"

"Was?"

"He died."

"No. I have no idea."

"Cho."

"Son-of-a-gun. Can you elaborate on a more interesting connection?"

"I can." She smiled and waited.

Bettye upheld her part of the charade and said nothing.

"Today?"

"Sure."

"Please do."

Bettye was enjoying every minute of Kate's act.

"As far as we can tell, Rosie Cho, also known as Sung-Sook Cho, was Mrs. Shin's youngest daughter."

"Aha! I'll be damned."

"Yes, indeed. But wait, there's more."

"You mean if I call within the next ten minutes you'll super-size my order?"

"I certainly will. You mentioned Mrs. Shin's son whose name is, of course, Cho. Han-Me Cho to be precise. You said he owned a produce market in Oak Ridge."

"Yes, Park told me that."

"Well, your lovely desk sergeant called the Oak Ridge PD and learned that not only is his name Cho—you would have figured that out by yourself, but he owns a two-family house right behind the market."

"So?"

"Wait for the punch-line. You'll love it."

"Please hurry. I don't know if I can keep up this heavy breathing much longer."

"It's the same address that your Mr. Boo uses on his driver's license."

"Well, well, well. I'd say aha again, but it might sound redundant."

"You remember I noticed Mr. Boo's given name was Cho-Hung? Cho being what they call a generational name."

"Yes, ma'am."

"The INS lists Cho, Han-Me, Mrs. Shin's oldest son and famous greengrocer of Oak Ridge, as Boo's sponsor...and his cousin."

"Hot damn. You guys are good, and this is really cool. I don't yet know what it means, but my cunning imagination is starting to dream up a great possibility."

"We can believe that," Bettye said.

I used a really deep East Tennessee accent to impress the girls, "Ladies, y'all done real fine. I 'ppreciate yer he'p. I shorely do."

They told me how pleased they were to assist, and Kate added, "How about some place fancier than Wah Lum for our lunch?"

"There's always Howell's"

"Samuel, Howell's is a dive."

"But it's a nice dive."

"Come on, Sammy. What would you have done without us?" Bettye said.

"You're right. Okay, lunch at a place of your choosing. I'll even agree to drinks."

Kate said, "That sounds better."

"You would have bought drinks anyway," Bettye said.

Some women are never satisfied.

"Let's go to the Villa Napoli," I said. "Nick will give you two a special bottle of wine because you're beautiful, and he loves to flirt. And his grandson, Vinnie the bartender, will try and look down your blouses."

"Does he always act like this?" Bettye asked.

Kate was quick on the uptake. "Most of his life."

"You ladies are speaking about me like I'm not here."

They both seemed content to ignore the man who wasn't there.

"Sorry to disappoint Nick and Vinnie," Kate said, "but I've been told the peanut-coated catfish at Aubrey's is the best anywhere. I might like to try that."

"My daddy had that a couple of weeks ago and said it was dee-licious." Bettye added a lot more country to her accent than usual.

"Aubrey's than?" I asked.

They both nodded.

"Good. They have oodles of draught beers. Have your people call my people with a date, and we'll do lunch. And I appreciate what you did. Good job! I love you both. With my guidance and your information, we'll help the Knoxville cops clear a couple of murders."

Both girls smiled.

"And you know I'll give you the credit."

Fred and John walked out into the lobby looking like they had done a hard morning's work.

"Prater's in a cell," John said. "My paperwork is all done and ready to go to court with him. I'll call Bobby when you finish yours."

I nodded to John, stood up, spun the chair around again and sat down between Kate and Bettye.

"Have I got news for you guys," I said, ready to tell them about the Cho and Boo connections.

"I can't wait, but I need food first," Fred said.

"Yeah, you must have lost six ounces already. The stress of the day has been grueling."

As if on cue, Mr. Lum's daughter, Mai, walked into the PD carrying a brown shopping bag with our lunches. I paid. She left. I spoke again to Freddie.

"See the difference between that Chinese woman and the Koreans?"

"No."

"Can you tell the difference between a Sicilian and someone from Umbria?"

"No." He laughed.

"Why do I bother?"

"Hey, thanks for lunch," Mazzio said.

John looked at me, got a big stupid smile on his face and dug into the bag looking for what he and our prisoner had ordered.

"Yeah, Boss, thanks for lunch," John said.

"Did I say I'd buy?" I asked. "I just offered to call."

Fred laughed.

Then John said, "You know, Boss, that was pretty clever how you got the kid to confess to both murders. If you worked for the CIA at Guantanamo they wouldn't have to do that *surfboarding* on terrorists."

Kate and Bettye laughed.

Fred shook his head. "That's waterboarding, you idiot."

"I don't think so, Freddie. It's surfboarding. Right, Boss? Who ever heard of waterboarding?"

"John," I said, "how can you remember a complicated word like Guantanamo and confuse something simple like waterboarding and surfboarding?"

"It's not surfboarding?" He seemed shocked.

"No, John, not surfboarding," I said.

"Could it be snowboarding?" Kate asked. "Or maybe washboarding?"

Bettye giggled again. Kate looked proud of herself.

I pointed at Kate. "You boggle my mind as often as John does." Then pointing at Bettye, "And you, Ms. Desk Sergeant, you laugh at her. Where's your loyalty? You see what I have to live with, Frederick?"

"Quit bitchin'. Except for John, they're too good-looking for you to complain."

"You're no help. Where can I find a loyal partner?"

Chapter Seventeen

After we finished lunch, I prepared my share of the paperwork. At 3:40, Bobby Crockett and Dallas Finchum walked in ready to take Prater McKendry to court before they finished a regular tour of duty and began their special assignment of guarding the lovely bodies of the girls from Kisaeng. Kate had gone home, Bettye and John were back to their regular work, and Fred had decided to spend some of his Smoky Mountain vacation time with his neglected wife.

I handed Crockett and Finchum the arrest and prosecution paperwork and briefed them on the particulars in case someone at the courts asked.

"He told you all that *and* signed a gat-dag confession?" Bobby asked.

"Sure," I said. "He likes me."

"Copped ta both murders and never asked for no lawyer?"

I grinned. "Why would he need a lawyer when he had me to help him?"

Bobby shook his head. "Lord have mercy."

"Guess he never heard about conflict of interest," Dallas said. "Is all that legal?"

"Sure. He waived his right to counsel and signed permission to search for the gun."

"I've got me a lot ta learn," Dallas said.

"And you didn't have ta thump on him?" Bobby asked.

"Of course not." I tried to sound indignant. "I may scare people half to death with the possibilities of what might happen if they don't

166

cooperate, but I never beat anyone."

"Someday," Crockett said, "we're gonna hear about a landmark federal case called U.S. vs Jenkins."

Dallas allowed himself a respectful laugh.

"You better hope not, smartass. If I end up in Leavenworth, you might get a serious guy for your chief. Maybe even an ex-Fed."

"Don't need that," Bobby said.

Dallas smiled again, and I asked him to give me his handcuffs.

"I'll get your prisoner and meet you at the back door," I said.

Five minutes later, I brought Prater McKendry from the cellblock and met Bobby standing in the hallway between the squad room and the rear entrance.

"Where's Dallas?" I asked.

"Went up front ta give Miss Bettye a couple o' field reports for the blotter. Don't know why he ain't back yet."

"Hang onto Prater. I'll get him."

When I arrived in the lobby, I not only found Bettye, John, and Dallas, but apparently Darnell Means had stopped by to introduce himself. When I joined the group, Darnell stopped speaking to those three and looked at me.

"Chief." He nodded slightly to acknowledge my existence. "I just dropped in ta say hello and introduce myself."

I smiled. "Hi there."

"Dallas here tells me y'all arrested a man for the double murders."

"We did. Officer Finchum and his partner were just about to take him for arraignment."

Before you interrupted our orderly world.

"I hear ya got a confession."

"Right again."

"Who's his attorney? Maybe I know him."

"Or her." In my peripheral vision, I saw Bettye smile "He didn't ask for a lawyer. The kid's got no money. He'll probably request a public defender."

"Y'all shouldn't take a confession without an attorney being present. The defendant can always recant."

"He waived his right to counsel in writing. And we have physical evidence linking him to both murders. He can recant until the cows come home, and I'll still get the confession through any hearing they throw at me."

"Mebbe, mebbe not. The Supreme Court says—"

If I wasn't used to dealing with administrative pains-in-the-ass, I would have seen red and attacked young Means right there in the lobby. But I didn't and also didn't adhere to the axiom of not verbally assaulting an employee or member of the management team in public. I thought it was time to show a select example of upward discipline.

I cut him short. "I know you've never made an arrest. How many homicides have you prosecuted?"

I have no doubt that Darnell turned out to be the one seeing red; at least his face showed the appropriate amount of anger. "I'm an attorney, not a prosecutor."

I knew that was a lie. "I thought you were a deputy mayor."

"Yes, well, uh." He skipped a beat for a brief moment. "May I see your paperwork?"

"The chief ADA is always satisfied with my paperwork. I'm happy to let her check my spelling. But thanks for the offer. Now, if you don't mind, we've got a judge waiting."

And the prisoner might have escaped while you're standing here annoying me.

Means scowled and tried to make his pasty face look angrier. "Right. Don't want to keep a judge waitin'. We'll talk about this at a later date when we discuss some of the changes I'll be making. Like reviewin' arrest paperwork."

I smiled again. "Perhaps. Thanks for stopping by." I turned to Dallas and gave him a look saying I wasn't pleased. "Meet me in my office."

He followed and stepped into my room as I continued down the hall.

"Your partner and I need to have a chat," I told Bobby who stood near the back door holding Prater by the arm.

"He in some kinda trouble?"

He didn't see a happy look on my face. "Ask him when you leave the Justice Center."

I turned and headed for my office.

Bobby mumbled, "Uh-oh."

I closed the door gently and looked at Dallas who waited for me with his hat in his hand. "Sit." I pointed to one of the guest chairs.

I waited a long moment, letting the kid squirm.

"Did you know Darnell Means before he got here?"

"Yes, sir. He's a friend o' my Uncle Claude. They were both on the county commission."

"Is he a friend of yours?"

"Not exactly. I've seen him at barbeques and get-t'gethers my uncle has. Spoke ta him a few times. He seemed like a friendly guy."

"Before I hired you, we discussed the politics your family is involved in. You know I am not a fan of either one of your uncles."

Dallas dropped his eyes and nodded.

"I'm sure my predecessor, your Uncle Buck, must have attended these parties, even though a major stipulation in the agreement of him not being charged criminally for selling those confiscated guns was to leave Blount County. I know he bought a place in Florida, but he still owns a house in Maryville and lives here part of the year. Correct?"

"Yes, sir."

"Is Darnell especially close to Buck?"

"I don't know, sir."

I shook my head and could have cheerfully shot Darnell Means.

"Do you want to work here, Dallas?"

He looked shocked. "Uh, yes, sir."

"Then consider Prospect PD exactly like Las Vegas."

"Do what?"

"Come on, son. You've seen the commercials. What happens here, stays here. That means no gossip. No telling war stories to your family or buddies. And certainly no discussing PD matters with that young shithead politician. Capische?"

Dallas didn't know *capische* from *cavatelli*, but he took my meaning.

"Yes, sir, but I figgered him bein' the new deputy mayor and all... I thought he'd be proud o' what you done."

"You figured wrong, Dallas. He's not a cop. He's not even a real lawyer. He's a bullshit artist, and I still haven't figured out how he ended up as deputy mayor. But I'll find out."

"Yes, sir."

"The important thing to remember is he is not a cop. He is one of them—and that means he is *not* one of us. He's not to be trusted. Don't ever let this happen again. Are we clear?"

"No, sir. I mean yes, sir. We're clear. I'm sorry."

"And forget about local politics while you're on probation."

"Yes, sir."

"Maybe you should move to Tibet so your family doesn't get you into any more trouble."

"Sir?"

"Forget it. Go find your partner, and get the prisoner arraigned."

He remained sitting.

"You can do that now."

Dallas popped up and put on his cap. "Yes, sir." He did an about-face and left.

I walked out to the lobby. Bettye was assembling a permanent case folder for the Prater McKendry arrest, and John typed a few new calls into the blotter. They stopped when I arrived.

"Sounds like the deputy mayor is on your shit list, Boss," John said.

"You might say that."

Bettye gave me an annoyed look. "I never would have guessed." Obviously, she considered me her bad little boy.

"You sound more like my wife every day."

She smiled. "It must be you."

"Ya know, Boss," John said, "That guy reminds me of a young version of Marty the Moose. You hated him, too."

"And he hated me. It was a nice relationship."

"Marty the Moose?" Bettye said.

"I'm sure Big Mouth Gallagher will tell you all about our former deputy police commissioner."

"Why did you call him the Moose?"

"Most people thought I called him that because he got his antlers caught in all the new paperwork he generated. But he was a *big* guy with an ass two nightsticks wide. I referred to him as a *moose* one day, and it stuck."

Bettye smiled, and I turned to leave.

But she still had more to discuss. "What was that about the changes Darnell has in mind?"

I was glad she reminded me and turned to face her. "I guess we'll find out. But there is no way that simpleton is laying a hand on my paperwork. Now we need something that I can use to cancel out anything he wants. First chance you get, Betts, make that call to the court and see what they know about Darnell. A guy who can't pass a bar exam isn't smart enough to get these jobs by himself. Find out who his rabbi is."

"Rabbi?"

"Political benefactor. His horsepower."

Bettye nodded. "Another New York expression?"

"Exactly."

She smiled again.

"John," I said, "start digging into this guy. Find all the dirt. All the skeletons. He didn't serve on the county commission without doing something that could get him into trouble. You might have to do some road time, but get the answers. Call Freddie, and tell him to help."

"Freddie will wanna set him up and take pictures."

I smiled at the idea. "Hmmm. He just might."

I started to leave again.

"Sam Jenkins, just what are you plannin'?" Bettye asked.

I waved my right hand in the air and exaggerated a laugh. "Ha, ha, ha."

* * * *

At four o'clock, Sergeant Stan Rose walked in.

"The bars are open back there. Who was in the cell?" he asked.

"Young Prater McKendry, killer of Korean women," I said.

"No kidding? You got him?" Stan settled into one of my armchairs and stretched out his long legs.

"Yes, Tonto, this wrongdoer has been brought to justice. But our work here is not done."

Stan decided Tonto should speak in Ebonics. "What else y'all doin', Ke-mo-sabe?"

"Well, trusty scout, there are more crimes to be solved. More victims to be avenged."

171

"Y'all got a bottom line fo' me, masked man?"

His skin looked dark next to his khaki uniform shirt, not exactly like Jay Silverheels.

I dropped the Clayton Moore voice and told him, "Yep. Thanks to a couple of lovely women who worked on the Korean connection. I'm sure, if given a little time, we can put the arm on the villain who killed Ha and Park."

"We, Kemosabe? Those be Knoxville cases."

"Yes, but we've got all the information and all the theories. Without us, Renfro's got as much chance of finding the killer as a one-legged man in an ass-kickin' contest."

Stanley shifted back to his Los Angeles accent. "Why not just give him the info? You know, inter-agency cooperation and all that jazz."

"Sure, but think of all the fun we'd miss." I probably sounded like a little kid.

Then he went back to Uncle Remus. "Yo gonna git me kilt some day, massah. Yessuh, yo surely is. Man yo lookin' fo got him a big-ass gun."

"You really could star in *Song of the South*, you know."

"Sometimes y'all put da fear o' da Lord in me, white man."

"Surely not, big, strong boy like you."

With a protective vest under his shirt, Stanley looked rather large.

"Boy?" He scowled and tried to look offended. I knew better.

"Listen to this, and then tell me what you think. Number one, Mrs. Shin, Park's housekeeper, was Rosie Cho's mother."

"No kidding? Mrs. Shin killed Ha and Park? Why would she do that if someone else killed Rosie?"

"I'm getting to that. Hold your horses. Remember I told you Park said Mrs. Shin's son owned a market in Oak Ridge?"

"Yeah."

"Mrs. Shin doesn't look like she'd pop two hoods with a .45, but this Mr. Han-Me Cho, Mrs. Shin's son, is thirty-six-years-old. He may know how to use a handgun."

"Two people named Cho are Mrs. Shin's children?"

I nodded. "I'll explain the name thing later."

"Okay, but why? Why would those two think Park or Ha killed

Rosie?"

I shook my head and changed my focus. "They might not."

"Mrs. Shin knows Park is a hood and might think he'd kill her daughter to stick it to you or Sunny Kim?" he asked.

I shook my head and smiled.

"Why not hit one of the other massage parlor employees if he could send the same message and not hurt his housekeeper?"

"Good point," I said, "but slow down, and listen up. After Park was killed, Renfro told me the only lead they had was a neighbor spotting a red Audi on the street near Park's home. Well, Roni Keeble owns a red A4."

"Roni Keeble killed Park?"

"No, Stanley, no, but that led me to more information and gave me the idea about Prater McKendry. That and the oil drip thing."

"Oil drip?"

"Forget the oil drip for now. Out of all this, I like Mr. Boo for killing both Ha and Park."

"Boo? You think he'd kill his employer and friend?"

"Why not? Bettye and Kate learned that Boo is Mrs. Shin's nephew. And who said Ha was Boo's friend?"

"Jesus, you didn't tell me that." Stan pulled his legs up and sat forward in the guest chair, tossing his PPD ball cap onto the edge of my desk.

"If you'd stop interrupting, I'd have a chance."

"Back to the same old question...why?"

"Well, think about it. Boo assumed that Park told Ha to kill one of Sunny's employees and the victim ended up being Boo's niece or second cousin or whatever Rosie was to him. Or it's about Ha and the prostitutes."

"Ha and the prostitutes?" It looked like that surprised him. For a smart guy, Stan gets confused easily.

"See, you miss a day, you kiss a lot. You snooze, you lose, big guy," I said.

"Fascinating. I'm still listening."

"When I went to confront Roni Keeble and Sunny Kim about why one or both of them went to Park's house—of course that was a bluff

173

because Renfro didn't even have a model of Audi, much less a plate number. Anyway, I also wanted to ask Chun-He about the oil drip."

"Sure, the oil drip again."

"I said forget that. But under pressure and before I ever mentioned the oil drip, Chun-He admitted she and the other two girls were hooking on the side, and Mr. Ha was their pimp."

"Good God. Who wrote this script, Elmore Leonard?" Stan really looked interested now.

"That led me to Prater. That and the oil drip."

"Of course. Why would he care that Rosie and the other girl, what's her name, were hookers?"

"Her name was Kum-Ok. It means golden beach in Korean. It's a very traditional name, very old." Stan needed another lesson in Korean folklore.

"Fascinating," he said again and shook his head. "I'm in awe of your language skills."

"Prater was engaged to Rosie and found out she was a pros."

"Killed her in a rage. Okay, I'll buy that. But why kill Kum-Ok?"

"To throw us off the track, or so he says."

"He admitted that?"

"Yep."

"Cold guy."

"I thought so. He doesn't act like it though."

"So why don't you like Prater for at least killing Ha, if not Park?"

"He's not smart enough."

"I'm confused."

"Me, too. But I'm ready to bet Boo thought Ha killed Rosie on Park's order to snuff an employee of Kisaeng Massage. Boo would know that Ha was a cold-hearted bastard who wouldn't care if the victim was a co-worker's relative, and Boo rightfully resented that."

"We're getting complicated again."

"Stay inside Boo's head with me now," I said. "Rosie might have looked like the most convenient victim when Ha was in a killing mood. Boo, being the local tough guy from the Cho family, felt duty bound to restore family honor and avenge Rosie's murder."

"You gonna sell this plot to Hollywood?"

I let his rhetorical question fall by the wayside. "He was wrong about Ha killing Rosie, of course," I continued, no doubt thrilling Stanley with my deductive reasoning. "Maybe Boo thought Park actually used Ha to run the business-girls for him...but he didn't. At least I don't think so. Ha supposedly acted independently, or so says Chun-He Lee. Maybe Boo killed Park because he resented Rosie being recruited as a prostitute, and he considered Park responsible for that as boss of the operation. Killing those two is no big thing for the rest of humanity, but they actually ended up getting a raw deal—assuming Boo's the killer, that is."

"And you can prove this how?" Stan asked.

"I can't...yet. If I know all this and I can't prove it, how would you expect the Knoxville cops to prove it?"

"I'm not sure they could even follow your outline."

"Exactly. So, what do you say we go to Knoxville—or Oak Ridge—tonight and try to get the proof?"

"I ask you this every time...why me? Shouldn't you be training one of the enthusiastic young cops to do these things? I have a bunch of patrolmen to supervise. What about those two old guys? Wouldn't they feel left out if you didn't take them along?"

"They probably would. Okay, we'll invite them, too. But on the road, Stanley, we're a team. Like Bettye is my inside partner, it's you and me on the road. Right?"

"When you get me killed, I expect you'll explain yourself to my wife."

"Sure, I'll send flowers. All girls like flowers. But right now I should call Renfro and tell him what's up and see if he wants to play with us."

Chapter Eighteen

My call to Dee-Dubyah's cell phone found him out of the office, investigating a house burglary. I told him about the arrest of Prater McKendry, clearing the Cho and Kyeung murders and what Kate and Bettye dug up on the Shin/Cho family. He agreed that making a run at Mr. Boo would be a good first step. And he wanted to bring Oak Ridge PD into the loop and coordinate the effort once they allocated backup personnel.

Then he dropped a grenade in my lap.

"You're really gonna git ta hate what I tell you, but there ain't no way this is gettin' any easier."

"Here I am on cloud nine after nicking that kid for two murders and learning all that good stuff about the Cho connection, and you decide to go and pee on my leg like a junkyard dog."

"Well, so ta speak."

"Okay, I'll close my eyes and take it like a man. What?"

"The .45 slug our M.E. got from Park ain't the same as the two taken from Ha. Not the same gun neither."

"Hell, I've got two different .38s. Maybe Boo has a pair of .45s?"

"Mebbe. Let's hope so. Ha was shot with two one-hunnert-and-eighty-five grain holler points, most likely Remin'tons. Park got tagged with one two-hunnert-and-thirty grain military hardball round."

"Hmmm. Boo looks more like a hollow point man," I suggested.

"Be my guess, too. That copper half-jacket on the holler points had enough riflin' marks to compare with the all copper hardball. Different guns or different barrels, at least."

"Or at worst two different shooters," I said. "Boo's disappeared, so it's reasonable we follow him and ask about his former co-workers. I don't see how we could get a warrant to search Cho the grocer's place for a second gun. That makes life difficult."

"I hear that."

"So what time do you want to have a sit down with Boo?"

"We'll be done here in a half hour, mebbe forty-five minutes. I'll call Oak Ridge PD. Grab yerse'f somethin' ta eat, and meet us in Oak Ridge around six o'clock. You know where the grocery store is?"

"Nope."

"How about Oak Ridge PD?"

"We'll find it," I said.

"You find the owner of that Audi yet?"

"I thought it may be someone I knew, but they had a good alibi."

I crossed my fingers, so that wasn't really a lie.

"Too bad," he said.

"Life's not easy."

"I hear that."

"Do I need to know anything else before making the drive?"

"Nope. See y'all at the PD then."

"Okey dokey, podna."

"Yer soundin' more local all the time," he observed.

"Hey, I'm the one who gets to do the jokes."

* * * *

The city of Oak Ridge, Tennessee grew up during the Second World War when the federal government decided that the Oak Ridge National Laboratory would make a good home for their super secret Manhattan Project. Einstein, Oppenheimer and a small army of physicists banded together in that sleepy little town to invent the atom bomb.

Today the ORNL, more commonly called Y-12 by the locals, is still operational with their nuclear reactors reacting accordingly. Lawsuits abound from seriously ill government employees, and there are periodic demonstrations urging a shutdown of the plutonium cookers. So far, those efforts have been unsuccessful.

In a little Polish restaurant that Kate and I visit occasionally, not only can you order pierogi and galumpki like babcia used to make, but you can often find a table of ten or twelve eighty-something-year-old men with eastern European accents and 180 IQs eating lunch and talking about the good ol' days in 'the secret city'.

I drove north on I-140, the Pellissippi Parkway. Stanley sat in the passenger's seat, and John and Fred relaxed in the back. North of Interstate-40, the main east-west road in Tennessee, the Pellissippi becomes Route 162, a locally maintained road. Closer to Oak Ridge, it's called Illinois Avenue.

Oak Ridge PD is housed in the city municipal building on South Tulane Avenue. I didn't really know where I was going, but with my basic knowledge of the town that glows in the dark and the GPS system in my Crown Victoria, I ended up taking the long way. I found the Oak Ridge Turnpike, turned right and then made a quick right on Tulane. We parked in the visitor's lot, walked past the fire department and into the lobby of the PD.

I resisted the urge to bluster up to the reception desk and tell them we were the pros from Prospect there to show the locals how to put the arm on an oversized Korean thug. Instead, I opted to act like an ambassador and kept Fred and John in the background.

I spoke to a sixty-something-year-old man at the reception desk who looked like a civilian. "Hi, I'm Chief Jenkins from Prospect PD. We've come to see a Detective Renfro from the Knoxville Police and someone from your investigation division."

"Do whot now?" he said.

I tried again, same story.

"Don't got no Dee-tective Renfro workin' here," he said.

I swallowed my impatience, took a breath and started my story again. "I know. He's from... *Why should I bother?* "Can I speak to any one of your detectives?"

"Shore, he'p yerse'f." He pushed a phone at me and scratched an itch beneath the front of his plaid short-sleeved shirt.

I sighed. "Uh...how would I call them?"

The old boy looked annoyed. "Ya kin try 2401 or 2402."

I smiled like a vinyl siding salesman. "Thanks a bunch."

I got a response from 2401; a Detective Wells answered. I explained my reason for being there one more time.

"Renfro? Yeah, he's rot here. Y'all from Prospect, ya say?"

"Right. There are four of us."

"Y'all hang in there. I'll come up front an' git ya."

Wells greeted the team and me with a big smile and handshakes all around. He looked about fortyish, had short brown hair and wore a red flowered Hawaiian shirt out of his pants. I wondered if he and Mazzio would swap tailor's addresses.

Back in the squad room, we found Renfro and Maples sitting next to Wells' empty desk. The ORPD chief had assigned two uniformed cops and Detective Hubert Wells to assist us. After more introductions, Wells told us we could find Cho's grocery market, Dae Han Fresh Produce, on Tennessee Avenue in the northeast section of town. We drove there in three cars.

The market fronted on Tennessee Avenue, the main drag, and occupied the corner of Florida Road. Just behind the market and its parking lot, we found the two-family-home of Mr. Cho.

Boo's digs could be accessed from a side door. There were no lights on inside his apartment and no response to our knocking. Either Boo wasn't home, or he was playing 'possum. We tried the Cho residence.

A good-looking Korean woman in her mid-thirties answered the door. She wore a tan sleeveless blouse and a wraparound print skirt. On her feet were traditional Korean rubber shoes called komo-shin—no relation to Mrs. Shin.

I greeted her in Korean and introduced myself. Stan and I entered the home. The other troops tried to remain inconspicuous outside and kept an eye on Boo's place. The woman told me she was Cho's wife. Her name was Chae. When I asked to see her husband about Mr. Boo, she left us in the living room and retrieved her hubby.

He was a good-looking man, a little taller than the average Hangook, with a medium length expensive-looking haircut. He wore a pair of wrinkled khaki pants and a white athletic T-shirt. It appeared that he'd spent a hard day with the vegetables. After offering a formal greeting and introducing myself and Stanley, I got down to business.

"Two of his co-workers have been murdered, and we haven't been able to contact Mr. Boo," I said. "We thought he may be in trouble himself. Have you seen your cousin lately?"

Cho told us Boo left home that morning, but had not yet returned. He came home at six o'clock the evening before; both Cho and his wife had heard him. Both readily confirmed that, but they didn't know if he went out later last night, as he sometimes did.

They also confirmed that Boo still drove a 2003 black Caddy that was nowhere to be found. He gave us Boo's cell phone number since there was no landline in the apartment. I called the number, but got no answer. Lastly, I asked if we could look in the apartment. Cho surprised me by agreeing. I had yet to mention the Rosie Cho murder. Neither did he.

Mr. Cho opened the green raised panel door to Boo's apartment and switched on the lights. Before we entered, I took several pieces of mail from an old-fashioned mailbox on the outside wall of the house, the metal kind with two hooks to hold a newspaper.

The apartment consisted of a combination eat-in kitchen and sitting area, a separate bedroom and a small bathroom. It was clean and tidy and looked just a little bigger than an extended stay motel room. Several framed prints that looked like things Cho purchased from The Dollar Store hung on the walls in the living room. The place appeared very impersonal.

I struck up a conversation with Mr. Cho while Stan looked in the bedroom. I knew he'd toss the closet and drawers, and I didn't want Cho to watch and have an opportunity to object. I kept talking while Stan moved and checked the bathroom. He came out of the john and gave a quick shake of his head. I took that to mean he found nothing of interest.

I picked up the stack of four envelopes the mail carrier left in the outside box, three pieces of junk and a bill from US Cellular. I opened that envelope. Boo was being charged for two different cell phone numbers. I wrote down the second one.

I handed Mr. Cho my card, thanked him for his help and gave him the standard line of call us when his errant cousin returned, reiterating that we were worried about Boo's safety.

Cho didn't look like a killer, but neither did Prater McKendry. I'd have Bettye double check TBI files for a recorded handgun purchase by Cho.

That scenario finished a little after seven. We were all disappointed. I told Renfro and Maples I'd interview Mrs. Shin the next day. They were glad to get my help because neither thought her English was good enough for any extensive questioning. I disagreed. I've always found that people who speak English as a second language often speak less fluently than they're capable of doing when they deal with police officers.

"I guess we can figure Boo may be on the run," I said.

"Seems strange he ain't here, if he's jest an innocent bystander," Renfro said.

"I guess putting out an alarm on his car and calling the airport PD is in order."

"I'll do that t'night."

"Maybe the Nashville airport, too," was my next thought.

"Good idea," Maples said.

"I'll let you know what Mrs. Shin can offer," I said.

"We 'preciate it." Renfro again.

I addressed both the Knoxville and Oak Ridge cops. "Thanks for the backup, guys."

"Thanks fer workin' our case," Renfro said.

"Talk to you tomorrow."

"Y'all be careful now."

Chapter Nineteen

I strolled around to the east side of a large colonial-style home in west Knoxville where Ahn-Na Shin rented an apartment. Two minutes earlier, the thermometer in my car read eighty-one degrees. The big powder blue sky didn't have a cloud in it. I passed a shiny, dark blue Kia Rio parked on a cement strip off the main driveway. Maybe Gallagher was right. Korean women might be *calvanistic.*

Brick steps led to the basement entrance, and a green and white striped aluminum awning protected the doorway from the elements. Shade provided by an ancient oak covered the entry area, and green mold had discolored the red brick exterior walls around the door.

I pushed the bell button, and a startling buzzer sounded within the house. Sixty seconds later, Mrs. Shin answered the door. She wasn't wearing the domestic uniform of Mr. Park's housekeeper. From her outfit, I assumed Park paid her a good salary. Her black slacks and blue print blouse were not from some cheap, outdoor flea market. I greeted her in Korean and thanked her for seeing me. As I expected, she averted her eyes, returned a greeting and asked me to come into her portion of the house, built in a typical 'mother-daughter' configuration.

Mrs. Shin led me down a short hallway to a small sitting room. I don't think I've seen many fat Korean women, and Mrs. Shin was no exception. For her age, she had a trim figure. As I followed, I found myself looking at her shiny black hair that Mother Nature had liberally flecked with gray. She smelled of sandalwood shampoo.

Two closed doors took up most of the rear wall of the room. I assumed they were to a bedroom and a bath. A wet-bar, mini refrigerator and electric hot plate on a modular kitchen cabinet provided her with a place to cook. The spotless apartment had no formal kitchen.

Steam emanated upward from the spout of an electric teapot sitting on the cabinet top. She poured two cups of black tea, and after a respectful interval, I began by telling her something I doubted she thought I knew.

"I am very sorry that you lost your daughter, Sung-Sook."

Her countenance turned from a patient, emotionless look to an embarrassed, painful one. I allowed her a moment and continued.

"The ladies she worked with said Rosie was a lovely girl. They liked her very much. I offer my sympathies to you and your family." I bowed for a brief moment to show respect.

She thanked me in Korean and went on to say, in accented English, that she heard it said on television that I had arrested the young man who killed her daughter and the Kyeung girl. I half expected some tears, but Mrs. Shin was a tough soldier. She presented a stoic persona even though her heart must have been broken.

Mrs. Shin admitted her ignorance of Rosie's intention to marry Prater McKendry. She explained that her family was ashamed of how Rosie had chosen to make extra money. In Korea, hooking on the side wouldn't be acknowledged, but rather silently tolerated by family members who knew it might be the only way to survive.

Trying to soften the blow, I reminded her that being a business girl in Korea was not a crime. In America, it was only a minor offense, not much more than a traffic ticket. I assured her that Rosie was not connected to other crimes such as theft or drug use as so many American business-girls are. Though I doubted it helped any, I felt obligated to try and mitigate her shame. Then I moved to a different topic.

"Shin, Pu-yin," I said, "I think your son has told you that he and I spoke last night at his house."

She nodded.

"We were looking for Mr. Boo."

Another nod.

"Your nephew, Mr. Boo."

"Yes." She sipped her tea quietly and didn't look surprised that I knew her relationship to Boo.

"He left his room at your son's house. No one knows where to find him."

"Yes." She settled the cup and saucer in her lap and nodded slowly.

"I think two things about your nephew, Shin, Pu-yin. I am not sure which is correct."

She waited without comment. I paused for a long moment and sipped from my teacup.

"Cho-Hung Boo is either in danger," I waited to let that sink in, "because the person who killed Mr. Park may also want to hurt him." Another exaggerated pause. "Or Cho-Hung killed Mr. Park and thinks he can escape us."

"Anyo!" she whined. "No, no, no! Boo, Cho-Hung not there when Mr. Park died. He leave early."

"Did Cho-Hung come back and kill Mr. Park?"

She hesitated, then shook her head and answered quickly, "Moo-la imnida. But he would not do that," meaning she didn't know, but doubted he would.

I left that one alone for the time being.

"I know that two women came to see Mr. Park the night before you found him dead—a blonde American and a Korean, both very beautiful—epun yeoja. Were you there when they arrived?"

She momentarily closed her eyes and then stared directly into mine. "Yes. I answered door."

I wasn't surprised that she hadn't told the Knoxville cops about my two girlfriends.

"Did you hear what they discussed with Mr. Park?"

"No, I stayed in kitchen."

I wasn't sure I believed that.

"Were you there when they left?"

"Yes."

The times jived with what Roni Keeble had told me. Mrs. Shin added that she went home shortly after the two women left. Mr. Park sat alone then, drinking and watching television.

"Was Mr. Park expecting anyone else that night?"

"He did not say. I do not think so."

"Who do you think killed Mr. Park?"

"I do not know. Mr. Park had many enemies...I think." She stopped abruptly.

I waited a moment before speaking. "There is no doubt that Mr. Ha was responsible for your daughter and other women becoming business-girls."

She dropped her eyes, shook her head and answered softly. "I-goo."

"Ha arranged for them to meet men at motels near the Knoxville airport in Alcoa. Ha kept more than one-half of the money the girls were paid. Do you think Mr. Park was the man behind that business? Was Park the honcho?"

She answered quickly. "I do not know these things."

I spoke slowly so she would grasp my next message. "I was told that your daughter asked Mr. Ha to allow her to stop being a business-girl. She wanted to get married. Ha said no. He *forced* her to stay in that business."

I made sure not to give up Chun-He as my informant. Mrs. Shin stared at me intently as if she were expecting me to disclose the meaning of Life.

I continued with, "Do you think this business had something to do with Mr. Ha's death?"

"These things, I do not know. I am...I *was* only Mr. Park's housekeeper. I think maybe Mr. Ha also had enemies." Her face took on a pained look. With her left hand, she slipped a few strands of hair behind her ear and sipped more tea.

"Shin, Pu-yin, forgive me, please, but Mr. Ha was the man who caused your daughter much trouble. And I think he caused you much pain. Were you and your son enemies of Mr. Ha?"

She nodded vehemently. "I disliked Mr. Ha."

"Did you know how Ha and Rosie were connected?"

"No."

"Did your son?"

"I do not think so."

Those answers were hard for me to believe.

"Did Mr. Boo know what Ha was doing to your daughter?"

"Ask Mr. Boo, please."

"Did Mr. Boo kill Mr. Ha?"

"You must ask Mr. Boo."

I should have anticipated that answer.

"I will, if you help me find him."

She said nothing.

"Right now, the Knoxville Police are looking for Mr. Boo," I said. "They think he killed both Mr. Ha and Mr. Park."

"Would never kill Mr. Park!" She was emphatic.

"Perhaps so. But those policemen think he did. I am not sure. They know Boo has a gun. They think he is a criminal like Park. He is a suspect in a murder investigation. You understand what that means?"

She nodded.

"If the police find Cho-Hung Boo and he tries to run, they may kill him because he flees."

"I-goo!" Her eyes contained tears, welled up and ready to release. Mrs. Shin appeared stressed to the max and about ready to lose it.

I leaned forward and placed my hand over hers. She didn't withdraw it.

"Yes, exactly. Some day the police will find Mr. Boo." I shrugged. "It is inevitable. If he talks to me, I promise, I will listen to his story. I want to know what he has to say."

She looked into my eyes, intently, as if trying to view my soul.

"I'll protect him. I promise you. Will you help me call Mr. Boo on the telephone?"

She thought about that for another moment, still looking deeply into my eyes, searching for that spark of truth.

"Just talk?" she asked.

"Yes, just talk. I assume he speaks good English."

"Yes, very good English."

"Okay, can we do this?"

"Yes, just talk on telephone."

I nodded. "Yes, talk only."

She got up and brought back a cell phone. I showed her the slip of paper with the two numbers I had.

"Which number?" I asked.

She pointed to the one I found on the US Cellular bill. She touched the keys. Someone answered. She spoke rapidly in Korean. I understood

186

only a portion of what she said. She handed me the phone.

"Yobosayo?" I used the standard Korean telephone greeting.

In return, I heard, "Nay, nugasayo?" He had asked who I was, but I assumed he already knew.

"Chief Jenkins, imnida. Chusayo, yongarul mal imnika?" I asked him if he would speak in English.

"What do you want?" His voice sounded much younger than I expected.

"You must know the Knoxville Police want to see you about the deaths of Mr. Ha and Mr. Park."

"I know nothing of Mr. Ha or Mr. Park being killed."

"You know they are dead. The police still want to speak with you."

"I don't think so."

"Believe me, it's true. The police will not stop looking for you. They will not go away."

No response.

"Things we have learned make us think you may have killed those men," I said.

"I killed no one."

"Mr. Ha caused problems and shame for your cousin Rosie Cho. You knew that. Ha was a bad man, and he hurt your family member. Mr. Park was Ha's boss. Maybe those men deserved to die."

"I killed no one."

"Then maybe Mrs. Shin and your cousin, Cho, Han-Me killed them. They were hurt by Mr. Ha, also, and maybe even Mr. Park. They would feel much shame, too. Maybe if you do not talk to us we have to arrest Mrs. Shin and Mr. Cho."

Boo probably thought I was a cold bastard.

He snapped back an answer. "You cannot. They know nothing."

"So you say. You are hiding, and that is not good. Why should I believe you?"

No comment.

I tried again. "Mr. Boo, you know where Prospect is. If you won't talk to me now, you can call the Prospect Police—anytime. But can I meet you? Sometime soon?"

He hung up abruptly. I turned my focus on Mrs. Shin.

In Korea, most people are apprehensive about dealing with the police; the national or local cops can be rather totalitarian at times. I know how people who are afraid of the police act. Sometimes I don't blame them because I understand their fears. I just can't understand why everybody doesn't love me.

I quickly decided only one thing would break Cho-Hung Boo from his hiding place—family loyalty.

"Mrs. Shin, I think you have to come with me."

She didn't argue.

"Please get your purse and whatever you need." I handed her the cell phone. "We have to stop and pick up your son before anything else."

Again, she offered no argument.

We drove to Oak Ridge, where I found Han-Me Cho working at his produce market with his wife and a Mexican helper. I persuaded him to accompany me to Prospect PD. He asked only one question—was he or his mother under arrest."

"No, we will just talk."

"Okay, just talk," he said.

Chapter Twenty

Once I got into the car, my first phone call went to Rachel Williamson's cell. She picked up immediately.

"I'm going to need you for something that's very important, very soon," I said. "Are you going to be home or somewhere I can call you?"

"I'm home now, but I'll leave for the station around four o'clock. What's up?"

"I'll tell you later. Answer your phone, please."

"I will."

"Can you send Leckmanski down to the PD right away?"

"Why do you need a camera?"

"Don't ask...yet."

"Sam, they won't send a cameraman all over just on my say-so, without an explanation. I need more information."

"I can't right now." I hoped she understood.

"Okay. You promise to call me again?"

"I will...soon. But for now, tell John to say he's going to lunch in Prospect or something like that, and have him see me. I'll only need him for a couple of minutes. I'll give him all the information you'll need, and then I'll call you. Trust me here. I'd never leave you hanging out to dry. Okay?"

"Only for you, Sammy."

"Thanks, kiddo. You're a peach."

"Yeah, yeah, yeah."

Next, I called D.W. Renfro.

"I'm going to do something that may cause your bosses to get excited. I'll call you with a heads-up shortly. I'll be at my office. Are you going to be near a phone?"

"Call the cell number I gave ya."

"Okay. With luck I'll need you and a few others as backup."

"Fer what?"

"I'll tell you later."

"No hints?"

"You don't want to know before it happens."

"Lord have mercy."

* * * *

I drove fast toward Prospect, using the Pellissippi 'Speedway' to leave Oak Ridge and pass through Knoxville and into Blount County. At eighty-five, I passed every car on the road, but they were also clipping along, well above the sixty-five-mile-per-hour limit, so my speed didn't seem that outrageous. When I glanced into the rearview mirror, Mrs. Shin and her son didn't look like they feared for their lives, so I pressed ahead and hoped the state troopers hadn't set up radar on the blind side of a hill just before the exit to Alcoa Highway and the airport. They often do, and I hate to grovel in front of one of the 'big hats' to get out of a ticket or a lecture.

I was lucky, sailed along past another two exits to where I got off onto Broadway and took the back roads to Prospect.

I ushered Mrs. Shin and Mr. Cho to the squad room, tried to make them comfortable and buzzed Bettye's phone.

"I've just brought in two people. They're not under arrest, but I want Gallagher to sit with them for a while. Tell him to make conversation, and get them to relax. He can ask them about Korean food. John will eat almost anything, so he'll act interested. I'll be up in a minute. I have a few phone calls to make"

"Oh, Sammy," she moaned like a disappointed mother. "What are you up to now?"

"Trust me. I know what I'm doing."

"I certainly hope so."

"Have faith, Betts. It's just a little scientific criminal investigation."

"Oh, Lord have mercy."

I told my detainees I'd order lunch for them and have tea brought in. Sometimes it's not all that bad being one of Jenkins' prisoners. When John took over, I went up front to explain the details of my cunning plan to Bettye. That took less than two minutes. She closed her eyes and shook her head only once.

Then I got back on the phone with Rachel.

"Can you get a special bulletin on the air as soon as Leckmanski takes his film?"

"I don't own the network, Sam. I'll need a good story to sell this to the station manager before they break into regular programming."

"You'd only be interrupting *Beverly Hillbillies* re-runs, for God's sake."

"What do you want me to say on this bulletin? It really has to be good."

I thought for a moment. An outright lie would be best, but it would damage Rachel's credibility with her boss. My wording would be critical if this was going to work. It took me a few seconds to answer. Rachel waited patiently.

"Okay, take this down exactly as I dictate it. The wording is very important—to you and me, and to those who hear it and may want to cause trouble in the next day or so. Don't change anything."

"Trouble?"

She paused for a moment, perhaps waiting for an explanation. I invoked my right to remain silent, and she finally gave up with a sigh.

"Are you ready to copy?"

She groaned before speaking. "Why do I let you get me into these things?"

"There's a reason, but I won't mention it. I'll only say it's because I'm your good buddy."

"Ha. Do you know how often I hate you?"

"You often tell me, and I know why you say that."

I might have heard a soft growl on her end of the line.

"If you were here, I'd punch you," she said. "You're such a creep."

I shrugged. "Yeah, fact of life. Okay, get all this down phonetically, and I'll give Leckmanski proper spelling for the Korean names when he gets finished with his camerawork. I'm ready, are you?"

"Yes, but not too fast. I don't take shorthand and don't have my *thingie* handy."

"My goodness, Rachel, it's an iPod."

"You are pushing your luck, mister."

"Surely you don't mean that." I didn't allow her time to comment. "Okay, tell me to slow down if necessary. Here's your text: The mother and brother of Rosie Cho, one of my murder victims, have been brought to Prospect PD on suspicion of complicity in the killings of Chang-Hai Ha and Hee-Chul Park. Chief Jenkins believes they thought Ha and Park were responsible for the murder of Miss Cho. Jenkins now knows that is not true, but because of the circumstances and Miss Cho's relationship with Mr. Ha, Rosie Cho's family may have blamed those two for her death and took action before knowing the truth. Knoxville PD has the open cases on the murders of these two men."

"And you're arresting them instead of Knoxville?"

"I'm not arresting them, but you can't say that. Leave it vague...that's the most important part. Okay?"

"Vague? News is not supposed to be vague. Tell me what you're doing."

I wanted to say, 'Inaccuracy never stopped a reporter before, so why is vague not permissible?', but I didn't want to annoy my ally before she did her part to help flush a killer out of a kimchee pot. I needed a show of blind faith from Rachel because time was a'wastin', but I could see her point.

"Oh, if I must," I sighed.

"Stop the act, please."

"I think Park's other hired hand, a man named Cho-Hung Boo, is the killer. Well, at least he killed Ha and maybe Park. He's disappeared, but I know he's close by. Earlier today, I spoke to him on the phone. Koreans are very honorable when it comes to family. If I make Boo think his aunt and cousin...Oh, I didn't mention that relationship to Mrs. Shin and Mr. Cho, did I?"

She interrupted me. "How in God's name can you keep all this straight in your head?"

"That's why I get the big bucks, doll-face."

It was Rachel's turn to sigh. And I thought she exaggerated for theatrical effect. "You love every minute of this, don't you?"

I chuckled. "Sure, police work can be lotsa fun at times. Anyway, if Boo, who's hiding out somewhere—probably killing time watching TV—hopefully your station—sees that his aunt and cousin have gotten collared for his crime, I think he'll call and turn himself in."

"Talk about a convoluted story. What makes you think he'll be watching NXX?"

"You get the best ratings. That's because you're the best looking woman on Knoxville TV."

"Oh, brother. You have some line of...crap."

"Me?"

"And this is your *best* idea to catch the killer?"

"What else can I do?"

"I can't imagine."

"Can we pull this off?"

"You mean can *I* pull it off, good buddy?"

"Well...yeah."

"You really have these two in custody?"

"Custody is too strong a word. They're in the squad room talking with John Gallagher. Then I'll give them lunch...and tea. If Leckmanski gets here soon it would look better if they were filmed without a Chinese lunch in front of them."

"I can see the production value in that detail."

"Good, I thought you would. Where's Leckmanski?"

"He's on the way. Are you going to serve him lunch, too?"

"I guess. A man's got to eat."

"You can't even imagine what you'll owe me for this."

"I am, madam, your most humble and obedient servant. Call upon me any time of the night or day. Your wish shall be my command."

"Oh, God, I hate you."

"No, you don't."

She hung up on me.

I dialed an extension in the squad room, Gallagher picked up.

"John, just listen, and don't say more than yes or no. Understand?"

"Yes?"

I explained the whole deal to him. "I'm calling over to Wah Lum for lunch. The Koreans would probably like Chinese food. Can I get you something without MSG?"

"Yes."

"What? You can say what you want."

He didn't answer immediately. "*Moo goo foo goo.*"

I sighed. "Does that mean Moo goo gai pan?"

"I guess so."

I buzzed Bettye and asked her about lunch. Now that she's on a constant diet, she's abandoned her former favorite sweet and pungent pork for Buddhist's delight with no rice, but that's too Spartan for me. As I made notes about lunch, John Leckmanski walked into my office. A heavy-looking camera bag hung off one shoulder and a big TV video camera balanced precariously on the other. He offloaded his gear and sat down without invitation.

Leckmanski is a cool customer. He's been around the block more than a few times. I trust and like him. But his wardrobe leaves something to be desired. He's one of those cameramen who feel obligated to always look like a combat photographer. His summer uniform consisted of an old Led Zeppelin T-shirt, six color, desert camo field pants and a Chicago Cubs ball cap.

"Officially, I really don't want to know more than what goes out on the air," he said, "but Rachel just called and told me what you told her. It's none of my business, but is what you're doing legal?"

"Actually, these folks are free to walk out at any time. And they know that," I said. "I'm not questioning them any longer, and they've not asked for an attorney. I'm not interfering with their free locomotion, so to speak. So, in answer to your question, yes, it's legal. Or more properly it's not illegal. I assume I'll raise a few eyebrows soon enough and get a few obscene phone calls, especially from someone in Knox County." I shrugged. "I think we'll make out quite well in the end. By the way, I was about to order Chinese takeout for everyone. Have you eaten?"

* * * *

I walked John Leckmanski to the back room. Gallagher sat near Mrs. Shin and Mr. Cho talking quietly. I felt sorry for the two Koreans. Speaking with John Gallagher could set their understanding of the English language back a decade. Mrs. Shin looked sad, a little confused, and like a proper lady. Cho just looked like a hardworking, blue-collar guy. Neither one your stereotypical one-shot-to-the-head killer type.

Leckmanski took some candid footage. John Gallagher knew not to look at the camera, and neither of the Koreans wanted to. They were not told why the film was being taken and didn't ask. In only a few minutes, Leckmanski completed the job.

He had declined my offer of lunch, so I looked at him seriously and said. "Go with God, my son. Ride…ride like the wind."

He didn't laugh at my attempted humor, but hefted the gadget bag and camera and shook his head. "And you're supposed to be one of the good guys?"

"Oh, ye of little faith, get outta here."

John turned and walked out our private back door, something no other news guy would dare try.

I called Rachel again. After a short discussion, she read me the copy that would be given to the daytime newscaster, a recently hired, thirty-something blonde who needed to smile more often.

"Super, exactly what I wanted," I said. "Now, let's hope our man Boo is watching."

"When I get fired for this, will you hire me as a policewoman?"

"That's a sexist title. I'll let you be a detective like Gallagher."

"Gallagher is a clerk-typist."

"Picky, picky, picky."

She said the bulletin would go on the air in less than an hour, and they'd repeat it every fifteen minutes. Later on, it was destined to be part of the regular news at 5:15 and Rachel's show at 6 o'clock. After Rachel hung up, I waited, but not for long.

The message first aired at 12:45. At 1:05, my phone rang, but it wasn't Mr. Boo.

"Moira Menzies for you," Bettye said. "She doesn't sound happy."

Moira is the chief assistant district attorney general for Blount County. She never sounds happy. After knowing her for a couple of years, I was convinced she had her period for twenty-eight days each month.

"Hi, Moira, you doin' all right today?"

"Just what the hell are you doing arresting two people in Knox County—without a warrant—for murders occurring in Knox County? The last time I looked, you do not work there."

"Nice speaking with you, too. Do I hear the sound of disfavor in your voice?"

"Goddamnit, Sam, I've just gotten a call from the Knox County DA after your girlfriend at WNXX put out that bulletin starring the one and only Sam Jenkins. A reporter at the News-Sentinel picked up on it right away and called the DA for an official statement. He, of course, called my boss. What the hell are you doing?"

"I understand Linda Crowley aired that story on WNXX. She and I have never met. I don't know what you mean about a girlfriend."

"Don't play dumb with me, mister. You know damn well what I mean. I'll ask again…what the hell do you think you're doing?"

"Right now, I'm eating a delicious red curry with chicken, vegetables and steamed rice. Mr. Lum at our local Chinese restaurant has added a few Thai specials to his menu. My new friends, Mrs. Shin and Mr. Cho, are sitting in the squad room with Detective Gallagher. They are also eating lunch. At my suggestion, Mr. Lum made something the Koreans would like, a spicy chicken with zucchini and yellow squash. Also with steamed rice. Only an American would ask for the salty fried rice they serve in most Asian restaurants, you know."

"Spare me your *feeble* attempt at *pathetic* humor, please. Do I have to ask the same question a third time?"

"The Koreans are not under arrest. They never were. We had a chat first, and they voluntarily accompanied me here for some free grub. Someone have a problem with that?"

"What?"

"The news bulletin, through no fault of mine or Ms. Crowley's, may have been misunderstood by someone who didn't listen *carefully* and may be prone to fly off the handle. Lawyers are sometimes like that, and

ADAs are no exception. If you heard it, I'm confident *you* would not have come to the same hasty conclusion that your counterpart in Knoxville jumped all over."

"You belong in jail."

"Surely you don't mean that. Let me continue, and I'm confident you'll see the wisdom in my actions."

"Humpf."

I envisioned steam escaping from her ears and her eyes rolling around like a slot machine. Moira is really quite attractive, but becomes unglued too easily.

I continued, "I'll paraphrase Ms. Crowley to make this quick, but I can give it to you verbatim if that's what you want."

She made no comment and waited for me to elaborate.

"The bulletin said that the mother and brother of murder victim Rosalind Cho were brought to Prospect PD under suspicion of complicity in the Knoxville murders of Messrs. Ha and Park. Period."

"That's it?"

"I never arrested them. I never questioned them after they got here. This was not a custodial interrogation. They never needed nor asked for legal representation. I just wanted to run a few ideas past them, and I have a terribly suspicious nature. You'd be surprised at what I think you're capable of."

"Don't smart mouth me, Sam Jenkins. I—"

A couple of bleeps interrupted whatever the ADA was about to say. Bettye had another incoming call for me.

"Excuse me a minute, Moira. I have another call. Don't go away."

"Sam, goddamnit—"

I switched to the call waiting.

"What are you doing?" I recognized the voice.

"Well, Mr. Boo, since you say you didn't kill either Ha or Park, and you are not willing to talk to me in person, I thought arresting your aunt and cousin for murder would be the right thing to do."

"You think my aunt is a killer?"

"She had motive, opportunity and a gun is easy enough to find around here. With the help of her son, sure, she could have killed both Ha and Park. I figure we should let a jury decide."

197

"Gae-sikee-ah!" He growled a derogatory remark that, by the way, is street-Korean for son-of-a-bitch.

I didn't take offense. "Of course, the expense of a good lawyer or two will mean a lot of cash. Maybe a guy like you who drives a big Cadillac would want to help them pay."

"Why do you do this?"

"Why do you think, chingo? You worked for Mr. Park. He was a genuine bad guy. You know the story. It's time for you to act like a man and take responsibility for what you did. Or you can hide and let your aunt and cousin, hardworking honest people, be punished for something you did."

He may have missed my entire statement, but objected to my use of the word *chingo*. "I am not your friend."

"Didn't you hear anything I said after that?"

He didn't answer. I tried again, speaking slowly.

"They killed no one." Boo sounded really angry.

"There is no reason for us to be enemies, Mr. Boo. We both know you killed Chang-Hai Ha. I think maybe Park, too. I caught you. It's time to pay for what you did. If you cooperate, I will ask everyone in Knoxville to go easy on you. Considering the circumstances, I'm not sure that I wouldn't have killed Ha myself—if I were in your place."

"You will let my aunt and cousin go free?"

"Of course. After you and I take care of business." I sighed. "I like your aunt and cousin. And I'll treat you like a gentleman. I promise. You and I can walk through this with dignity."

"I can come to your police station?"

Not a good idea.

"You tell me where you are, and I'll pick you up. Then we drive to the Knoxville Police station, but I'll stay with you. Agreed?"

"You are not lying?"

"I am telling the truth. An cuji mal."

"Can chom sumnida! It is okay then?"

"Yes, everything is agreed."

Boo gave me the address where he was staying in Knoxville. We agreed to meet in two hours or less, when I would call him again.

When I tried to get back to Moira, I found that she had hung up. I'd have Bettye call her back with the new information and forestall another hissy fit. I should offer Moira a free Chinese meal someday.

As soon as I cradled my phone, it rang again. Bettye was on the line.

"Sam, the mayor called down. He said the Knox County DA called him directly and wanted to know what you were doing making arrests in his county without tellin' him first. You'd better go upstairs and see Ronnie. He wasn't exactly mad, just kinda flabbergasted. Y'all know how he can get."

"I've got a couple of calls to make first. Then I have to leave immediately for Knoxville. First, you call Stanley, and get him here right away. Then call Ronnie back, and tell him if I have time, I'll come up and see him, but if I can't, he has to trust me. I'll call him as soon as I get this squared away. I really don't want Darnell to know anything about this. I don't trust him, and he may call someone and spoil my plans."

"You're gonna give the mayor a heart attack."

"Nonsense. That last call I got was Mr. Boo. He said he'd turn himself in...to me only. I'll pick him up in Knoxville and take him to KPD to process his arrest for at least one of the Korean murders. Call Kate for me, and tell her I'll be late for dinner. Got all that?"

"Lord have mercy, yes. Anything else you need?"

"Was that a note of sarcasm, Mrs. Lambert?"

She sighed. "Course not. You be careful, Sammy, you and the rest of the guys."

"You bet, Blondie. I'll call and let you know what we've accomplished when we're finished."

"Don't you call me Blondie."

I laughed, hung up and buzzed the squad room again. John answered.

"Call Freddie. See if he wants to go to Knoxville to arrest Mr. Boo for murder. Stan's coming in. We can all go together. Then call someone in from the road, somebody who'll work a little OT. He can sit with the Koreans until we have Boo in custody. After that, he can drive those two back to Knoxville and Oak Ridge."

"Can I say more than yes or no?"

"Yes."

"Okay, boss, I'll do it."

Then I called Renfro.

"Can you and Maples and maybe two uniforms meet me in about an hour? Boo says he'll surrender and admit to Ha's murder. I agreed to walk him through everything. You process the arrest at your place."

"Shoot, we only got two burglaries and a li'l ol' armed robbery to check on, but since it's fer you, sure why not? And since ya done already started makin' arrests on yer own, we may as well accept yer invite, don' ya think?"

I gently slapped my forehead. "I guess I forgot to call you about my slick plan to flush Boo out, didn't I?"

"Uh-huh. I guess ya did." He sounded a little annoyed.

"Now don't go getting excited, Dee Dubyah. I didn't arrest anyone yet. And don't get testy and don't believe everything you hear on the news. I'll explain all that later—to your boss if necessary. But for now, I'll see you at the corner of Southerland Avenue and Lebanon. There's a Korean grocery on the corner. You know where that is?"

"I do," he said.

"The house is down Lebanon on the right. Something Park owned. Meet us in the store parking lot, okay?"

"Okey dokey, we'll be there with bells on."

* * * *

Fred Mazzio was the first one to roll in. He was all smiles when he swaggered into my office in yet another Luau shirt, a green and yellow one.

"Hey, madman, you're goin' out to pick up that big Odd-Job-looking guy, Mr. Boo?"

"We are. He's too big for just me."

"I hear ya. When do we leave?"

"As soon as Stanley gets in. Come here a minute," I got up and walked across the room and opened the door to the evidence closet.

On the middle shelf, my Glock 19 lay in a holster with two extra loaded magazines in a double belt-pouch. I unbuckled my belt and slid off the holster holding my Smith & Wesson Combat Masterpiece.

"Here," I handed the Smith to Freddie. "You remember how to use one of these?"

"As good as you. Well...almost maybe. Can I carry concealed in Tennessee?"

"Not really, but it's okay with me."

"How about the rest of the cops in the state?"

I shrugged. "Who knows? I can probably get your sentence reduced."

"Heh, heh, heh, you're so good to me."

"I don't know why, but I am."

He picked up his shirt and started to unbuckle his belt.

"Can you find the buckle by yourself?"

"I'm not that fat."

"You want some help?"

"Shut up."

I put on the other holster, pushed the Glock into it and then snapped the magazine pouches onto my belt.

A few moments later, Stan Rose walked in and asked the inevitable question, "You think that big guy will go quietly?

"He says he will."

"And you believe him?"

"For lack of anything better to do."

"Oh, great."

"Got plenty of bullets?" Fred asked him.

He patted the holstered Glock hanging under his left arm. "Only need one."

"Oh, shit, another egomaniac," Mazzio said.

"You wearing that Steve McQueen shoulder holster again?" I asked.

"Sure," Stan said.

"You were born too late," I said. "They went out of fashion in the 1970s."

"I know," Stan said. "I should have been your partner when you were young."

"I'm still young."

Stanley laughed. "Not lately."

"See, Freddie, these kids have no respect."

Then John walked in.

"Hi, Boss. Hi, Sarge. Hi, Freddie." John looked like an overweight leprechaun in his green sport jacket. "I got Lenny Alcock to sit with the Koreans. I'll call him when we arrest the big guy, and he'll drive them home."

"Thanks, John. You're a brick."

"A what?" Fred asked.

"Brick, you swine, with a B."

"Swine?"

I ignored him.

"Ahóndele', amigos. Come, we ride," I said.

Chapter Twenty-One

The blacktop parking lot of Arirang Groceries consisted of cracks and patches upon patches. The sidewalk in front of the store suffered from its own case of the cracks, with each section tilted and uneven, moved drastically by the frosts of many winters. The high curbs surrounding the property were chipped, and in places, sections were missing. This did not look like the high rent district of Knoxville.

The Korean grocery store, in a former 7-11 or Piggly-Wiggly, was a low, single-story building of unmistakable design. Signs, taped to the glass, covered the front windows. One said, 'Yoju rice is number one rice.' I agreed with that. Another advertised a Korean brand of low-sodium soy sauce. Still another spoke of a Korean musical show to be held at the Tennessee Theatre in three weeks.

We found Renfro's white Impala facing toward the street, parked under a big oak tree. Three plainclothesmen sat in the car. A white and blue Knoxville PD cruiser, parked driver's door to driver's door next to the Chevy, held two uniformed cops talking with the detectives.

I pulled into the last spot near the corner of the store, walked over to Renfro's car and hopped into the back seat.

"Hey," I said, "did I miss the PBA meeting?"

"We're glad y'all are havin' so much fun," Renfro said. "Kinda feel privileged to be in-vited."

"Yeah, I love my job." I recognized Wit Maples sitting in the front seat, but turned to the officer next to me. "Sam Jenkins. How are you?"

"Howdy. Gabriel Earlywine. Good ta meetcha."

We shook hands. He had an intelligent face and a friendly smile. His dark crew cut had grayed at the temples.

"Gentlemen, how're you doin'?" I waved to the two patrol cops.

Renfro took over the introductions. "Driver's Billy Dean Hoskins. T'other one's Farley Deaton. Both good boys. Y'all kin trust 'em."

They were a pair of blonds in dark blue PD summer uniforms.

"I don't expect a problem with this guy, Boo," I said, "but it's always best to be prepared."

A bunch of heads nodded their agreement to that thought.

"How does this sound?" I asked. "Dee Dubyah, you, me and Stan Rose, the big guy with me, go to the front door. You four and the other two guys from Prospect cover the front and back. When we come out, we'll take Boo in my car and head for your squad room. I'll need somebody to give my two extra men a ride there."

"I'll do it in this car," Maples said.

"Boo's a big, potentially mean customer," I said. "He knows his aunt and cousin are in custody in Prospect. That's why he's agreed to surrender. Just keep yourselves safe here."

More nods.

"Well, I guess we better git'er done," Renfro said.

"Okay," I said, "third house down this street and on the right."

I got out of Renfro's car and quickly briefed the Prospect troops. We made the short drive and parked a safe distance from the house where Boo told me he was hiding.

It looked like a typical, one-story rental on the wrong side of town. Some misguided soul had painted the asbestos shingles avocado green with a lighter, but incompatible putrid green trim. It appeared as if the windows hadn't been washed since the end of the Korean War, and the sparse amount of grass on the front lawn hadn't been cut in months. An eclectic assortment of weeds poked up here and there between the scrawny foundation plants.

I called Boo's cell phone from mine. "We're outside. Are you ready to do this?"

"Yes, ready," he said.

I spoke slowly to avoid confusion and a possible problem. "So all these policemen don't get nervous, open the front door and stand there. Rest your hands on the door frame so we can see you don't have a gun."

"Okay, can do. Where is my aunt?"

"She's in Prospect. A policeman will drive her and your cousin home when I call and say you and I are together."

"Okay. Cho-sumnida." He thought all that was good.

"When you open the door, three of us will walk up to you."

"Can chana." He thought that was okay, too.

After Boo opened the door and assumed the proper position, we all took a deep breath and began the festivities. Boo had no tricks planned, and everything went off without a hitch. Stan, D.W. and I entered the house. Boo sat on the sofa and offered us tea. *What a guy*. I declined.

"We will talk later at the police station," I said.

He nodded.

"Do you have the gun?"

"Yes."

"Tell me where. We'll get it."

"On the bed." He gestured with his head. "In there."

"Just one gun?"

"I have only one."

"A .45 automatic?"

"Yes, .45."

Stan and Renfro retrieved the gun, a brushed nickel Colt with dark wood grips.

"May I see that?" I asked.

Renfro handed me the gun butt first. I dropped the magazine, pushed the slide to the rear and locked it open with the slide-stop. There was no round in the chamber. I looked at the bullets in the magazine.

"Hundred and eighty-five grain hollow points." I said, looking at Boo.

"Yes." He gave a quick nod.

"The same round killed Mr. Ha. Did you shoot him?"

"I will say what you want me to say."

I shook my head. "I want you to tell the truth."

"Yes, I killed Mr. Ha."

"When we get to the Knoxville police station, you can tell us the details."

"Okay, can do," he said.

"When we leave, four detectives will search this house. Will they find another gun?"

Boo shook his head. "No, no other gun."

I nodded. "We have to put handcuffs on you."

He gave another quick, single nod, stood up and put his hands behind him, as if he had been in that position before. His arms were so big I didn't think one pair of cuffs would reach from wrist to wrist.

"In front is okay," I said. "Sergeant Rose will do that."

Boo turned and thrust his hands out in front of him, palms together. Stan cuffed him, gave him a friendly pat on the shoulder and walked him out. Renfro and I followed.

* * * *

We sat in an interrogation room at Knoxville PD—Boo, Stan, Renfro and me. The uniformed cops went back on the road with my thanks. John and Fred were in the detective's squad room with Maples and Earlywine and anyone else willing to listen to their New York war stories.

Boo admitted killing Ha and dumping the body in I.C. King Park. He knew enough detailed information for us to believe that he was, in fact, the killer. The TBI ballistics lab would test the Colt Government Model automatic Boo carried and would no doubt match it to the two rounds taken from Ha's body.

Boo told us he learned about Ha's secret enterprise of using the three girls from Kisaeng Massage and several other Korean women, employed elsewhere, as out-call prostitutes. He knew about Cousin Rosie being involved, but could live with that because he thought it had been her choice. Hearing Ha brag about how he sampled the girls himself whenever he felt so inclined pushed Boo over the edge.

The big fellow never liked nor trusted Ha, whom he considered an opportunist and potentially disloyal to his employer and comrades. Boo, on the other hand, was an old-fashioned standup guy. He took his salary from Hee-Chul Park, and for that money, he gave Park one-hundred-percent loyalty. Traditionally, in the gangs of Korea, that was expected. Boo thought Ha was competent, but wasn't a team player. In Korea, you either play for your home team, or they expect you to ship out to

Pyongyang.

That still left us with one question: Who Killed Mr. Park? Boo said not him—emphatically. While Stanley and D.W. took a break and went for liquid refreshment—Boo had asked for an orange soda—I tried a little friendly casual conversation to find out why Boo remained so adamant in his denial.

"You used your gun and the hollow point ammunition to kill Ha."

He nodded slowly. His expression made me think he was trying to figure out why I began revisiting territory already discovered.

"Those Remingtons are good rounds," I said. "Hot ammunition, very efficient. Do you ever use other bullets?"

"No, those are good. Very fast. Very good."

I agreed with him and nodded with a smile.

"Where do you go to practice?"

"Practice?"

"Yes, shoot at targets."

He grinned. "Don't practice."

Ah, a real egomaniac. Even I practice. I abandoned my next question of did he use inexpensive military ball ammunition when he shot at paper targets.

"You were very loyal to Mr. Park, and you swear you didn't shoot him. Do you know who did?"

He shook his head for a long moment and then said, "No, if I know that, maybe I shoot them for killing my friend, Mr. Park."

I could understand his point.

"Was there someone who Mr. Park called his enemy? Someone in the same business maybe, who would kill Park to take over his area?"

Another shake of his head. "No, not here."

"But from someplace else maybe? From Los Angeles? Atlanta?"

"Maybe, but I don't think so."

"Mr. Park is special to you. Why?"

"He was like opa—like father."

"How long have you known him?"

"Many years, many—takusan."

"Can you explain more? Why was he so special to you?"

"Mr. Park good to my father—paid him money. When my father

died, Mr. Park paid money to my mother." He shrugged. "And he gave me job."

"Your father worked for Park?"

"No, Park owed father debt."

"Explain, please."

"You know Mr. Park was slicky-boy in Seoul?"

I nodded. "Yes."

"My father was taxi driver." He pronounced it tock-shee. "PX taxi at Me-pol-gun, Yongsan."

That meant U.S. 8th Army Headquarters at Yongsan Compound, Seoul.

Boo continued his explanation. "Mr. Park and his people all the time steal from Me-pol-gun—anything, all the time—make much money on black market."

"I remember the Itaewan black market—big money."

Boo smiled and nodded. "Umm, big money." Then he continued. "One night, Mr. Park bribe Korean security guard at main PX-ou to look away—let slicky-boys take refrigerators, TVs maybe. This guard only had to walk to other side of building and do nothing. But instead, he call his sergeant. They catch three slicky-boys. Not Park...three others. Guards call MPs. All slicky-boys go to jail."

Stan walked in and handed Boo a bottle of Sunkist. Boo nodded his thanks and wiped the bottleneck with his hand as if that would chase away any germs and then damn near drained the bottle in one pull. After that, he made a satisfied sound and continued his story.

"Mr. Park was not happy. The guard took his money and betrayed Park. Another night, Park goes to see this guard, a man named Yim. Park could never forget—bad for reputation. Park asks the man why he arrested three slicky-boys when he took money to look away."

He stopped for a moment to hold up the soda bottle and look at it carefully, but he didn't drink.

"Park offer Yim cigarette before Yim explain," he said. "When Yim light the tombay, Park shoot him." He poked a finger onto his forehead. "One shot—dead."

Boo sounded pleased with Park's efficiency.

"My father sitting in his taxi and saw this happen. But my father does not run away and tell American MPs. My father kept Park's secret. Park forever show thanks."

He drained the soda bottle, looked at Stan and nodded. "Umm, orangey soda number one. Com op da."

Stanley shrugged. "My pleasure. Want another?"

Boo shook his head. "No. Later maybe." Then he smiled.

Stan had made a friend.

Well, it was a story. Maybe Boo's affection for Park bred the greatest loyalty the world had ever seen. Who knows? Boo's tale and rationale may have been true.

"Look, Mr. Boo," I said. "You have admitted to killing Ha. I'm sure Detective Renfro could talk to his district attorney and make sure you got no extra punishment if you also pled guilty to killing Mr. Park. It's called concurrent sentences. You understand?"

"Yes, I know this. Didn't kill Mr. Park. Ha, yes. Mr. Park, no. I disliked Ha."

"Once we leave here, you can't get a good deal again. If we learn you killed Mr. Park you get two separate sentences—big jail time."

"Did not kill Mr. Park. I cannot say so."

I shrugged. "Okay, let's write a statement."

* * * *

After spending a lot of time with him, Boo was finally ready for formal booking and the identification process: mug shots and fingerprints. Wit Maples would show a new detective working that day the ropes, and they would take care of that. The rest of us sat in the squad room.

"I've got an armed robbery of a little restaurant up in North Knoxville I'm getting' nowheres with, jest in case there's more po-leece work y'all would like ta do here in my town," Renfro said.

"No, thanks," I said. "But I'd be curious to find out who killed old Park."

"You and me both. You git any more on that Audi?"

He didn't want to let go of that damn Audi, his only clue.

"As far as I can tell," I said, "that's a dead issue. From what I've heard today, I think I'm barking up the wrong tree, but I'll see if I can learn something more on that."

"Well, we 'preciate ya handin' over this arrest. Shore makes the bosses happy. Y'all ever need sumthin', give us a holler, hear?"

"Actually, I could use a favor. I owe a TV reporter something, and if you could give her a call and tell her the story of Boo's arrest before you send out a general press release that would sort of square things and get me off the hook."

"You'd really do sumthin' fer a reporter?" He sounded as if I had suggested playing Russian roulette, something a cop just didn't do.

I shrugged. He probably expected that. "Without her, Boo would never have called me and surrendered."

"I unnerstand. This reporter kinda set up that li'l sideshow fer ya."

"Yeah, exactly, a sideshow. Here's her name and number." I handed him a small slip of paper.

He read it and smiled. "Oh, yeah, I know who she is. Good-lookin' whoaman. I'd do her a favor, too, it was me."

I smiled too. "Uh-huh, here's your chance."

"Well, I'll git'er done fer ya. The loo-tenant takes care o' them press releases, and he ain't none too speedy. I'll call her when I git a minute. Thanks again, and remember what I tol' ya."

"You bet. It was my pleasure. Good doin' business with ya, Dee-Dubyah."

We all shook hands, everyone mumbled a few good-byes, and the four of us left. Outside Stan put his hand on my shoulder. I looked up to see what he wanted.

"Dee-Dubyah?" he said. "You sound like you've been hanging around Bettye too long."

"Just think what I'd sound like if you did your Uncle Remus act more often."

He showed an exaggerated grin. "Lor', Massah Sam, I jest cain't 'magine, I sho'ly cain't."

Not being able to let that go, I said, "I needs ta git home now, Stanley. Yessuh, I damn sho does." I jingled my car keys in the air. "Feet don' fail me now."

Chapter Twenty-Two

I drove back to Prospect, dropped everyone off in the parking lot and opened up the shop. The main lobby of the municipal building looked extremely dark; only an eerie security light mounted high on a lobby wall appeared visible from the main doors to the PD. Our reception area, where Bettye and John sit, languished in total darkness, as did the rest of our rooms, except for my office. It always makes me feel melancholy, sitting in a PD facility alone with most of my world in darkness. I called Kate to report in.

"Everything go off okay?" she asked.

"One Hangook gangster charged and booked for murder, Dano."

"Just like Hawaii Five-0."

"Almost. Park's murder is still open. I'll tell you about it when I get home. I'm in the office, almost ready to close up. But I need to call Ronnie before he has a stroke. And I'll make a couple more calls. Be finished in less than a half hour."

"Have you eaten?"

"Nothing."

"I shall take care of you, my love."

"I thought you wanted to feed me."

"Well, that, too. You're so bad—most of the time."

"You're too hard to resist."

"Oy, such a smoothie."

"I hope you've got plenty of ice handy. I'm going to want at least one tall, cool one."

"Plenty of ice, plenty of lime. I suppose I can rustle up a little gin and tonic to go with that."

"You're a good woman. Remind me to let you stay around another couple of decades."

"Smoothie doesn't begin to describe you."

"You're all heart, and cute, too. See ya later, alligator."

"Okay, Bill Halley. Say hello to the Comets for me."

My next call went to the Lambert homestead. "Hey, Donnie, how ya doin'? Your wife around?"

"Hey, Sam, you doin' aw rot today?"

They never wait for an answer.

"Bettye's rot here. Y'all hang in there."

I hung on, but only for a moment.

"Sammy, you okay?" she asked.

"Yes ma'am, just fine. Stan and the two fat boys are good, too. And everything went off without any bumps. Just wanted to let you know."

"Thanks for callin'. I'm glad you're okay. I don't mind sayin', I'm happy this arrest is over. Where are you now?"

"In the office. I've got another call or two to make, and I'll close up for the night."

"Need me to do anythin' for you?"

"Yikes. What an offer. There's no one else in the building, and you say something like that—I'm lucky I didn't have a heart attack."

"Oh, stop actin' like an over-sexed school boy. I was tryin' to be helpful."

"And I appreciate it. I'll go home now and dream about what you offered."

"Someone needs to beat the fool outta you, Sam Jenkins."

"That might be impossible, but someday, maybe."

"Darlin', did you wear your vest tonight?"

I knew that might come up. It usually does.

"What vest?"

"How many times have I asked you to wear that...damn vest when you go out to arrest a man like this Mr. Boo?"

"I know, I know. But it's hot, and it makes me look fat."

"See what I mean? With all due respect, Mr. Sam Po-leece Chief Jenkins, you can be such an idiot at times."

"Yeah," I laughed, "that remark just oozed with respect. I'll see you in the morning, Betts. Have a good night."

"You, too, Sammy. I'll see ya."

Third call: "Mission accomplished," I told Rachel. "Thanks to you and John Leckmanski. Another horrid murder is sol-ved, mon cheri, or my name is not Chief Inspector Clousseau."

I thought I heard a sigh of relief. At least I hoped so.

"Are you okay? Is everyone else okay? Where are you now?"

Rachel often asks multiple questions.

"Yes, yes, and back in the office. Did you get a call from a Knoxville detective named Renfro?"

"I haven't checked my office voice mail recently, but not yet. Why?"

"I asked him to call with the details before putting out a press release. In case he forgets, this is what happened...

Minutes later, she said, "I knew you'd find the killer. Didn't I tell you that?"

"You did. But I...well, Knoxville still has another murder to clear. I'm not sure where to go with that."

"Are you going to continue with their case?"

"I don't know. Well, yeah, maybe. I guess so. I'd really like to know who killed Park."

"Then you'll find that killer, too, Sammy—just like you found this one." She laughed. "I personally guarantee it."

"Oh, you do? Well, good for me. With a coach like you, I could solve all the mysteries of the last century."

"Maybe you could, lover. What are you up to now?"

"I'm going home, having a drink, or two and something to eat."

"Good. You deserve a rest. Have a good evening, and thanks for calling. Can I put this story on the air at eleven?"

"You should hear from Renfro before that, but if you don't, shame on him, air your story. And thank you for having faith in my less than conventional scheme."

"You're welcome. Will you call me tomorrow?"

"Yes, ma'am, soon as I think you're awake. I'll let you know how much trouble I'm in after I speak with the mayor."

We made a couple more non-business related remarks, not quite phone-sex as Fred suggested, but a little flirtatious, and then we hung up.

Finally, I made my last call. I knew the mayor was anxious to hear from me.

"Hello, Ronnie, did Bettye get back to you while I was in Knoxville with the KPD people making that arrest?"

"Sam, y'all are gonna drive me ta drink." He sounded slightly exasperated. "Ya know how many phone calls I got this afternoon? Lord have mercy. Y'all ruffled lotsa feathers this time, ya surely did."

"Yes, well, I guess some people have to learn how to take a joke."

"Now, I unnerstand y'all had Bettye let those two Ko-rean people ya had in custody go."

"They were never in custody, uh...per se. I never arrested anyone. The TV station sent my message out as I requested, worded the way I wanted." I slowed down and spoke very clearly so Ronnie would understand the finer legal points of my plan. "Those who jumped to conclusions never listened as carefully as they should have done. But, the real killer heard the newscast and called to turn himself in and save the other two Koreans—his family members—any hassle. That's why I asked Rachel to air that newscast. The killer is under arrest, after confessing to one of the outstanding murders."

"Lord have mercy, Sam. You do things in unusual ways."

"Desperate times call for desperate measures, Ronnie. Didn't Winston Churchill say that?"

"Do what? Yes, well, maybe he did. I'll have to look that up. By the way, Darnell told me ya coulda gotten us in real trouble fer what ya did."

I saw red. I saw stars. I cannot convey how...annoyed I got. "Pardon the expression, Mr. Mayor, but your new deputy is a child-like dipshit and doesn't know his ass from a hole in the ground. Don't use that numbskull as your legal advisor."

"Now, Sam, Sam, Sam. Darnell's told me that y'alls have gotten off on the wrong foot. He says he ain't very happy with ya."

I took a moment to allow the fumes to escape from my brain. "Ronnie, screw him. If he interferes with one of my investigations again, I'll arrest his ass for obstructing governmental administration. I don't take advice from a law student who can't pass the goddamn bar exam.

And don't expect me to act as his training officer. I coordinate everything with the chief assistant district attorney, and she seems to be quite happy with my actions." That may have been stretching the truth a little, but Ronnie didn't need to know all the gory details of my relationship with Moira Menzies. "May I respectfully request to keep that young bastard away from me, or I'll strangle his fat neck?"

"Sam, ya puttin' me between a rock and a hard place."

I thought, 'Tough shit,' but I said, "And I don't mean to do that. Just please tell him to slow down and not try to change anything in a police department that isn't broken."

"Change somethin'?"

"His words, not mine. He wants to check my paperwork before I send it to the courts."

"He said that?"

"Yes. And that's not gonna happen."

"Oh, Lord have mercy, Sam. Now, don't git excited. I'll see what he's got in mind."

"I'd appreciate that. But tell him to plan on pissing off. I'll kill him before allowing him to be part of Prospect PD."

"Okay, Sam, calm down. I'll take care o' this for ya. Don't you worry. Now, I'd appreciate a favor, too."

"Sure."

"Can I count on you to make a couple of phone calls tomorrow and smooth over all o' those feathers ya ruffled?"

"Yeah, boss, I'm a born diplomat. Give me a list and a few dimes, and I'll start calling."

"Y'all are okay, Sam? All of the boys are okay, too? No trouble with the arrest?"

I took a deep breath. "Everything's fine," I assured him.

"Good. Oh, one more thing a'fore I let ya go. I've seen a kinda, uh...what should I say? Uh...outgoin' an' loud feller hangin' around the po-leece d'partment last couple o' days. Feller who wears Hi-wiian shirts. He a friend o' yours?"

I snickered. "Yes, he is. I'll tell you all about him tomorrow. He's basically harmless...and sort of helpful. The women in the building have nothing to worry about. I promise."

215

"Okay, Sam. Thanks for the call. See y'all tomorra. Night, now."

* * * *

"I heard your name mentioned twice today," Kate said, as she sat on the green plaid love seat. "I saw John Gallagher, too, with a couple of not very dangerous looking Koreans."

The floor lamp next to her made the white streaks in her hair shine. Her big brown eyes were doing their share of sparkling, too.

"Ex-cel-lont, Kato." I winked at her. "How did you like my old show-the-false-suspect ploy?" I heard a voice much like Peter Seller's speaking to my wife.

"Didn't work on me," she said, sounding very Oriental. "I know your tricks, Inspector."

Who other than my wife can imitate Bert Kwok?

"Chief Inspector, Kato, my little yellow friend."

"Well, Chief Inspector, are you now ready for my old gin-and-tonic ploy?"

"Ah, yes—yes. Yes," I sighed. "Yes."

"You are so predictable, Chief Inspector."

"Not when I wear my hunchback disguise, Kato."

"Yes, your hunchback disguise…the one with the inflatable hump."

I squinted at her. "The very same, Kato." I took the first gulp from my gin and tonic and, switching back to a Long Island accent, said, "Anyways, my liddle yellah friend, t'anks ta you trackin' down Korean family connections fuh me, I waz able ta get anudder confession and the moidah weapon ta solve one more case. But da gangster Park's killer is still out there, and it beats the merd outta me who dat may be."

"Maybe Knoxville will get lucky and find him." She tucked Bert in for the night and sounded like Kate again.

"Probably not. It's up to me, really."

"You are so vain."

"Didn't Carly Simon say that?"

"She didn't know you."

"Hey, she's a New York girl. How can you be sure we weren't acquainted? She never identified the subject of that song."

"Then maybe it was you. You certainly fit the description."

"I'm not vain—just brilliant, talented, lucky...sometimes and fairly modest."

"Oh, pa-leeze."

"Don't start."

"That's my line, buddy boy."

"What was it you said about taking care of me?"

"Dinner first, Sambo."

"Always the romantic."

Chapter Twenty-Three

I walked into the office almost an hour early and only fifteen minutes after Bettye arrived. I knew Ronnie Shields would like to hear a full account of my exploits and how I intended to assuage those Knoxville politicians with ruffled plumage so, at nine o'clock, I'd call him first.

After I spoke to Ronnie, I intended to call Moira Menzies and try to smooth her over. She often annoys the hell out of me, but it's not a bad thing to have the chief assistant DA on speaking terms with you.

After Moira, I'd call one of the nitwits at the Knox County DA's office and schmooze them into a state of relative happiness. That's what I intended. Then my phone buzzed.

"Sam, Bobby's on the line," Bettye said. "He and Dallas are helping the county with a four car wreck on their end of the thirteen curves. One car went over that steep embankment, you know where it is, and two others rear-ended a rubbernecker. They expect to be there for some time."

"Oh, crap," I said. Not the way I like to start my morning.

Bettye continued. "Another deputy and a trooper are on the way to assist, but Bobby says he needs someone to pick up *those women*."

I laughed inwardly. "Those women?" I said. "What women would *those women* be?"

"Don't you mess with me this early, Sam Jenkins. You know perfectly well what women *those women* are—your blonde and her friends—*those women*."

"The only blonde who's mine, baby, is you. But I understand what you're saying. I'll take care of transporting Mrs. Keeble and her co-workers."

"I thought you might."

"Don't get catty, Mrs. Lambert. We've had this conversation before."

"I'm hangin' up a'fore I start cussin'. Yew do whutever yew wont, darlin'."

"You sound like such a hillbilly when you get mad."

"Yew are pushin' yer luck, mister." She hung up.

Women know how to put me in my place.

On my way out, I kissed Bettye on top of her head, told John Gallagher to make sure he told the mayor what I was doing and insure Bettye didn't boil over, and then I drove to Keeble Manor in the Yorkshire Dales subdivision of Prospect.

It had been two years since I'd last been in Roni Keeble's home. When we conducted the initial interview, Bettye took an instant dislike to Mrs. Keeble. Maybe it was something she said. Roni and I seemed to have gotten along quite well from the beginning.

At five to nine, I pulled into the driveway. After sniffing the fresh air and looking at the lovely landscaping, I rang the bell and waited. Then the door opened.

"Oh, hi, Sam," Roni said. "I was expecting Bobby and Dallas."

The widow Keeble wore a silky dark blue robe with a half million flowers embroidered directly into the fabric. Involuntarily, I wondered if she had anything on beneath it. Her hair and makeup were flawless, and as usual, she looked ravishing. I couldn't wait to see today's outfit.

"He's busy with that pesky police work we sometimes get into," I said. "Being the boss, I get to taxi all the pretty girls around when no one else is available."

"Well, aren't you sweet?"

Just her smile was worth eight-hundred an hour.

"I'm here to protect and serve you ladies."

"I'm the only one left this morning. Sunny and Chun-He drove in together a few minutes ago. They had a nine o'clock appointment scheduled today and couldn't wait for some handsome guy to show up. They promised not to stop anywhere and thought they'd be safe."

Their lives—who was I to argue?

"Then, madam, I shall be your private chauffeur. Whenever you are ready, I am at your disposal." I chose to speak with a dreadfully stuffy British accent.

She touched my shoulder. "Give me a couple of minutes, sweetheart, and I'll be right with you."

"Sure, pretend I'm not here."

She disappeared, toward the master bedroom, I supposed.

I wandered around on my own, looking at the knick-knacks and a few photos scattered around the living room. One 5x7 caught my attention, three soldiers standing together, shoulder to shoulder, all of them holding trophies and handguns. From the subdued insignia sewn to their obsolete olive drab fatigues, I assumed the picture was from the late 1960s or early '70s. One of the three, a staff sergeant, wore a Kozlowski nametape. Kozlowski was Roni's maiden name. I assumed he was her father. He looked taller and beefier than the other two NCOs, a good-looking guy with a big smile. It was easy to understand him having a beautiful daughter. In the photo, he held a Colt Gold Cup .45, the target model of the GI service automatic.

As I looked at the picture, Roni snuck up behind me. "Okay, Mr. Chauffeur, I'm ready."

I turned around and looked at her outfit, a watermelon-colored short-sleeved V-neck blouse, navy blue slacks and a pair of comfortable-looking flats. If she had been the receptionist at my doctor's office, I'd have made more appointments.

"I was just looking at this photo. Is the staff sergeant your dad?"

"He is. Mike Kozlowski, career soldier."

"I didn't know you were an Army brat."

"I wasn't really. My parents divorced when I was eight. Mom and I went back to Chicago, and Dad stayed in California. He was assigned to Fort Ord then."

"I guess this shot was taken long before he pulled the pin?"

"I think so. He served for thirty years, retired in '95 as a master sergeant, and settled in Havre de Grace, Maryland, not too far from Aberdeen Proving Grounds where he'd been stationed a few times."

"That's a nice post. They have a good museum there."

"It is. I never visited the museum, but went to visit him there occasionally."

"You remember a lot about the Army. I guess you two got along well."

"Oh, yeah." She showed me another big smile. "When I was a kid, I used to stay with him for a few weeks during the summers. He was a good guy. He and Mom just couldn't get along after a while."

"That's a neat gun he's holding. I guess he was a bulls-eye shooter?"

"Yes, he was on different pistol teams over the years. Somewhere along the line he was one of the top hundred something."

"The President's Hundred?"

"That's it, yes."

"Pretty good shooting. I'm impressed. Where's your dad now?"

"He was killed in a traffic accident six years ago. That gun, the flag from his coffin and a couple of pictures are all I have left."

"You have that gun...the .45 automatic?"

"Yes, he taught me how to shoot, but I never did anything by myself. Dwight was a fisherman. He wasn't into hunting or guns. But I couldn't get rid of it."

Things started racing through my mind. Park was killed with a .45 caliber military bullet. Roni's Gold Cup was a .45, well suited to shoot 230 grain hardball ammunition. The night Park was killed, a neighbor saw Roni's car sitting outside Park's home. She admitted being there. I hated to ask the first question that jumped into my mind.

My face must have changed, looked overly concerned, because she frowned and tilted her head.

"What's wrong? What did I say?"

I didn't answer directly, but after a long moment, shot a question at her. "Did you go back to Park's house after you and Sunny left him the night he died?"

A shocked look altered the beauty of her face. She frowned and snapped her answer at me. "No! Where did that come from? I thought that Park business was behind us. Why do you think that?"

"Park was killed with a gun just like the one you inherited."

She shook her head. "Oh, Christ! And that's the only gun like it in Tennessee? Give me a break, Sam."

I couldn't argue with that logic. "Of course it's not."

"But you still think I killed him?" She crossed her arms defensively across her breasts and tilted her head again. Her body language showed lots of frustration.

"I'm just asking."

"Damn it, Sam!" She didn't look pleased with me.

"That's not an answer."

"I can't believe this." She dropped her arms and placed her hands on her hips. "I already told you I had nothing to do with Park's death. Neither did Sunny. What's your goddamned problem?" Her tone sounded harsh, more than annoyed.

"I'd sure like to believe you, Roni. Will you show me your father's gun?"

"I should tell you to go get a warrant."

I really didn't need to hear that. "Oh," I sighed, "I love it when people think they know a little about the legal system. If you insist, I'll call my office and have someone get a warrant, while you and I sit here and stare at each other."

"I don't understand why you don't believe me. Why would I kill Park? He did nothing to me."

"He did something to your friend...and her three girls. This gun throws one more item onto my list of things to consider. Park's murder is still an open case. Will you show me the gun?"

"I can't."

"Explain that, please." I started to feel frustrated, too.

"I don't have it."

I closed my eyes for a brief second and shook my head. "I hope you're not going to tell me it was stolen during an unreported burglary."

She shook her head, but said nothing.

"We can clear this up in a day," I said. "If the gun doesn't match the murder weapon, you're home free. I'll offer a humble apology. I'll even get down on one knee. Once you accept, I'll be on my way. It couldn't be easier."

She closed her eyes for a moment and sighed. "Sam, can't you let this go? Park was not a good person. He was a bastard, a truly bad man. He hurt people, here in Tennessee and for most of his life. You told me that."

I didn't know how to interpret her last statement. "You can't go around killing the bad people of the world, Roni."

"Oh, Sam, I didn't." Everything about Roni and her recent attitude softened up. She stepped in very close and took my hands in hers. "And I don't have to tell you that I'd take care of you for as long and as often as you'd like. We get along great, and you know how I really like you." She smiled again, and I couldn't help thinking how well she was playing me. "It could be even better." She rested her hand on my chest. "No one would have to know, and please don't give me that Boy Scout stuff about being married and in love."

I shook my head. "I can't let this go, Roni, no matter what fringe benefits I might derive. I want that gun, please."

She backed up and became all business. "I said I don't have it."

I didn't think acting tough would get her cooperation. I kept my question soft. "Where is it?"

She shook her head, but again offered no answer.

"Please don't make me call for a warrant and a bunch of cops to search your house."

"I gave it to someone."

"Sunny?" Things became clearer.

She hesitated again. "Sam, please don't do this. Just let it go."

I took a turn waiting. I said nothing, just looked at her. She appeared uncomfortable with the silence.

"All right," she said with a sigh. "I gave it to Chun-He."

"Did she kill Park?"

"I don't know!" Roni was on the threshold of losing her temper. She raised her voice much too loud to answer that simple question. "I didn't know what kind of gun killed Park until you just told me."

"Jeez, Roni. You're trying your best to protect her, and it sounds like you think Chun-He may have killed Park. And you gave her the gun to do it."

"I gave her a gun to protect herself. She's a nice kid, Sam. And her two roommates were murdered." Her volume dropped back to a friendlier level.

"I remember. Look, someone's going to answer for Park's murder. I don't want it to be you or Sunny. Maybe Chun-He has a good answer, a good reason. Maybe she was justified in what she did. Maybe she didn't do it. I won't know until...I take the gun away and talk to her. Is she on the run?"

"On the run? I don't think so."

"Where is she now?"

"Like I said, at work, with Sunny."

"Does she have the gun with her?"

"I doubt it. The purse she took this morning wasn't that big." She ran a hand through her blonde hair, almost desperately, messing up the work she did before I arrived. "This isn't some kind of conspiracy, you know."

I have a hard time browbeating someone that beautiful.

"Where's her room?" I asked. "It's your home. Give me permission to search her room."

After asking, I reconsidered that idea. If Roni gave her a place to stay, Chun-He had a basic expectation of privacy in that room. At least the courts would think so. Technically, I should obtain a search warrant to toss Chun-He's temporary dwelling for the gun and ammunition. But, did I, at that point, have probable cause to believe Chun-He used a borrowed gun to kill Park? I didn't think so.

My knowledge that a gun *similar* to what Roni loaned Chun-He was used to kill Park amounted to nothing more than a proven fact. The idea that Chun-He used Roni's gun to kill Park was only a possibility, my suspicion. I couldn't put Chun-He at Park's home during the time of the shooting, and I didn't know of a good reason why Chun-He may have wanted to kill Park.

If I scooped up the gun first and then confronted the girl, even if she confessed, the gun would be suppressed as evidence at a hearing because it would have been a bad search. Her confession could be recanted at any time, and no gun meant no match to the bullet in Park's head. Things they call 'fruits of the poisoned tree'. I knew all this from experience, not any legal assistance from Darnell "Shit-for-brains" Means.

Again, I saw a need for more unconventional thinking.

"Forget what I just asked. I don't want to see the room yet. Does the gun you gave Chun-He still look like the gun in your dad's photo?"

"Yes, I guess so. Sure, I think it does. Why?"

I held up a hand to stop further conversation and used my cell phone to call Bettye.

"Do we have anything important going on at the moment?" I asked.

Roni looked at me, expecting an answer to her question and probably wondering what I was up to.

"Bobby and Dallas are almost finished with the wreck I told you about," Bettye said. "Junior is handling a stolen bicycle call, and Will is out patrollin'. Why?"

"Send Will to my house. I want him to pick up my Army .45. I'll call and tell Kate where it is. Have Bobby and Dallas come to Mrs. Keeble's house as soon as possible. I want them to sit in her guest room and be sure no one goes in or out. As soon as he gets here, Mrs. Keeble and I will be driving into town. I'll talk to Will on the radio. He can meet us behind Kisaeng Massage in the town parking lot. And one last thing, tell me again what kind of car Chun-He Lee drives."

It only took Bettye a minute to come back with an answer.

"Chun-He Lee owns a red 2007 Kia Optima, Tennessee tag HKS-537."

"You're sure it's red?"

"That's what the registration information says."

"It's unusual for a Korean. Red is an unlucky color."

"Can I assume it may be her unlucky day?"

"Maybe. I'll let you know. What else are you doing for me?"

"Sending Bobby and Dallas to the Keeble house and Sparks to your place."

"Yes, ma'am, perfect. Thanks."

"You need more help than Will?"

"No, he'll do just fine."

"You be careful, Sammy."

"Always, Betts. Thanks again. Gotta go."

I called my home number. Roni didn't seem to be getting any more impatient as she watched me work.

"Kate, listen carefully. This is important," I said. "Go downstairs to the safe, and look on the third shelf from the top. There are two black plastic cases. Take the GI .45 in the larger case. Stick one of the magazines into it, and give it to Will Sparks. He'll be there in a few minutes. You know which gun I'm talking about?"

"Sure, I know what an Army .45 looks like. Can you tell me what you're doing?"

"No time right now. Oh, give Will a new Ziploc bag big enough to hold the gun. I'll call you as soon as I can."

"Okay, love. One GI .45 with a magazine and one plastic bag coming up."

"Thanks, kiddo."

"You be careful if there are guns involved."

"Yes, ma'am, just for you."

"I love you, Sammy."

"You, too, Kats. See ya later."

My Army .45 wasn't a Gold Cup, but I had added new sights and spruced it up from the out-of-the-box gun I bought years ago. It would probably fool Chun-He into thinking it was the same gun she received from Roni. At least I hoped it would. I looked back at Roni Keeble.

"All the girls tell you to be careful, don't they?" she asked.

"Yeah, I guess some women have that motherly instinct."

"Sure, right. I don't think Chun-He took the gun with her, but since you're determined to go through with this, I'll say it, too. Be careful, please."

"Thank you, Roni, I will. Now, before we leave for town, why don't you go powder your nose or do whatever girls need to do before they hit the road. Don't hurry. We have to wait for Crockett and Finchum to show up."

She frowned. "I don't have to *powder my nose*."

"Sure you do. It will probably take you ten minutes if I'm not mistaken."

She nodded. "Okay." I think she knew what I had in mind. "But I don't know why I should help you."

"Because you're a good person, and this is the right thing to do."

"Do you get sick of being right all the time?"

I smiled the shy little boy smile I practice in front of the mirror for such occasions. "Yeah, it's a curse."

Even that serious situation didn't dampen the million-dollar smile she gave me. "Tell those two if they want to guard Chun-He's room, it's upstairs to the right, second door," she said, being more helpful than I expected.

"Thanks, I'll tell them." *And thanks for the tip.*

She closed the door to the downstairs bathroom.

I took the steps two at a time. I didn't have plastic gloves so I used a handkerchief to open the bureau drawers. I did it the quick way, like a burglar, starting at the bottom so I didn't have to waste time and close them before opening the next.

I suggested the powder room thing because I didn't want to put Roni in a position to testify that she saw me searching Chun-He's room before I obtained a warrant.

When I got to the top drawer, the last one—it's always that way—I found the pistol beneath a couple layers of clothing. It was still cocked, but at least the safety was on. I picked it up by the checkered walnut grips with two fingers. Using my hankie again, I pushed the magazine release and caught the clip in the cloth. It was quite a juggling act. The ammo loaded in the clip, and the bullet in the chamber were copper jacketed, 230 grain, military ball rounds.

I replaced everything and went back downstairs, feeling a bit more confident with those tactics and just a little safer.

Roni Keeble was a sharp piece of work. She waited until she heard me walking on the first floor before leaving the bathroom.

"Well," she said, "I guess I needed to powder my nose more than I thought."

"You know these things when you get to be my age."

"I'll bet."

"Do you know what Chun-He's car looks like?"

"I've seen it before, yes."

"Is it something like yours?"

She thought for a moment.

"Sort of. It's the same size, same color. Both have four doors. I guess you could say that."

Unsure of what an '07 Kia Optima looked exactly like, I planned on finding out.

"Okay, then," I said. "I think I just heard the police arrive."

* * * *

The weather had turned surprisingly cool. A Canadian cold front and a jet stream dipping all the way down into northern Georgia brought us overnight temperatures in the fifties. I loved it.

After leaving Bobby Crockett and Dallas Finchum sitting in overstuffed easy chairs, reading magazines in Roni's living room, she and I took a short walk to my car sitting in her driveway. I held the passenger's door open, and Roni got in without a comment on either the weather or my chivalry. I fired up the engine and began our trip.

"Beautiful morning, isn't it?" I asked.

"The weather is, yes," she said, obviously not in the mood for small talk.

I had just accused her of murder, and for all she knew, I might be planning to arrest one of her co-workers. I'm basically selfish, but even I couldn't blame her for not holding up one end of the conversation.

At 9:35, the thermometer on the Ford's dashboard told me the air temperature was sixty-two. Roni wore a lightweight cardigan to ward off any cool breeze. My summer sport jacket felt just right.

During her powder room interlude, Roni touched up her self-tousled hair and reapplied lipstick that needed no attention. She was the most demure looking ex-hooker I'd ever seen, more like a lovely actress playing a girl-next-door role. She seemed content to make the ten-minute ride in silence.

We passed Ginty's used car lot. The portable sign at the road announced: *Consignments! Let us sale your car.* Colloquial pronunciation generally trumped the rudimentary rules of spelling and usage.

Just a few hundred yards down the road, I noticed that Prospect Bottled Gas had added a new sign. In front of the large submarine-shaped propane storage tank, a white, four-by-eight sheet of plywood with red block letters told me, *Jesus Loves You!* Perhaps He knew what a nice guy I was.

A handful of tiny, high altitude clouds dotted the otherwise clear and startling blue sky. The contrail from an airliner recently launched from nearby McGhee-Tyson Airport striped the sky as the plane flew northward.

The digital thermometer on the Prospect Citizen's Bank confirmed the sixty-two-degree temperature, and a continuous strip of electronic information, scrolling above their weather report, quoted the interest rates on various types of loans. All dreadfully interesting, but I started getting uncomfortable with the silence.

"It's nice and cool now, but it's supposed to get into the eighties by late afternoon," I said.

"Yes, I heard that on the weather this morning."

"That doesn't sound too bad, but I hate the heat."

"My dad said the same thing when he came back from Vietnam."

"A lot of guys disliked heat and humidity after a year over there."

"I can imagine."

I paused for a few seconds, but couldn't keep myself from saying, "No, you probably can't."

She turned her head and looked at me. I saw an expression of understanding in a pair of blue eyes that shined like polished lapis.

She flashed a brief and crooked little smile. "I suppose so."

I bounced over the speed bump blocking the entrance lane of the municipal parking lot behind the massage parlor and found a spot fairly close to the rear entrance of the business.

Sunny Kim's Black Honda Accord sat next to Chun-He's Red Kia. Again, I remembered John Gallagher's comment about Korean girls buying Korean cars—*calvinistic*. Sunny was an exception. I'd probably use John's word so often in jest, I'd forget that *chauvinistic* was the proper thing to say.

Looking at Chun-He's car, I realized that an '07 Kia had lines very similar to Roni's Audi, same rounded corners, same size and styling. Auto industry designers weren't above borrowing ideas from the competition. Renfro's witness may have confused the two cars in the dark. Roni and I sat quietly and waited for Will Sparks.

"Prater McKendry was a nice young man, wasn't he?" I asked when the silence again bothered me.

"He seemed like a nice boy, yes," she said. "He was quiet and polite. Did a good job, I guess."

"Chun-He seems nice, too. Charming girl, pretty, a lot like you and

229

Sunny."

She turned and looked at me again. "Where are you going with this?"

"I just want you to know I can't let every nice guy or charming girl go free if they commit murder. If they had a good reason to do so, one that the law recognized, and they tell the jury a compelling story, they either go free or that story is considered at sentencing. I don't mean to lecture you on the criminal justice system. I just wanted you to know that."

"It matters to you what I think?"

"I guess it does."

She considered that for a moment. "It sounds like you've been thinking about what you've just said for a while."

"Maybe."

"Sounds like an issue."

I hesitated answering and thought of my first case in Prospect. "Yeah, maybe."

"Oh."

Will Sparks pulled up and parked in the row behind us. He and I got out of our cars at the same time. Will handed me the black pistol case. I opened it and took out my combat .45. I checked to see that it was unloaded, re-seated the empty magazine, then dropped the gun into the plastic bag and slid the Ziploc across the opening."

"I ain't even gonna ask what y'all are doin'," he said.

"That's a good idea."

Will rolled his eyes, and I wrapped the loose plastic around the gun and slipped it under my waistband at the small of my back, under my navy blue blazer.

"Thanks, partner," I said. "I want you to hang out here a bit. I'll call and let you know what's happening."

"You got it, boss. I'll be right here waitin'."

Even in a sharp khaki and green police uniform, Will looked like a thirty-year-old version of Opie Taylor.

I opened the car door for Roni.

"Let's take a walk inside," I said.

She swung her legs out of the Ford and stood up, but still didn't look happy. She tried to pull off a half-hearted smile and started toward the back door of Kisaeng Massage.

The time for confrontation loomed close at hand, and Roni must have been uncomfortable thinking a co-worker and friend may soon have her life changed immeasurably. I thought killing Park may have already done that to Chun-He.

Chapter Twenty-Four

Roni opened the back door before I could, and we entered, walked the full length of the hallway and stopped in the front room.

We found Sunny sitting at the reception desk turning the pages of a recent *People* magazine. Immediately, she seemed to sense it was not going to be one of those average mornings. She looked at Roni and then at me.

"What's wrong?" she asked.

Her furrowed forehead and downturned mouth gave away her apprehension.

"I need to speak with Chun-He," I said. "Is she with a patient?"

"Yes, Mr. Suttles came in at nine o'clock."

I looked at my watch; it was 9:45.

"What time does she finish?"

"Ten o'clock, maybe little later. What is wrong?"

Sunny seemed to be getting upset; her Korean accent sounded more pronounced.

"I think Chun-He killed Mr. Park," I said.

"No! Why would she do that?"

"I don't know. I'll have to ask her."

"No!"

"I think so. We'll see. Can you take over for her? Tell Mr. Suttles it's an emergency."

"No, not Chun-He."

"Please," I said. "I won't bully her. I promise."

Sunny nodded reluctantly, got up and walked toward the treatment room, shaking her head.

Roni took a seat at the reception desk. I looked at the nearest painting on the wall. A pretty Korean girl wearing the traditional two-part dress, the chi-ma and chogo-ri, sat in a park-like setting, playing an ancient-style drum, the changgo. I thought it was too bad Chun-He wasn't destined to just sit around, like a kisaeng girl, tapping out her own version of *Arirang,* the Korean national anthem, on a changgo.

A few minutes later, Chun-He met me in the reception area. I took her into Sunny's office and left the door open. Roni remained at the reception desk.

No other patients were present and no additional morning appointments scheduled. Chun-He sat. I remained standing.

I advised her of her rights in a friendly but businesslike manner. No matter how kind I try to sound, that's a shocking message to an average person.

"Why do I need lawyer?" Her accent thickened immediately. She sounded frightened.

"Because I think you shot Mr. Park." Using the word *shot* sounds less serious than killed.

"No! Why do you think that? I shoot no-body."

"Do you want to talk to me now, or do you want a lawyer?"

"No lawyer. I do nothing wrong. Don't need lawyer." She sounded a little defiant.

"Okay, but let's stop the 'I did nothing' story. I looked in your room, and guess what I found?"

She gave me a hard stare. Her dark, almond eyes narrowed to tiny slits, and for the first time, she looked a little sinister.

I took the gun from under my coat, smoothed out the plastic bag and laid it on the desk. Her eyes widened. Her expression changed. I received her undivided attention.

I continued to speak softly, without threat. "I'm going to have the FBI test the gun and match one of those bullets to the bullet the doctor found in Mr. Park."

I lied about the FBI doing the test, but from experience, I've always thought Koreans were overly impressed with the mystique of the FBI. I doubted Chun-He knew who the TBI was. They would actually conduct the test.

"*Effu-V-I?*" she asked with a horrified look.

"Yes, FBI, the best. They never make a mistake." I wished Ralph Oliveri could have heard that.

"Why are you doing this?" she asked. "Mr. Park was bad man."

"Yes, Park was a bad man. I know that. And you are a nice young woman. If you tell me the truth, now, with no more lies, I can help you."

She listened closely, looking at me intensely while I spoke.

"I can talk to the district attorney and the judge and say you cooperated." I paused because the next part was important for her to comprehend. "I think maybe you had a good reason to shoot Mr. Park. And Mr. Park was a very bad man. If you talk to me, you can tell your story. Tell everyone just how bad he was."

Her beautiful eyes searched my face, probably wondering if I was telling the truth.

"Tell me your reasons," I said. "Then we can tell everyone what bad things Mr. Park did. Maybe Park tried to do something bad to you?"

I watched as she lipped the words I spoke. She followed me very carefully in her own way and began nodding after my last sentence.

"If you refuse to say anything, Chun-He, I have to show the judge the gun that killed Park, tell him you had it, and you won't explain your reasons. People will just see you as a killer. They'll think, maybe, you had no good reason. Please, Chun-He. Let me help you. You're a nice girl. You need to tell people your story."

Her face hardened, and she shook her head. "You know I was business-girl. You don't think I am nice girl."

I sighed and genuinely wanted her to understand. "That's not true. Sometimes people must do things when they have no other choice. Ask Sunny. Ask Roni. They know I don't think like that."

"I want to see Sunny, please." She started blinking rapidly, swallowing more often than necessary. Her tension showed.

I shook my head. "Not yet. Tell me the truth first. No truth. No Sunny. No truth. I put you in jail until the FBI tells me your gun killed Mr. Park. Then no more time for deals. No time for help. You go to jail with no friends."

She shrugged. "I go to jail anyway. How long?"

"Tell me your story first. The law is complicated. When I know *why* you shot Mr. Park, I can answer better."

"You will help me? Honest? No lie?"

"I'll help if you cooperate. Honest. I promise. I have no reason to lie."

She thought for a long moment, stared at me, ran a hand over her mouth, and then dropped her eyes again, sitting perfectly still with both hands laying palms down on the desktop.

She had used pink nail polish to match the pink knitted top she wore. Suddenly she shrugged again and began her story.

"Late that night, I drive to Mr. Park's house-su. I see Roni's car there. I don't know why she is there. I want to go in, but I wait. Then I see Sunny and Roni leave. I hide so they don't see me."

I never take notes when a suspect goes on a roll. A cop feverishly jotting down statements tends to stifle the free flow of information.

"Short time later, I see Korean woman leave and drive away in little blue car that was parked in driveway.

"Then I park my car where Roni's car had been. I go to door, and Mr. Park let me in." She paused for a long moment to collect her thoughts. "He take me to his back room, and we sit. He all the time smiling. Make me takusan uncomfortable…Very uncomfortable. Very. Then he offer me whiskey, but I say no. We talk then." She paused again and raised her stare to meet mine. Tears welled up in her dark eyes, just waiting to cascade over her cheeks.

"What did you talk about?" I asked.

"I ask him, 'What happens now that Mr. Ha is dead?' I say, I need money. Have no roommates any more to help with house-su money. I need money for my sister. Mr. Park, he say, I need money so bad, I go back to Oak Ridge and work. He say…"

The more she spoke, the more excited she got. She began twisting her hands, and a few tears rolled over her high cheekbones, carrying a trace of black eyeliner downward. She started talking over my head, making little sense. I interrupted.

"Chun-He, slow down. Please. Everything is going to be okay."

Easy for me to say.

"Start at the beginning. Talk slowly. Let me ask you a few questions. I don't know anything about Oak Ridge. Tell me about that first."

"The beginning? You mean when I come here from Korea?"

"Sure, why not?" *I'm easy.*

It appeared to be an effort for her to make the words come out.

She nodded for a few seconds. "My brother work for Mr. Park. Not paid gompay like Boo or Ha, but he work for Park, too. My brother, he help me come to America, but I don't know he is man like Park. I must have job to stay here, so my brother get me job in massage place at Oak Ridge. But not real massage place like here—sex only, all the time sex."

She stopped and hung her head again. It wasn't easy for her to admit what her life had been like, and what her brother had done to her.

I watched two small flies buzzing around the room. Occasionally they would land, on a file cabinet, on the desk where Chun-He sat or on the walls.

"Is that where Park wanted you to go back and work?" I asked.

"Yes, Oak Ridge, near big highway. All the time truck drivers come for sex. Oak Ridge massage place owned by Mr. Park."

"What's your brother's name?"

"Lee, Jin-Ho."

"Does Jin-Ho run the massage place?"

"No, Miss Yang, Yang, Su-Dae is manager."

We were building a cast of thousands. I needed a scorecard.

Chun-He's story of Jin-Ho selling her into prostitution wasn't exactly a shocker, just one of those things you don't forget.

Briefly, I found myself back in Korea, in the early summer of 1970. I had parked my jeep on a side street just off the MSR, a main supply route, between Yongsan and the village of Itaewan and beyond, where an old-fashioned market hummed day and night. I needed a birthday gift for my wife and the jewelry vendors there were always ready to bargain.

After chaining the steering wheel to the brake pedal to keep the slicky boys from boosting my ride, I started walking toward the market when a kid, no more than eight-years-old, stepped up beside me.

He asked, "Hey, GI, you want cherry-girl?"

I shook my head, but like all the mini-pimps of the area, he displayed persistence not unlike a hawk waiting on a branch above an unsuspecting chipmunk.

"I give you number one cherry-girl, mister, number one! Only five-hundred won."

These kids knew as much about the U.S. Army as the average draftee. He pointed at the rank insignia on my collar.

"Only five-hundred Won. You officer, you can afford. Cherry-girl, my sister, you be first, I know for sure. Only five-hundred Won." The little weasel sounded sincere and desperate.

I remember a wave of sadness washing over me. The kid would sell his sister for less than a buck-and-a-half. I shook my head and fished a hundred Won note out of my pants pocket. I handed it to the kid and told him, "Kada!" Get away.

He turned and began to run. Then, over his shoulder, he called out, "Thanks, GI. You number one," and he broke into a sprint, probably heading somewhere to try his act on another horny soldier.

I came back to the present and resumed my conversation with Chun-He.

"Okay," I said, "go back to your talk with Mr. Park. What did you ask about the arrangement you had with Mr. Ha?"

She took a deep breath and let out a sigh. "I say I have to still do. I maybe get more girls like Rosie and Kum-Ok. I tell him I can do Mr. Ha's job. I *need* money for my sister. If I do Mr. Ha's job, I should get same money."

Somehow, I didn't think Park was an equal opportunity employer.

"Why did you talk to Mr. Park if Ha was running the business girls himself?"

"What I say before not true. Mr. Ha does not do all by self. Nothing Korean happens here without Mr. Park saying okay. Nothing. Mr. Park must get some money all the time from everybody who has business."

"So Park *was* involved with Ha's business girls all the time?"

"Yes! Mr. Park *do* nothing, but still get money from Mr. Ha."

"What did he say to your idea?"

"He say forget Prospect. I can work, but for him in Oak Ridge. Plenty customers. Plenty money. But I could not have own business, just

237

work like before. He say I am very pretty. Men would ask special for me after they know me, pay more for me. More customers, more money."

"But you never wanted to go back to Oak Ridge?"

"No! Oak Ridge job is number ten! No good!"

More tears rolled down her right cheek. Her eye makeup was a mess. She looked like a pathetic little girl who had used her mother's cosmetics and gotten caught.

"Truck drivers not like businessmen at motels," she said. "Sometime not clean, not nice. Drunk maybe. Sometime drugs. You know."

Chun-He whined out her answers showing the stress and emotion she felt. Still more tears came. I picked up a box of tissue from the top of a file cabinet and placed it on the desk near her hand. She pulled out a pair of Kleenex and wiped her cheeks, dabbed at her eyes and looked at the smears of black on the tissue.

"I cry too much," she said. "Now look ugly."

I shook my head. "You look fine. Never ugly. Take a minute and relax."

The pair of flies landed on the desktop again. They stood face to face, both rubbing their front legs together. They looked like two bantamweight wrestlers facing off against each other.

Chun-He sniffed a few times and took another deep breath. "Okay now."

"What did you say then?" I asked.

"I say I don't like Oak Ridge. Oak Ridge job is no good. I stay with Sunny and get second job maybe. Make more money. Maybe give up house-su. Sleep here." She pointed toward the floor. "Maybe sell my car. I don't know. Oak Ridge is bad!"

"And what did Mr. Park tell you?"

"He laugh. He say why do I think I have choice? He say Prospect is over. No money in Prospect. He say *you* are too much trouble, Mr. Sam. He say I go to Oak Ridge. Have no choice."

Her voice cracked with the last sentence, and she stopped again to wipe more tears from her cheeks.

"And what happened next?"

"I say no."

"He didn't want to hear that?"

"No. He say if I not go to Oak Ridge, okay, but then my sister must work at Oak Ridge. I say, please, my sister only seventeen-year-old, still in high school. She live with my brother because she need home and law say she must go to school. But I think maybe my brother will send her to Oak Ridge place anyway when school is over for her. That is why I need money for her. So my sister, Lee, Yeun-Ja, can live with me. Maybe get real job for her, maybe more school. Not Oak Ridge massage shop."

"What did Park do then?"

"He get up from chair, put whiskey down and stand in front of me. Then he slap me hard. Then he go back to couch, touch cushion and say time for me to take care of him. He point and say I do that, then plenty time for me to go Oak Ridge later. He say if I be very good to him, maybe I stay at his house-su, not go Oak Ridge at all. He say I can be his yobo. But I have to show him first. You see how bad Mr. Park is?"

I nodded and tried to look sympathetic. The sympathy part wasn't difficult.

"I did not move." Her expression turned to a scowl, and her eyes narrowed again. Chun-He looked quite angry. "I say, I not take care of him! Not want him in my mouth. Park is twagey. You know twagey?"

I nodded, remembering *twagey* is the Korean word for *pig*.

"So he shout at me. Say he will hit me again. Then I take gun from my purse-su and tell him no!"

"You knew the gun was loaded?"

"Yes. I load and make ready."

I didn't ask where she learned her way around GI .45s. I figured that was a question for the prosecutor.

"What happened next?"

"He say, okay, I have gun now and maybe walk out tonight, but I have no place to go. He say I should give him gun or sister and I will work in Oak Ridge now and forever. He say my brother will not help me. My brother work for him. Then he unzip pants and say again I take care of him now."

I doubted a quick hundred Won from me would have made any difference to Park or Chun-He's skell brother.

She cried heavily, her story punctuated with sobs and her accent thick. Her eye makeup still ran down her cheeks as if there was an endless supply. She took another tissue and wiped her eyes, making additional black streaks on her face.

I took the gun off the desk and slipped it back into my waistband.

"And you had to shoot him?" I asked.

"Yes, yes, Mr. Sam, I had to. No choice. Had to protect sister." Chun-He shook her head violently. "No choice."

One of the flies made an exceptionally loud buzz and took off out the office door. A moment later, the second one followed.

"Because you thought he would force you to give him sex?" I suggested.

"Yes, I *was* afraid. I am *so* tired of sex. Please, adjosh-ee, you promised. Help me, please!"

Everything rang true. Perhaps with a little embellishment, but nonetheless probably based on fact.

"I will. You and I will talk to your lawyer."

"What lawyer?" She sounded surprised.

"The one Roni is going to call for you. Sit here and wait. Do you want a glass of water?"

Jenkins, the tough guy, does it again.

"Yes, please." Chun-He pushed her short black hair behind her ears. She looked small, young and beyond pathetic. The beautiful girl who walked into that room had taken a hiatus.

I stuck my head out of the office doorway. Both of the flies zeroed in on me and buzzed near my ear. I waved my hand to chase them away.

"Roni, can you come here, please?" I said.

She left her desk and in only a few seconds stood next to me.

"Will you get Chun-He some water?"

"Of course. Is she all right?"

I nodded, and Roni disappeared for a moment.

I took out my wallet and found a dog-eared business card for Joe Costello, arguably the best criminal attorney in the area. Roni came back with a short plastic bottle of cold water. She handed it to Chun-He. I gave the card to Roni.

"Call this number. The secretary's name is Stephanie. She's nice. Tell her I suggested you call on Chun-He's behalf. Explain that she'll be arrested for Park's murder. See if Costello is available, and have him meet me at Prospect PD. If he's in court, have her send an associate right away. Call me at the PD one way or the other. We'll be there."

"She looks awful. What happened?"

"Just what I thought. Chun-He confessed. But she's got one hell of a story. Costello won't have a problem painting a picture of Park as a monster. He can make Chun-He look like a victim. Her life has been one big mental trauma. He'll probably claim a sufficient amount of duress influenced her into killing him. Or Park's actions were coercive enough that Costello may get the jury to believe she was justified in preventing her from getting sodomized or raped that night. Joe's good...the best chance she's got."

"And why are you doing all this? Don't you just want to solve the murder?"

I looked at her without immediately answering. I didn't have one handy nor did I want to give a complicated reply. I settled for the simple truth.

"Because I'm a schmuck, sweetheart. A sucker for a sob story. And I don't like guys like Park or Ha or Chun-He's brother."

I didn't give her an opportunity to ask about the brother.

"Make the call, please." I stepped out of Sunny's office, leaving Roni and Chun-He to deal with the flies.

I looked at my watch again. Quarter after ten. I glanced down the hall and watched one of the massage room doors open. A man in his early-seventies stepped out. He walked with a limp. As we passed in the hall, he smiled and nodded. I looked into the treatment room. Sunny had already bundled up a sheet and began taking the case off a pillow.

"I need your help," I said. "Chun-He needs a friend and would like to see you."

"What happened?"

"She killed Park—with good reason. Roni is calling a lawyer. I want to talk with him before I call the Knoxville cops."

"You are going to arrest her?"

"Not me. I'll take her into custody and drive her to Knoxville after I speak to her lawyer. I have to pick up the gun at Roni's house first. After I speak to the lawyer, I'll know if I need a warrant or not. I'm thinking I won't and that he'll let Chun-He sign permission for me to search her

241

room. I'm trying not to hurt Chun-He, believe me. I think she had good reason to shoot Park." I shrugged. "Hell, I'd shoot him myself if I knew about this." I paused and realized I had a world-class tension headache. "Right now Chun-He's upset, and you can give her more comfort than me. She's in your office."

Chapter Twenty-Five

Joe Costello didn't contest the idea of Chun-He allowing us to search her room. When she told her lawyer I already had the gun she used, I admitted that gun was mine, and I had played a trick. Costello assured her that cops are allowed to use deception to elicit the truth.

But Chun-He wanted the last word on that topic. "Oh, you koogie-mal," she said and even managed a little smile and wiggled a finger at me.

Koreans appreciate a cunning plan better than most.

I thought she felt a bit more secure with Costello sitting in her corner. He's not a big, protective-looking guy, but his confidence is palpable and comforting to defendants.

When we agreed on a course of action, Joe and I shook hands. He's one of the only lawyers I trust to keep his word.

Then I called D.W. Renfro in Knoxville.

"Hey, Dee-Dubyah, yew doin' aw rot t'day?"

"That don't sound much like Noo Yawk ta me," he said.

"Yeah, I'm assimilating into the Appalachian community. Hey, listen, I'm in the office with a Miss Chun-He Lee and her lawyer. They walked in about an hour ago. Miss Lee wants to confess to shooting He-Chul Park. I've got our crime scene guys retrieving the gun as we speak. She's got a good story behind everything—it's worth hearing. I think she might have been justified in shooting. Mr. Costello here would like her to cooperate fully. I'm going to have them escorted to your shop. Want to do some more paperwork?"

"You're givin' us another one?"

243

"Sure. Christmas comes early in Prospect."

"Well, I'll be derned. I guess I really owe y'all somethin' big."

"It's nice to meet a gentleman who offers before I have to ask."

He laughed. "Hot damn. What am I gittin' m'se'f inta?"

"Tell you what," I said. "You take plenty of time and consider what Miss Lee has to say and be sure you do the right thing. Manage that, and we're even."

"Y'all are a piece o' work, Chief. I'll keep an open mind and take what ya say serious like. I think I'm hearin' ya tell me somethin', so don't worry about it."

"Thanks, partner. Pleasure doin' business with you."

"I got any questions, I'll holler at ya."

D.W. and I hung up.

"That was a bit more than we had agreed on," Joe said. His short, almost black, curly hair shined from Brylcreem or some modern equivalent.

"Isn't all this lawyer-talk supposed to be confidential?" I asked.

He nodded and grinned.

"Then please confidentialize everything you heard me say. I have an image to uphold. Who wants to be seen as a softie?"

"Confidentialize? Y'all talk funny."

* * * *

Once again, I was late for lunch. John had already gone out. I called his cell phone and asked him to stop at Wah Lum and bring back several gallons of won ton soup. He laughed and said he'd pick up a quart. I sat down next to Bettye, wondering what all the Chinese food I'd eaten recently might do to my constitution.

"You drum up a lot of business for Joe Costello," she said.

"You're right. I should ask for a finder's fee."

"When you refer people to him, I know you feel sorry for them."

"Yeah, I'm a real schlep at times."

"The first day you came to work here you used that word. I didn't know what it meant, so I asked your wife. I don't think you're a schlep."

"Thanks."

"Gonna tell me what happened?"

"Sure." And I did.

At five to one, John walked back in with my won ton soup. Fred Mazzio followed him wearing yet another brightly colored Hawaiian shirt, this one red with big white and yellow flowers.

"Hey, Boss, how's it goin'? Here's your soup," John said.

"Thanks, John. How's it goin', Freddie?"

"Hey, big guy. I met John on the street. You got another bowl? I'll share the soup with you."

"Why didn't you get your own?"

"I didn't want a whole quart."

"They sell pints."

I must have sounded exasperated. Bettye laughed.

"Yeah, but I wanted to share with you."

"Jeez, Frederick, you are such a—"

Betty cut me off before I could finish."Gentlemen, I'm outta here. Y'all have a nice lunch. Bye." Again, she made the sheep sound.

"See ya, Betts."

"See ya later, Sarge."

"Ta ta, beautiful," Freddie said.

"John, do we have a dish for the great Hawaiian islander?"

"I'll look, Boss."

"Make it a small one. He can live off the fat of the land."

"Hey, after all the help I've given you!" Mazzio protested.

"I admit, you've helped," I said.

"So, I ain't worth half a container of soup?"

"Sit down. Eat. When John gets back, I'll tell you what happened this morning."

A half hour later...

"You bastard," Freddie said. "You were in that blonde's house?"

"Yeah, she doesn't live far away."

"Where is she now?"

"When I left, she was in the shop."

"I should go for another massage." Only Mazzio would say that.

"I think they're a little short on trained personnel at the moment."

"You think they'll go outta business, Boss?" John asked.

"I hope not. They're trying to make an honest buck. They deserve a chance."

"Give me a call when they're back in business, will ya, Sam?" Fred asked. "I'll come back up. Maybe I'll invite the blonde out for a ride on the Harley. She's single, right?"

"What would Mary do if she knew you were out farting around on your bike with Roni Keeble?"

"I don't know. Go shopping, I guess."

"Why don't you ask?"

"You crazy?"

I shook my head and changed the subject. "Good soup, huh?"

"Yeah, good."

"You ate most of it."

"No. You sure?"

"How'd you know it was *Chung-Lee* who shot Park," John asked.

"I didn't really consider *Chung-Lee*," I grinned at Freddie and then turned my attention back to John, "as a suspect until Roni told me she gave her the .45 automatic for protection—back when she was still at the double-wide, after the other girls were killed. Then I remembered it might be a good possibility that Veronica and Sunny really left Park's house before ten o'clock that night, but Park's neighbor still saw a red car at the curb later on. I didn't know what a Kia Optima looked like, but then I saw that it looks a lot like Roni's Audi. So those two things made me think it could have been Chun-He with Park after everyone else had gone. I just took a shot in the dark."

"You're pretty soft on these good-lookin' killers, big guy," Fred said.

"That's why girls all like the Boss, Freddie," John said, "and if you remember, you couldn't even get laid in a whorehouse."

"Yeah, John, you probably got run out of Boca by all your rich neighbors, you shanty-Irish sleazebag."

John laughed, Fred fumed, and I stood up and dabbed my lips with a napkin, ready to go back into my office.

"I've got to make a few phone calls, and then I'll face the music and see the mayor. This is big stuff. He'll have a press conference tomorrow morning. You two are invited if you behave yourselves."

"No kiddin'? I can come?" Fred asked.

"Do you have anything to wear that's not from the Don Ho collection?"

"No, it's summertime."

"Jesus Christ."

I returned to my office and called Kate.

"I can't wait to hear what you did this morning," she said.

I told her.

"Your gun in a Glad bag, you clever old dog."

"When I told Chun-He Lee about the trick she called ma a koogie-mal."

Kate laughed; she knew the term.

"You are an accomplished liar, Sammy."

"I don't lie to you."

"Yeah, right."

"I omit certain facts at opportune times, but I don't lie."

"Aren't you sweet?"

"Sweet enough to take you to dinner. Freddie ate most of my lunch."

"My poor boy. What are you thinking of? Chinese, Mexican or Italian?"

"I heard Aubrey's makes peanut coated catfish that's supposed to be good."

"Oh yeah, who told you about that?"

"Can't remember…some hot-looking babe, I suppose."

She laughed.

"I checked their website the other day. They have nice side dishes, too," I added.

"Such as?"

"Squash casserole and mushrooms in burgundy sauce are but two that tickled my fancy."

"You buy me dinner, big feller, and I'll tickle your fancy."

"I don't mean to take you for granted, but talk like that keeps me going out with you."

"Such a smoothie."

"You've said that before."

"I'll have an aperitif waiting for you, sweetie."

"Thanks, kiddo. See ya later."

"Alligator."

"Ha."

* * * *

I tracked down Rachel at the TV station. The operator said she was in a meeting. I said the message I had for her was more important than the meeting. The woman believed me, and in three minutes, Rachel picked up the phone.

"What's wrong? Are you okay?"

"What's wrong? Nothing, everything's right. I've cleared another homicide, and you get the story before anyone else."

"Another murder arrest? That's four in a week. I'm impressed."

"Six days actually, and you should be. Four bodies, three killers, and they're all mine. Am I good or what?"

"I admit, yes, you are. But I sometimes I wonder if I'm attracted to you because of your inflated ego or your physical attributes."

"I won't comment on that, you being a married woman and all. But I mean really, Mizz Williamson, what am I to think?"

"I only meant that, well, uh...how can I put this? Uh...I...was only kidding."

I'd never heard her stammer before and responded with a big laugh.

"Oh, shut up!" she said.

"I know exactly what you meant, and you're almost sputtering—very unprofessional for a media person. I'd like you to think of me as a sex object. I'm flattered. As long as you never tell anyone I'm a mindless sex object."

"Oh, you're such a pig. Oink, oink."

"Stop the barnyard noises. Do you want to hear the story?"

"Of course I do."

I told her.

"Now call that Knoxville detective, D.W. Renfro and get him to tell you. If he's still dealing with Joe Costello and Miss Lee, ask to speak with his lieutenant. I understand he's in charge of press releases, and if I'm any judge of character, he'll have the hots for you after two minutes of conversation. He'll tell you everything including his credit card number."

"Do you know how easy it could be to hate you?"

"Impossible for any woman and you know it. Hey, are you getting used to that Mustang yet, or are you still doing eighty up Broadway?"

"I have to admit, I like it. Yes, I'm getting used to my hot car. I should thank you for that, too."

"Just another service from your friendly neighborhood policeman."

"I'm lucky."

"When you're ready to dump that soccer mom thing you drive, let me know, we'll go car shopping."

"Cool. You think I'm a Cobra kind of girl?"

"Yikes, what a question. I think it's time for you to go out there and scoop the competition."

She gave a sexy laugh. "See ya, Sammy."

* * * *

After that racy conversation, I walked upstairs to see the mayor. Ronnie Shield's secretary, Trudy Connor, sat in the outer office typing up a storm on her computer. She stopped when I stood in front of her desk. Darnell Means sat at another station only twenty feet from Trudy. He looked up when I walked in, but said nothing. I ignored him, too.

"Hi, Ms. Connor, is the great white leader available?"

"Oh, hello, Mr. Jenkins. My, but haven't you been famous lately? I saw your name mentioned in the paper and heard what you said twice on TV. Three murders solved in less than a week. I know the mayor will be impressed.

I gave her the little-boy-smile and said, "Shucks, Ms. Connor, but it's four murders now. I made another arrest this morning."

She shook her head. "Well, bless your heart. Let me buzz the mayor and tell 'im so yew can let him know *allll* about it."

I gave her a minute to speak with Ronnie and wondered if she had gotten to like me or was just reacting to my recent celebrity status.

Trudy smiled and dropped the phone back onto the console. "Go right in. He's a'waitin'."

I closed the door quickly, hoping Darnell would take the hint and not try to interrupt Prospect's resident hero while he spoke to the mayor. I dropped down into one of the green leather chairs in front of Ronnie's

249

desk, looked around and noticed he had added another stuffed fish to the wall since last I'd been in his office. A largemouth bass with a red and white surface plug hooked to the poor thing's lip occupied a place of honor.

"Trudy said you solved another murder this mornin', Sam. Congratulations, I'm im-pressed." After the kind comment, he dug his spurs in just a little. "We haven't had much chance to talk recently, not as much as I'd like. Y'all need ta bring me up ta speed on everything that happened before the press conference t'marrah. Four murders cleared an' three killers caught in a week, Lord have mercy."

"Six days, actually, but who's counting?"

Ronnie smiled and nodded. "Before ya start yer story, Sam, let me ask if you've had a chance to call our district attorney yet and his counterpart in Knoxville?"

Our mayor not only looks like a Southern preacher, but he's interested in doling out penance for my sins.

"No, not yet. Things were a wee bit hectic this morning."

"Well, I kin imagine. But please, Sam, give those folks a call soon as ya' kin. Ya didn't do anythin' today that'll git them bent outta shape, did ya?"

"Probably not, but you never know with lawyers, do you?"

He smiled again. "They're a breed all ta themselves, huh, Sam?"

"You bet."

"Well then, let's hear all about what ya done."

Not one of the dirty-blond hairs on Ronnie's head looked out of place. I think a wholesale distributor sends cases of hair spray to his home on a regular basis.

I told my story, got a couple more compliments and another reminder to call all those I had previously offended. After clearing four murders, I was more inclined to say *screw them*, but I have to live with Ronnie. I'd make the calls.

I walked out of the mayor's office, winked at Ms. Connor, ignored Darnell and left the second floor. On the way down the polished marble steps, I decided to make one more personal call before smoothing the ruffled feathers of two district attorney generals... Or was it district attorneys general? I tried to remember if they came under the same rule that applied to sergeants major and mothers-in-law.

I called Kisaeng massage. Roni Keeble answered.

"I didn't know if you'd still be there."

"We're both here. We've been on the phone to schools, colleges, employment offices and anybody else we could think of trying to get a couple of therapists or PTAs to work here, even part-time or temporarily."

"I wish you luck."

"Thank you. We're trying."

"I just wanted to tell you what's happening with Chun-He. She went to Knoxville PD with her lawyer not too long ago."

"We know. The Knoxville cops let her call Sunny. They were on the phone a long time. She said the detectives were being nice to her. She told Sunny what you did. Her lawyer says she'll be out on fairly low bail tonight. She'll stay with Sunny for a while."

"Good. I hope things work out for her."

"We'll see. I have my fingers crossed."

"I know I shouldn't say this. It's not what a cop should do, but I wanted to call and apologize to you and Sunny if I caused you any hard feelings. This sounds corny and maybe a bit theatrical, but I did what you pay me to do, you both being part of the Prospect community."

She laughed. "Tillie Spoon said you reminded her of the sheriff in a cowboy movie. She's right. You're a real straight shooter—a classic hero, aren't you, Mister Jenkins?"

"You don't sound mad."

"I'm not. I got upset at the time, but I understand. So does Sunny. We're okay."

"Good. If I can help you get the business back in gear, let me know."

"We need customers. You want a massage? I'll do that one personally."

"And people say I'm bad."

She laughed again.

"The mayor is having a press conference tomorrow morning. They're usually held in the wing of the lobby outside the PD. I'm sure I'll be asked to speak. I plan on mentioning your business—in a complimentary way. You can come and watch if you'd like."

"I've never been to a press conference before. I'm sure Sunny hasn't either. Okay, I think we could take some time from our busy schedule. Can we stop and see you?"

"I'm never certain what the mayor thinks about my personal activities, but sure, why not? I'll see you in the lobby."

"Until tomorrow then."

Actually, I couldn't give a hoot what Ronnie thought. It was Bettye who carried the gun and acted subjectively about my dealings with the ladies at Kisaeng.

* * * *

For the first time in days, I planned on taking a break. I'd tired of working, it was afternoon, and I had already done more than what my meager salary demanded. I decided to sit down and bother Bettye.

"I must say, you seem rather pleased with yourself today," she said.

"Who? Me? Surely not. I'm too modest to sit around and rest on my laurels."

"If I didn't love ya, darlin' I'd laugh at ya."

"Thanks, I think. Hey, you deserve a fair amount of ink in the story of solving the great Korean murder mystery. How about sitting outside with the two fat boys and me tomorrow at the press conference?"

"Thank you, Sammy, but I really don't want to be on TV in uniform. It's not my favorite outfit."

"I hate uniforms, too. Wear whatever you want. Greater Knoxville will think you're a movie star."

She smiled. Bettye is more like me than she'd like to admit. I could give her a medal, but a well-placed compliment means more.

"Okay, I'll call Joey Gillespie and have him come in to work the desk."

My troops were ready to meet the press.

Chapter Twenty-Six

Press conferences can be a drag, especially when you have more than one case to discuss. That morning we had three. They were all somehow interrelated, but the four murders involved three very different and separately motivated defendants.

I anticipated making an opening statement that would answer most everything a reporter could want to know. However, four murders would bring out all the network anchors and newspaper heavies. Those people generally like to hear themselves talk, and they all want their time on camera. Far be it for me to be clear, concise and complete, and in doing so, deter them from asking the questions they had written down on the clean part of a napkin that morning at breakfast.

My only other problem came from having to remember what witty comebacks and snide remarks I made about one case and not duplicate those when equally inane things were asked about another. Just hang out with reporters for a while and you can dispel the myth that there is no such thing as a stupid question.

I wore a summer-weight beige suit that I purchased in the 1980s. It was in perfect condition and still fit as well as it did back then. My button-down, light blue shirt was relatively new and looked natty next to the MacDonald tartan tie I wore. The tie was my way of alluding to a Jenkins/MacDonald alliance by marriage many generations ago. If anyone made a comment about my lack of adherence to current fashion, I'd grit my teeth and try to scare them off by saying I hadn't been faithfully attending my court ordered anger management classes.

I looked at my watch. 9:30. Ronnie Shields, or more probably Trudy

Connor, had scheduled the extravaganza to kick off at 10:00. The lobby had been set up and was ready to go since the night before.

John Gallagher dressed for the occasion and looked like an old detective from Palm Beach PD with pastel green slacks, a salmon-colored blazer and a pale yellow shirt. The outfit made him look like he had emerged from a tub of rainbow sherbet.

Fred Mazzio showed up looking like Detective Kahanamoku of Honolulu PD. Those two wouldn't be asked to comment during the discussion, but it's traditional to allow your helpers to stand in the background and be seen on TV.

John walked into my office carrying a coffee cup.

"The Sarge tell you what she learned about Darnell Means?" he asked. "About his uncle being chairman of the county commission? Guy named *Micro* something."

I smirked. "Micah Blevins?"

"That's him."

"Yeah," I said. "I wouldn't say Darnell was sent here to mess with me, but because of a few past incidents, Blevins won't be joining my fan club anytime soon."

"That bad, Boss?"

"I locked up Micah's brother for murder, let him go and ended up charging his sister-in-law."

"I guess he was pissed."

"You think?"

John laughed.

"Then I locked up another commissioner for bribery and his son for possession of drugs with intent to sell."

"You never liked politicians."

I shrugged. "I just let the chips fall where they may. And there might be a couple more things that would frost Uncle Micah's cupcakes. I'm not his favorite cop."

"Sorry I couldn't dig up any dirt on this guy Darnell. But the Sarge's friends at the court said they'll ask around some more."

"You tried. Something may turn up."

"I started soon as you asked. You know me, Boss. I don't let any hair grow under my toes. But nobody'll talk to me."

John was trying to sound sincere, but I wanted to laugh. "I know, John. Maybe he's clean."

"Freddie wanted to buy a whore and lure him into a sleazy motel."

I laughed at that. "He would."

"Only he didn't know any local whores, other than the ones who got shot or arrested."

"Good. Let's skip the whores."

John set his cup on my desk and looked out the door. "The reporters are coming in, and Freddie just got here."

"Won't be long now."

"Yeah, wanna go outside?"

Ronnie would kick off the dog and pony show with an opening statement. He was second to none when it came to being an emcee. If he ever left politics, he should consider starring in a revival of *Hee-Haw*.

I stood next to Bettye's desk and looked out into the main lobby. She had decided to show the reporters her sleeveless burgundy dress. A good choice. If I allowed Bettye to wear civilian clothes every day, none of the cops would stay on the road. My desk sergeant comes fully equipped with a world-class figure.

I heard Officer Joey Gillespie as he puttered around in the file room waiting to take over the desk when Bettye left.

As John said, the participants were beginning to arrive. I saw a few of the TV news personalities familiar to everyone in the Knoxville viewing area as well as a few cameramen I'd seen at similar gatherings. The Knoxville and Blount County papers were represented, as were two news service bureaus. This wing-ding promised to be a biggie.

The back door buzzer buzzed, sounding like a sick dinosaur needing to purge its stomach. I took the walk and let Rachel and John Leckmanski in through our private portal. No other reporter would dare try something that personal with me.

Before going into my office, Rachel stopped to give Bettye a quick hug and sisterly peck on the cheek. She wiggled her fingers at John Gallagher and, I guess, wondered about our representative from the Sandwich Islands. Leckmanski gave a friendly wave to everyone.

It was no longer a secret around the Knoxville Press Corps that Rachel had an in at Prospect PD. The other members might make pointed comments about that at opportune times, but they had to live with it.

In my room, Rachel gave me a platonic kiss on the cheek. John and I shook hands.

"You look nice all dressed up," she said.

"Thanks. So do you," I said.

She wore a navy blue suit with a straight skirt and a white wrap-around blouse—sort of *LA Law* style.

"You've got great legs for a short girl," I added.

She's used to my candor, but still blushed.

"And John, you look snazzy in your foreign correspondent's outfit. You get those duds at Dan Rather's yard sale?"

He'd worn his formal outfit, a khaki bush jacket and freshly pressed jeans.

"How'd you know?" he asked.

"I suppose we have to take this abuse to get allowed in early?" Rachel suggested.

"Sure. It's the only fun I'll have today. Would you guys like coffee?"

I knew Rachel would say no, and John would go to the pot and fix his own. Rachel and I sat in guest chairs in front of my desk. John used my big swivel chair. She crossed her legs and showed almost four inches of thigh.

I took an exaggerated look. "You do that just to make me crazy, don't you, you evil vixen."

She tried to pull the skirt down, but had little luck.

"Don't do that on my account," I said.

"Oh, stop that." She could only hold a frown for a few seconds before smiling.

John snickered and sipped from a large coffee mug.

"You want to know any more than what I've already told you?"

"I can wait. Maybe I'll throw you a trick question and get you flustered."

"You wouldn't—and I wouldn't."

"I know."

We were interrupted by someone knocking on the doorjamb. Fred

Mazzio's smiling face and large body filled up most of the thirty-inch doorway.

"Excuse me, Sam," he said, "but I seem to be the only one not acquainted with your guests."

"Maybe there's a reason for that, Frederick." I hinted, but it wasn't enough to deter him.

Mazzio stepped into the room and up to where Rachel and I sat.

He turned on the oily charm. "Hi, I'm Fred Mazzio, for many years right hand man to a certain Lieutenant Jenkins. He'll never admit it, but I came here on vacation and helped him solve four homicides. Didn't I, Samuel?"

I forced a smile. "Ex-Detective Mazzio often exaggerates. He played a minor role in the clearances we'll speak about this morning. Frederick, this is Rachel Williamson and the gentleman is John Leckmanski."

He shook Rachel's hand and said, "It's my pleasure." He bowed. I thought he might kiss her hand, but didn't.

She giggled. Mazzio can be an idiot with precious little effort. He stepped around to my desk and shook hands with John.

"Didn't we know a Leckmanski back on the Island?" he asked.

"Yes, he did wire taps and that sort of technical work," I said. "No relation."

Fred nodded. "Well, it's very nice to meet you both. I hope the chief answers all your questions. If not, don't hesitate to see me. I've always been a friend to the press."

"Thanks for stopping in, sport. Now get out," I said.

Fred shook his head and rolled his eyes. "He's so harsh with his co-workers."

"Out!"

He left smiling and swaggered toward Gallagher's desk.

"I guess you've known each other for a while?" Rachel asked.

"We were in the police academy together. And then he worked for me for a few years. Yes, a long, long time."

The sound of someone tapping on the microphone at the podium in the lobby made its way into my office. We heard Ronnie Shields asking the crowd to take their seats.

"Looks like it's show time," I said.

257

We walked through the reception area. I looked at John and Fred.

"Hey, Curley and Moe, fall in." They followed. Bettye led the police procession.

After a brief greeting and introduction by Mayor Shields, it was my turn to perform at Prospect's public relations festival.

"Good morning, people," I said. "It's been a while, but it's good to see all of you again. I wish we could get together under more pleasant circumstances, but it seems every time we have these discussions someone has suffered a catastrophe. Let's try for a PD versus press softball game and picnic sometime."

That got a few smiles and one or two chuckles from the audience. Then I needed to look for serious material.

"The Korean community in and around Knoxville has suffered over the last two weeks." I began. "As you know, two young Korean ladies, residents and workers in Prospect, were killed, and two Korean men from Knoxville were also murdered.

"There's an old Korean proverb that says, 'To die is not such sorrow, but to suffer pain is the real sorrow.' That can be interpreted two ways. The victims all died quickly and felt very little pain. So, to those family members who lost loved ones and are now feeling sorrow and pain, we in Prospect extend our sympathies."

I paused for a long moment and looked out over the crowd. The reporters waited patiently. The cameramen were filming, and the still photographers snapped a few shots, their flashguns blinking in the rear of the audience.

Roni Keeble and Sunny Kim stood to my right near the back of the group looking like two attractive professional women. After reciting the old Korean proverb, I saw Sunny dab her eye with a white hankie.

"Four people died in three separate incidents," I said. "The investigation of the murders of two women who died in Prospect, subsequently tied in to both of the killings which occurred in Knoxville. We coordinated efforts with detectives of the Knoxville Police to clear both of those cases. The press releases Sergeant Lambert sent to you were quite detailed. So I won't revisit all those areas.

"I do, however, with considerable embarrassment, want to take a little time to apologize—again—to the people at WNXX News. I draw your attention to the time when I jumped the gun, so to speak, and gave cameraman John Leckmanski, who was here on a totally unrelated matter, early information about two subjects who voluntarily came in to answer questions relative to the murder of a Mr. Chang-Hai Ha. A few people misinterpreted my information. Those two subjects were never arrested. They were never in actual custody and are, as far as we're concerned, totally uninvolved with any crimes."

The attempt to mitigate my ploy of flushing out Mr. Boo drew more snickers from a few sharp reporters than my joke about the softball game.

Darnell Means sat next to Ronnie Shields two seats to my left. He cleared his throat a bit louder than necessary after my comment. *Screw him.*

"Later that same day," I said, "we were able to locate Mr. Ha's killer who surrendered peacefully. So, to Mr. Leckmanski, Ms. Rachel Williamson, who received the information and wrote the story and to their station manager, I apologize to you all, here in front of your colleagues. Okay, I think I've lectured—and groveled, enough. I assume you have questions."

Allen Peters, a tall sandy-haired guy who loves to break my chops, jumped up with the first obnoxious question.

"Chief Jenkins, what do four murders in a very short period of time, all involving Korean nationals, say about that segment of our community?"

I couldn't let him get away with that, but I also couldn't call him an idiot in front of his comrades. Instead, I rolled my eyes before answering. "It says that we have to multiply the four Korean victims by a much larger number to know how many people were injured emotionally by these tragedies."

He showed his displeasure with my answer by making a face.

Up his.

"I have a great affection for Korean people," I said. "I lived in South Korea for more than a year a long time ago. Koreans are not violent people, and these incidents should not imply to anyone that they are. They love their family members. They're very religious while not being hypocritical." *Take that you fundamentalists.* "And they have a great liking for Americans."

Sandy-hair must have realized that I'd never play his game. He sat without further comment.

"Look, people," I said, feeling like a sixth grade teacher addressing a class, "two of the victims were members of an organized criminal element. All ethnic communities in this country end up with a few bad apples who attempt to make a dishonest buck off the backs of their countrymen. That's what happened here. If anyone has any doubts about Korean people, go to a Korean restaurant and see how nicely you're treated." I exaggerated a smile. "I love the food. You might, too."

Choke on that, Peters.

After a few more grins and snickers from the crowd, a tall, over-thirtyish blonde from another network stood up. She was built like a *Sports Illustrated* swimsuit model, but didn't look as smart as a watermelon. I smiled for her. Girls like that need a break, too.

"Chief, two of the victims and two of the people arrested were employees of a massage parlor here in Prospect. What kind of business is this?"

Her last sentence conveyed an implication, and I didn't care for the way she delivered the question. *So much for her break.*

"The term *massage parlor* makes us think of a sleazy, back-ally joint offering sex for money under the guise of therapy. Kisaeng Massage is a legitimate business with patients having legitimate medical needs."

Miss Swimsuit had trouble hiding her emotions. Her affected countenance told me she had hoped for a juicier answer. Poker would never be her game. I continued as if her attitude never bothered me.

"Prior to any murders, I investigated this business and confirmed its legitimacy. Unfortunately, as we know, they lost their roster of licensed and qualified massage therapists. I understand that the owner, Miss Soon-Wha Kim and her colleague Mrs. Veronica Keeble, both residents of Prospect, are currently recruiting new, qualified employees from schools and colleges with health care programs. They are state licensed, receive referrals from physicians and even accept insurance payments. We all wish them luck and hope they can get back to business so they can serve the patients that have come to depend on them for pain management."

Swimsuit sat down, looking no more satisfied than Sandy-hair. Then Rachel stood up and tossed me a beauty.

"Chief, there seemed to be very little in the way of physical evidence available to you in any of these cases. Can you tell us how you were able to solve four murders so quickly?"

I couldn't hide my wide grin. "Ms. Williamson, did the mayor pay you to ask that question?"

She smiled and sat. I scored my third round of moderate laughter.

"If he didn't, please stop at my office and pick up your check."

I dropped my eyes and tried to make the crowd think I was embarrassed. I wasn't.

"Well, with this opportunity to toot my own horn," I continued, "I'll have to be honest and give credit to other personnel who did some extraordinary detective work which led our little task force to the three arrests that closed four murders.

"The two women from Prospect, Sung-Sook Cho and Kum-Ok Kyeung, were linked to one killer. I have to admit that we had little to go on, and our first ideas were way off base. Two auxiliary police officers, both retired detectives from another jurisdiction with collectively almost fifty years of experience, John Gallagher and Fred Mazzio Jr., spotted something in a crime scene photo that led us to apprehend a Rockford man who worked with both victims." I half-turned and pointed to the Dead End Kids, gesturing for them to stand and take a bow. They did, with as much grace as they could muster. John gave a small wave to the reporters and cameramen. Fred offered a polite nod.

"Sergeant Bettye Lambert, the officer on my right, investigated the very complicated family connections involved to determine who may have killed of one of the Knoxville men. Her results led me to apprehend that person."

I paused. Bettye took her cue, stood and bowed slightly. She returned to her seat with more class than Detectives Frick and Frack.

"We worked closely with Knoxville Detectives D.W. Renfro and Witford Maples to locate Mr. Cho-Hung Boo who confessed to killing Chang-Hai Ha. Unfortunately, those officers had a prior commitment and couldn't be with us today."

The day before the news conference, Renfro told me, *'We got us some real po-leece work ta do and don't want no part o' no bunch o' reporters.'*

"Later, when I learned what kind of handgun and what specific ammunition was used to kill Hee-Chul Park, I developed additional information leading me to the person who was subsequently arrested. After listening to her account of the incident, I'm inclined to believe she may have been quite justified in that killing, but that's a matter for the courts to decide."

I hoped that my editorial comment might influence at least a few of those potential jurors in the TV audience. I figured Chun-Hee needed as much help as she could get.

Maybe I am a schlep.

"Any more discussion about the defendants at this time would be inappropriate because of upcoming trials."

I may have done enough damage already.

As often happens, the remainder of questions were either inconsequential or redundant. After answering those, I thanked everyone and turned things back to Ronnie Shields, who spent a few minutes chatting before he ended the program.

That's always my signal to run away and hide in my office. Well, I ran away from the lobby and after a discrete period, Rachel joined me.

On my way back to the PD, I heard someone call. Roni Keeble and Sunny Kim walked over and waylaid me much too close to the rest of the crowd.

"That was a nice thing you said, Sam," Roni told me.

"Aw shucks, ma'am, it weren't nuthin'."

"You're acting like an Old West sheriff again."

"You guys deserve a chance. I want to see you back in business again soon."

"Thank you," Roni said and treated me to a smile that could illuminate a coal mine.

"Com op sumnida, Sam," Sunny said, "for trusting us and helping. I never met a policeman like you before." Her smile ran into in the seven-figure category, too.

"Chom ahnayo, Sun-Me. And you're welcome, Ms. Keeble. I meant what I said. I hope you guys end up with a prosperous business."

"You think your chubby friend will come in again to investigate us?" Roni asked.

"My chubby friend may be your best customer if he decides to vacation here next year. But his investigating days are over. He didn't fool you, did he?"

"Only for a day. When he came back in with you to do police work...well, we thought you might have sent him. He looked like either a cop or a gangster, and gangsters don't vacation in Prospect."

"Thank goodness. I hope you took no offense."

"No, no offense. We are two pretty tough girls," Sunny said.

"Okay, ladies, I wish you good luck. If I can help, please call. Now I've got to run before a reporter corrals me. Bye."

They left me with two more beautiful smiles as I made my getaway back to the office.

Chapter Twenty-Seven

For ten minutes, I thumbed through the latest issue of *Smithsonian* magazine, deeply engrossed in an article about Tennessee's own Andrew Jackson, as true a psychopath as I've ever read about. If I were a Cherokee, I'd never carry a twenty-dollar bill in my pocket.

The next voice I heard didn't make me jump, but I did swing my feet off the desk and almost come to the sitting position of attention.

"Who were the two women you were talking to?"

Rachel surprised me with her question. I hadn't heard her walk into my office. How did she do that in high heels?

"Oh, hi, you snuck up on me. I must be getting old."

She looked at me, waiting for an answer. She gave me the woman's international signal for, 'Answer up, pal,' a tilt of the head and an intense stare.

"Uh, they were Roni Keeble and Sunny Kim from Kisaeng Massage."

"They're both quite pretty."

"Yes...they are, aren't they?"

I often wonder how women can make me feel so uncomfortable with so little effort. I waited for her to sit, but she didn't.

"They're the ex-hookers you mentioned?"

"I told you that?"

"You did. They certainly cleaned up nicely."

"They were pretty high-priced call girls. I doubt they needed much cleaning up."

She almost snorted. "You all seemed rather friendly."

Her body language didn't promise much affection. She dangled her black leather purse from her right hand and rested her left hand on her hip.

"Are you going to sit down?"

Finally, she sat on the edge of the chair, clutching her handbag like a weapon.

"Very friendly. I'd say they like you," she added.

"I was nice to them. And helpful, I suppose. Anyway, almost everybody likes me." I smiled for her and blinked a few times.

"Maybe not everyone."

I shrugged and tried another smile, a weak one.

"Thanks for your question," I said, reminding Rachel of what she had said earlier, desperately trying to change the subject. "It gave me an opportunity to offer the necessary attaboys. I appreciate it."

"I like being nice to you...and helpful, I suppose."

Was there an echo in the room?

"Have I annoyed you?"

"Why would you ask that?"

"My po-leece training makes me sense something." My third smile had no effect either.

"Well, I guess it's time for me to get back to Knoxville, isn't it?"

"You just got here, and you didn't answer my question. Are you in a rush?"

"I thought you'd have something important to do."

"I don't. I was waiting for you. I'm in no hurry to get anything done."

"Oh."

"If I've done something that's offended you, I apologize. But you have to tell me what it was." I pressed for an answer, but thought I already knew.

"I'm fine, really."

She didn't look any too happy.

"I owe you thanks for all your help," I said. "It was important. I'd like to elaborate on how grateful I am. We should go to lunch, and it should be someplace nice."

"Yes, I guess."

Neither happy nor eager.

"I asked if you'd like to try one of the Korean Restaurants up in town. I think you'd like the food."

"Oh, that would be appropriate, wouldn't it?"

Ouch.

"Now I'm thinking maybe not. Perhaps we should talk about it."

"I'll call you," she said, stepped around the side of my desk and gave me a fast peck on the cheek. It felt like I'd been kissed by a spastic hummingbird.

"Bye," she said quickly, and then she was gone.

I don't think my wife would get annoyed if she saw me talking with two former hookers.

Five minutes later, Fred Mazzio walked in.

"Your friend's gone already?"

"Had to get back to the station."

"Good-lookin' woman. I mean *good-lookin'.*"

"Yes, she is. She's nice, too."

"You bastard."

"Yeah, that's me."

"Hey, I gotta go. It's my last night here. Mary'll give me hell if I don't help her clean up and get ready to move out."

I nodded, still thinking about Rachel. "It was good seeing you, Freddie. Drive up again sometime. And thanks for the help. I'm still proud of you."

"Thanks for the honorable mention out there. John appreciates it, too."

"No sweat, GI. You guys deserved it."

He stuck out a hand.

"Well, I'll see ya, madman. I gotta de de mao."

"Say goodbye to Mary for me. And take care of yourself. Lose a little weight, huh?"

"Bite me."

"Maybe not."

He laughed, waved his arm and left. On the way out, he stopped and kissed Bettye's hand. I sat and started reading again. Minutes later, my cell phone rang.

"Sam? I'm sorry. I was out of line. I…uh…"

"Where are you, Rachel?"

"In a ladies' room at a gas station, I didn't want John to hear me."

I laughed. "You're quite the secret agent. Do you have a phone in your shoe?"

"Stop the jokes, please. I need to apologize. I was…uh…"

"You don't have to explain. But thank you for calling. I don't want you to be mad—there's no reason."

"I have to explain. I had no right to…"

I interrupted again. "Was that someone knocking at your door? There may be a woman outside who's crossing her legs."

"Oh, you are such an idiot."

"I try my best."

"Okay, then. But I am sorry. Hey, what's Korean food like?"

"Lots of vegetables, lots of spices and if you don't eat all the rice, it's not fattening."

"Could I get a salad?"

"I'll order for you. You'll be happy."

"Is it very spicy?"

"I speak the language, I'll tell them, 'Ahn tugup sumnida'."

"What does that mean?"

"Not too hot for the little, round-eyed girl."

"Really?"

"Rachel, it's time for you to get out of the girl's room."

"You're right."

"I know."

"I'll call you," she said.

"I'll be waiting."

"Bye, lover."

"See ya."

* * * *

At quarter after twelve, I sat down next to Bettye.

"You're late for lunch again," she said.

"Life's a bitch, and then you starve."

"You look like you need a day off."

"I need a drink."

"No, you don't."

"I saw that slime-ball Mazzio kiss your hand when he left. What did he say?"

"He's not a slime-ball. He was being nice. He said when he comes back and isn't busy solving your cases, he'd take me to lunch as payment for all the computer work I did for him."

"For him? That fat..." I stopped short of my intended epithet. "What did you tell him?"

"I said I'd ask my boss if I could have some time off."

"Smart girl. You know that the computer work was for me, don't you?"

She smiled. "Course I do, Sammy."

"Is Joey still close by?"

"He is."

"Call him in to watch the desk until John gets back. I'm the one who owes you for all the good work. I'll take you to lunch. In addition to the one I owe you and Kate."

"Well, thank you, sir. Are we going for Chinese?"

"Any more Chinese food and I'll turn into a coolie. No, you're all dressed up. We'll go for a nice, quiet, classy lunch. We can go to Johnny Milton's steak house. How's that?"

"That would be lovely. I could get a salad."

I dropped my head and groaned.

"Yes, you can have a salad. I don't know why you'd want one, but you may have anything you want. Sure you wouldn't like the char-broiled tuna or swordfish?"

She shook her head.

"That way we could share one bottle of wine."

"White wine goes with fish and salad," she said.

"You're too smart for your own good."

* * * *

Bettye and I didn't get back to the office until 2:30. Joey Gillespie hit the road. Bettye took her position at the desk, John continued to do his thing, and I hung out in my office.

An hour later, PO Harley Flatt knocked on the door.

"Got a minute?" he asked.

"Sure, what's up?"

Harley is a big man who started shaving his head after his hairline began receding faster than the polar icecap. The shaved head and dark mustache makes him look like a professional wrestler.

I pointed to a chair, and he took a seat.

"Got somethin' here ya need ta see."

He stretched and handed me a 5x7 two-part departmental form—one of our field interrogation cards. I read over the handwritten document quickly.

Before I could comment Harley said, "Ya see the time and location?"

"Yeah. What took you into Townsend PD's territory yesterday at midnight?"

"Just before end o' tour, I got a disabled motorist call on the south end o' Main Street. Ol' boy who's a friend o' Vernon's car just up and died. Said his son was a mechanic and he'd tow it home t'day. So, him bein' a friend o' Vern Hobbs and all, I figgered I'd give him a ride home. I heard Billy Puckett sign on with the dispatcher, so I went out o' service, and me and this ol' boy headed fer his place in Townsend."

"Uh-huh."

"On my trip back this away, I found him." He pointed to the interrogation card.

"And this happened at the rest area on 321 across from the old rock quarry?"

"Yep. That's the one."

I cracked a big smile. "Interesting. That place is a famous spot for prostitutes and other sex minded people to hook up."

Harley nodded. "Sure is. And this one didn't offer much of an excuse fer bein' there at that hour."

I read a line on the PD form. "Tired and needed a break? That's pretty lame."

"What I thought."

"Have you told anyone else about this?"

"Just you. Subject there didn't even know I wrote it up."

I nodded and kept smiling. "I'll take care of this. Don't mention it to anyone."

Harley was in uniform, so I didn't need to ask if he was working a four-to-twelve tour.

"I'll call you later after I know more. Keep your cell phone turned on high."

He smiled. "You go it, boss."

We stood at the same time. "Thanks," I said.

Harley nodded. "Figgered y'all could have some fun with that."

Chapter Twenty-Eight

I folded the form and slid it into my inside jacket pocket. Harley left, and I strolled out and stopped at Bettye's desk.

She looked over the tops of her granny glasses. "You're lookin' rather smug, darlin'. Got somethin' to tell me?"

I shook my head. "Not just yet. In case anyone is looking for me, I'll be out for a while with my phone turned off."

She frowned.

"I won't be far."

"I don't like the sound of this."

John Gallagher stopped typing and looked in our direction. "Need some help, Boss?"

"No thanks, John. I can handle this alone."

"You look like the cat who ate the cheese, Boss. What's up?"

I laughed. "Canary, John."

"Canary?"

"It's, 'You look like the cat that ate the canary.'"

"You sure?"

I nodded and turned to walk out. "See you two later."

I skipped up the marble steps to the second floor and entered the mayor's office.

Trudy Connor replaced her telephone onto the cradle. "Hello, Mr. Jenkins. You lookin' for the mayor?"

"No, ma'am, but thanks for asking."

She wrinkled her forehead and gave a questioning look.

I smiled at Trudy and took two steps to Darnell Means' desk. "You

271

and I have business," I said. "Let's take a walk outside."

"I'm busy at the moment." He didn't hide a look of annoyance.

I leaned over and put my face close to his ear. "That wasn't a request, Darnell. Follow me, or I'll drag your ass out of here."

I doubted that Darnell ever fancied himself a tough guy in the physical sense, but the look of fear that crossed his face would cause anyone to lose a game of chicken.

He stood slowly and made a production of placing a hundred-dollar silver pen in the top inside pocket of his gray suit.

I pointed at the door, and Means started walking.

I smiled at Ms. Connor. "We won't be long."

She nodded. From her expression, it looked as if she'd just witnessed the Gestapo dragging her Jewish friend out of the office.

On the stairs, I said, "Out the front door and head for the town square."

"What's this all about?" His fear must have subsided; he didn't try to hide a bad attitude.

"You'll find out. When we get there, find a bench and sit."

"This had better be good. Y'all are on thin ice with—"

"Shut up. You finish that thought, and I'll need someone to restrain me from kickin' your ass."

Darnell's fear seemed to return, and he didn't speak again until we sat on a park bench in the middle of the square. The angle of the sun created lines and shadows on the grass. There appeared to be more birds than usual on the branches of the big tulip poplar trees—cardinals, jays, wrens, mourning doves. A flock of robins and assorted tiny birds bounced over the ground looking for worms and seeds.

I crossed my legs and took the field interrogation card from my pocket.

"Know what this is?" I asked.

I guess he still thought an attitude might work on me. "How should I?"

"It's a form we use to record suspicious persons—people a cop thinks may have committed or are about to commit an offense."

"That's very nice. What's it got to do with me?"

He must believe that the best defense is an offense. *Fool.*

I smiled. "Darnell, I think you and I have stepped off on the wrong foot in our relationship. That's going to change today."

"Oh?"

I heard a hint of apprehension in his voice.

"Yes. We're starting over, and our first implementation of the plan is you canning the attitude." He began to speak when I continued. "Unless you want me to ruin the rest of your life."

Maybe he began putting two and two together or he thought I was insane, but he chose to remain silent.

"This a record of a PO finding you parked in the rest area on Highway 321 just after midnight."

"I can—"

"Shut up. I'm not finished."

He closed his mouth and crossed his arms over his chest.

"Don't give me any crap about feeling tired and needing a snooze. No one would believe it. Even in heavy traffic, you live less than twenty minutes from Townsend."

"I—"

I tried to sound as friendly as possible and still convey my message. "What part of *shut up* don't you understand, son?"

He said nothing.

I made a production out of relaxing my shoulders and getting comfortable on the bench. "Here's the deal, Darnell. Everyone in the county knows all about that rest area. The Townsend and county cops are constantly troubled with men parking there at night hoping to hook up with the occasional prostitute who stops by offering a quickie. Prostitutes of both genders, by the way. And quiet often, homosexuals form temporary liaisons with no money changing hands. The place is well known to your former colleagues, the county commissioners, and it's even advertised in certain illicit publications. So, don't try to talk your way around what you were caught attempting."

His demeanor softened considerably. The look of fear returned. "Please, let me—"

I snapped at him. "Let you, my ass. I have no interest in your sexual preferences, but I do have a vested interest in the reputation of Prospect's leaders."

He unfolded his arms and placed his hands on his knees. Then he hung his head and nodded slowly.

"Let's change the subject, shall we?" I said. "Your uncle, Micah Blevins, chairman of the county commission, got you this job."

He turned to look at me, but said nothing.

"Sort of a leg up with your political career. And Micah doesn't like me because I caused his brother, your other uncle, Audie, a ration of grief. Then I locked up his buddy, Commissioner Finnbar McMillan and Finn's shithead son, Larry J. And let's not forget arresting Danny Swope, the Prospect councilman who beat his wife as often as he changed his socks."

He opened his mouth, but I cut him off at the knees. "Uh, uh, uh. I talk. You listen." I shrugged. "I could go on, but my memory isn't as good as it once was."

When I took a breath, he grasped the opportunity. "What do you want from me? Money?"

"I want a lot. But the money part is insulting. I should lock you up for bribery."

"What?"

"As an opener to our new relationship, quit breaking my balls. And never circumvent the chain of command and talk to one of my cops without me present."

"I'm the deputy mayor."

"Who cares? I've got your future in my hands."

He sat up straight and tilted his head in what looked like disbelief. "Say that again."

"You heard me, son. Keep out of our way. Forget Prospect has a police department. Assist the mayor, and behave yourself. If I ever see you overstep what I consider proper conduct, I'll let the world know about this *indiscretion* of yours, and they can draw their own conclusions."

"I'm guilty of nothing."

"I seem to be repeating myself. Who cares? I'll let our right-wing evangelical Christian constituents think what they want, and your political career will slide into the cesspool. Leave me alone, and I'll leave you alone."

He stared at me wide-eyed. "That's blackmail!"

I laughed. "See why you couldn't pass the bar exam? There is no statute called blackmail. This is simply coercion in the first degree. Study up, and maybe you'll pass next time."

"You can't get away with this."

"You could complain to someone, but in the big toilet of my life, you're just a little turd. You think I'd have trouble convincing the public that you misunderstood my intentions? And while I'd be playing the suffering hero, I'd tell the world about how you look for sex in dark roadside meeting places. Get real, boy. You want to be a politician. You can't do that in the South when those God-fearing voters know you break the commandments with impunity."

I stood up and looked at my watch. "4:35," I said. "Just enough time to go inside, say goodnight to my workers and head home. I could use a drink. How about you?"

"That's it?" he asked.

"Between you and me? Sure. I'll trust you to keep our agreement. If you have any doubts about me, ask around. My word is good."

He nodded.

"Oh, one more thing. Tell Micah to kiss my ass. And ask if he doubts whether I have enough horsepower of my own to bring a truckload of shit down on his head. If he tries to pull something like this again, he'll find out. Understand?"

I didn't wait for an answer.

Chapter Twenty-Nine

The next few days remained unseasonably cool. Those days turned into weeks. I couldn't remember a half dozen times that month when the temperatures rose anywhere close to ninety. For once, Mother Nature decided to send us adequate summer rain. The grass turned an Irish green, and the trees looked dark and healthy.

Kate and I relaxed on a blanket just outside the ruins of the 18th century Tellico Blockhouse near the village of Vonore. I leaned my back against a four-by-four post that supported not only me, but held a signboard telling the story of how the Blockhouse operated under the old U.S. Factory System that provided the Cherokee with trade goods. Kate sat on my right, in a very proper, yoga-like position. She never slouches; I do.

An old wicker picnic hamper lay open on the far end of our olive drab Army blanket. An assortment of crusty bread, three cheeses and red seedless grapes lay next to us on unbreakable plates.

"This cheese is nice," I said, pointing to one on the scrap of bread I held. "It's different. What do they call it?"

"The drunken goat. It's Spanish."

"There's red wine in it."

"It's soaked in red wine."

"Yahoo."

"Indeed."

"From the Fresh Market?"

"Uh-huh."

"The bread's good, too. It's seedier than a luncheonette in

Brooklyn."

"Sammy, you are so eloquent."

"Buy it in the same place?"

"No. Panera."

"You like the wine?" I asked.

"It's beautiful," she said and looked at the back label. "From Chile. Hmm. It says, 'Superb quality and craftsmanship are the hallmarks of our ruby red cabernet sauvignon. Elegant and balanced, its fruity aroma is dominated by berries, cloves and vanilla. While on the palate it delivers a fine concentration of flavor, suggesting juicy ripe fruit, plums, earth notes and leather; a true natural delight for your senses.' Do you agree with that?"

I frowned. "Leather? I've never drunk leather before. Maybe they use a blender. I think it's nice."

"Just nice?"

"Nice means good. You have to go a long way for me to rate something as nice."

"The master of understatement."

"It was only $6.99—on sale. Three bucks off. Pretty good deal for a nice wine. It scored an eighty-nine from some critic."

"You're not supposed to tell people how much you pay for wine."

"I thought you'd appreciate my shopping skills."

"I do."

I took another nibble of the drunken goat and a sip of the Chilean wine that delighted my senses as I looked over the grassy meadow and across the wide shimmering surface of Nine Mile Creek toward the log palisades of the reconstructed Fort Loudoun and beyond to Tellico Lake.

That spot had once been the confluence of the Little Tennessee and Tellico Rivers, but the Tennessee Valley Authority flooded the entire area in the early '70s to create one of their large, manmade recreational lakes. Many of the locals say they lost some of the finest brown trout fishing in the state after the project was completed.

The Chillhowee Mountains stood tall over the water and on the horizon, reminding me of a particular vista along the west shore of Loch Lomond.

"You know what I missed working these murders?" I asked.

"I don't know what you mean."

"Funerals. Park had paid for his plot and service a long time ago. A probate lawyer from Knoxville took care of him. Ha didn't seem to have any family, and the city will, sooner or later, bury that scoundrel."

Kate laughed. Her big brown eyes took on a bright and happy look. "Scoundrel?"

I shrugged. "And it wasn't until after Boo confessed to killing Ha that Rosie Cho's brother claimed her body. I'm still not sure what's happening with Kum-Ok."

"That is strange, isn't it?"

"It usually helps if we attend the funeral of a victim and see who shows up. You never know what surprises you find at a grave yard," I said.

"It was all very sad, wasn't it?"

"I felt sorry for all girls—in many ways. Park and his boys were just hoods. Who cares about them?"

"Uh-huh."

Thinking about so many victims began to dampen my mood. I wanted to change the subject. "We wouldn't be able to enjoy a summer picnic if we lived in Korea."

She thought for a few seconds and knew my meaning. "You're right...the monsoons."

"Remember that rain? Eighteen hours a day, seven days a week, from July to September. If you stood still too long, you'd mold."

"I remember. The springs and autumns were beautiful though."

"Yeah, but cold winters."

"Colder than cold."

"The many faces of the land of morning calm," I said.

"You should be a travel agent."

"Sure, another branch of Jenkins Enterprises. We could lead tours to various places in Southeast Asia and end up in Korea."

"That was a year I wouldn't trade for anything."

I nodded. "You know, we should go to those Knoxville Korean restaurants more often."

"They can get a little pricey."

"That shouldn't be an issue. What price can you put on nostalgia?

And who else serves OB beer and real yaki-mandu?" I asked.

"Do you remember that Korean place we used to go to upstate in Newburgh?"

"Sure, The Yobo. They made the best bulgogi this side of Yong Dong Po. We spent some nice weekends up there. A football game at West Point and dinner at The Yobo."

"The Newburgh Holiday Inn was a pretty place," she said.

"After a couple of sake martinis at The Yobo, the Holiday Inn was a pretty romantic place."

Kate reached over and touched my forearm. "Any motel with you, Sammy, is a romantic place."

"You want to go out tonight?"

"I have fresh salmon and asparagus that would be best if used today."

"I'm being romantic, and you're being practical."

"After dinner we could watch a movie. Netflix came this morning. That could be romantic."

"Okay, a movie and my best girl… Sounds good."

"I'll make popcorn."

"What kind of wine goes with popcorn? Chardonnay or pinot grigio?"

"Either would be lovely," she said and sipped a little cabernet.

"Champagne. I'll stop and get a cold bottle."

"Your mother should have named you Bacchus."

"Bacchus Jenkins? Sounds like an NBA all-star."

"Maybe not."

"Did I ever tell you about my great, great Uncle Bacchus? He fought with the Spartans at Thermopile."

"You had a Greek ancestor?"

"He was a Scottish mercenary. Fought all over the ancient world."

"Of course he did, sweetie."

"If the movie gets boring, we could neck on the couch."

"I'd love to neck with you, my passionate boy."

"Wanna neck right here?"

"Suppose somebody drives up?"

"At home then."

"Home is better."

"Okay, let's go."

Kate packed up the hamper, and I carried it to the Austin-Healey, parked twenty yards away on the gravel. While she folded the blanket, I took care of a personal chore before I started the car.

Kate sat in the passenger's bucket seat, and I settled in behind the wheel. I switched on the ignition, depressed the clutch and touched the starter. The engine growled, and I goosed the accelerator, getting a chorus of gurgles from the tuned, double exhaust pipes.

"Wow, sexy car noise. You're showing off," Kate said.

"Of course. It's how I impress the girls."

"Works for me."

I drove slowly out of the gravel lot. When I hit the blacktop, I double clutched to make the car sound even sexier. Kate smiled. She's cute as hell.

Heading north on US 411, I turned right onto Tennessee 72.

"You're taking the long way home? Not in a hurry to start necking?"

"It's not that long. And it's more scenic. Besides, it'll give the vitamin "V" I just took a chance to work."

"You keep Viagra with you?"

"Every time I'm out with you, baby."

"No matter what they say, Jenkins, you've still got it."

"Who are they?"

THE END

About the Author

Wayne Zurl grew up on Long Island and retired after twenty years with the Suffolk County Police Department, one of the largest municipal law enforcement agencies in New York and the nation. For thirteen of those years he served as a section commander supervising investigators. He is a graduate of SUNY, Empire State College and served on active duty in the US Army during the Vietnam War and later in the reserves. Zurl left New York to live in the foothills of the Great Smoky Mountains of Tennessee with his wife, Barbara.

Zurl has won Eric Hoffer and Indie Book Awards, and was named a finalist for a Montaigne Medal and First Horizon Book Award. He has written four novels and more than twenty novelettes in the Sam Jenkins mystery series.

Author Links:
Author website: http://www.waynezurlbooks.net
Twitter: http://www.twitter.com/#!/waynezurl
Facebook: http://www.facebook.com/waynezurl

Other books by the author at Melange
From New York to the Smokies
A Leprechaun's Lament
Heroes and Lovers
Pigeon River Blues

www.ingramcontent.com/pod-product-compliance
Lightning Source LLC
Chambersburg PA
CBHW031114030726
47496CB00002BA/538